Witchy

Volume 2

Ariel Slamet Ries

ONI PRESS

PUBLICATION

Designed by Sarah Rockwell
Edited by Shawna Gore

onipress.com 📘 🐦 🌐 lionforge.com

Witchy is a member of thehiveworks.com
Visit witchycomic.com to read the comic as it updates.

First Edition: February 2022

ISBN: 978-1-63715-018-4
eISBN: 978-1-63715-027-6

Printed in China.

LCCN: 2021940870

10 9 8 7 6 5 4 3 2 1

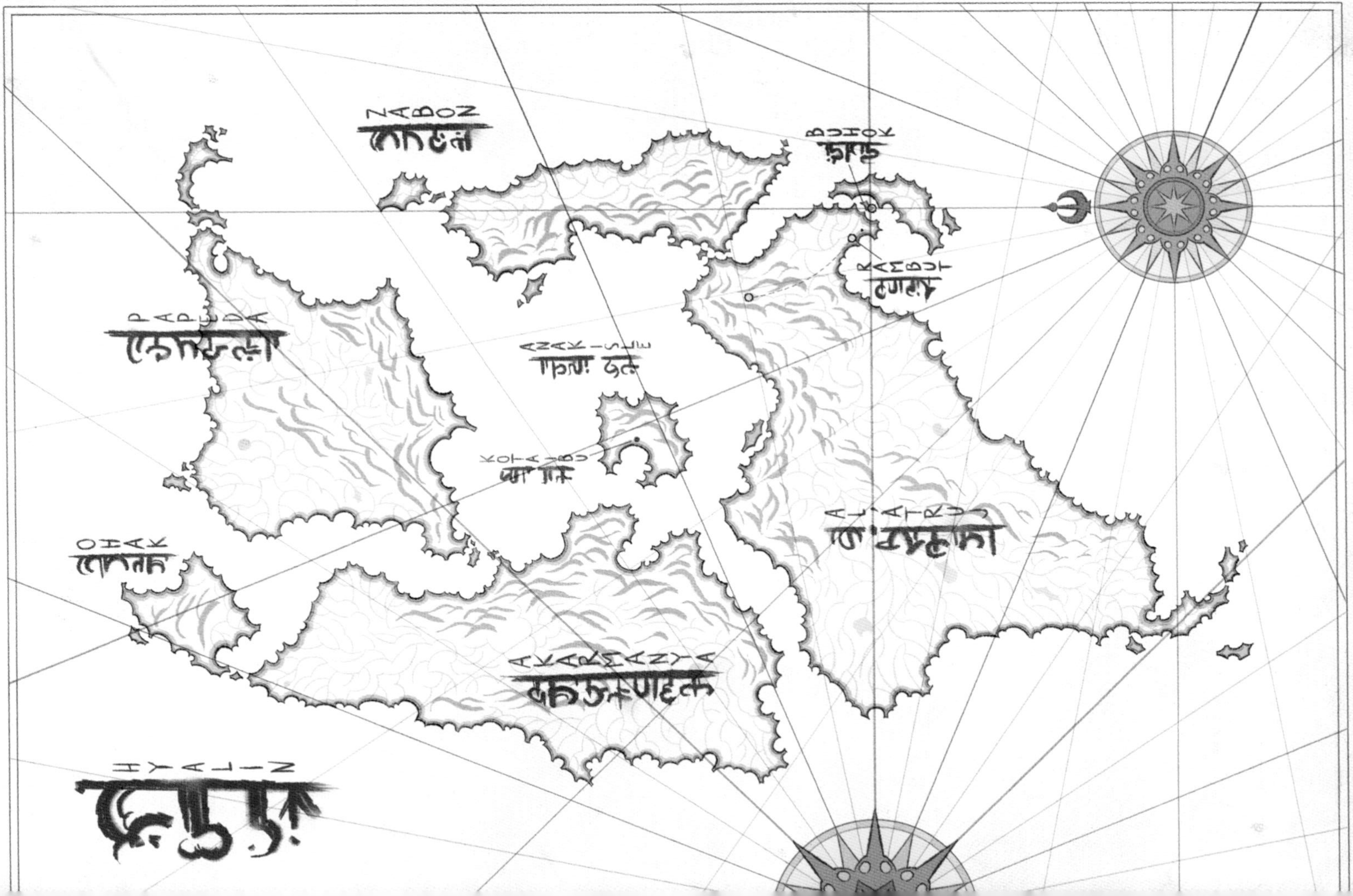
HYALIN
OHAK
PAPEDA
ZABON
KOTA BU
ANAKISLE
AKARMANYA
AL'ATRU
RAMBUT
BUHOK

THE STORY SO FAR...

In the midst of the Witch Guard's conscription exams, Nyneve's true hair length was exposed by Hyalin's de facto leader, Viceroy Jung. Disoriented and panicked after her recruitment, Nyneve committed the ultimate form of heresy—the severing of one's hair—and went on the run. Now, with her mother imprisoned for aiding her escape, and a fledgling rebellion on her side, Nyneve continues her journey to escape from the Kingdom's clutches.

WITCHY
CHAPTER FIVE

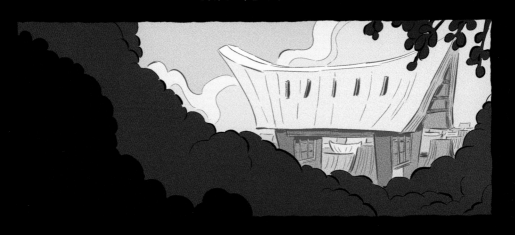

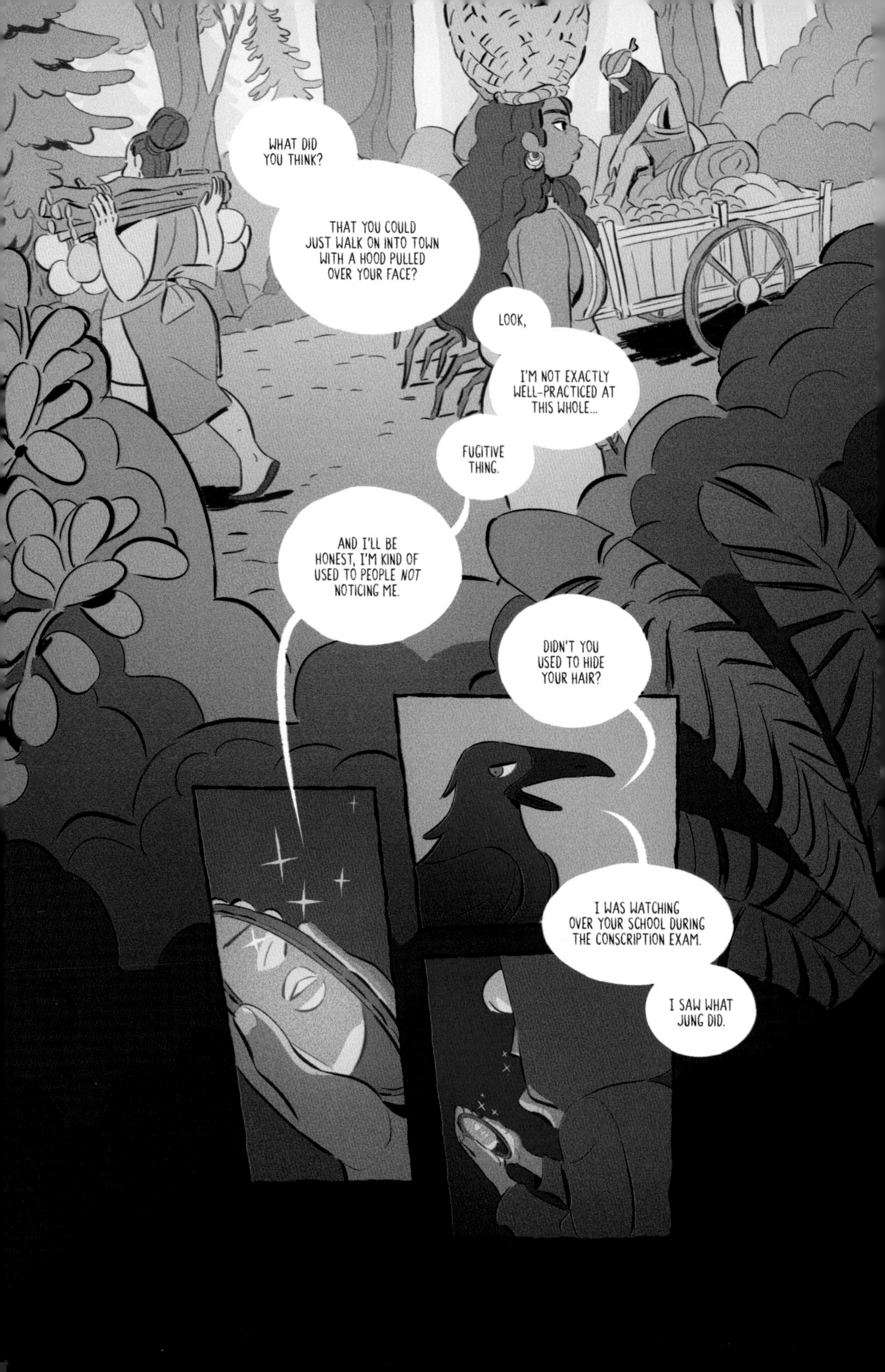
WHAT DID YOU THINK?
THAT YOU COULD JUST WALK ON INTO TOWN WITH A HOOD PULLED OVER YOUR FACE?
LOOK,
I'M NOT EXACTLY WELL-PRACTICED AT THIS WHOLE...
FUGITIVE THING.
AND I'LL BE HONEST, I'M KIND OF USED TO PEOPLE *NOT* NOTICING ME.
DIDN'T YOU USED TO HIDE YOUR HAIR?
I WAS WATCHING OVER YOUR SCHOOL DURING THE CONSCRIPTION EXAM.
I SAW WHAT JUNG DID.

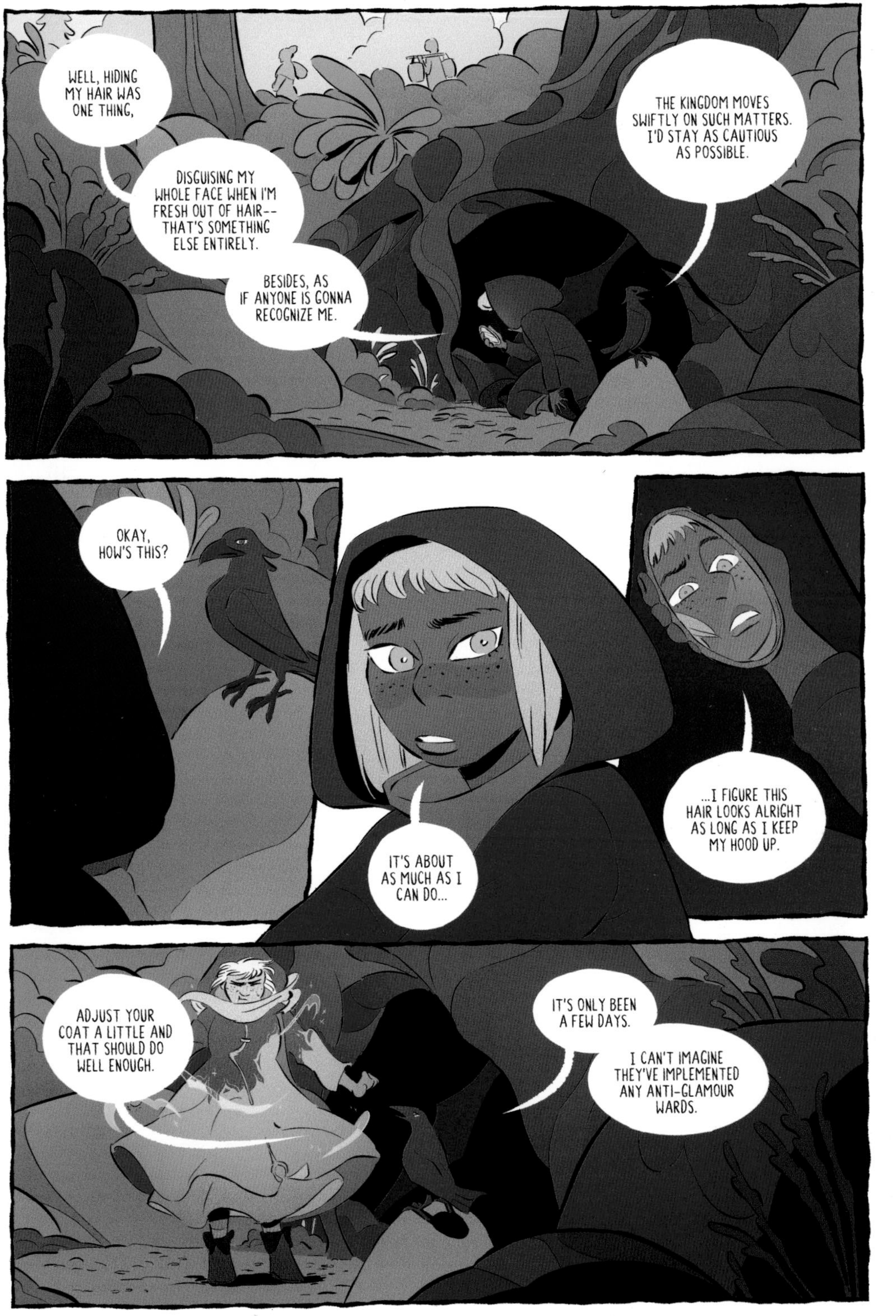
WELL, HIDING MY HAIR WAS ONE THING,
DISGUISING MY WHOLE FACE WHEN I'M FRESH OUT OF HAIR-- THAT'S SOMETHING ELSE ENTIRELY.
BESIDES, AS IF ANYONE IS GONNA RECOGNIZE ME.
THE KINGDOM MOVES SWIFTLY ON SUCH MATTERS. I'D STAY AS CAUTIOUS AS POSSIBLE.
OKAY, HOW'S THIS?
IT'S ABOUT AS MUCH AS I CAN DO...
...I FIGURE THIS HAIR LOOKS ALRIGHT AS LONG AS I KEEP MY HOOD UP.
ADJUST YOUR COAT A LITTLE AND THAT SHOULD DO WELL ENOUGH.
IT'S ONLY BEEN A FEW DAYS.
I CAN'T IMAGINE THEY'VE IMPLEMENTED ANY ANTI-GLAMOUR WARDS.

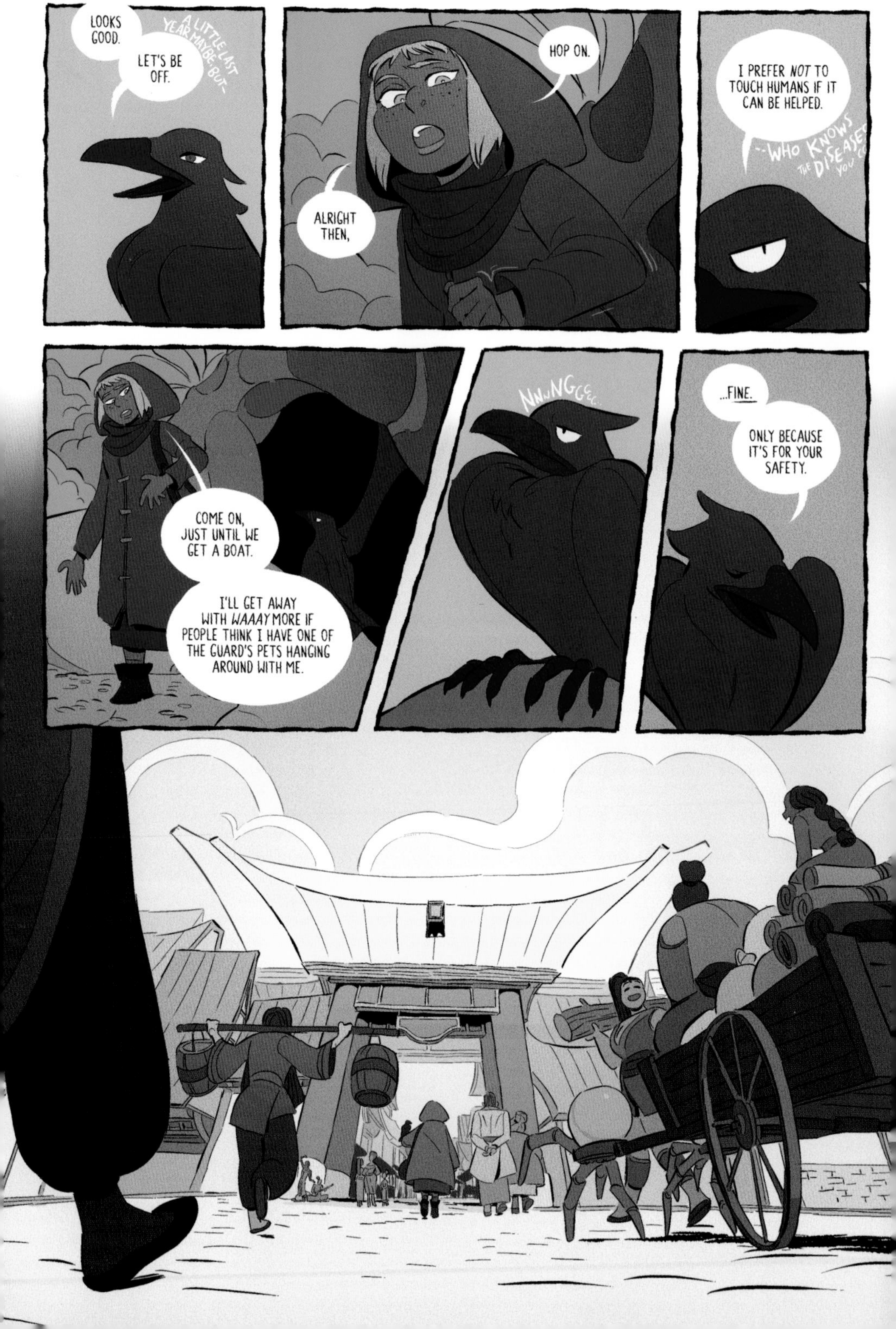
LOOKS GOOD.
LET'S BE OFF.
A LITTLE LAST YEAR MAYBE BUT-
HOP ON.
ALRIGHT THEN,
I PREFER NOT TO TOUCH HUMANS IF IT CAN BE HELPED.
--WHO KNOWS THE DISEASES
COME ON, JUST UNTIL WE GET A BOAT.
I'LL GET AWAY WITH WAAAY MORE IF PEOPLE THINK I HAVE ONE OF THE GUARD'S PETS HANGING AROUND WITH ME.
NNNNGGGG...
...FINE.
ONLY BECAUSE IT'S FOR YOUR SAFETY.

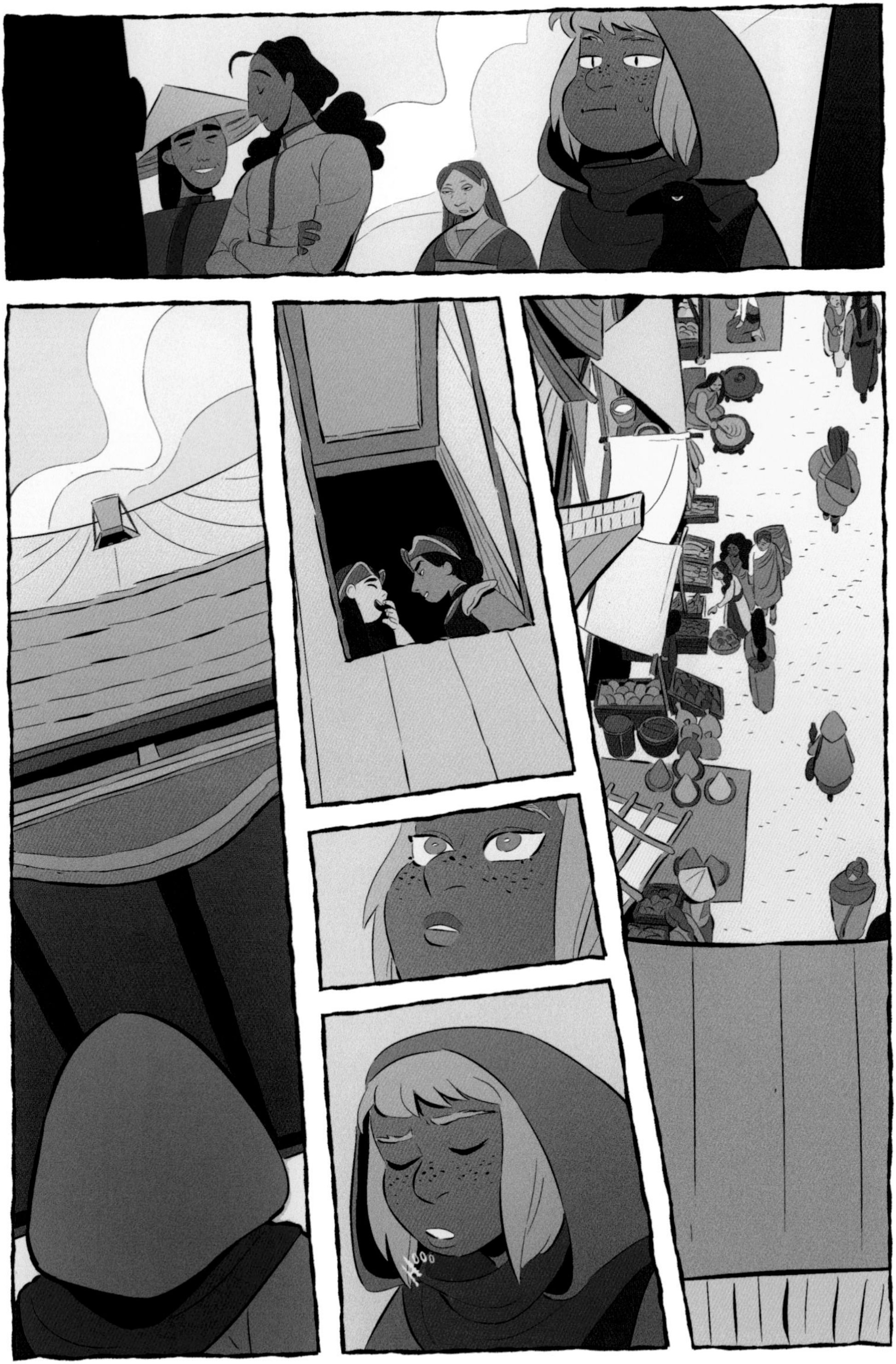
Hooo

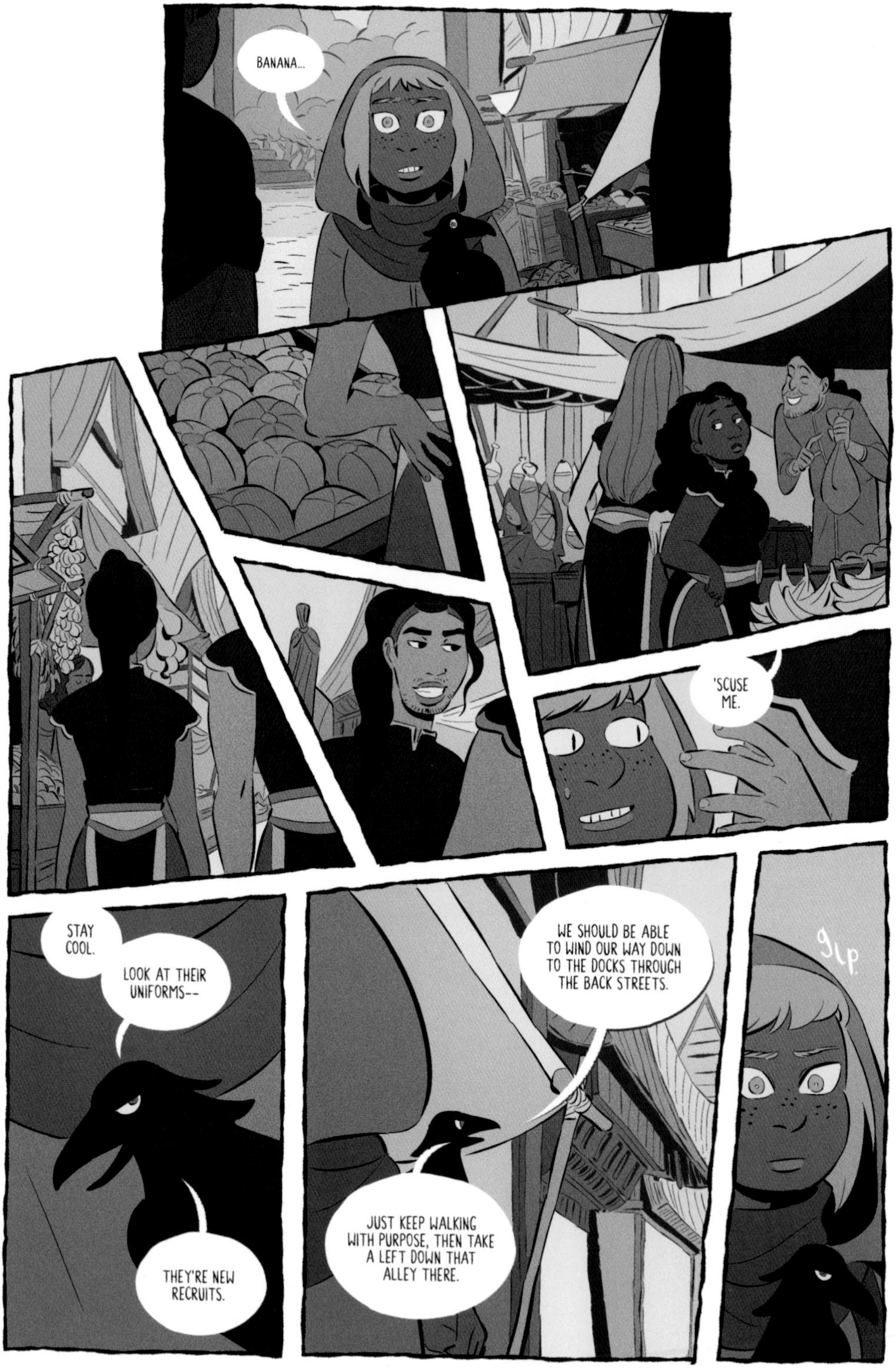
BANANA...
'SCUSE ME.
STAY COOL.
LOOK AT THEIR UNIFORMS--
THEY'RE NEW RECRUITS.
JUST KEEP WALKING WITH PURPOSE, THEN TAKE A LEFT DOWN THAT ALLEY THERE.
WE SHOULD BE ABLE TO WIND OUR WAY DOWN TO THE DOCKS THROUGH THE BACK STREETS.
GLP.

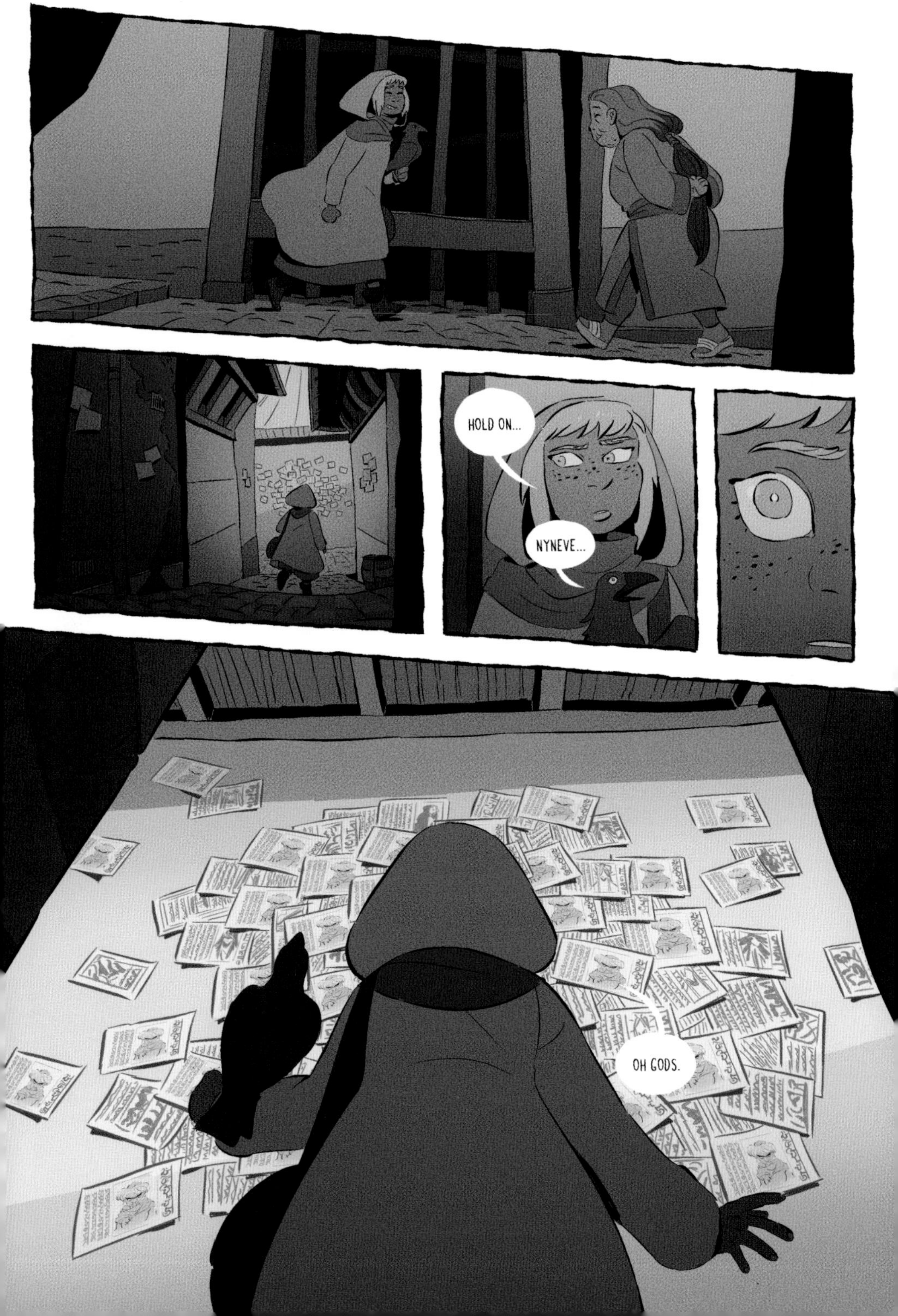
HOLD ON...
NYNEVE...
OH GODS.

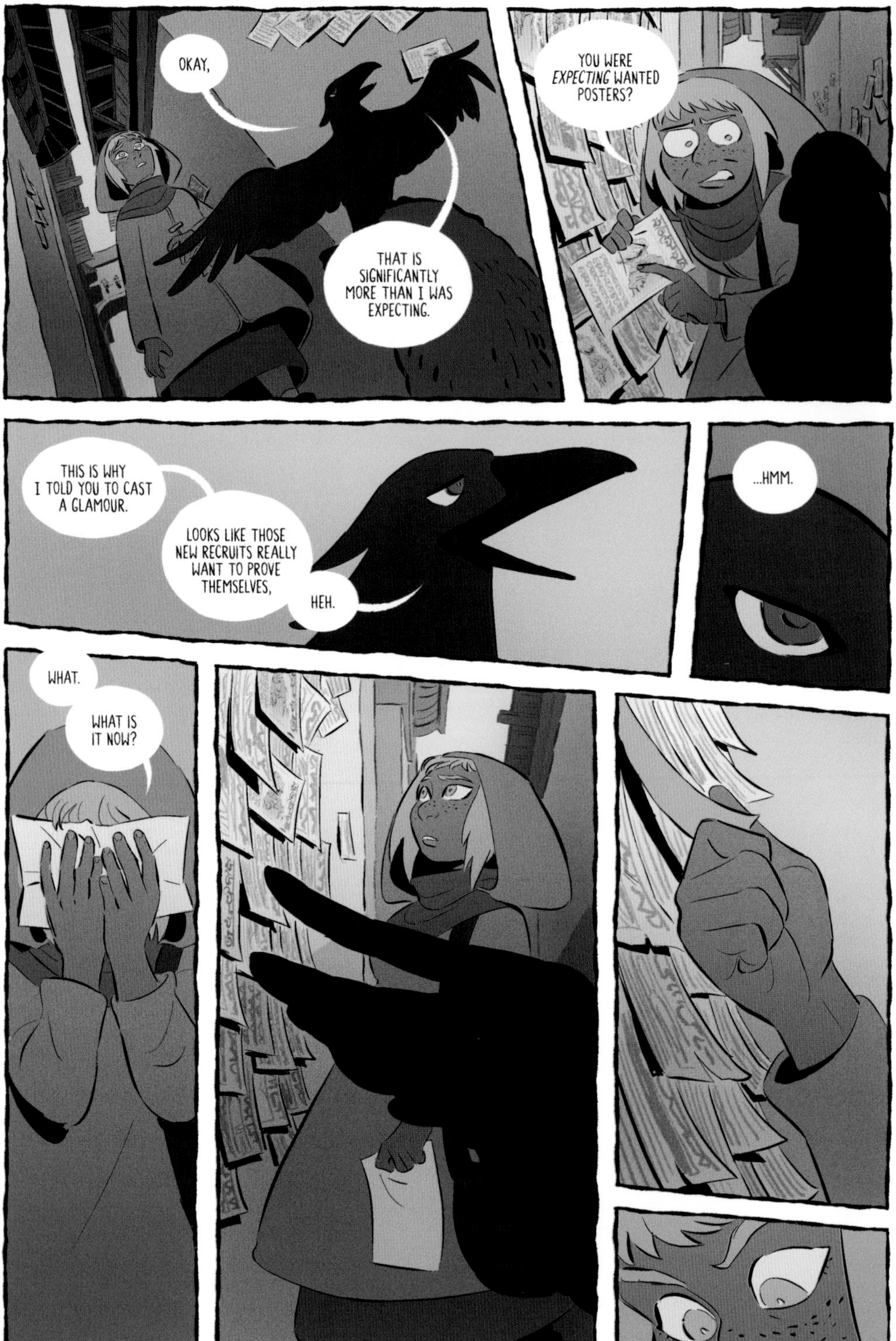
OKAY,
THAT IS SIGNIFICANTLY MORE THAN I WAS EXPECTING.
YOU WERE *EXPECTING* WANTED POSTERS?
THIS IS WHY I TOLD YOU TO CAST A GLAMOUR.
LOOKS LIKE THOSE NEW RECRUITS REALLY WANT TO PROVE THEMSELVES,
HEH.
...HMM.
WHAT.
WHAT IS IT NOW?

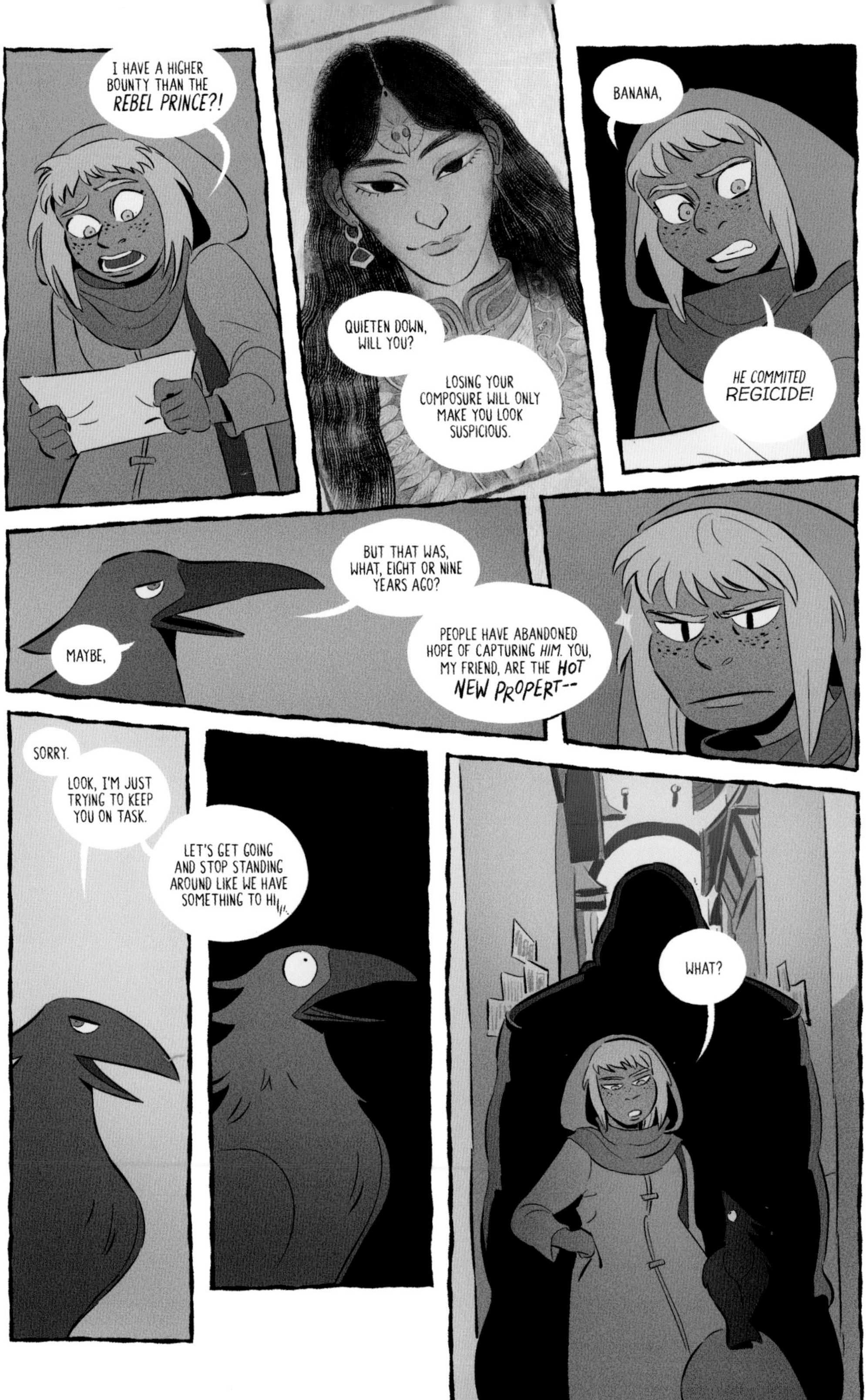
I HAVE A HIGHER BOUNTY THAN THE REBEL PRINCE?!
QUIETEN DOWN, WILL YOU?
LOSING YOUR COMPOSURE WILL ONLY MAKE YOU LOOK SUSPICIOUS.
BANANA,
HE COMMITED REGICIDE!
MAYBE,
BUT THAT WAS, WHAT, EIGHT OR NINE YEARS AGO?
PEOPLE HAVE ABANDONED HOPE OF CAPTURING HIM. YOU, MY FRIEND, ARE THE HOT NEW PROPERT--
SORRY.
LOOK, I'M JUST TRYING TO KEEP YOU ON TASK.
LET'S GET GOING AND STOP STANDING AROUND LIKE WE HAVE SOMETHING TO HI...
WHAT?

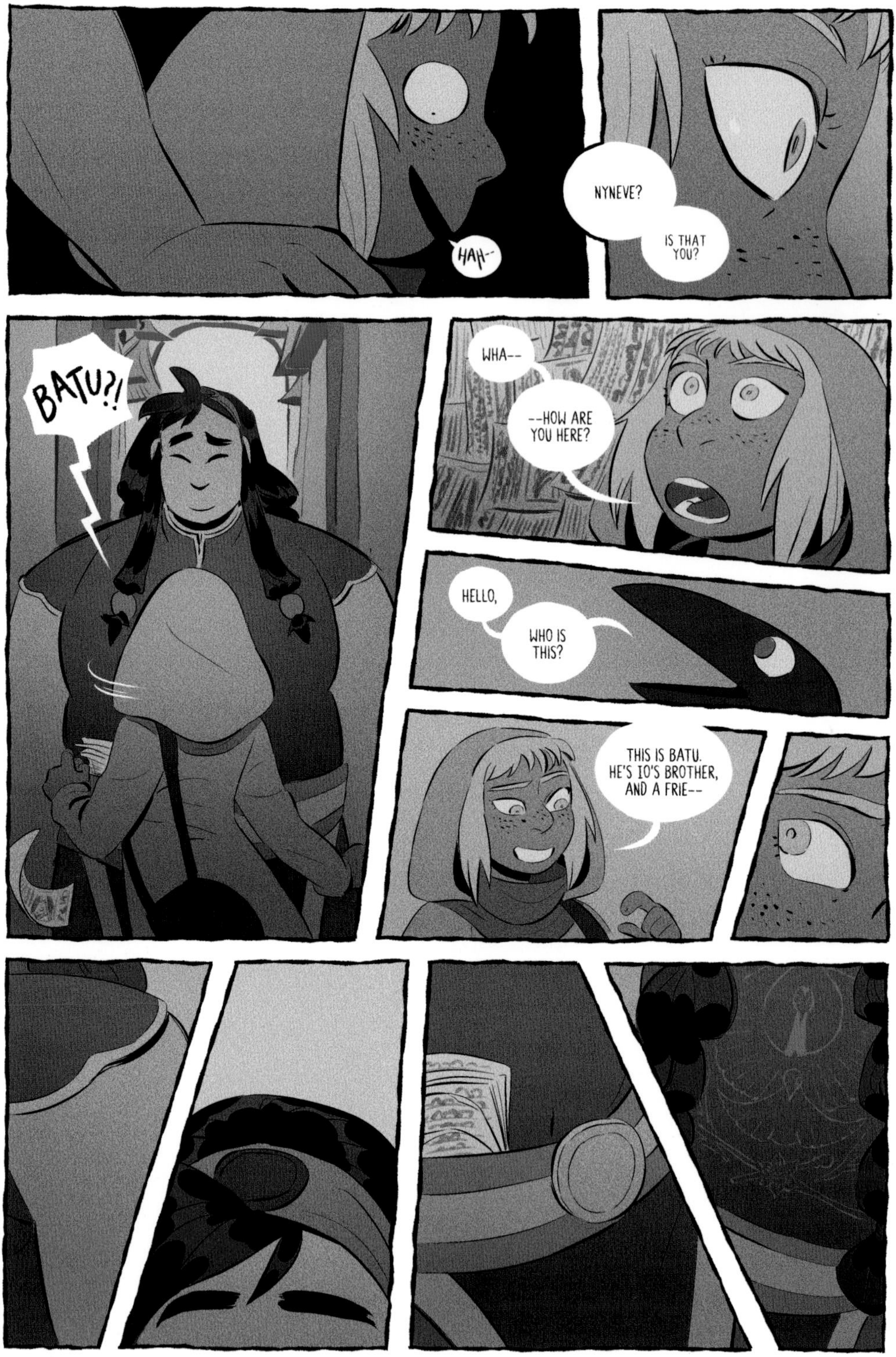
HAH--
NYNEVE?
IS THAT YOU?
BATU?!
WHA--
--HOW ARE YOU HERE?
HELLO,
WHO IS THIS?
THIS IS BATU. HE'S IO'S BROTHER, AND A FRIE--

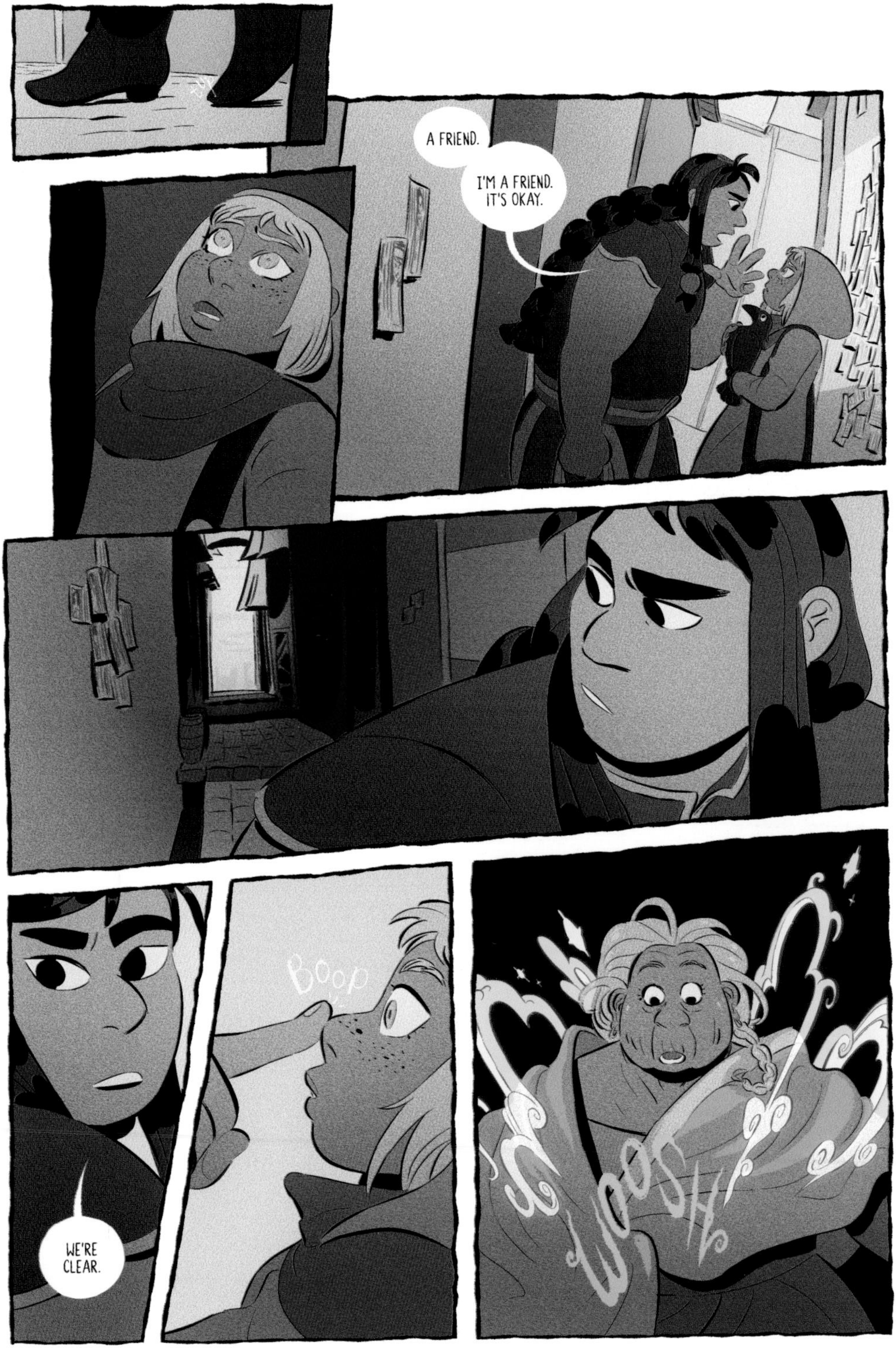
A FRIEND.
I'M A FRIEND. IT'S OKAY.
WE'RE CLEAR.
BOOP
WOOSH!

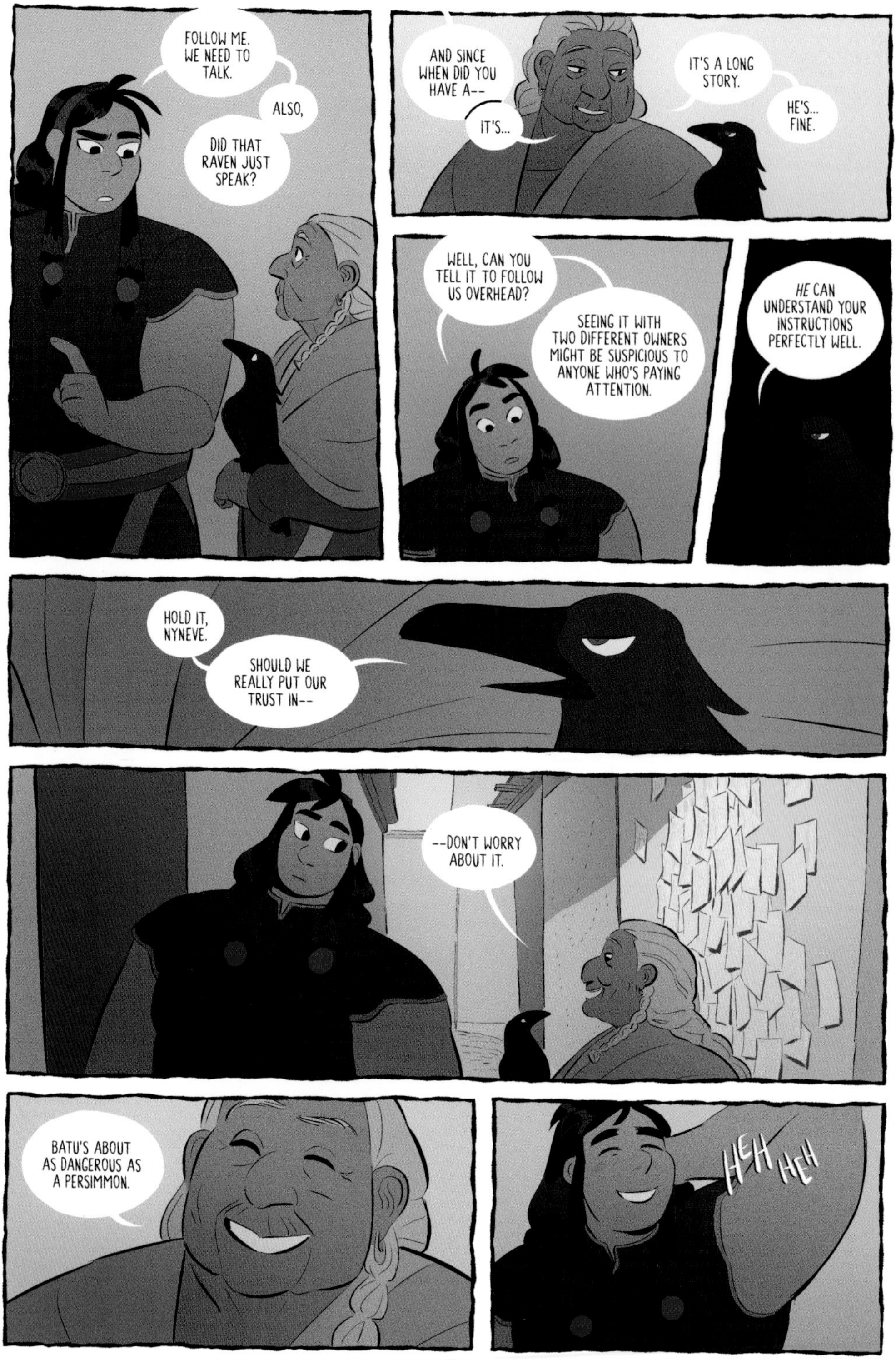
FOLLOW ME. WE NEED TO TALK.
ALSO,
DID THAT RAVEN JUST SPEAK?
AND SINCE WHEN DID YOU HAVE A--
IT'S...
IT'S A LONG STORY.
HE'S... FINE.
WELL, CAN YOU TELL IT TO FOLLOW US OVERHEAD?
SEEING IT WITH TWO DIFFERENT OWNERS MIGHT BE SUSPICIOUS TO ANYONE WHO'S PAYING ATTENTION.
HE CAN UNDERSTAND YOUR INSTRUCTIONS PERFECTLY WELL.
HOLD IT, NYNEVE.
SHOULD WE REALLY PUT OUR TRUST IN--
--DON'T WORRY ABOUT IT.
BATU'S ABOUT AS DANGEROUS AS A PERSIMMON.
HEH HEH

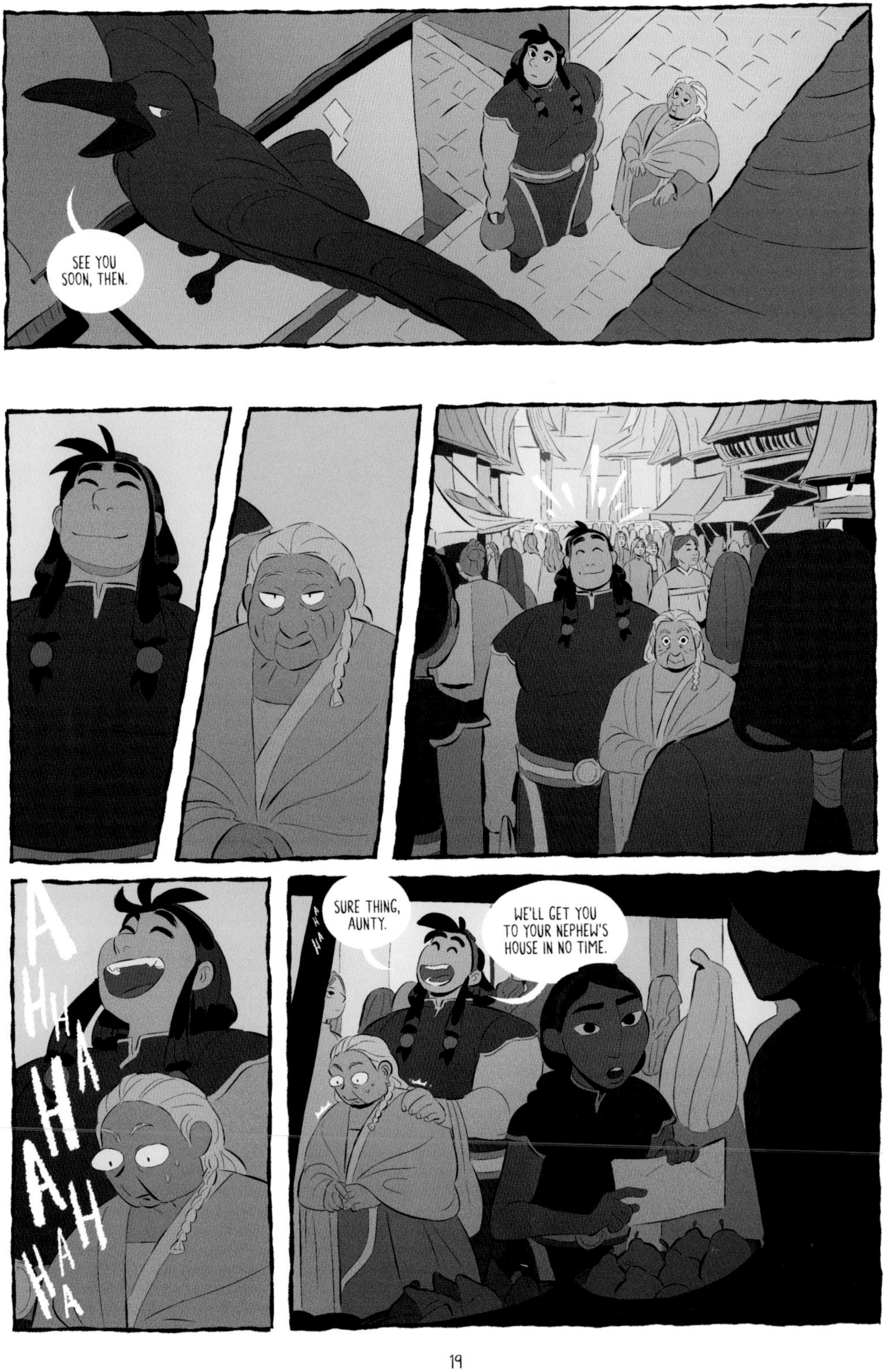
SEE YOU SOON, THEN.
AHHAHAHAHAHAHAHA
HAHAHA
SURE THING, AUNTY.
WE'LL GET YOU TO YOUR NEPHEW'S HOUSE IN NO TIME.

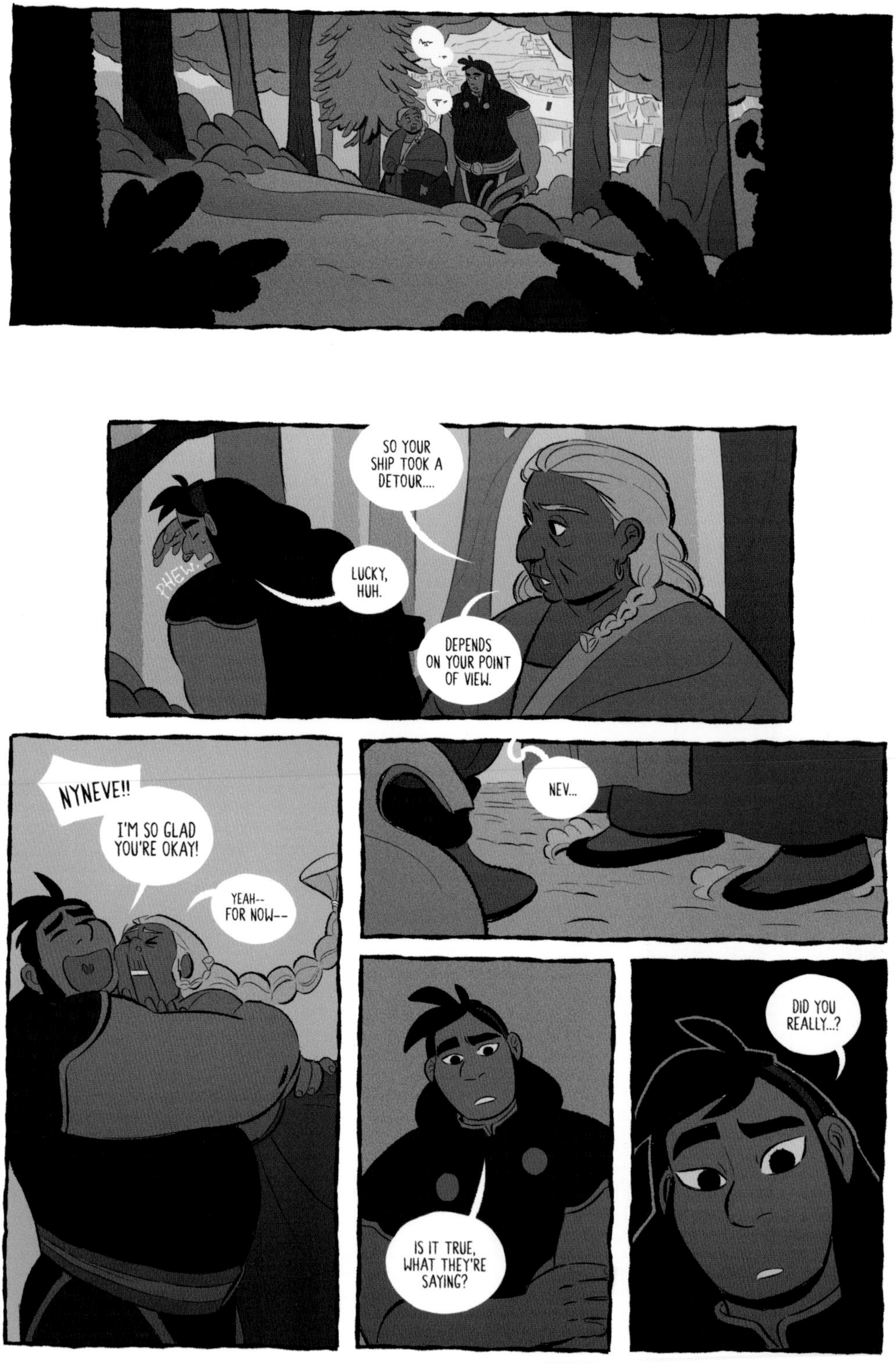
SO YOUR SHIP TOOK A DETOUR....
PHEW.
LUCKY, HUH.
DEPENDS ON YOUR POINT OF VIEW.
NYNEVE!!
I'M SO GLAD YOU'RE OKAY!
YEAH-- FOR NOW--
NEV...
IS IT TRUE, WHAT THEY'RE SAYING?
DID YOU REALLY...?

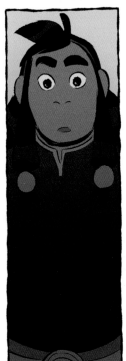

HAHA.

I AM *SO* SORRY.

I DIDN'T EXPECT IT TO LOOK SO...

CAN I TOUCH IT.

GO AHEAD.

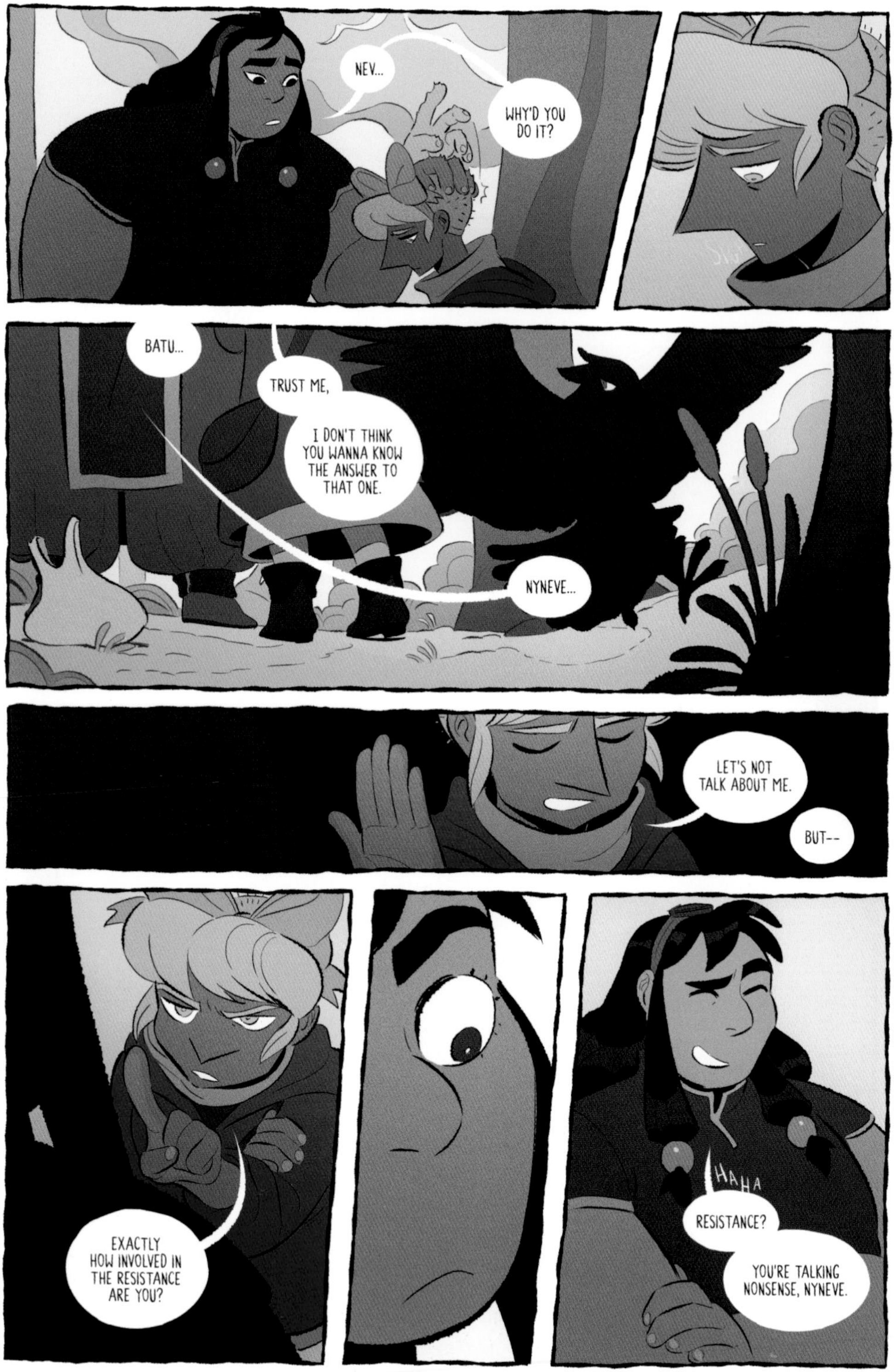
NEV...
WHY'D YOU DO IT?
BATU...
TRUST ME,
I DON'T THINK YOU WANNA KNOW THE ANSWER TO THAT ONE.
NYNEVE...
LET'S NOT TALK ABOUT ME.
BUT--
EXACTLY HOW INVOLVED IN THE RESISTANCE ARE YOU?
HAHA
RESISTANCE?
YOU'RE TALKING NONSENSE, NYNEVE.

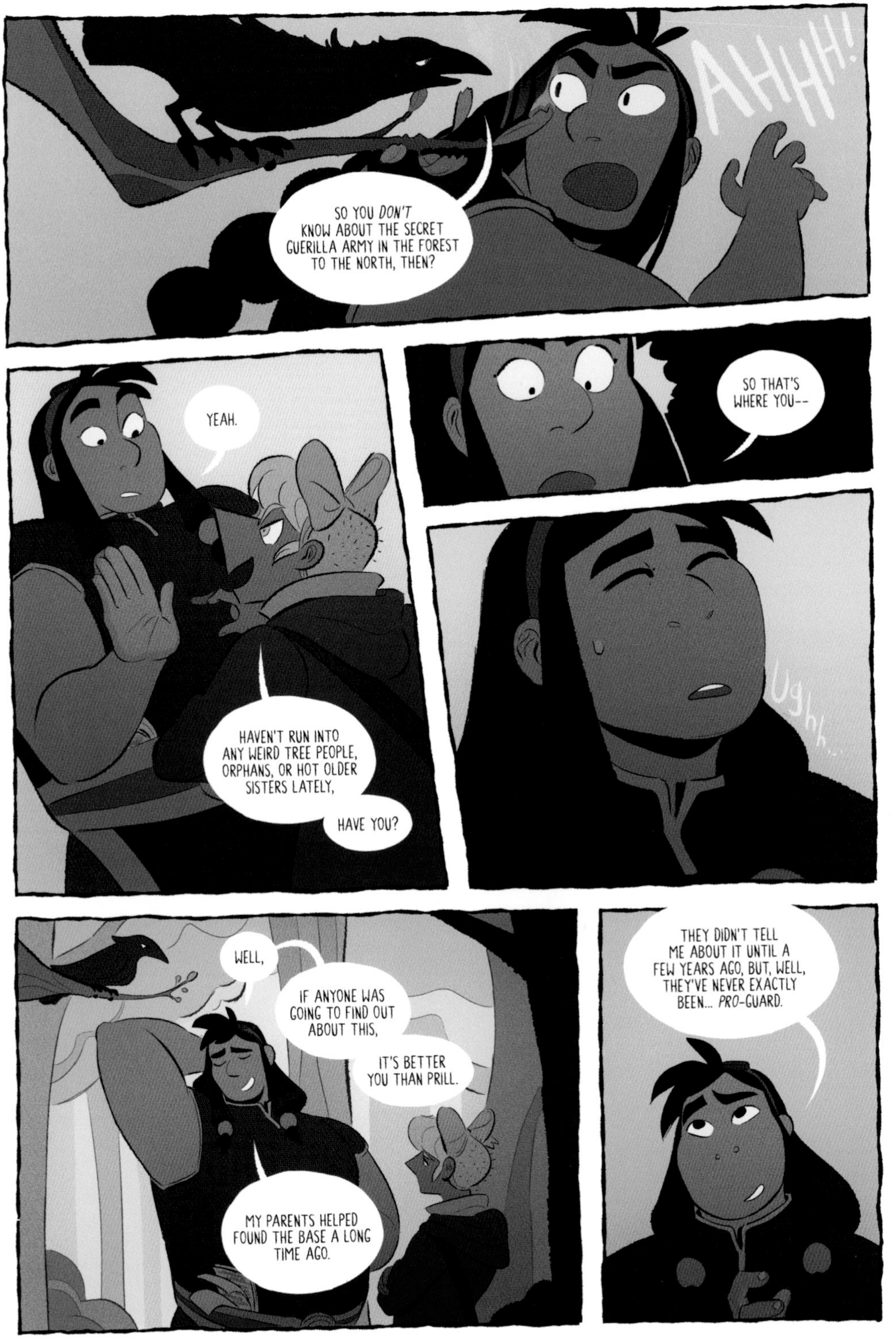
AHHH!
SO YOU *DON'T* KNOW ABOUT THE SECRET GUERILLA ARMY IN THE FOREST TO THE NORTH, THEN?
YEAH.
HAVEN'T RUN INTO ANY WEIRD TREE PEOPLE, ORPHANS, OR HOT OLDER SISTERS LATELY,
HAVE YOU?
SO THAT'S WHERE YOU--
Ughh...
WELL,
IF ANYONE WAS GOING TO FIND OUT ABOUT THIS,
IT'S BETTER YOU THAN PRILL.
MY PARENTS HELPED FOUND THE BASE A LONG TIME AGO.
THEY DIDN'T TELL ME ABOUT IT UNTIL A FEW YEARS AGO, BUT, WELL, THEY'VE NEVER EXACTLY BEEN... *PRO*-GUARD.

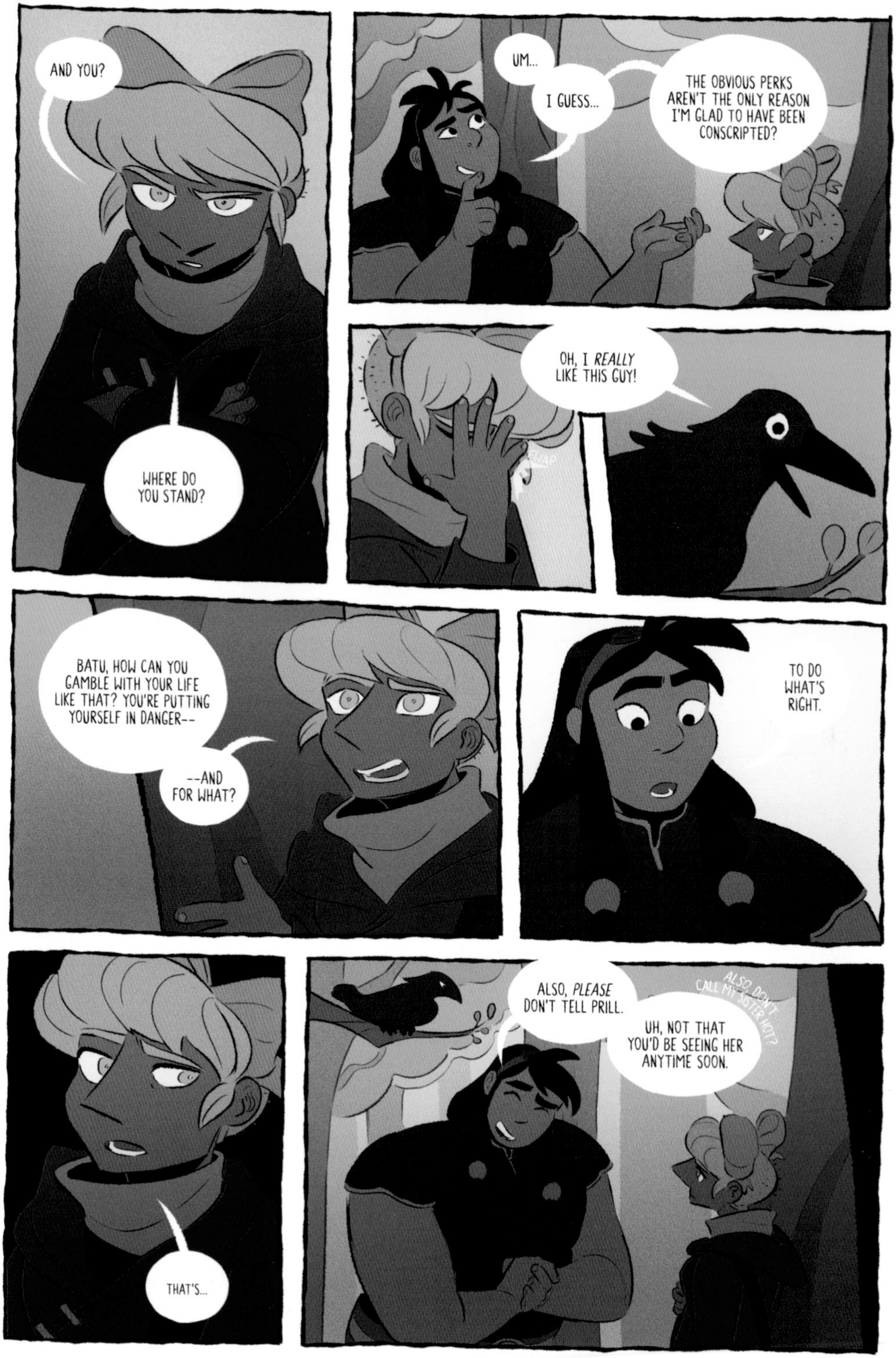
AND YOU?
WHERE DO YOU STAND?
UM...
I GUESS...
THE OBVIOUS PERKS AREN'T THE ONLY REASON I'M GLAD TO HAVE BEEN CONSCRIPTED?
OH, I *REALLY* LIKE THIS GUY!
BATU, HOW CAN YOU GAMBLE WITH YOUR LIFE LIKE THAT? YOU'RE PUTTING YOURSELF IN DANGER--
--AND FOR WHAT?
TO DO WHAT'S RIGHT.
THAT'S...
ALSO, *PLEASE* DON'T TELL PRILL.
UH, NOT THAT YOU'D BE SEEING HER ANYTIME SOON.
ALSO, DON'T CALL MY SISTER HOT?

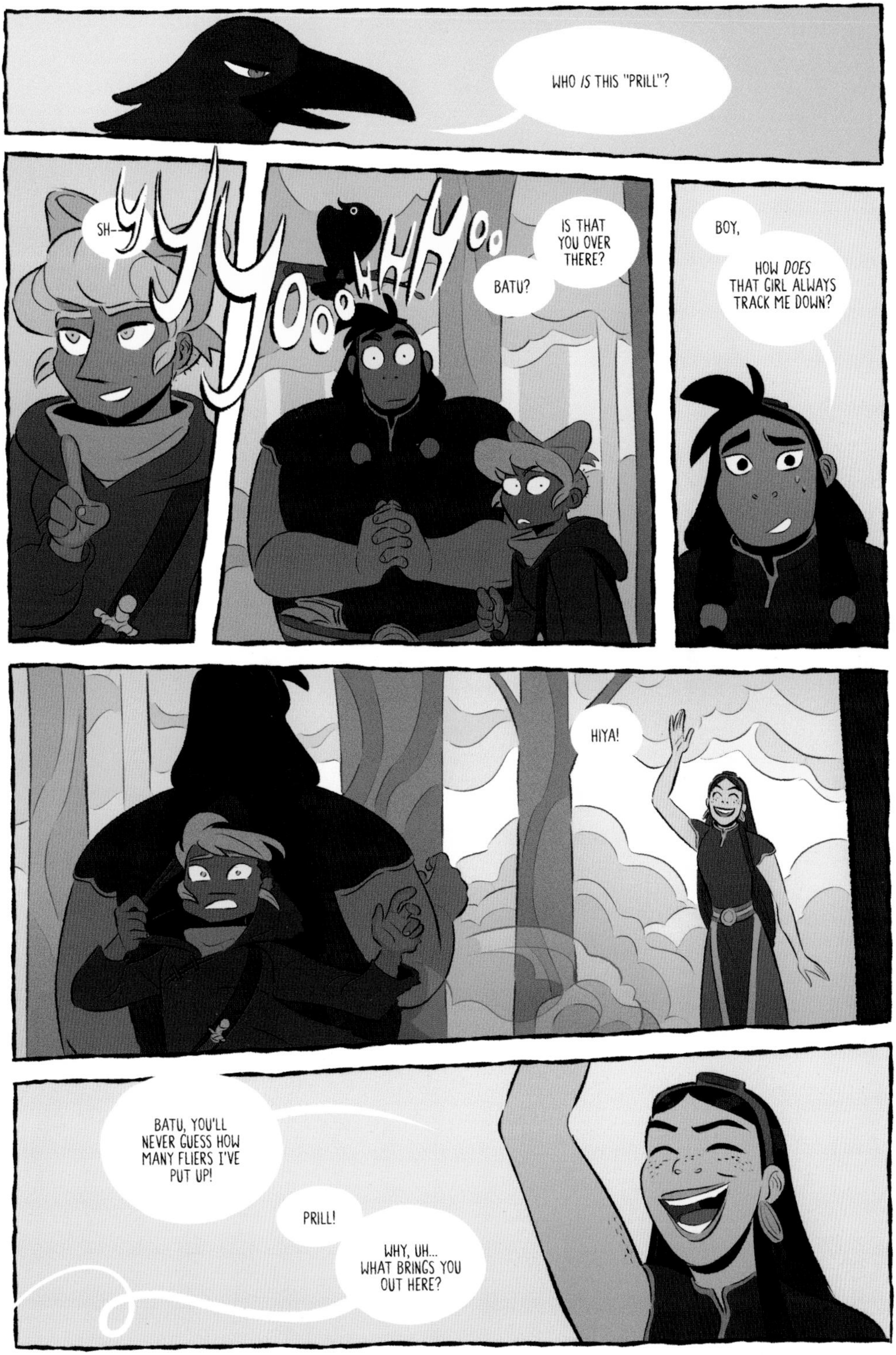
WHO *IS* THIS "PRILL"?
SH—
BATU?
IS THAT YOU OVER THERE?
BOY,
HOW *DOES* THAT GIRL ALWAYS TRACK ME DOWN?
HIYA!
BATU, YOU'LL NEVER GUESS HOW MANY FLIERS I'VE PUT UP!
PRILL!
WHY, UH... WHAT BRINGS YOU OUT HERE?

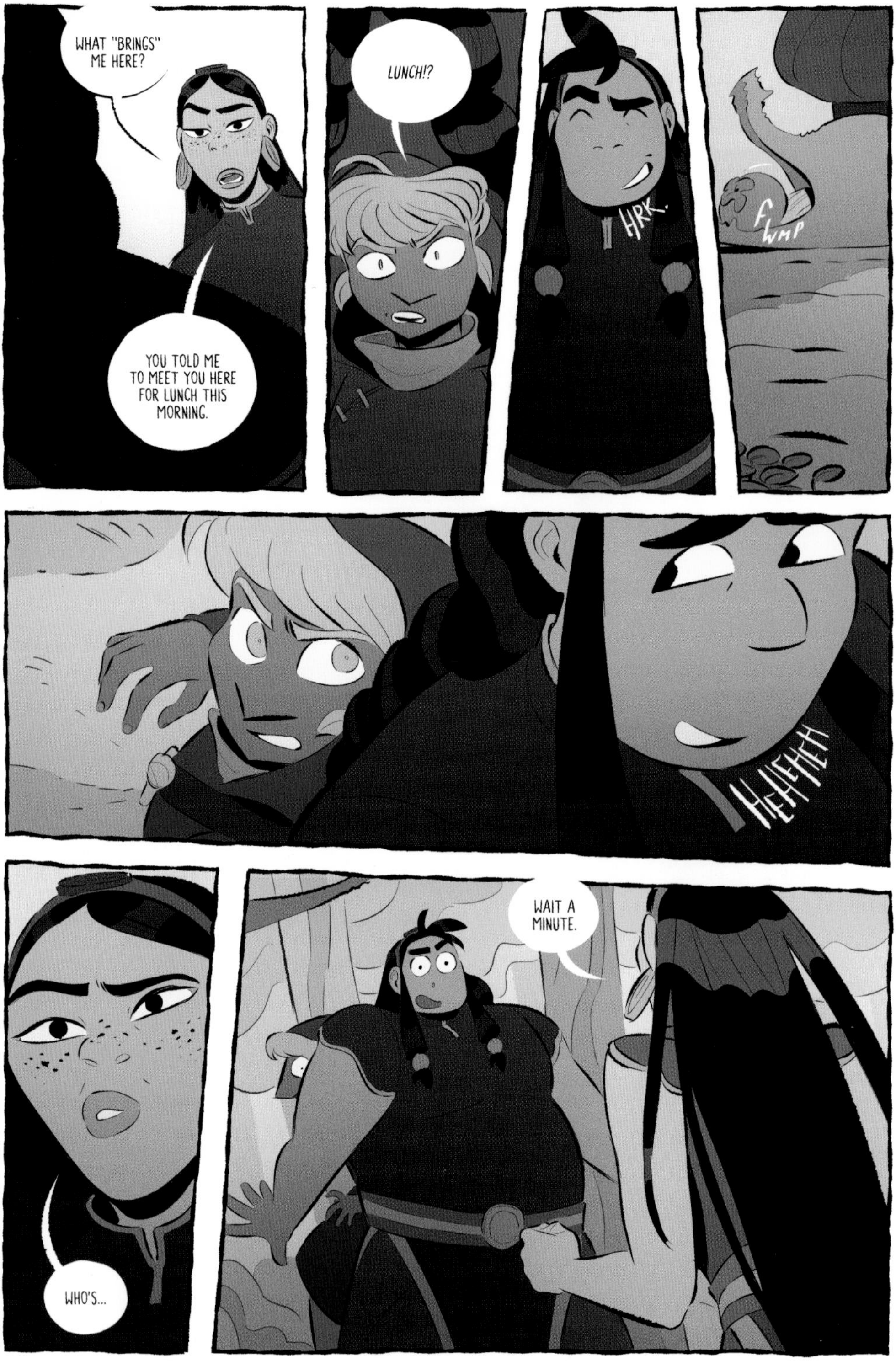
WHAT "BRINGS" ME HERE?
YOU TOLD ME TO MEET YOU HERE FOR LUNCH THIS MORNING.
LUNCH!?
HRK.
FWMP
HEHEHEH
WHO'S...
WAIT A MINUTE.

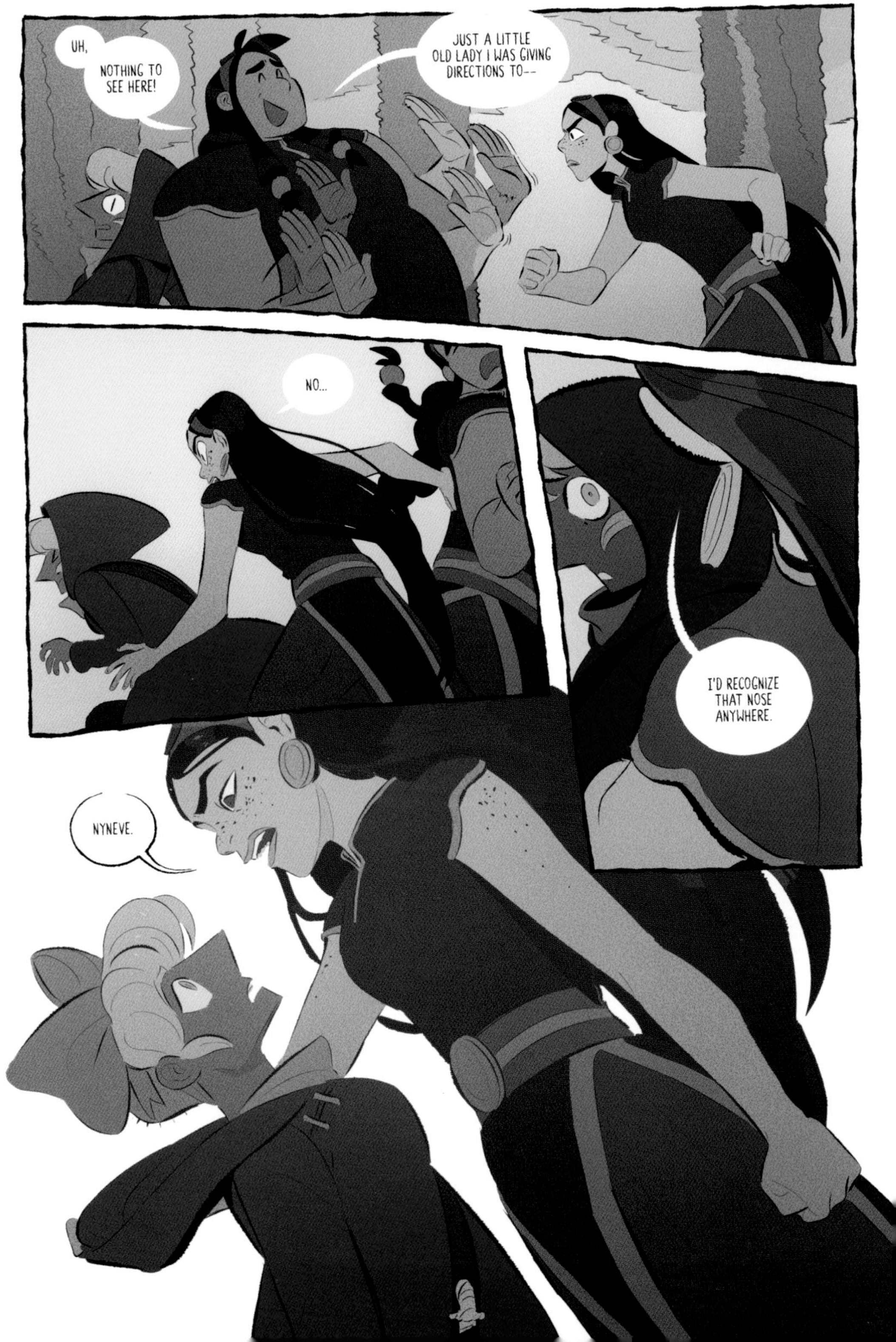
UH,
NOTHING TO SEE HERE!
JUST A LITTLE OLD LADY I WAS GIVING DIRECTIONS TO--
NO...
I'D RECOGNIZE THAT NOSE ANYWHERE.
NYNEVE.

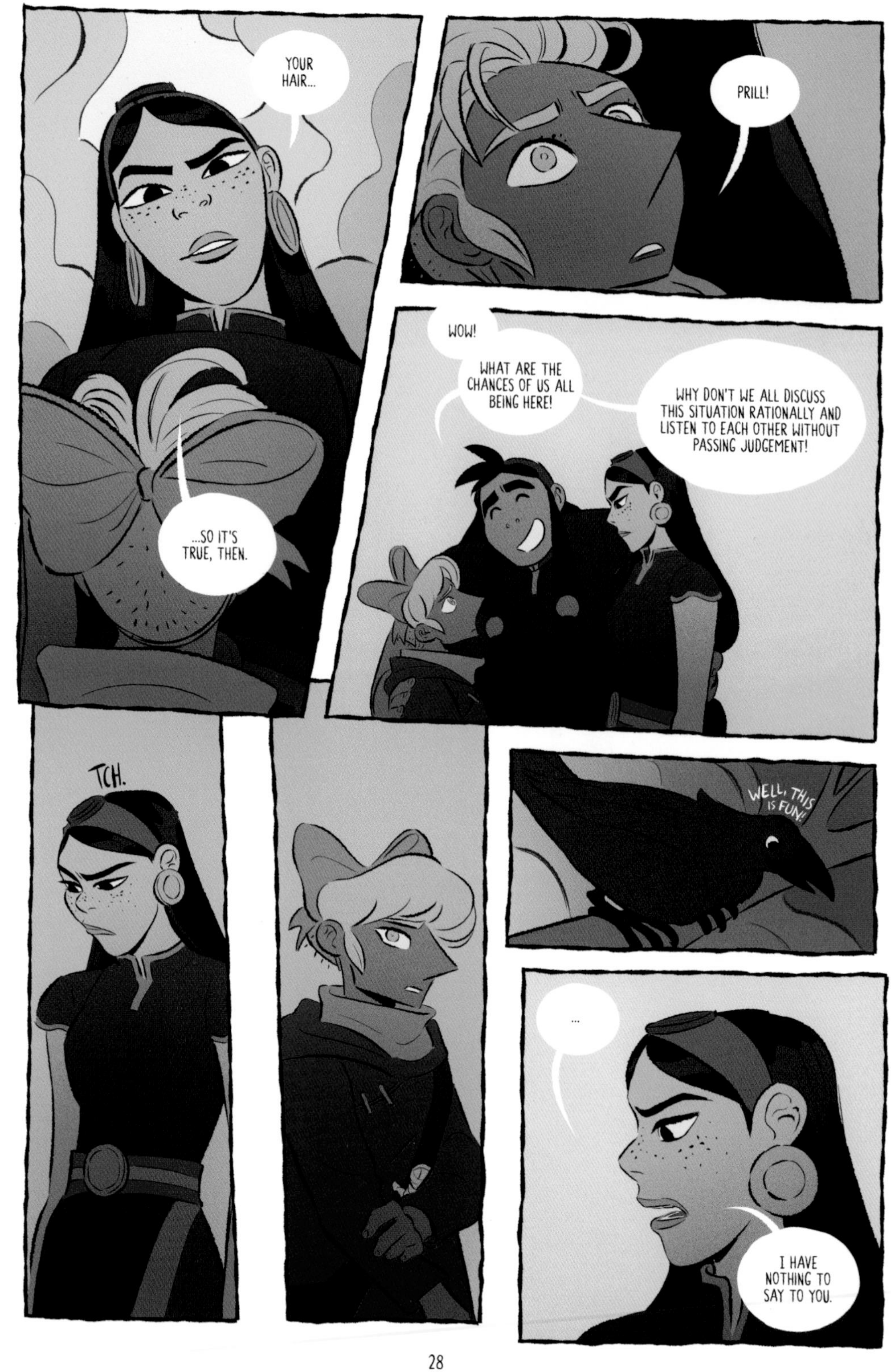

YOUR HAIR...
...SO IT'S TRUE, THEN.
PRILL!
WOW!
WHAT ARE THE CHANCES OF US ALL BEING HERE!
WHY DON'T WE ALL DISCUSS THIS SITUATION RATIONALLY AND LISTEN TO EACH OTHER WITHOUT PASSING JUDGEMENT!
TCH.
WELL, THIS IS FUN!
...
I HAVE NOTHING TO SAY TO YOU.

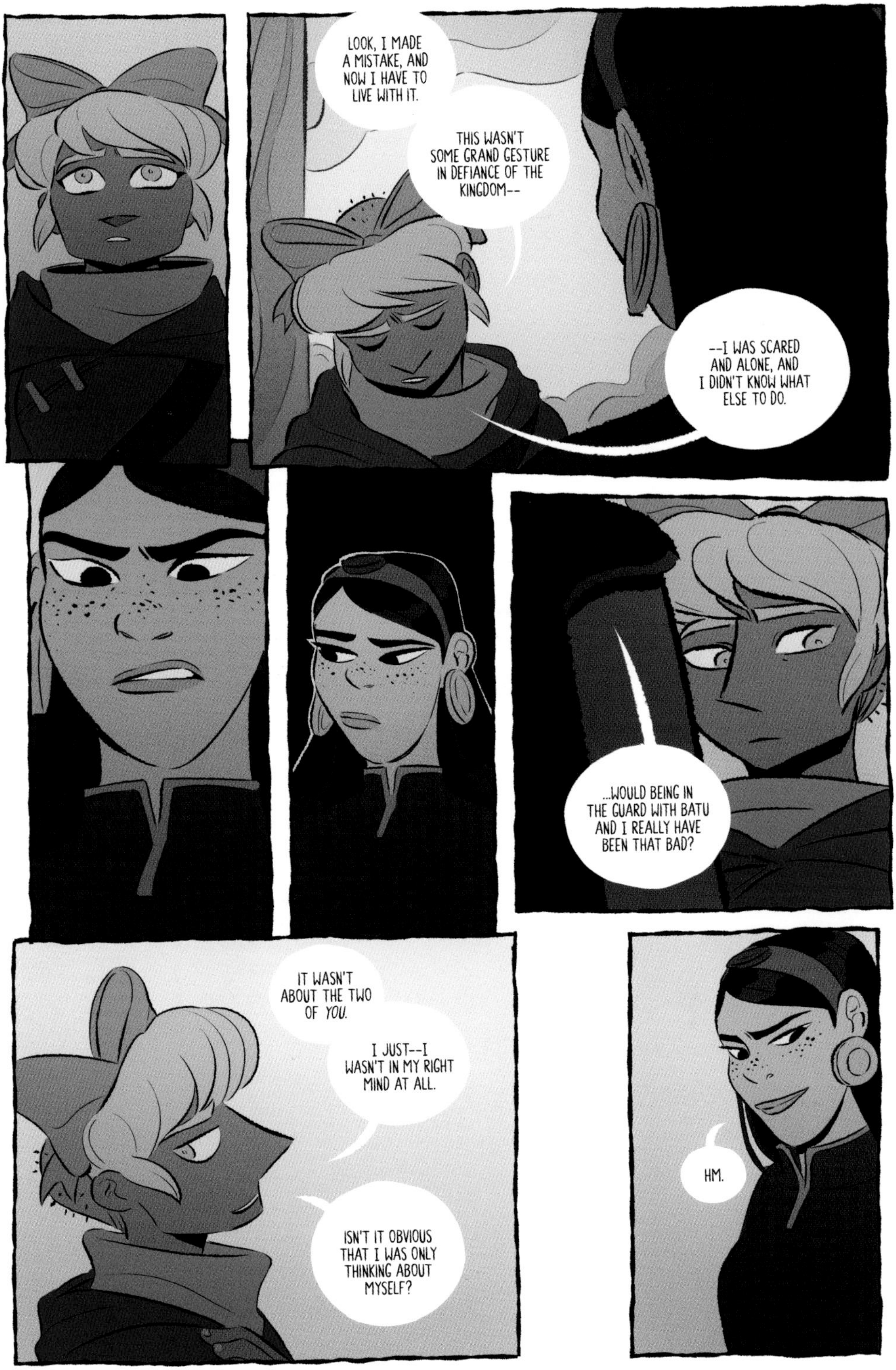
LOOK, I MADE A MISTAKE, AND NOW I HAVE TO LIVE WITH IT.
THIS WASN'T SOME GRAND GESTURE IN DEFIANCE OF THE KINGDOM--
--I WAS SCARED AND ALONE, AND I DIDN'T KNOW WHAT ELSE TO DO.
...WOULD BEING IN THE GUARD WITH BATU AND I REALLY HAVE BEEN THAT BAD?
IT WASN'T ABOUT THE TWO OF *YOU*.
I JUST--I WASN'T IN MY RIGHT MIND AT ALL.
ISN'T IT OBVIOUS THAT I WAS ONLY THINKING ABOUT MYSELF?
HM.

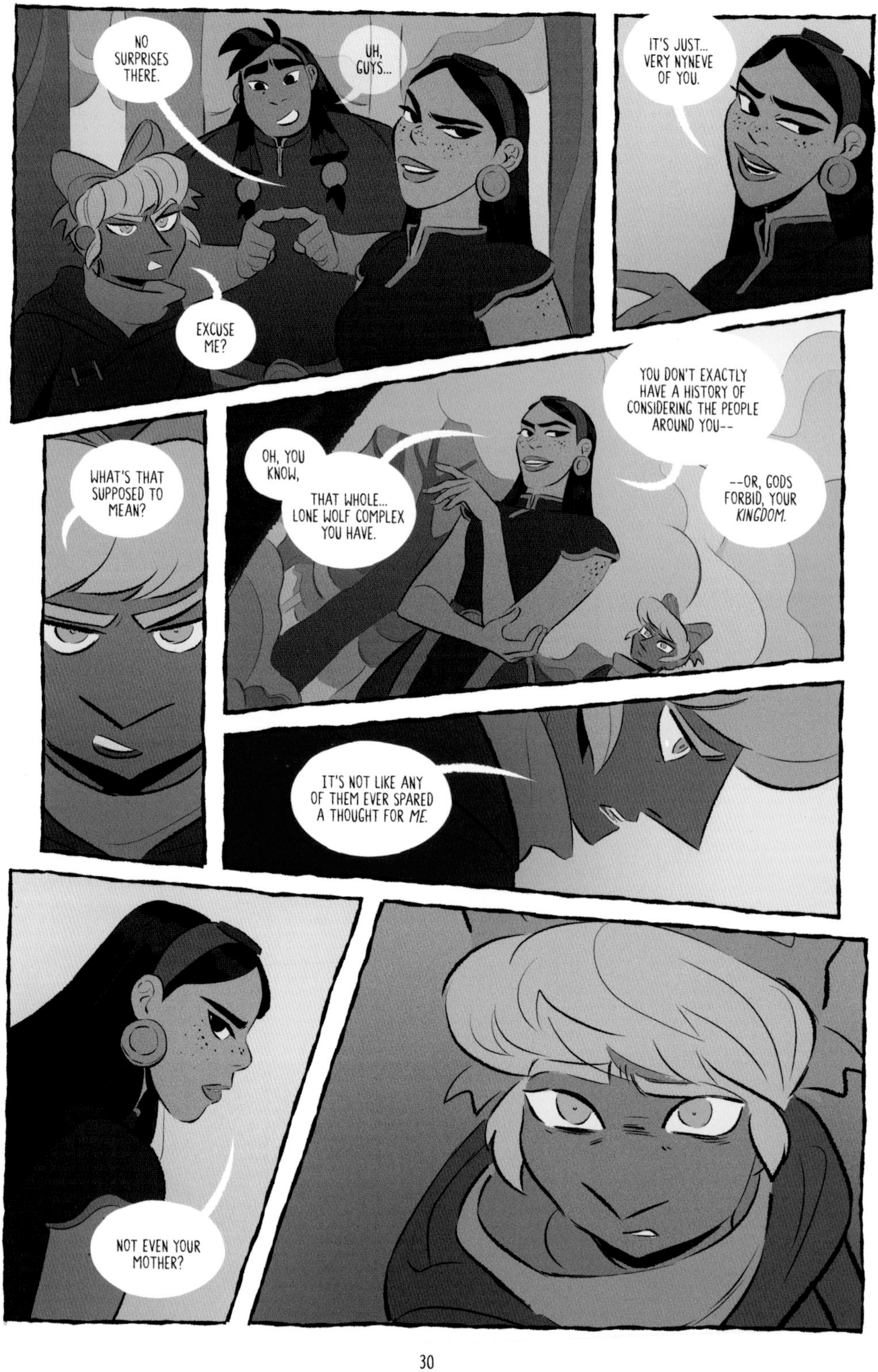
NO SURPRISES THERE.
UH, GUYS...
EXCUSE ME?
IT'S JUST... VERY NYNEVE OF YOU.
WHAT'S THAT SUPPOSED TO MEAN?
OH, YOU KNOW,
THAT WHOLE... LONE WOLF COMPLEX YOU HAVE.
YOU DON'T EXACTLY HAVE A HISTORY OF CONSIDERING THE PEOPLE AROUND YOU--
--OR, GODS FORBID, YOUR *KINGDOM.*
IT'S NOT LIKE ANY OF THEM EVER SPARED A THOUGHT FOR *ME.*
NOT EVEN YOUR MOTHER?

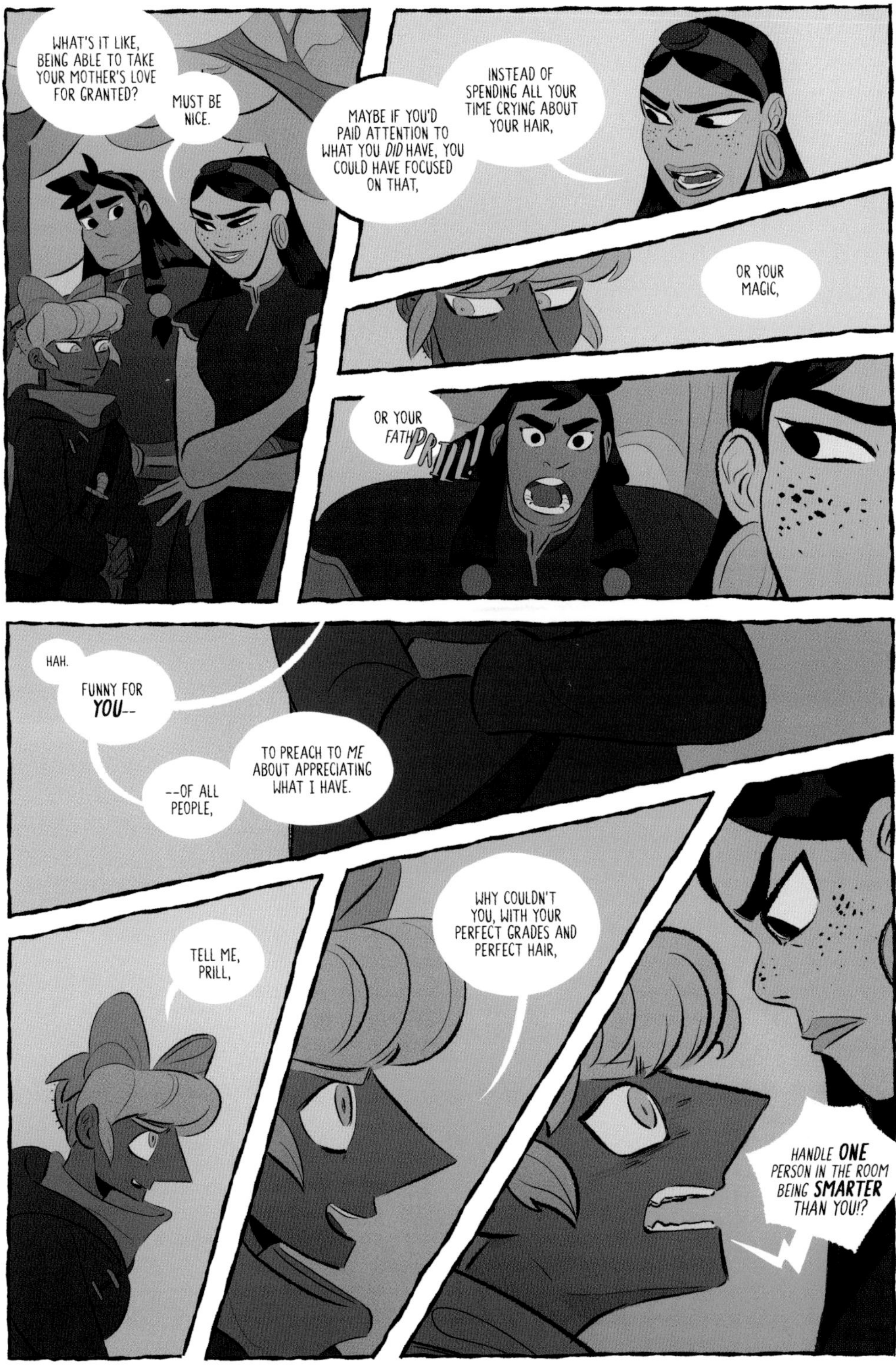
WHAT'S IT LIKE, BEING ABLE TO TAKE YOUR MOTHER'S LOVE FOR GRANTED?
MUST BE NICE.
MAYBE IF YOU'D PAID ATTENTION TO WHAT YOU *DID* HAVE, YOU COULD HAVE FOCUSED ON THAT,
INSTEAD OF SPENDING ALL YOUR TIME CRYING ABOUT YOUR HAIR,
OR YOUR MAGIC,
OR YOUR FATH
PRILL!
HAH.
FUNNY FOR **YOU**--
--OF ALL PEOPLE,
TO PREACH TO *ME* ABOUT APPRECIATING WHAT I HAVE.
TELL ME, PRILL,
WHY COULDN'T YOU, WITH YOUR PERFECT GRADES AND PERFECT HAIR,
HANDLE **ONE** PERSON IN THE ROOM BEING **SMARTER** THAN YOU!?

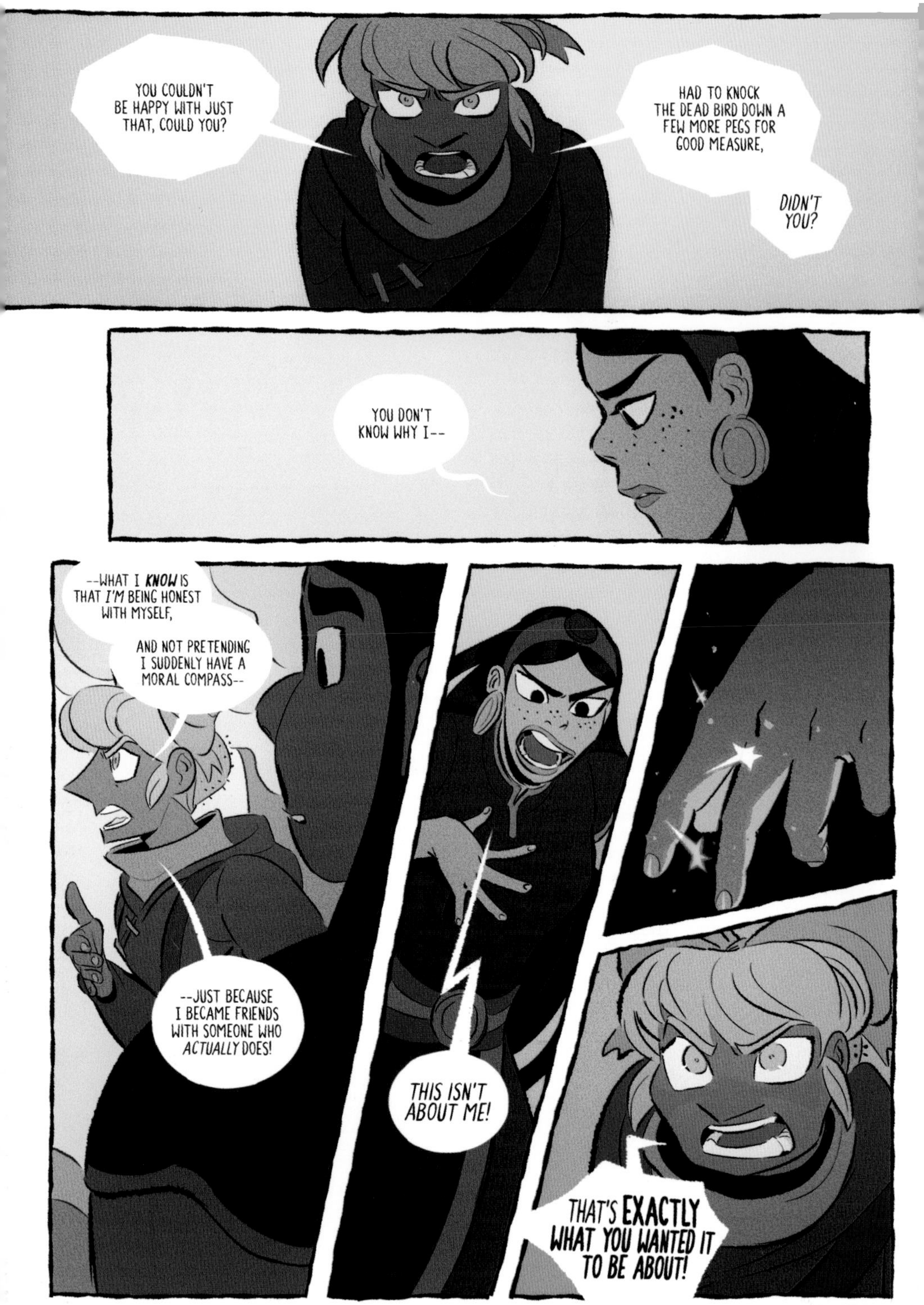
YOU COULDN'T BE HAPPY WITH JUST THAT, COULD YOU?
HAD TO KNOCK THE DEAD BIRD DOWN A FEW MORE PEGS FOR GOOD MEASURE,
DIDN'T YOU?
YOU DON'T KNOW WHY I--
--WHAT I **KNOW** IS THAT *I'M* BEING HONEST WITH MYSELF,
AND NOT PRETENDING I SUDDENLY HAVE A MORAL COMPASS--
--JUST BECAUSE I BECAME FRIENDS WITH SOMEONE WHO *ACTUALLY* DOES!
THIS ISN'T ABOUT ME!
THAT'S **EXACTLY** WHAT YOU WANTED IT TO BE ABOUT!

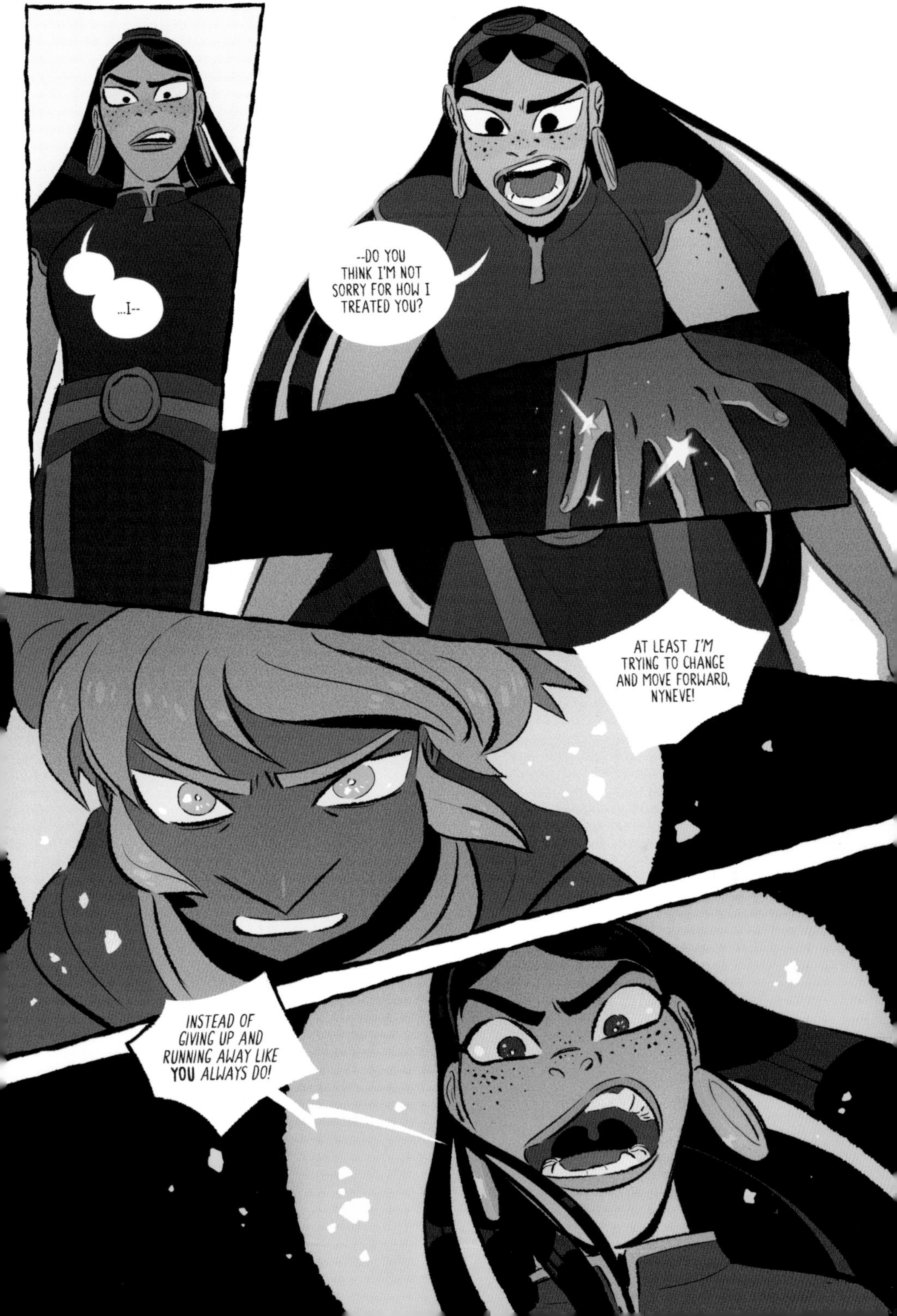
...I--
--DO YOU THINK I'M NOT SORRY FOR HOW I TREATED YOU?
AT LEAST I'M TRYING TO CHANGE AND MOVE FORWARD, NYNEVE!
INSTEAD OF GIVING UP AND RUNNING AWAY LIKE YOU ALWAYS DO!

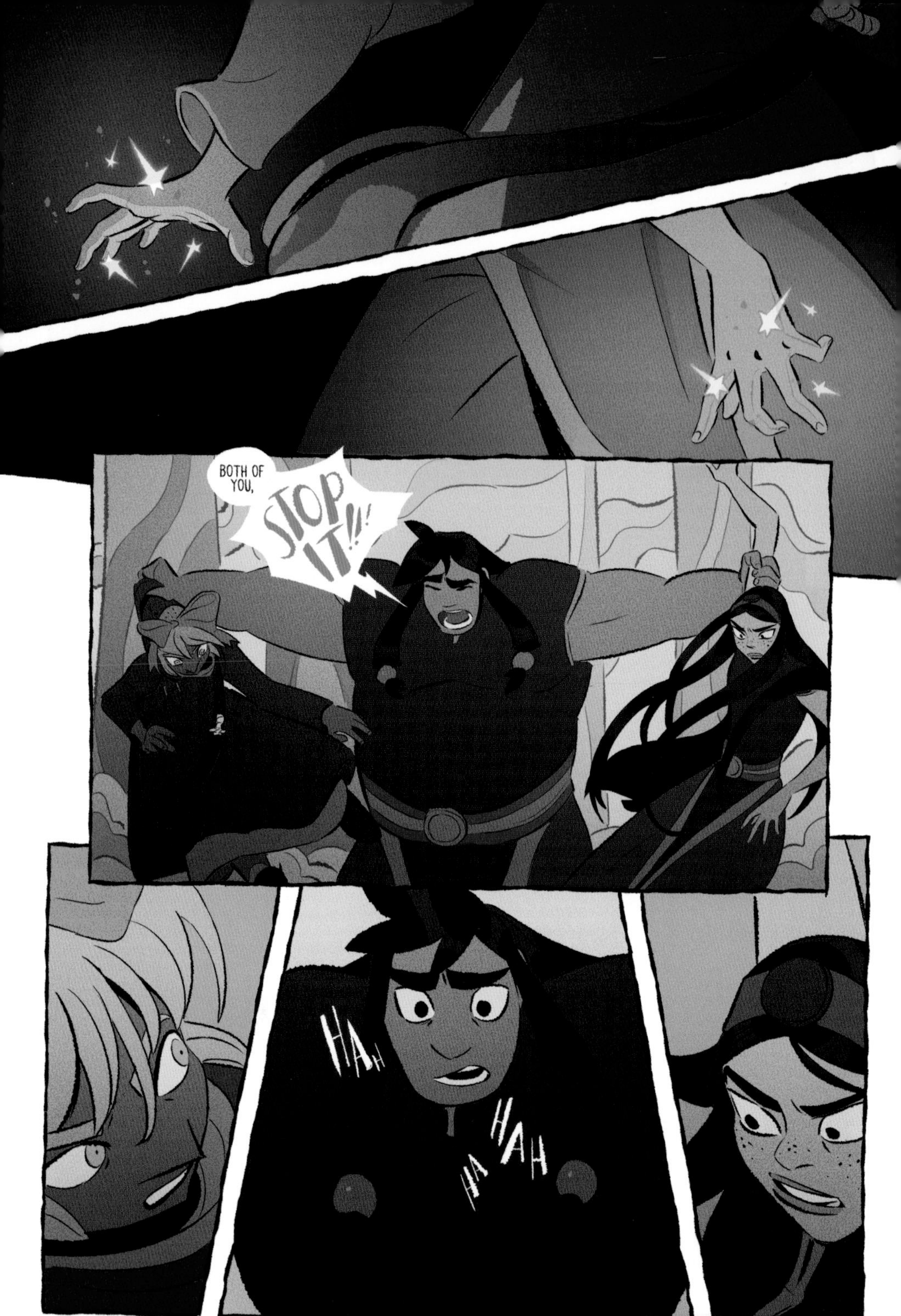
BOTH OF YOU,
STOP IT!!!
HAH
HAH
HA

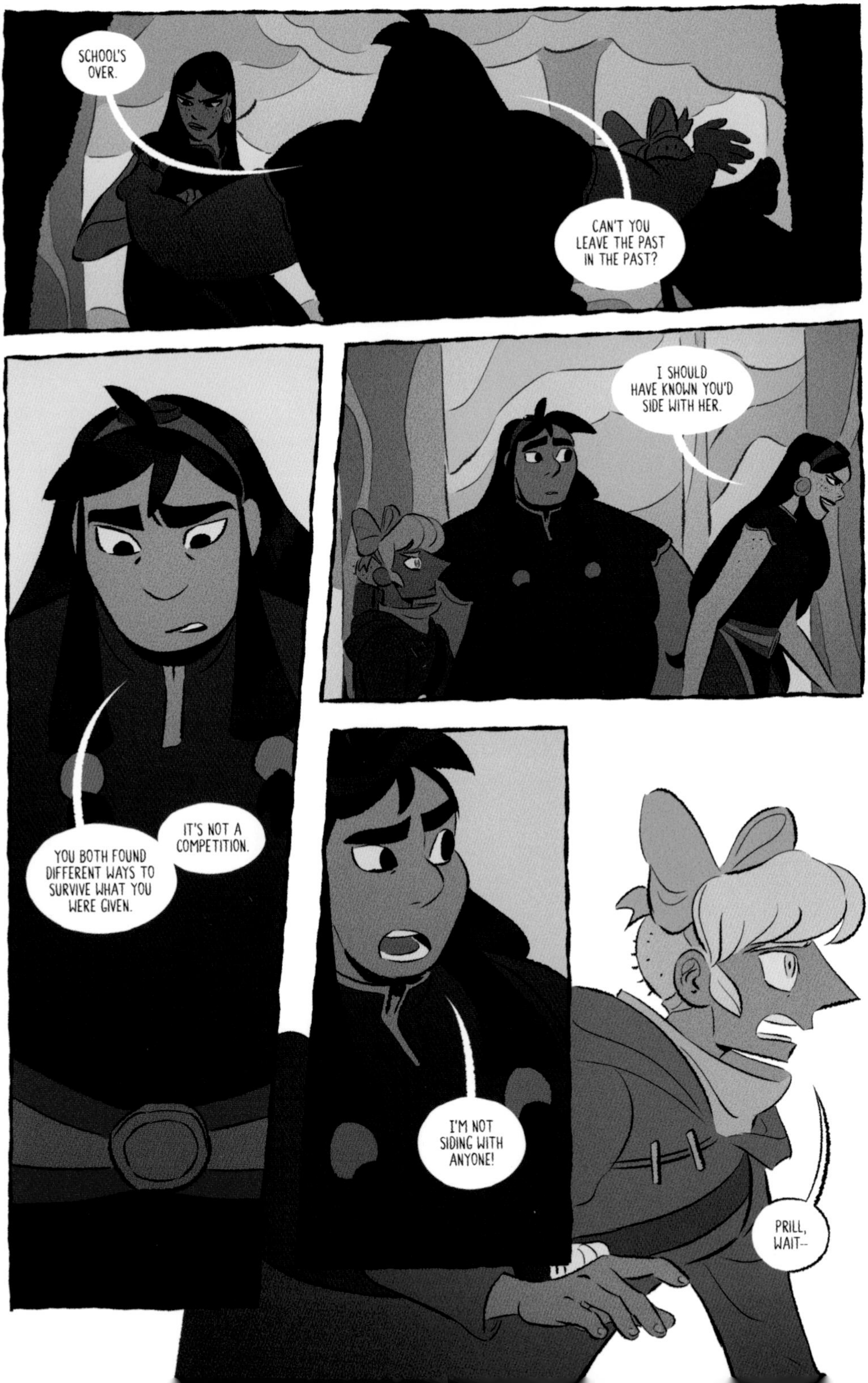
SCHOOL'S OVER.
CAN'T YOU LEAVE THE PAST IN THE PAST?
I SHOULD HAVE KNOWN YOU'D SIDE WITH HER.
IT'S NOT A COMPETITION.
YOU BOTH FOUND DIFFERENT WAYS TO SURVIVE WHAT YOU WERE GIVEN.
I'M NOT SIDING WITH ANYONE!
PRILL, WAIT--

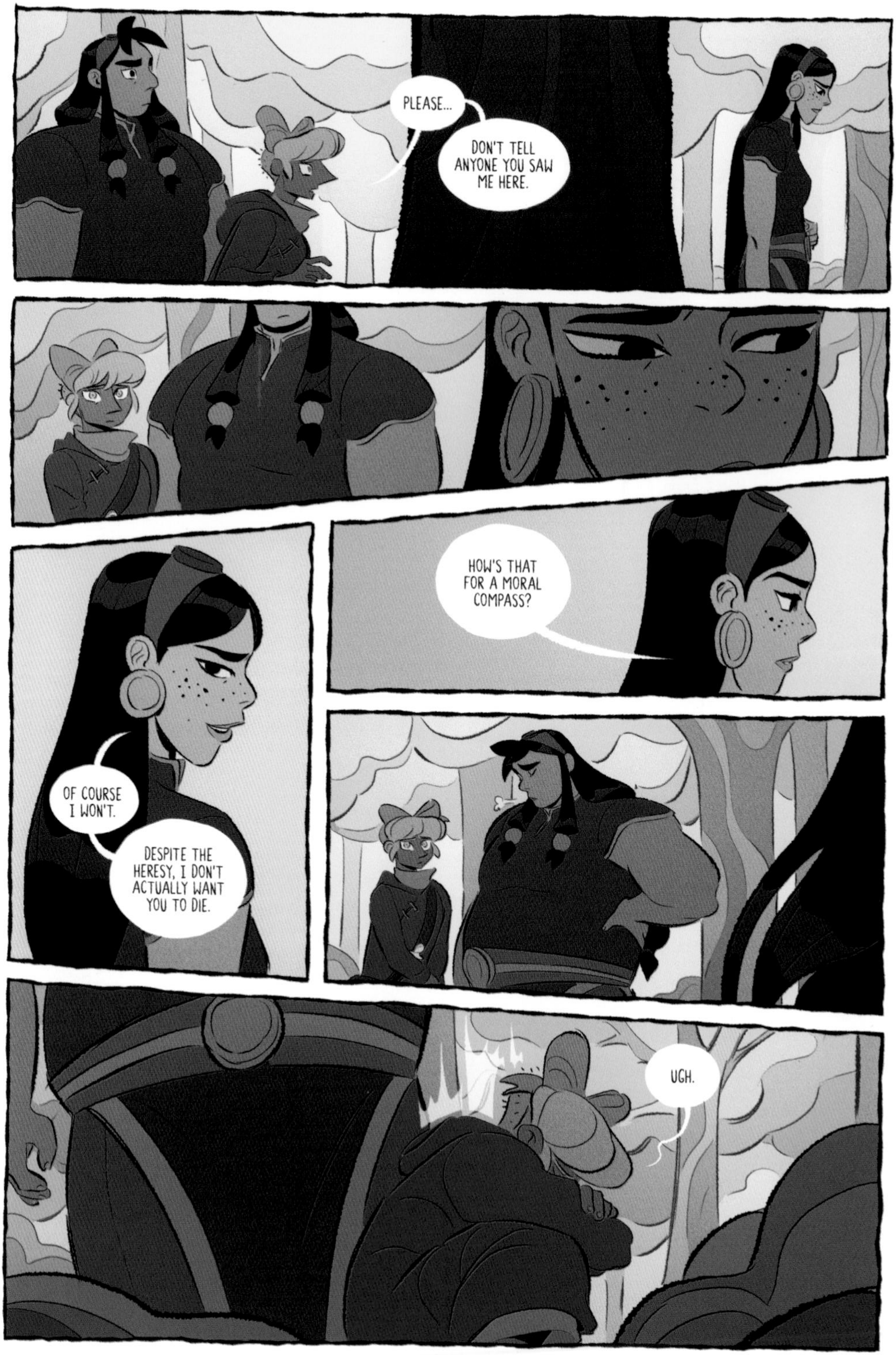
PLEASE...
DON'T TELL ANYONE YOU SAW ME HERE.
HOW'S THAT FOR A MORAL COMPASS?
OF COURSE I WON'T.
DESPITE THE HERESY, I DON'T ACTUALLY WANT YOU TO DIE.
UGH.

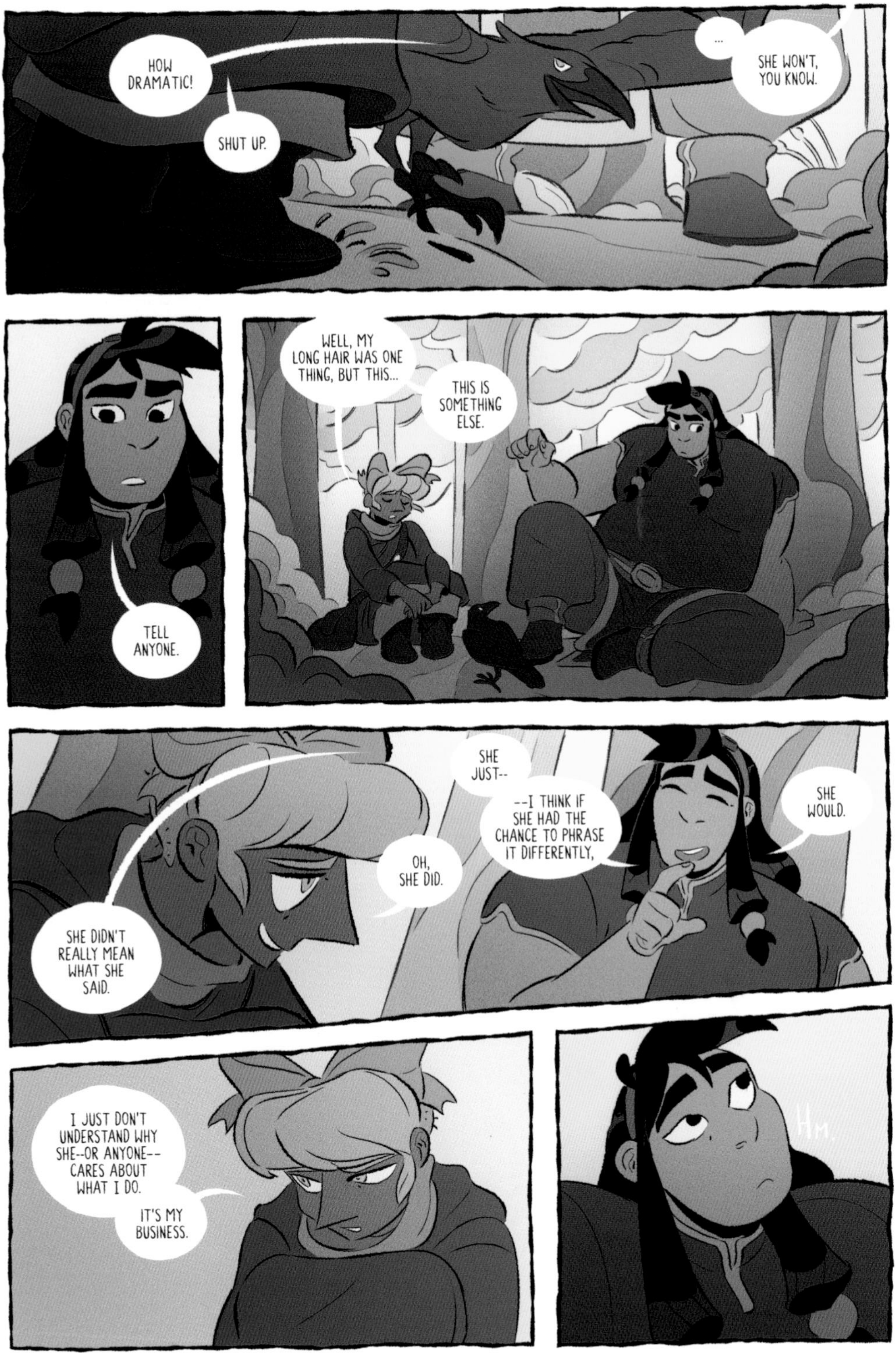
HOW DRAMATIC!
SHUT UP.
...
SHE WON'T, YOU KNOW.
TELL ANYONE.
WELL, MY LONG HAIR WAS ONE THING, BUT THIS...
THIS IS SOMETHING ELSE.
SHE DIDN'T REALLY MEAN WHAT SHE SAID.
OH, SHE DID.
SHE JUST--
--I THINK IF SHE HAD THE CHANCE TO PHRASE IT DIFFERENTLY,
SHE WOULD.
I JUST DON'T UNDERSTAND WHY SHE--OR ANYONE--CARES ABOUT WHAT I DO.
IT'S MY BUSINESS.
HM.

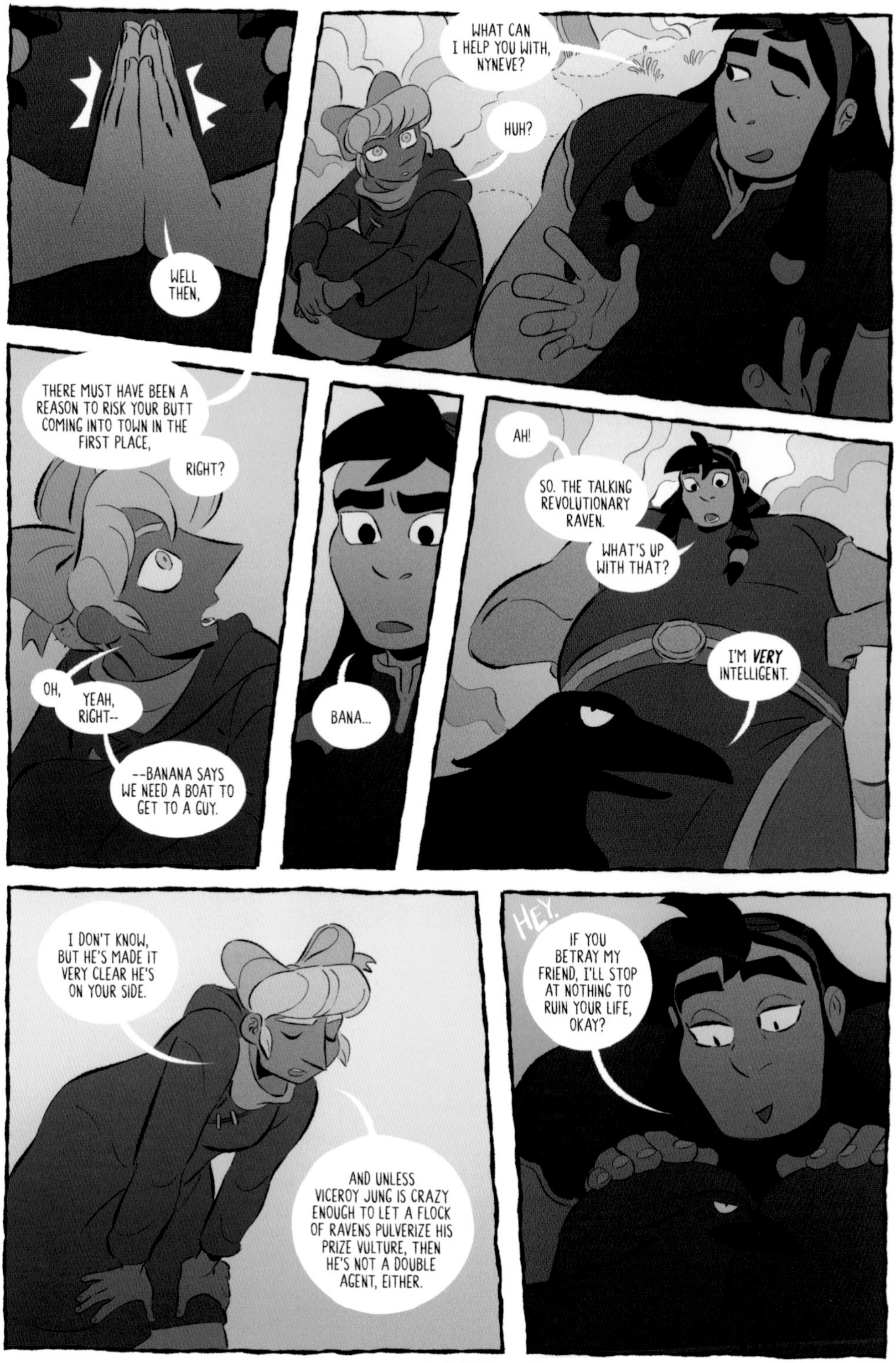

WELL THEN,
WHAT CAN I HELP YOU WITH, NYNEVE?
HUH?
THERE MUST HAVE BEEN A REASON TO RISK YOUR BUTT COMING INTO TOWN IN THE FIRST PLACE,
RIGHT?
OH,
YEAH, RIGHT--
--BANANA SAYS WE NEED A BOAT TO GET TO A GUY.
BANA...
AH!
SO. THE TALKING REVOLUTIONARY RAVEN.
WHAT'S UP WITH THAT?
I'M **VERY** INTELLIGENT.
I DON'T KNOW, BUT HE'S MADE IT VERY CLEAR HE'S ON YOUR SIDE.
AND UNLESS VICEROY JUNG IS CRAZY ENOUGH TO LET A FLOCK OF RAVENS PULVERIZE HIS PRIZE VULTURE, THEN HE'S NOT A DOUBLE AGENT, EITHER.
HEY.
IF YOU BETRAY MY FRIEND, I'LL STOP AT NOTHING TO RUIN YOUR LIFE, OKAY?

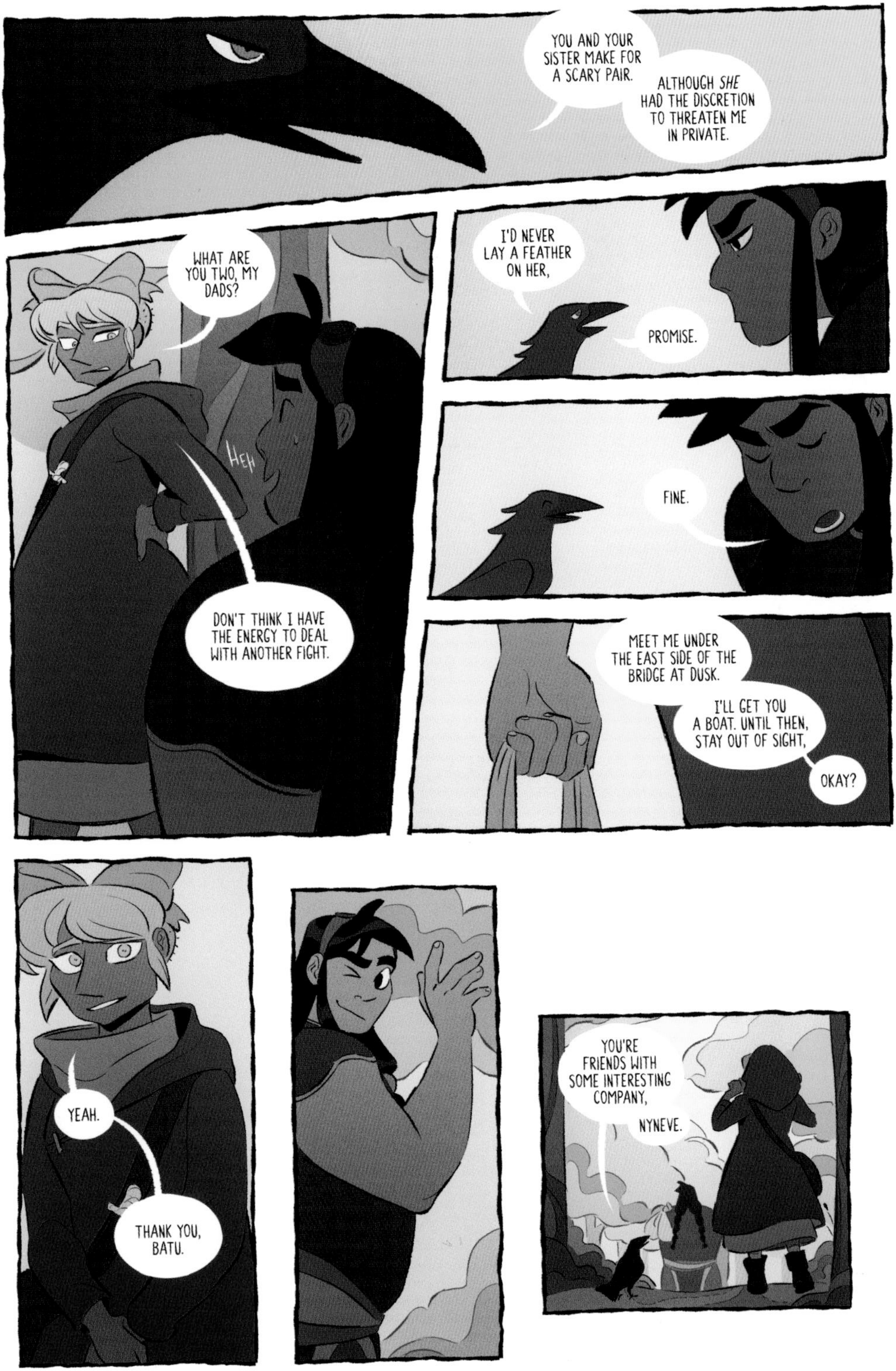
YOU AND YOUR SISTER MAKE FOR A SCARY PAIR.
ALTHOUGH *SHE* HAD THE DISCRETION TO THREATEN ME IN PRIVATE.
WHAT ARE YOU TWO, MY DADS?
HEH
DON'T THINK I HAVE THE ENERGY TO DEAL WITH ANOTHER FIGHT.
I'D NEVER LAY A FEATHER ON HER,
PROMISE.
FINE.
MEET ME UNDER THE EAST SIDE OF THE BRIDGE AT DUSK.
I'LL GET YOU A BOAT. UNTIL THEN, STAY OUT OF SIGHT,
OKAY?
YEAH.
THANK YOU, BATU.
YOU'RE FRIENDS WITH SOME INTERESTING COMPANY,
NYNEVE.

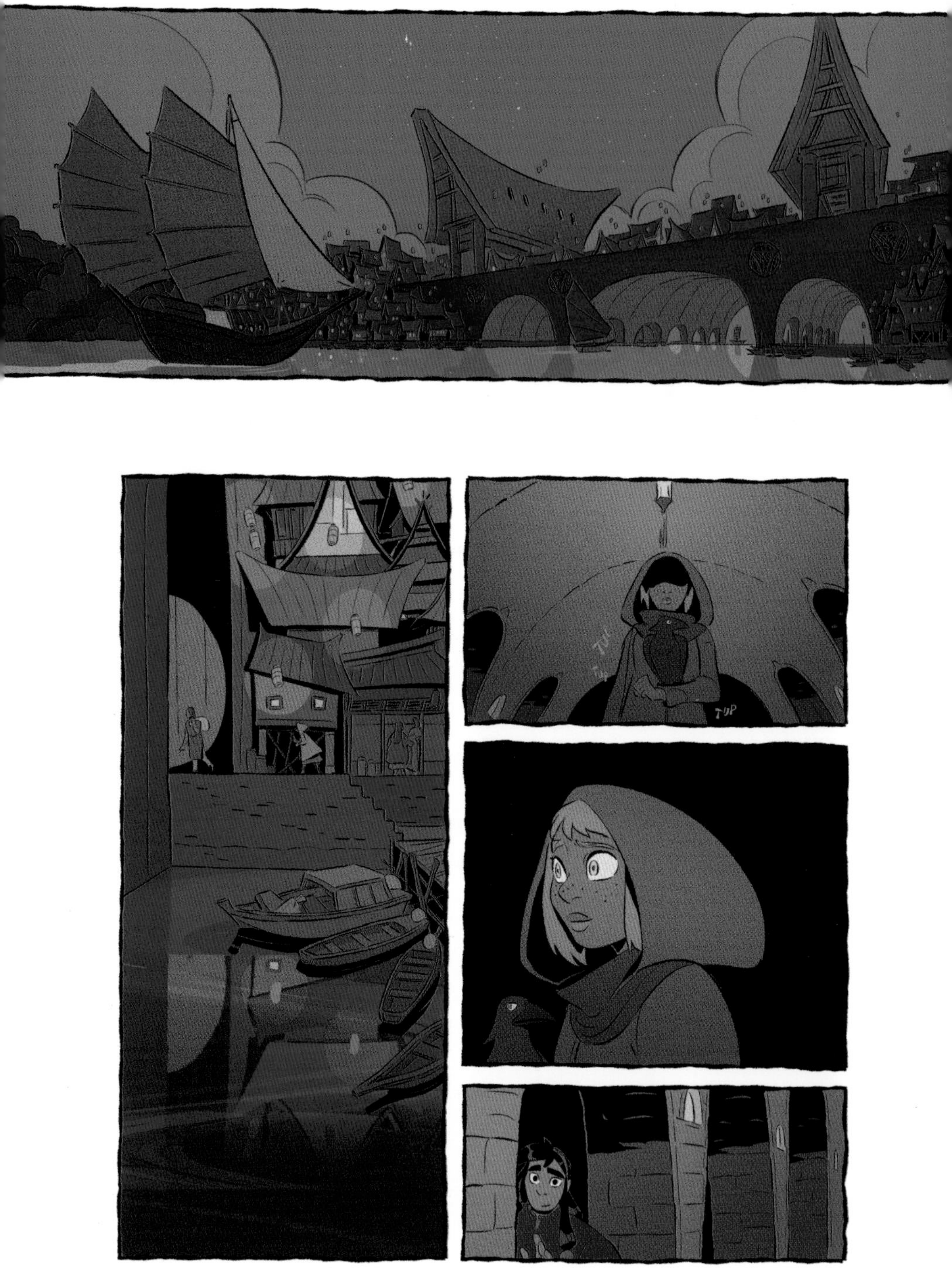
TUP

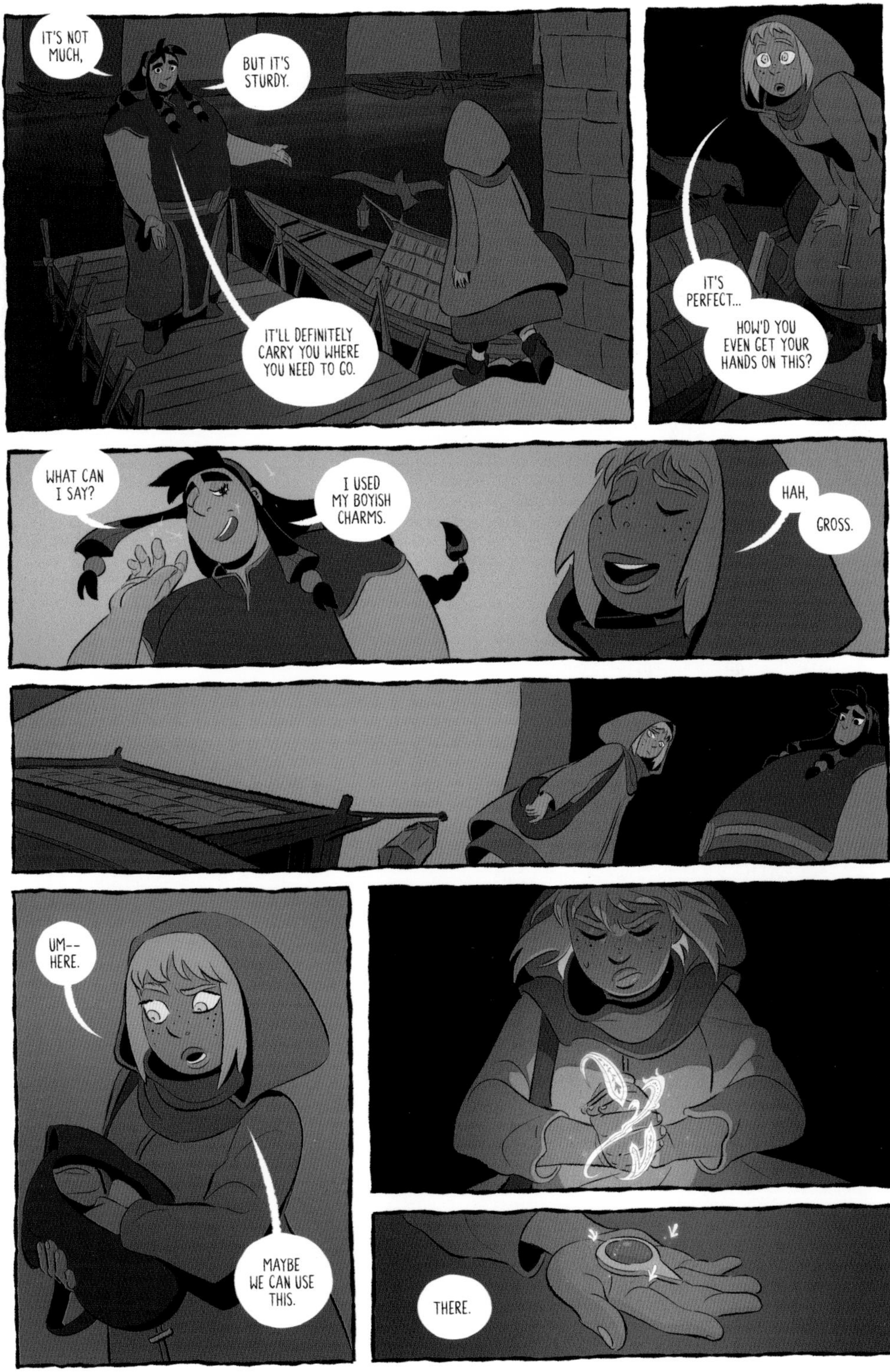
IT'S NOT MUCH,
BUT IT'S STURDY.
IT'LL DEFINITELY CARRY YOU WHERE YOU NEED TO GO.
IT'S PERFECT...
HOW'D YOU EVEN GET YOUR HANDS ON THIS?
WHAT CAN I SAY?
I USED MY BOYISH CHARMS.
HAH,
GROSS.
UM-- HERE.
MAYBE WE CAN USE THIS.
THERE.

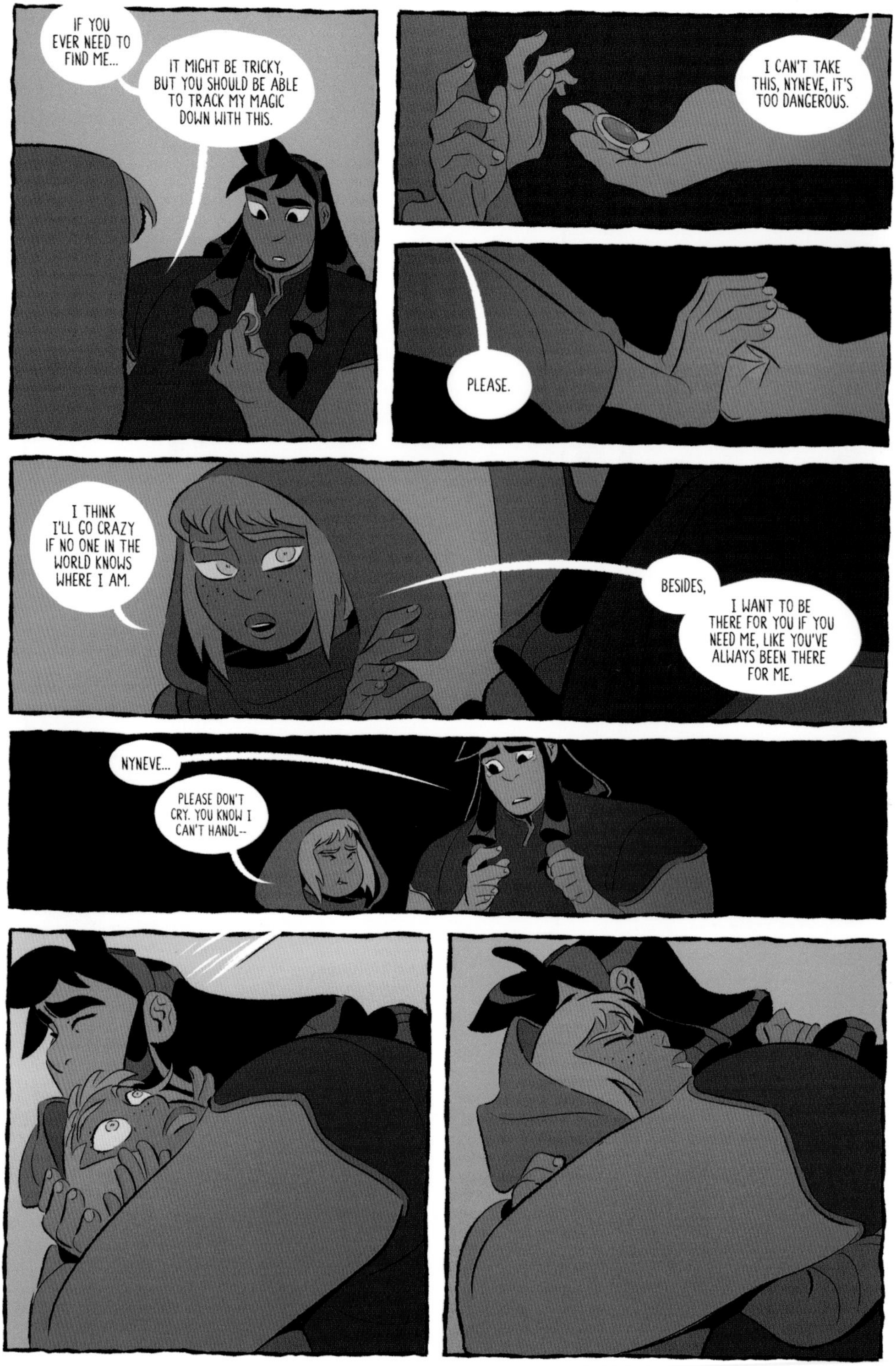
IF YOU EVER NEED TO FIND ME...
IT MIGHT BE TRICKY, BUT YOU SHOULD BE ABLE TO TRACK MY MAGIC DOWN WITH THIS.
I CAN'T TAKE THIS, NYNEVE, IT'S TOO DANGEROUS.
PLEASE.
I THINK I'LL GO CRAZY IF NO ONE IN THE WORLD KNOWS WHERE I AM.
BESIDES,
I WANT TO BE THERE FOR YOU IF YOU NEED ME, LIKE YOU'VE ALWAYS BEEN THERE FOR ME.
NYNEVE...
PLEASE DON'T CRY. YOU KNOW I CAN'T HANDL--

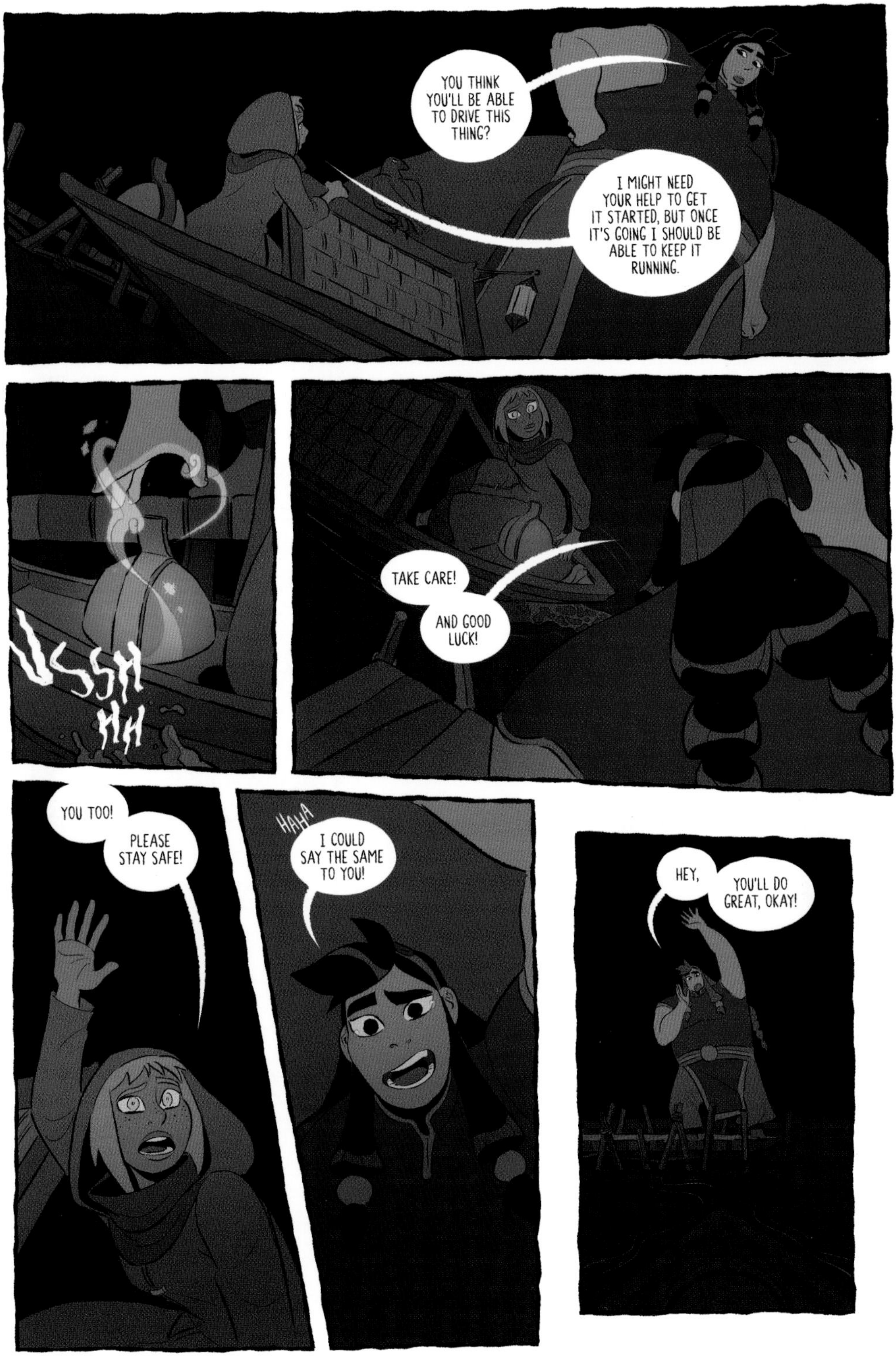
YOU THINK YOU'LL BE ABLE TO DRIVE THIS THING?
I MIGHT NEED YOUR HELP TO GET IT STARTED, BUT ONCE IT'S GOING I SHOULD BE ABLE TO KEEP IT RUNNING.
TAKE CARE!
AND GOOD LUCK!
YOU TOO!
PLEASE STAY SAFE!
HAHA
I COULD SAY THE SAME TO YOU!
HEY,
YOU'LL DO GREAT, OKAY!

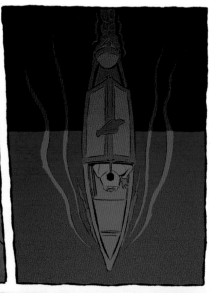

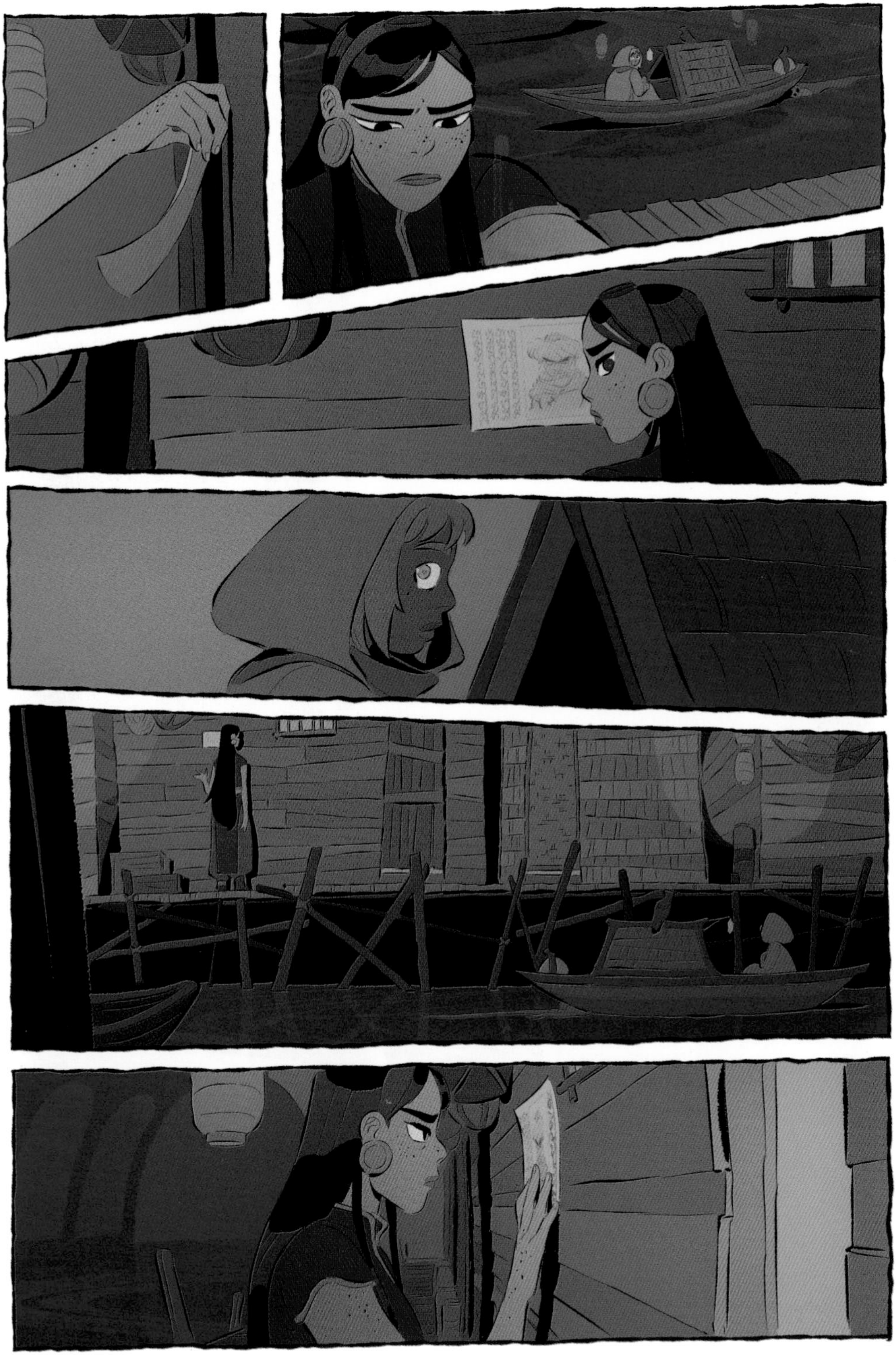

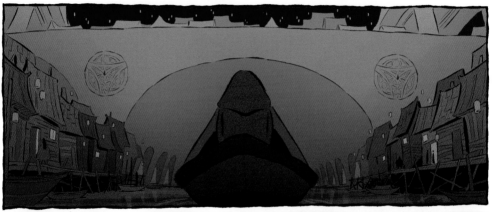

WELL,

I GUESS IT'S JUST YOU AND ME FOR THE NEXT COUPLE OF...

SNF

DAMN IT.

AH--

GODS...

SORRY.

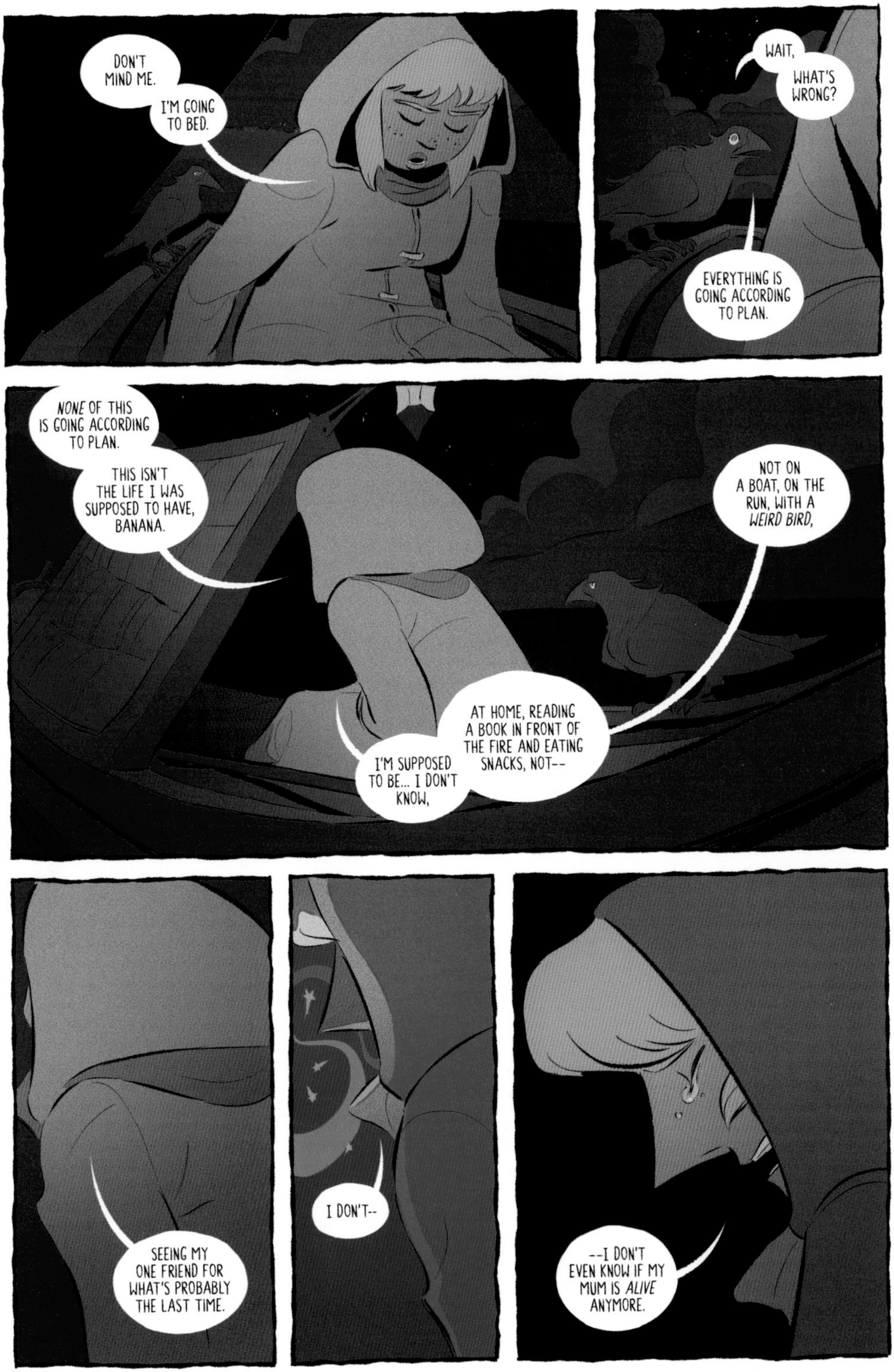
DON'T MIND ME.
I'M GOING TO BED.
WAIT,
WHAT'S WRONG?
EVERYTHING IS GOING ACCORDING TO PLAN.
NONE OF THIS IS GOING ACCORDING TO PLAN.
THIS ISN'T THE LIFE I WAS SUPPOSED TO HAVE, BANANA.
I'M SUPPOSED TO BE... I DON'T KNOW,
AT HOME, READING A BOOK IN FRONT OF THE FIRE AND EATING SNACKS, NOT--
NOT ON A BOAT, ON THE RUN, WITH A *WEIRD BIRD*,
SEEING MY ONE FRIEND FOR WHAT'S PROBABLY THE LAST TIME.
I DON'T--
--I DON'T EVEN KNOW IF MY MUM IS *ALIVE* ANYMORE.

WHY DID SHE MAKE ME DEAL WITH ALL OF THIS ALONE?

I'M SORRY.

I'M SURE... THIS WILL ALL GET EASIER WITH TIME, AND,

I DON'T *WANT* IT TO GET EASIER.

I DON'T WANT IT TO BE HAPPENING AT ALL.

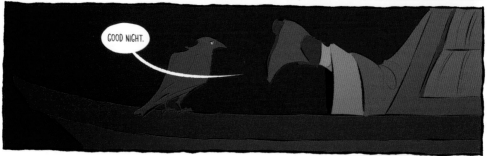

GOOD NIGHT.

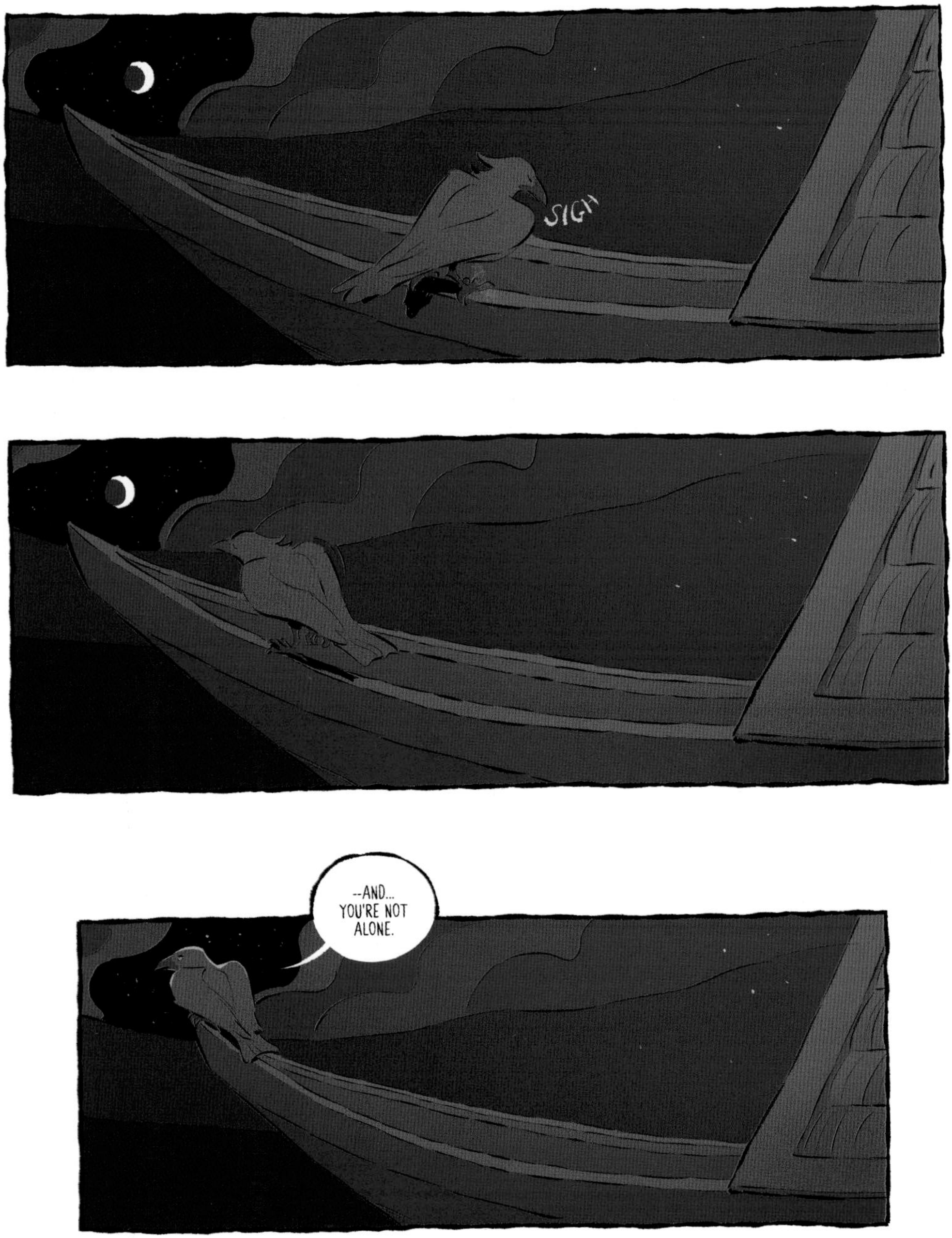
SIGH
--AND... YOU'RE NOT ALONE.

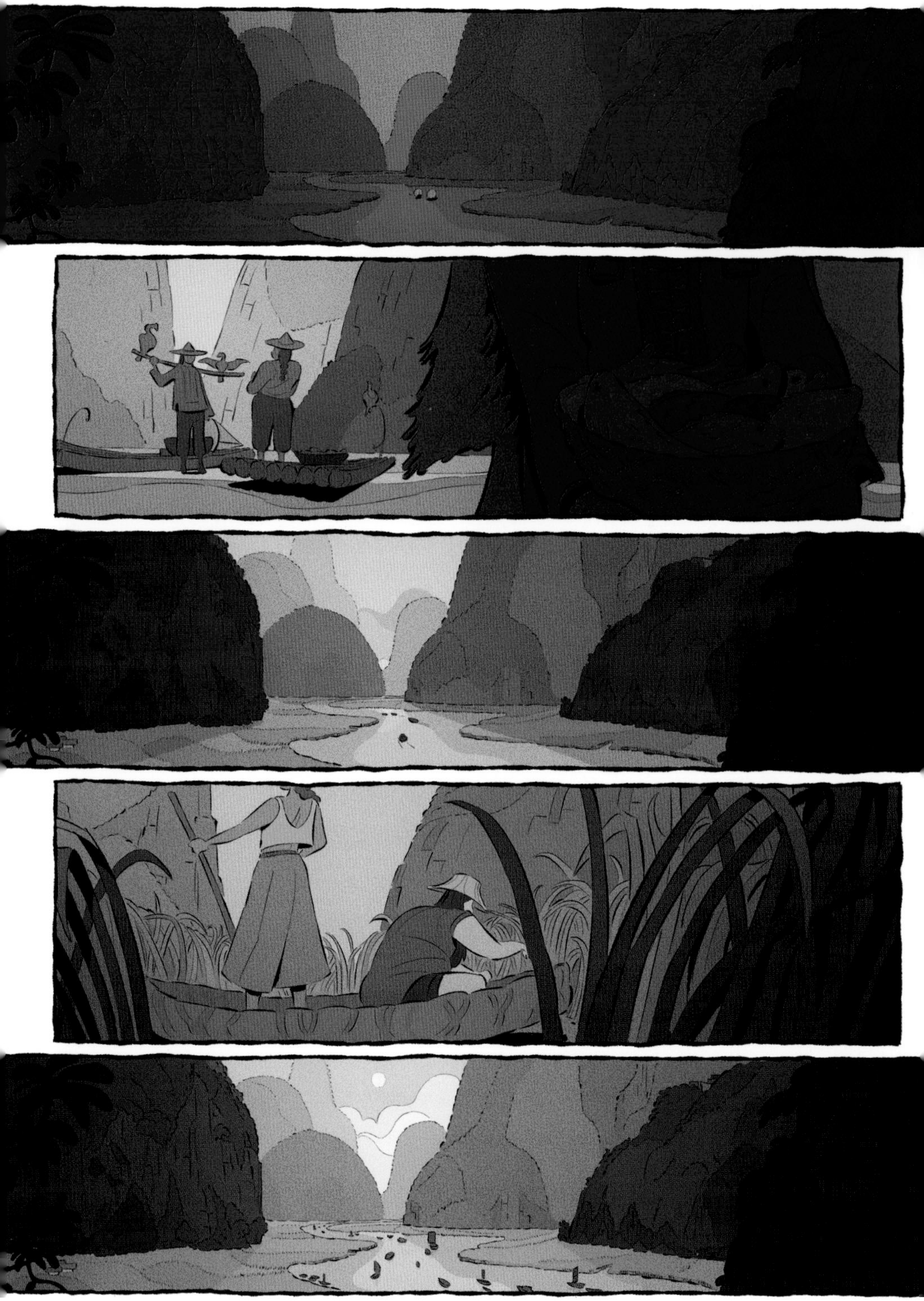

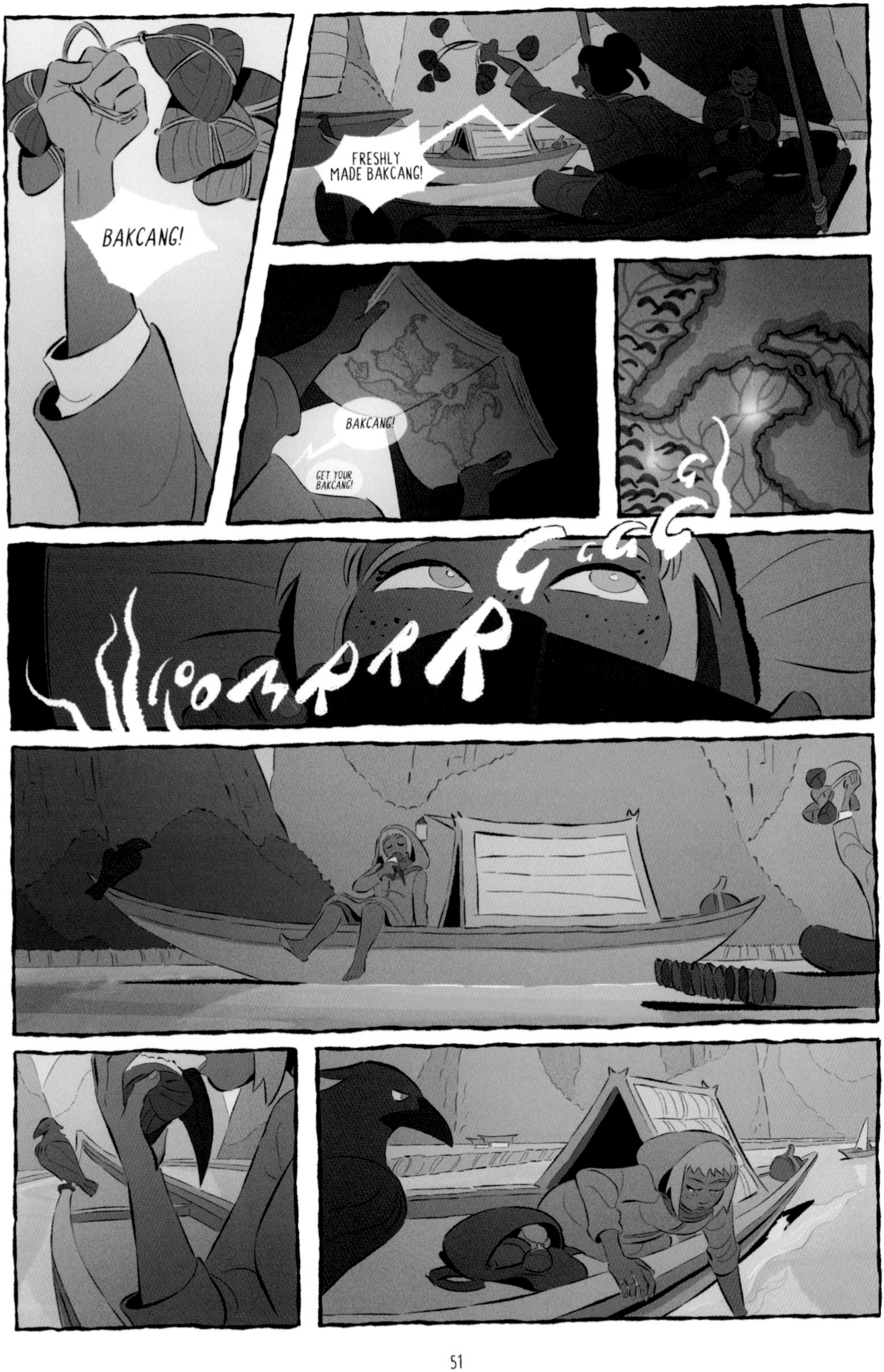
BAKCANG!
FRESHLY MADE BAKCANG!
BAKCANG!
GET YOUR BAKCANG!
OOMRRRRGGGG

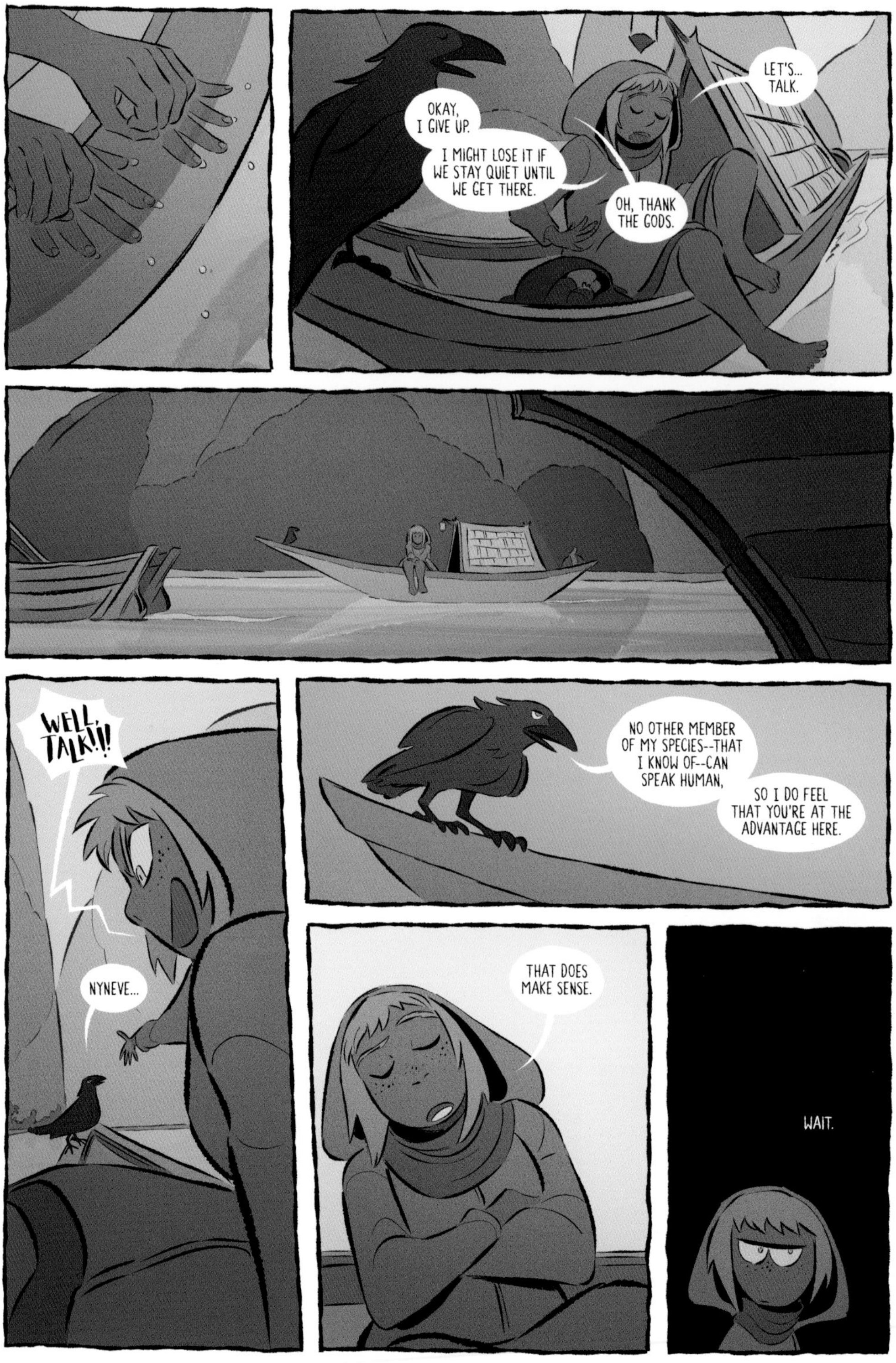
OKAY, I GIVE UP.
I MIGHT LOSE IT IF WE STAY QUIET UNTIL WE GET THERE.
LET'S... TALK.
OH, THANK THE GODS.
WELL, TALK!!!
NYNEVE...
NO OTHER MEMBER OF MY SPECIES--THAT I KNOW OF--CAN SPEAK HUMAN,
SO I DO FEEL THAT YOU'RE AT THE ADVANTAGE HERE.
THAT DOES MAKE SENSE.
WAIT.

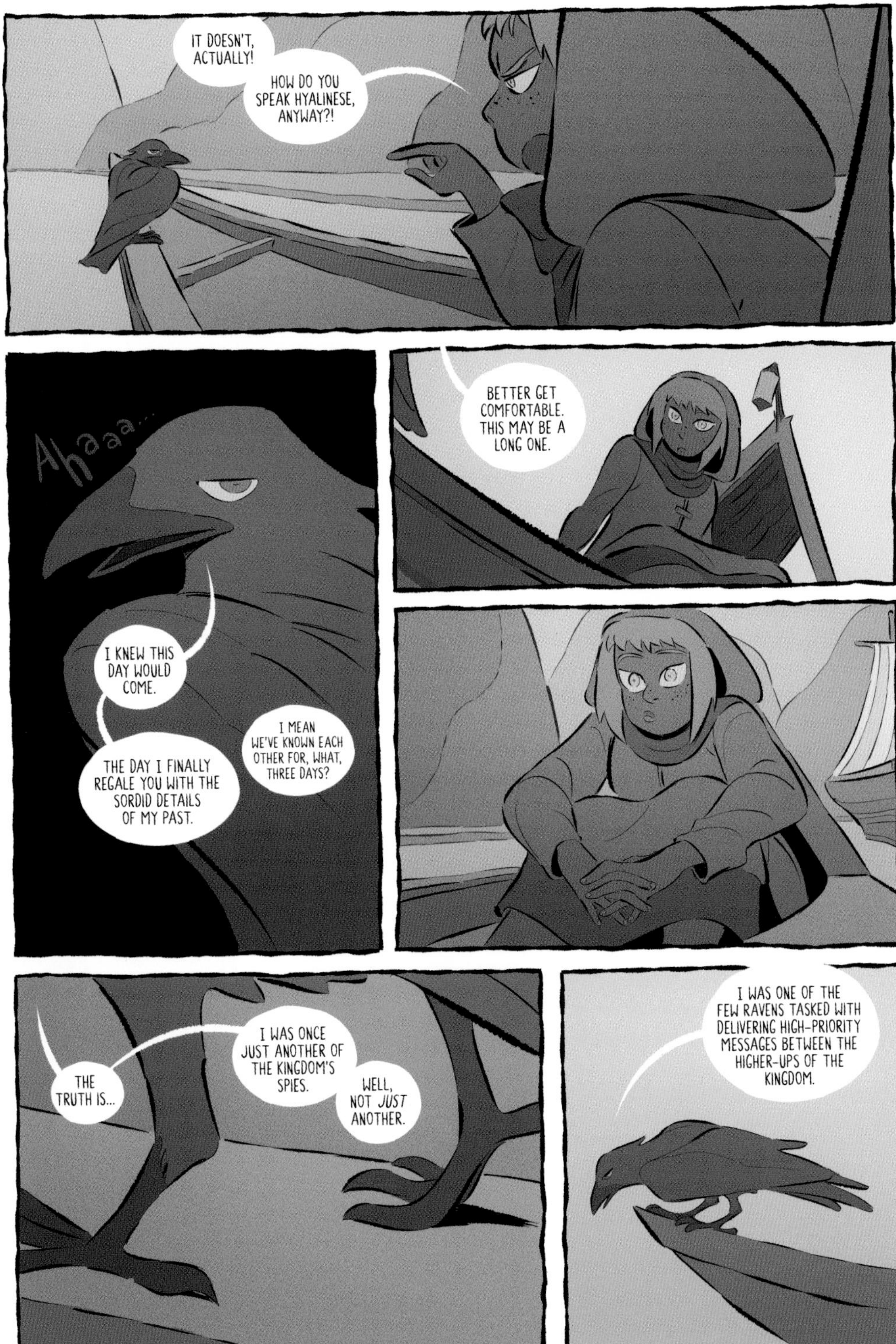
IT DOESN'T, ACTUALLY!
HOW DO YOU SPEAK HYALINESE, ANYWAY?!
Ahaaa...
I KNEW THIS DAY WOULD COME.
THE DAY I FINALLY REGALE YOU WITH THE SORDID DETAILS OF MY PAST.
I MEAN WE'VE KNOWN EACH OTHER FOR, WHAT, THREE DAYS?
BETTER GET COMFORTABLE. THIS MAY BE A LONG ONE.
THE TRUTH IS...
I WAS ONCE JUST ANOTHER OF THE KINGDOM'S SPIES.
WELL, NOT *JUST* ANOTHER.
I WAS ONE OF THE FEW RAVENS TASKED WITH DELIVERING HIGH-PRIORITY MESSAGES BETWEEN THE HIGHER-UPS OF THE KINGDOM.

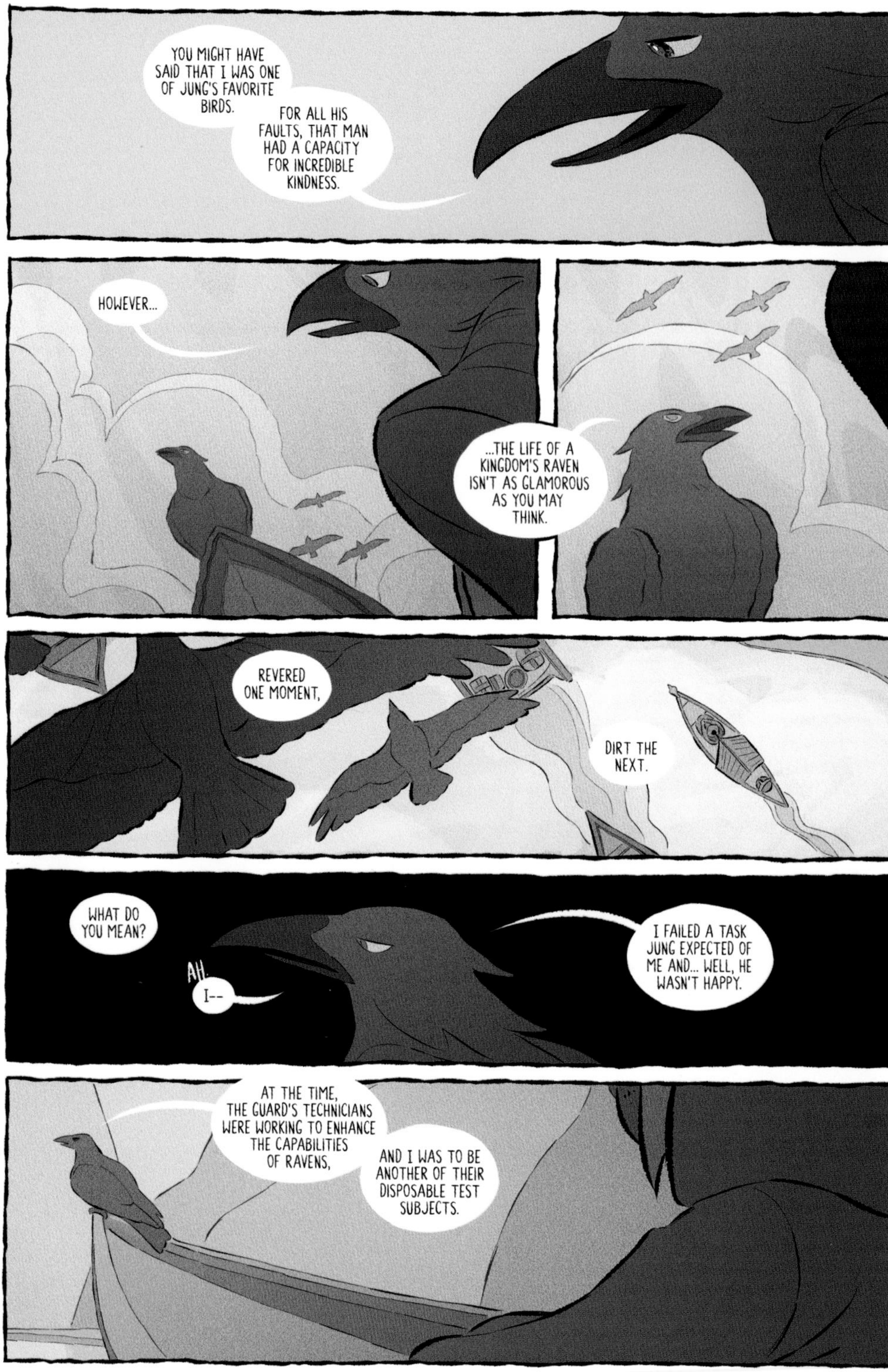
YOU MIGHT HAVE SAID THAT I WAS ONE OF JUNG'S FAVORITE BIRDS.
FOR ALL HIS FAULTS, THAT MAN HAD A CAPACITY FOR INCREDIBLE KINDNESS.
HOWEVER...
...THE LIFE OF A KINGDOM'S RAVEN ISN'T AS GLAMOROUS AS YOU MAY THINK.
REVERED ONE MOMENT,
DIRT THE NEXT.
WHAT DO YOU MEAN?
I FAILED A TASK JUNG EXPECTED OF ME AND... WELL, HE WASN'T HAPPY.
AH.
I--
AT THE TIME, THE GUARD'S TECHNICIANS WERE WORKING TO ENHANCE THE CAPABILITIES OF RAVENS,
AND I WAS TO BE ANOTHER OF THEIR DISPOSABLE TEST SUBJECTS.

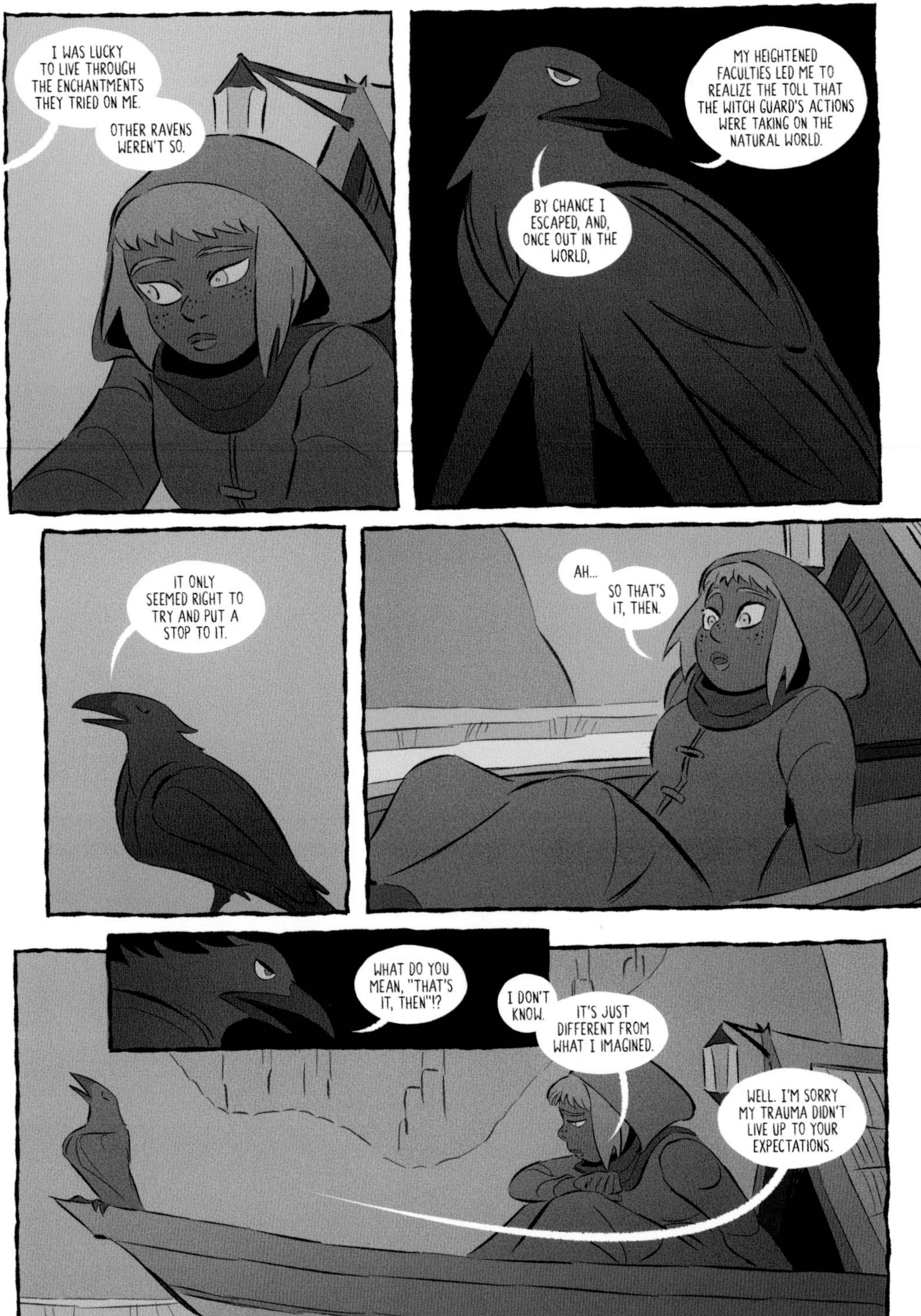

I WAS LUCKY TO LIVE THROUGH THE ENCHANTMENTS THEY TRIED ON ME.
OTHER RAVENS WEREN'T SO.
MY HEIGHTENED FACULTIES LED ME TO REALIZE THE TOLL THAT THE WITCH GUARD'S ACTIONS WERE TAKING ON THE NATURAL WORLD.
BY CHANCE I ESCAPED, AND, ONCE OUT IN THE WORLD,
IT ONLY SEEMED RIGHT TO TRY AND PUT A STOP TO IT.
AH...
SO THAT'S IT, THEN.
WHAT DO YOU MEAN, "THAT'S IT, THEN"!?
I DON'T KNOW.
IT'S JUST DIFFERENT FROM WHAT I IMAGINED.
WELL. I'M SORRY MY TRAUMA DIDN'T LIVE UP TO YOUR EXPECTATIONS.

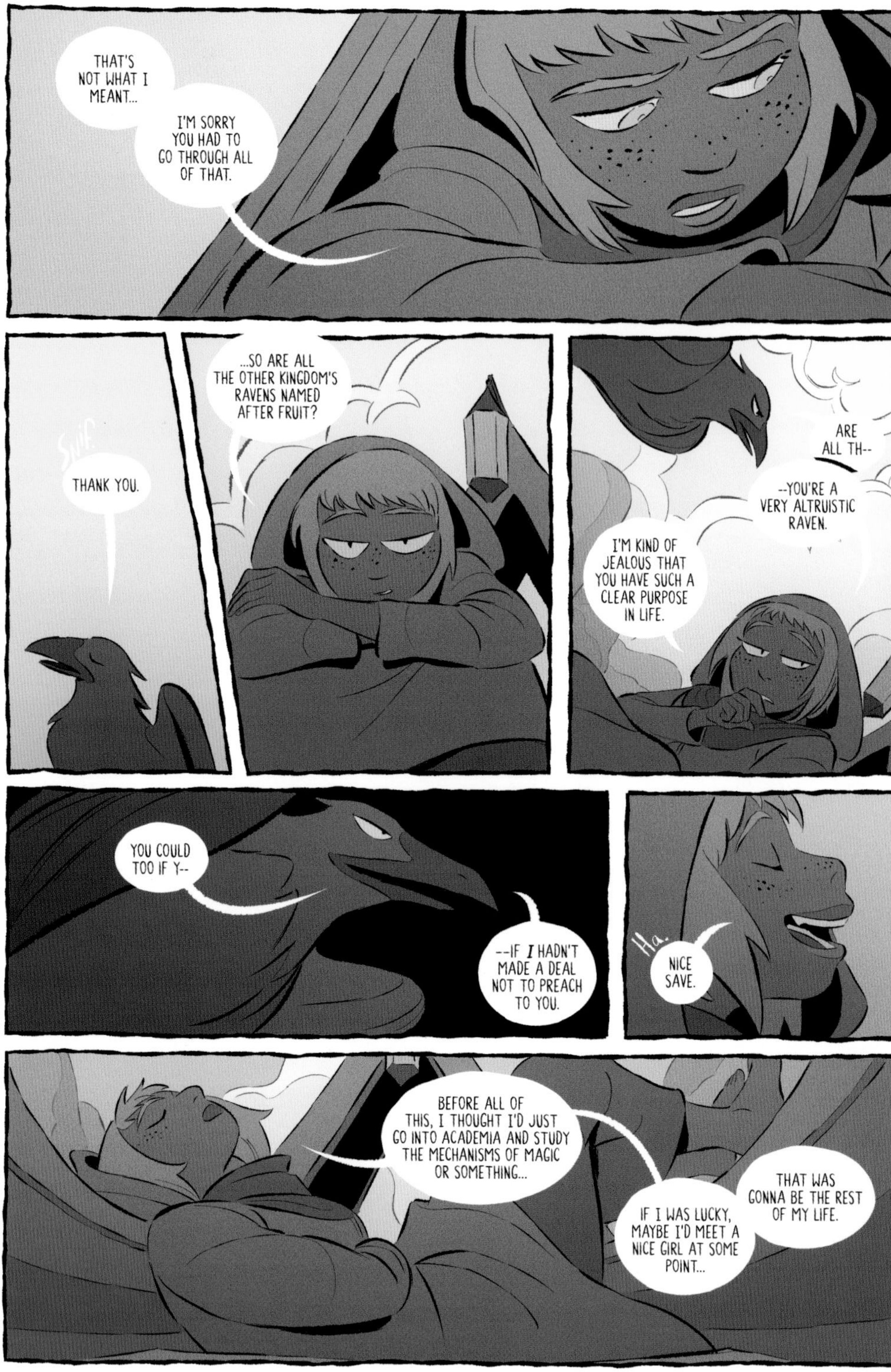
THAT'S NOT WHAT I MEANT...
I'M SORRY YOU HAD TO GO THROUGH ALL OF THAT.
SNIF
THANK YOU.
...SO ARE ALL THE OTHER KINGDOM'S RAVENS NAMED AFTER FRUIT?
ARE ALL TH--
--YOU'RE A VERY ALTRUISTIC RAVEN.
I'M KIND OF JEALOUS THAT YOU HAVE SUCH A CLEAR PURPOSE IN LIFE.
YOU COULD TOO IF Y--
--IF I HADN'T MADE A DEAL NOT TO PREACH TO YOU.
HA.
NICE SAVE.
BEFORE ALL OF THIS, I THOUGHT I'D JUST GO INTO ACADEMIA AND STUDY THE MECHANISMS OF MAGIC OR SOMETHING...
IF I WAS LUCKY, MAYBE I'D MEET A NICE GIRL AT SOME POINT...
THAT WAS GONNA BE THE REST OF MY LIFE.

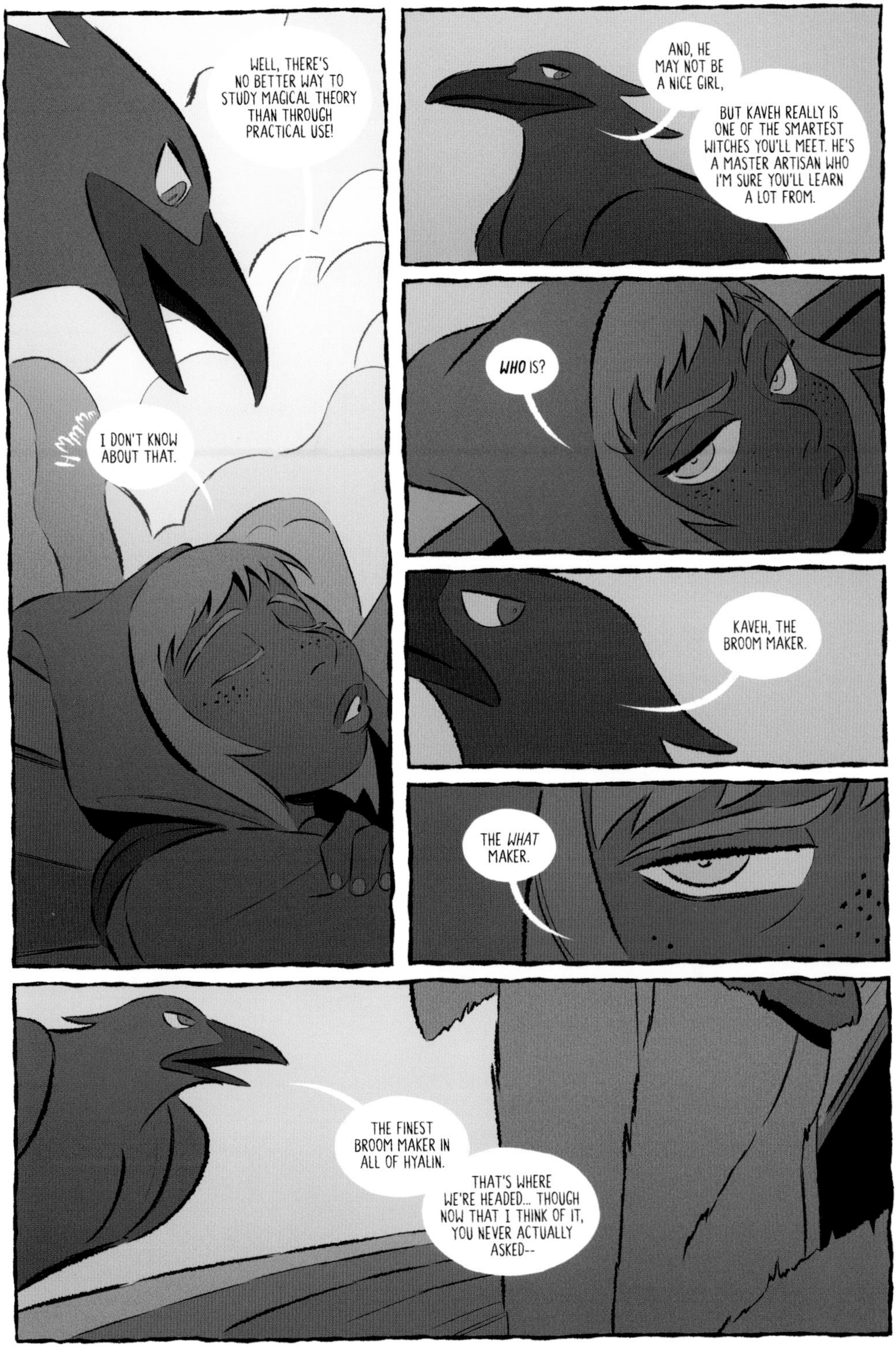
WELL, THERE'S NO BETTER WAY TO STUDY MAGICAL THEORY THAN THROUGH PRACTICAL USE!
HMMMM
I DON'T KNOW ABOUT THAT.
AND, HE MAY NOT BE A NICE GIRL,
BUT KAVEH REALLY IS ONE OF THE SMARTEST WITCHES YOU'LL MEET. HE'S A MASTER ARTISAN WHO I'M SURE YOU'LL LEARN A LOT FROM.
WHO IS?
KAVEH, THE BROOM MAKER.
THE WHAT MAKER.
THE FINEST BROOM MAKER IN ALL OF HYALIN.
THAT'S WHERE WE'RE HEADED... THOUGH NOW THAT I THINK OF IT, YOU NEVER ACTUALLY ASKED--

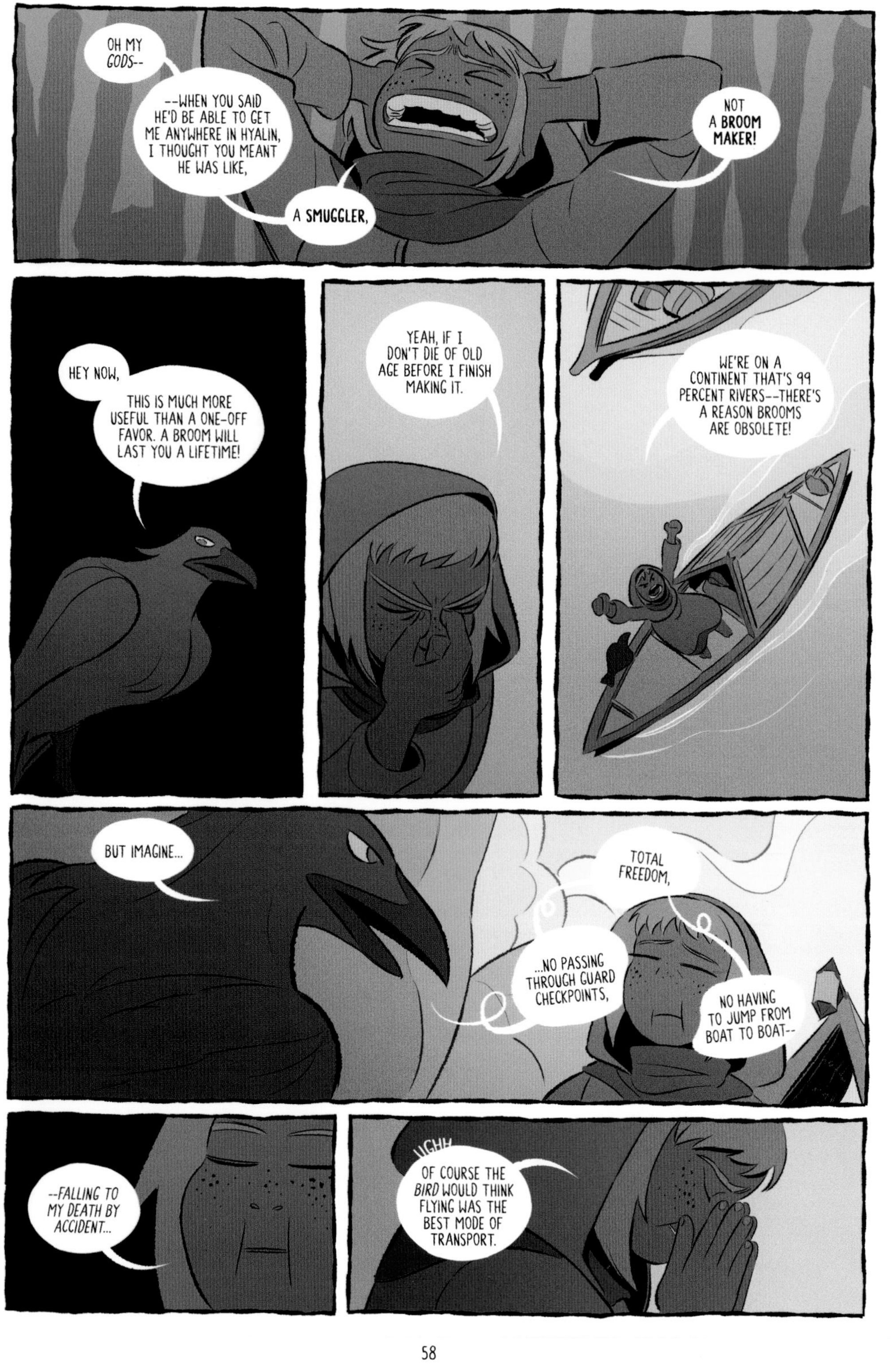
OH MY *GODS*--
--WHEN YOU SAID HE'D BE ABLE TO GET ME ANYWHERE IN HYALIN, I THOUGHT YOU MEANT HE WAS LIKE,
A **SMUGGLER**,
NOT A **BROOM MAKER!**
HEY NOW,
THIS IS MUCH MORE USEFUL THAN A ONE-OFF FAVOR. A BROOM WILL LAST YOU A LIFETIME!
YEAH, IF I DON'T DIE OF OLD AGE BEFORE I FINISH MAKING IT.
WE'RE ON A CONTINENT THAT'S 99 PERCENT RIVERS--THERE'S A REASON BROOMS ARE OBSOLETE!
BUT IMAGINE...
TOTAL FREEDOM,
...NO PASSING THROUGH GUARD CHECKPOINTS,
NO HAVING TO JUMP FROM BOAT TO BOAT--
--*FALLING TO MY DEATH BY ACCIDENT*...
OF COURSE THE *BIRD* WOULD THINK FLYING WAS THE BEST MODE OF TRANSPORT.

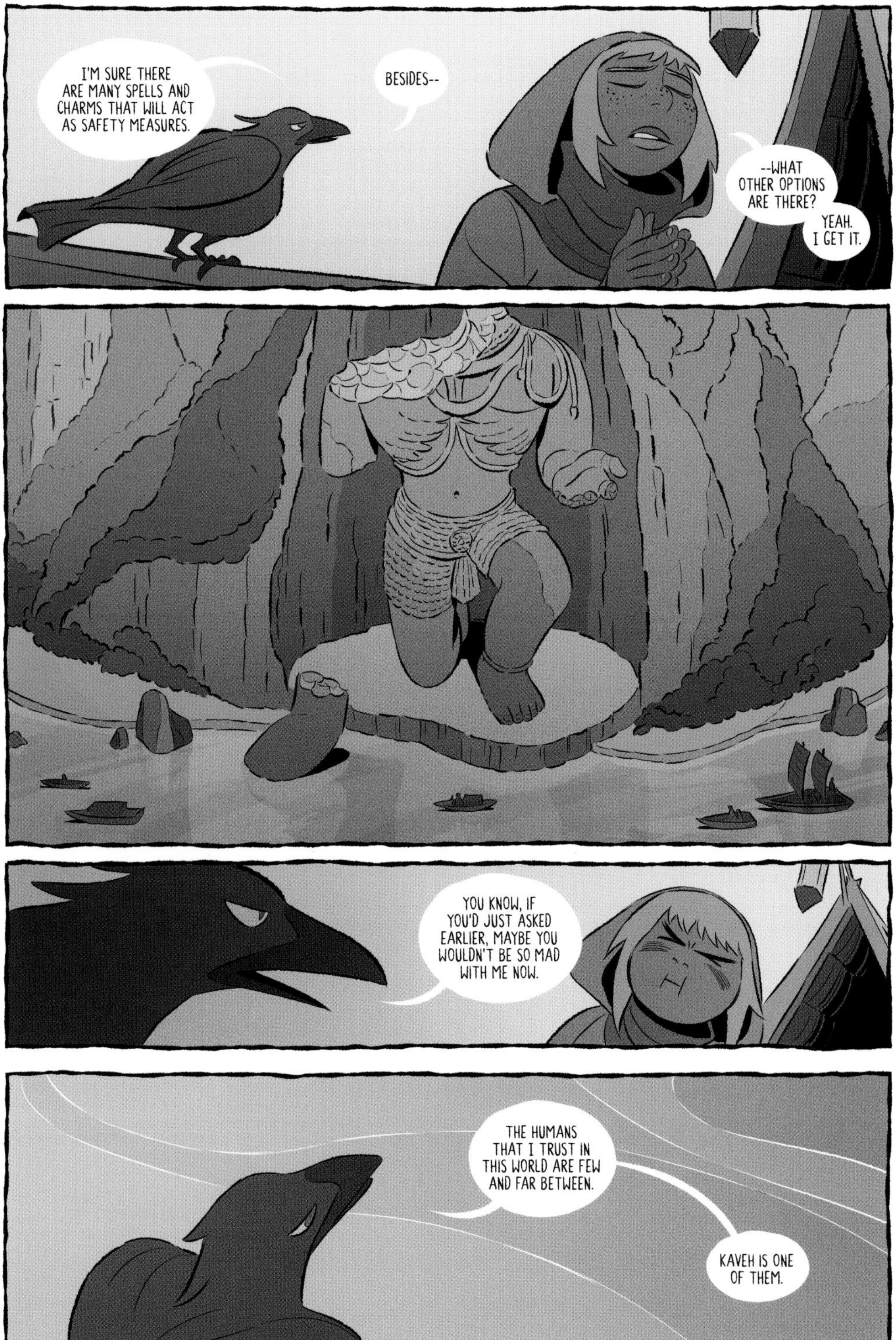
I'M SURE THERE ARE MANY SPELLS AND CHARMS THAT WILL ACT AS SAFETY MEASURES.
BESIDES--
--WHAT OTHER OPTIONS ARE THERE?
YEAH. I GET IT.
YOU KNOW, IF YOU'D JUST ASKED EARLIER, MAYBE YOU WOULDN'T BE SO MAD WITH ME NOW.
THE HUMANS THAT I TRUST IN THIS WORLD ARE FEW AND FAR BETWEEN.
KAVEH IS ONE OF THEM.

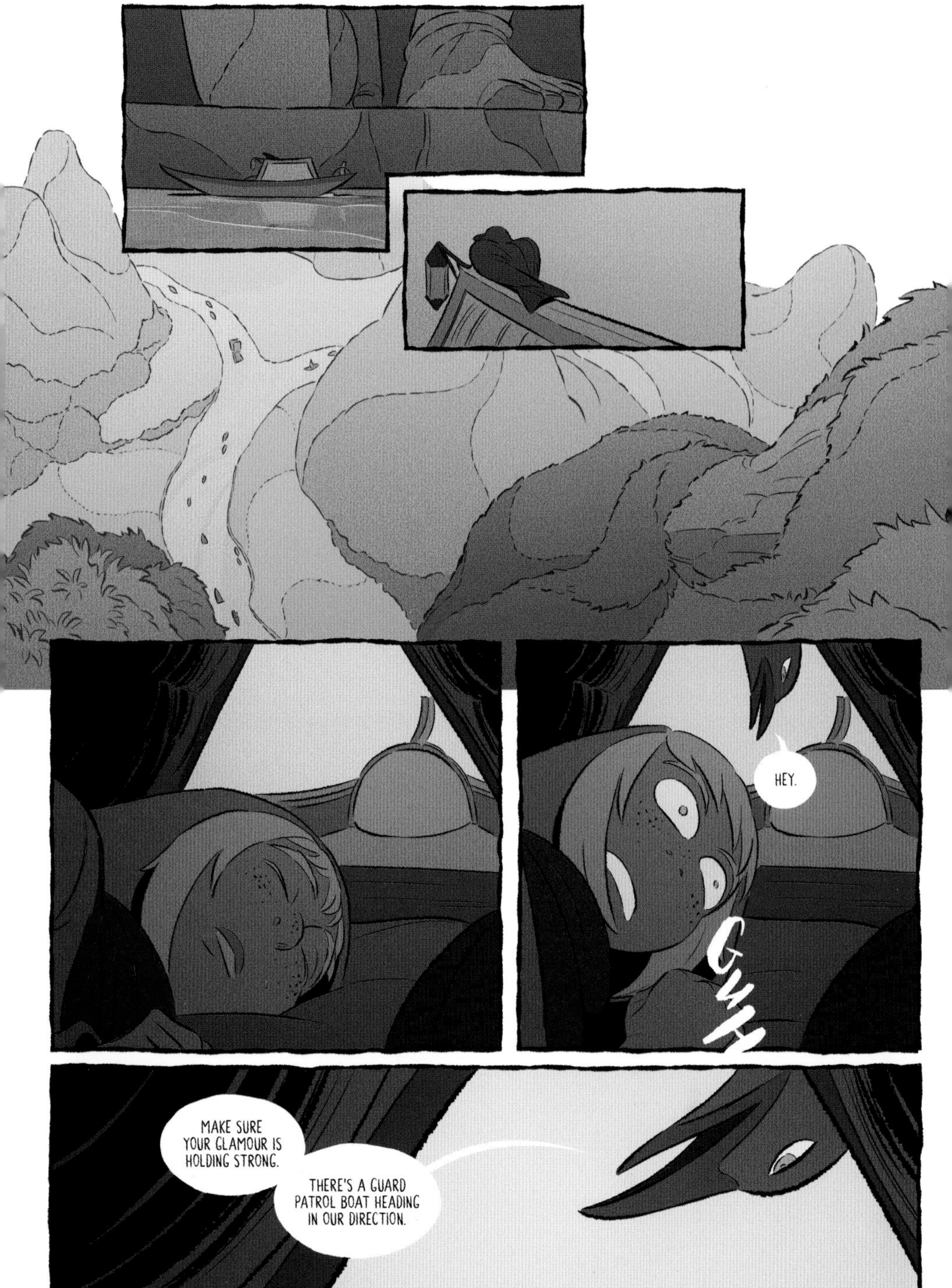
HEY.
GWH
MAKE SURE YOUR GLAMOUR IS HOLDING STRONG.
THERE'S A GUARD PATROL BOAT HEADING IN OUR DIRECTION.

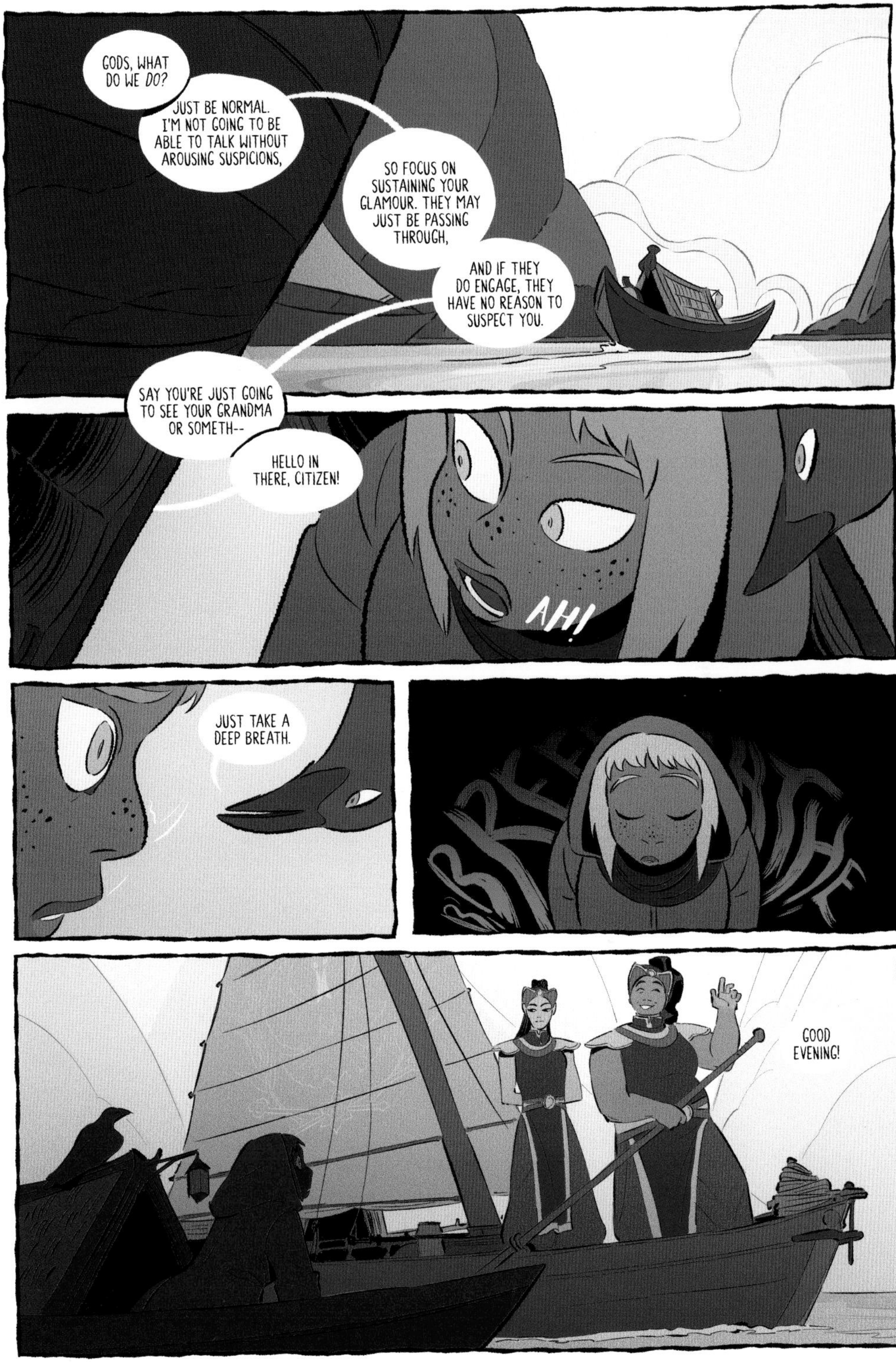
GODS, WHAT DO WE *DO?*
JUST BE NORMAL. I'M NOT GOING TO BE ABLE TO TALK WITHOUT AROUSING SUSPICIONS,
SO FOCUS ON SUSTAINING YOUR GLAMOUR. THEY MAY JUST BE PASSING THROUGH,
AND IF THEY DO ENGAGE, THEY HAVE NO REASON TO SUSPECT YOU.
SAY YOU'RE JUST GOING TO SEE YOUR GRANDMA OR SOMETH--
HELLO IN THERE, CITIZEN!
AH!
JUST TAKE A DEEP BREATH.
BREEEATHE
GOOD EVENING!

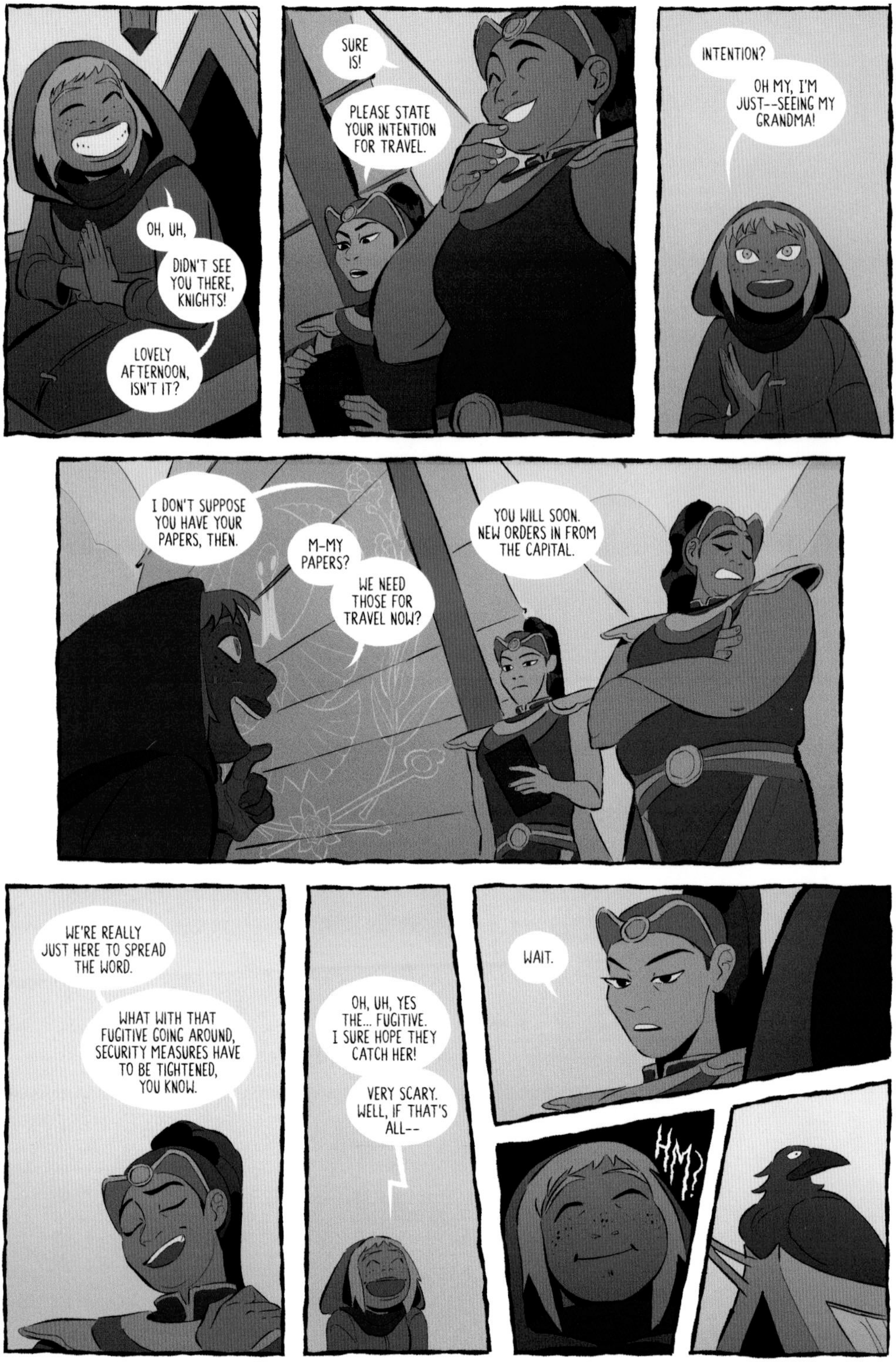
OH, UH,
DIDN'T SEE YOU THERE, KNIGHTS!
LOVELY AFTERNOON, ISN'T IT?
SURE IS!
PLEASE STATE YOUR INTENTION FOR TRAVEL.
INTENTION?
OH MY, I'M JUST--SEEING MY GRANDMA!
I DON'T SUPPOSE YOU HAVE YOUR PAPERS, THEN.
M-MY PAPERS?
WE NEED THOSE FOR TRAVEL NOW?
YOU WILL SOON. NEW ORDERS IN FROM THE CAPITAL.
WE'RE REALLY JUST HERE TO SPREAD THE WORD.
WHAT WITH THAT FUGITIVE GOING AROUND, SECURITY MEASURES HAVE TO BE TIGHTENED, YOU KNOW.
OH, UH, YES THE... FUGITIVE. I SURE HOPE THEY CATCH HER!
VERY SCARY. WELL, IF THAT'S ALL--
WAIT.
HM?

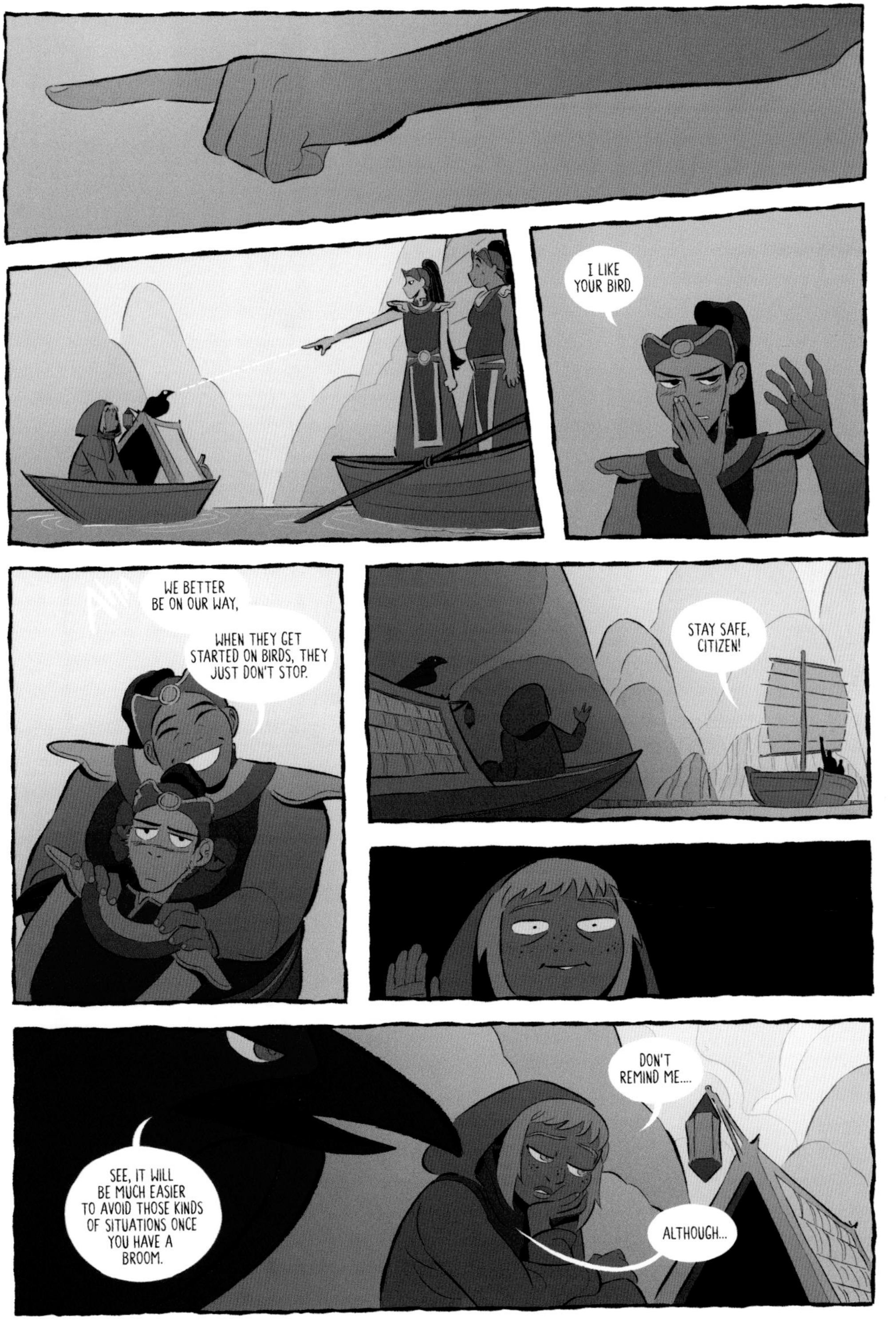
I LIKE YOUR BIRD.
WE BETTER BE ON OUR WAY,
WHEN THEY GET STARTED ON BIRDS, THEY JUST DON'T STOP.
STAY SAFE, CITIZEN!
DON'T REMIND ME....
SEE, IT WILL BE MUCH EASIER TO AVOID THOSE KINDS OF SITUATIONS ONCE YOU HAVE A BROOM.
ALTHOUGH...

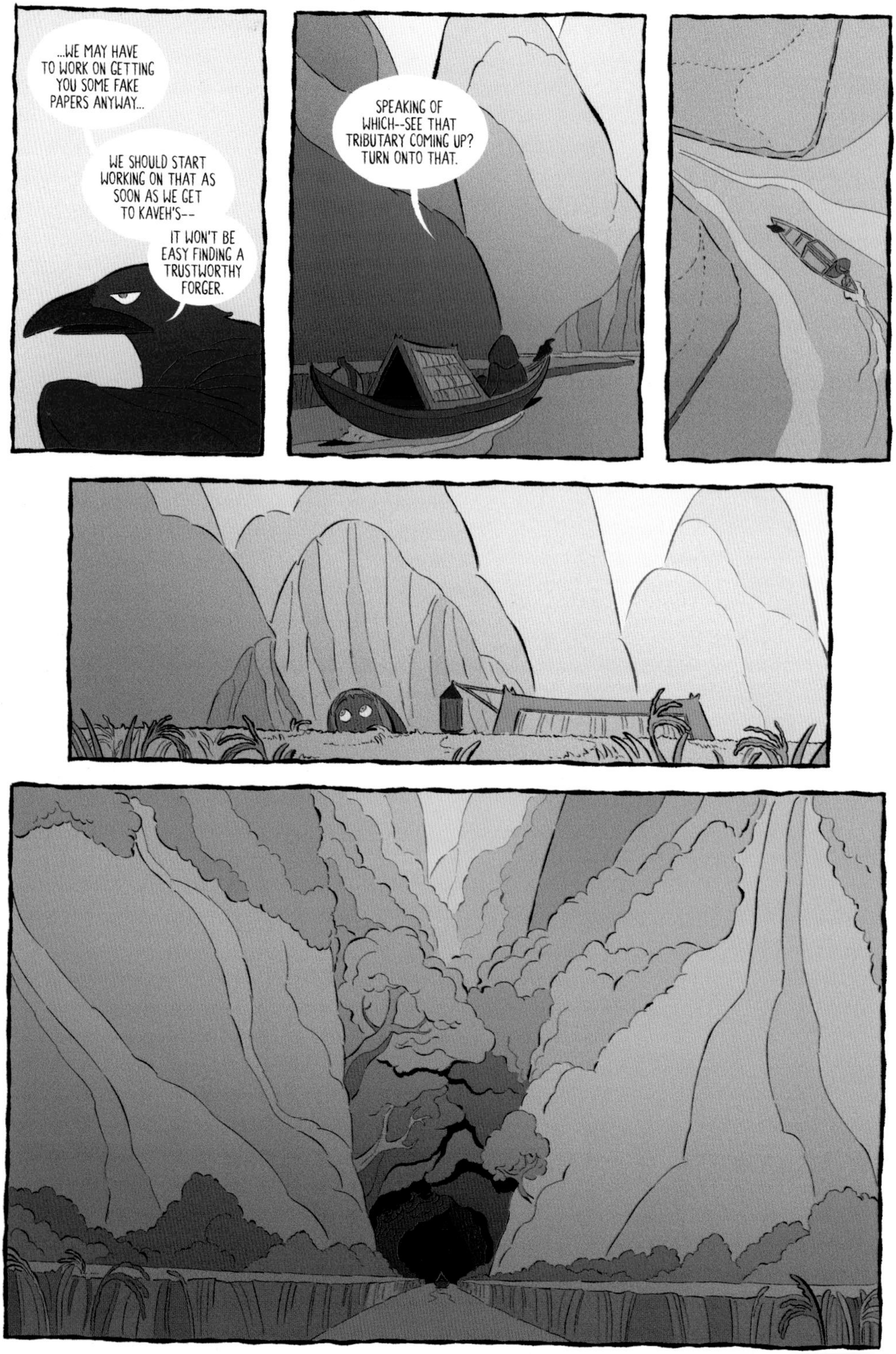

...WE MAY HAVE TO WORK ON GETTING YOU SOME FAKE PAPERS ANYWAY...
WE SHOULD START WORKING ON THAT AS SOON AS WE GET TO KAVEH'S--
IT WON'T BE EASY FINDING A TRUSTWORTHY FORGER.
SPEAKING OF WHICH--SEE THAT TRIBUTARY COMING UP? TURN ONTO THAT.

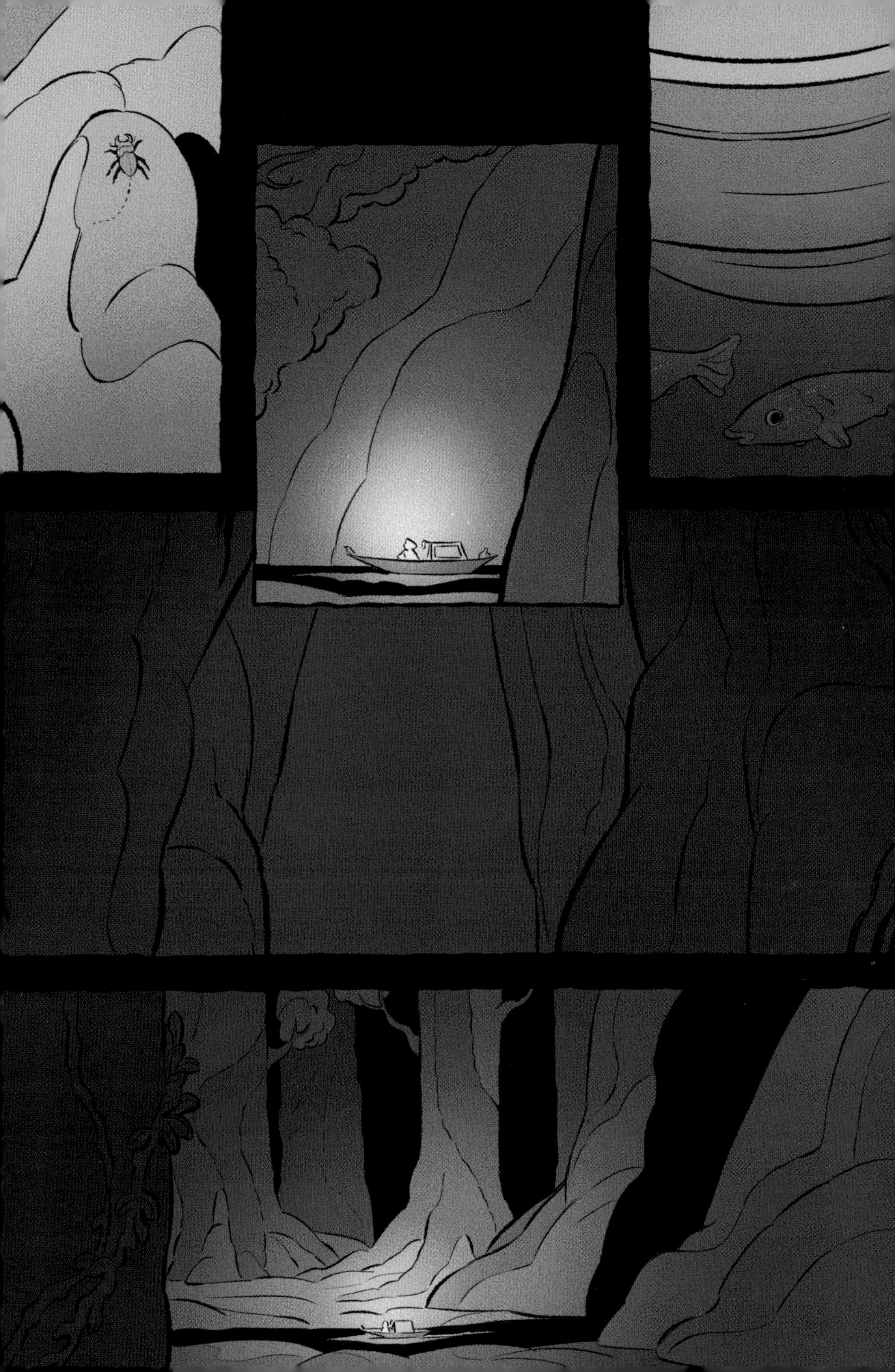

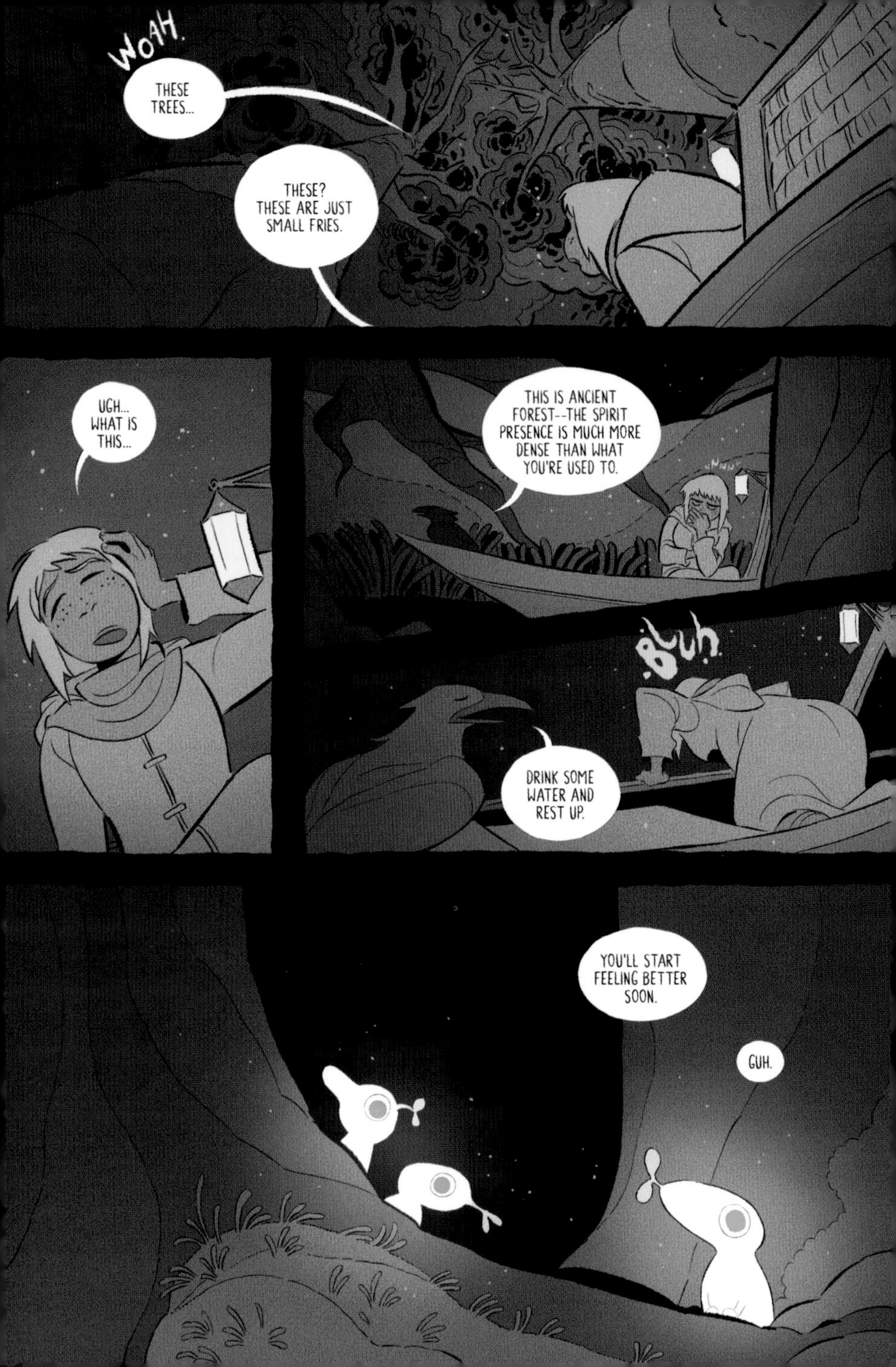
WOAH.
THESE TREES...
THESE? THESE ARE JUST SMALL FRIES.
UGH... WHAT IS THIS...
THIS IS ANCIENT FOREST--THE SPIRIT PRESENCE IS MUCH MORE DENSE THAN WHAT YOU'RE USED TO.
BLUH.
DRINK SOME WATER AND REST UP.
YOU'LL START FEELING BETTER SOON.
GUH.

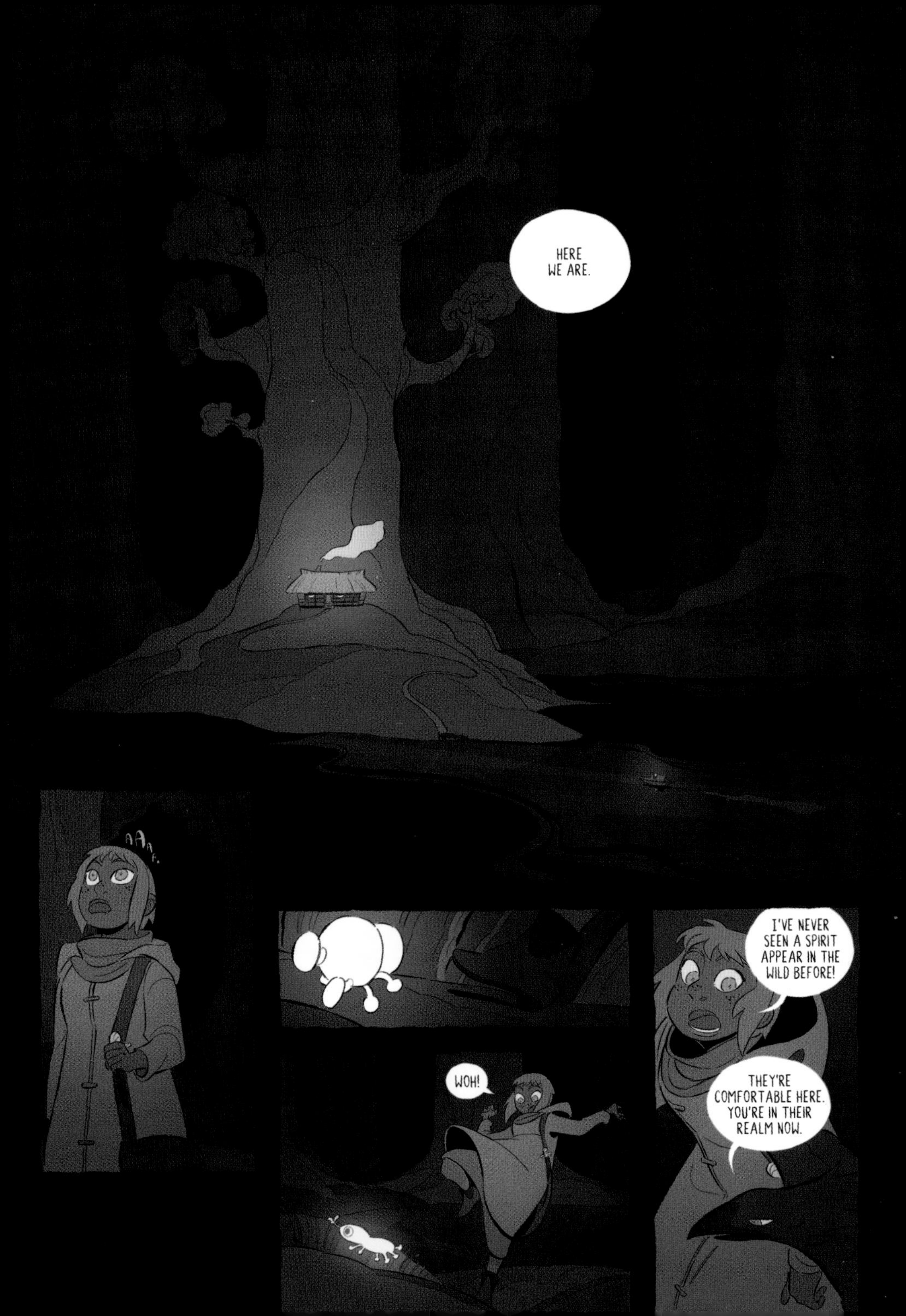
HERE WE ARE.
AAAF.
I'VE NEVER SEEN A SPIRIT APPEAR IN THE WILD BEFORE!
WOH!
THEY'RE COMFORTABLE HERE. YOU'RE IN THEIR REALM NOW.

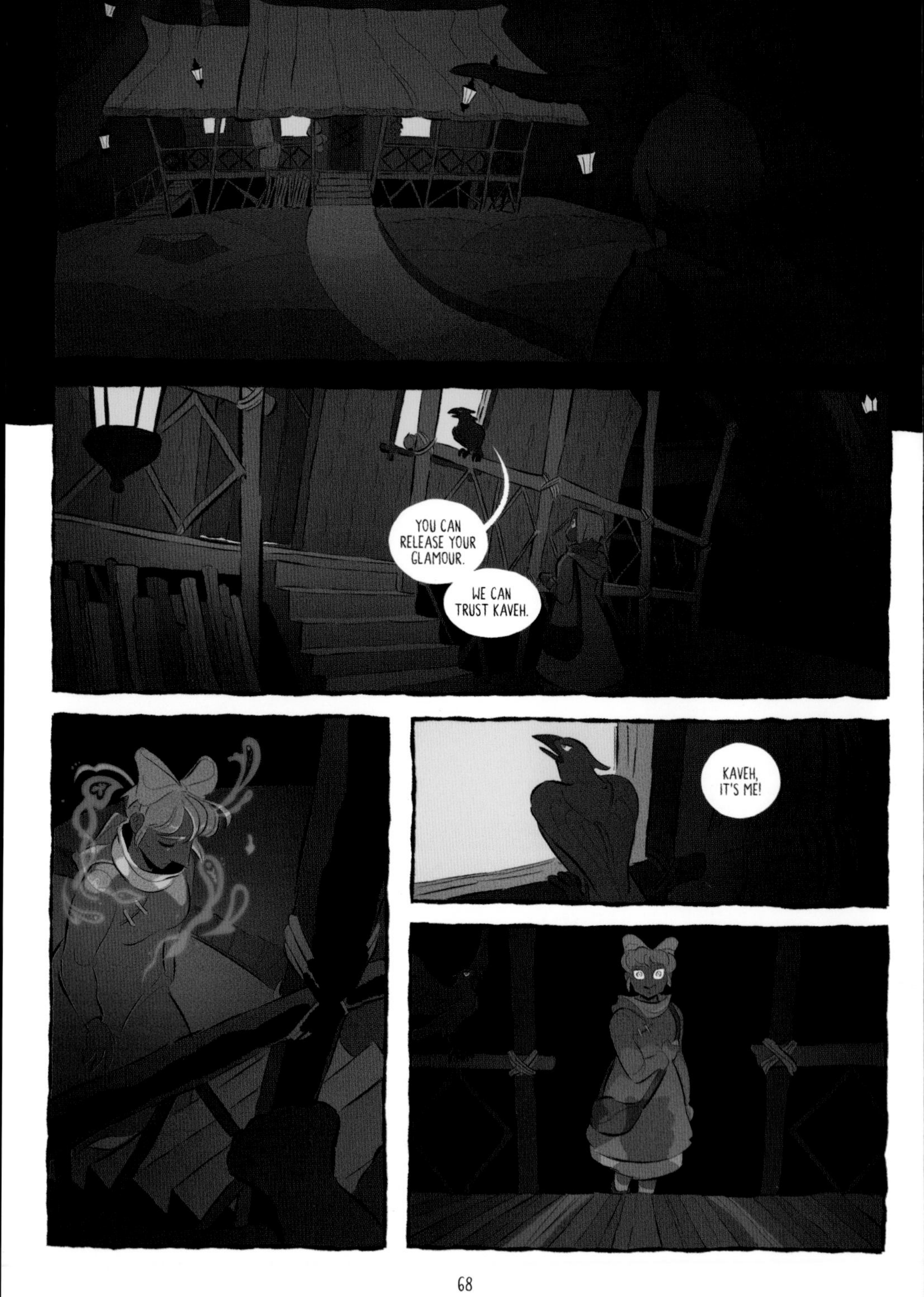
YOU CAN RELEASE YOUR GLAMOUR.
WE CAN TRUST KAVEH.
KAVEH, IT'S ME!

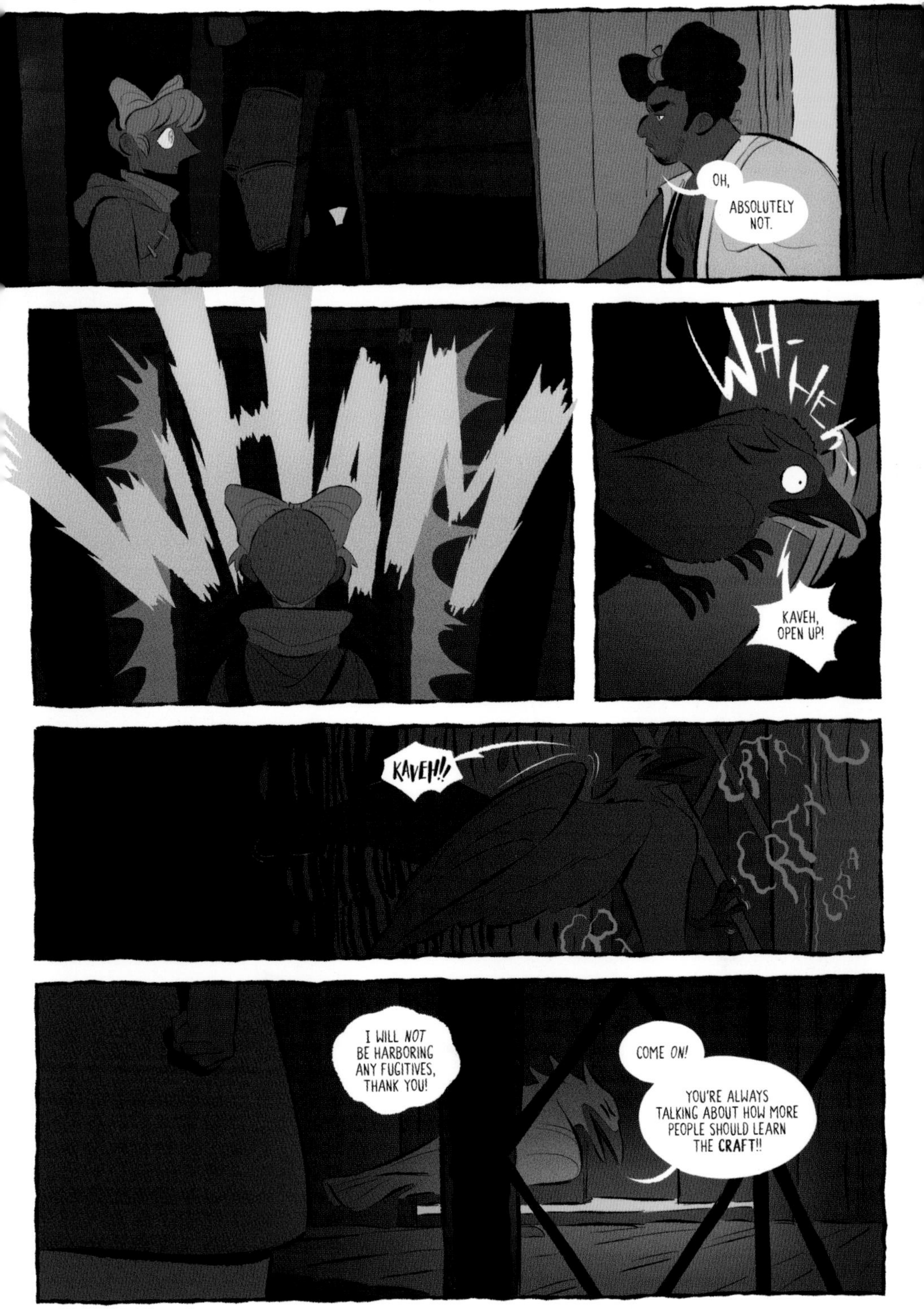
OH, ABSOLUTELY NOT.
WHAM
WH-HEY-
KAVEH, OPEN UP!
KAVEH!!
I WILL *NOT* BE HARBORING ANY FUGITIVES, THANK YOU!
COME *ON*!
YOU'RE ALWAYS TALKING ABOUT HOW MORE PEOPLE SHOULD LEARN THE **CRAFT**!!

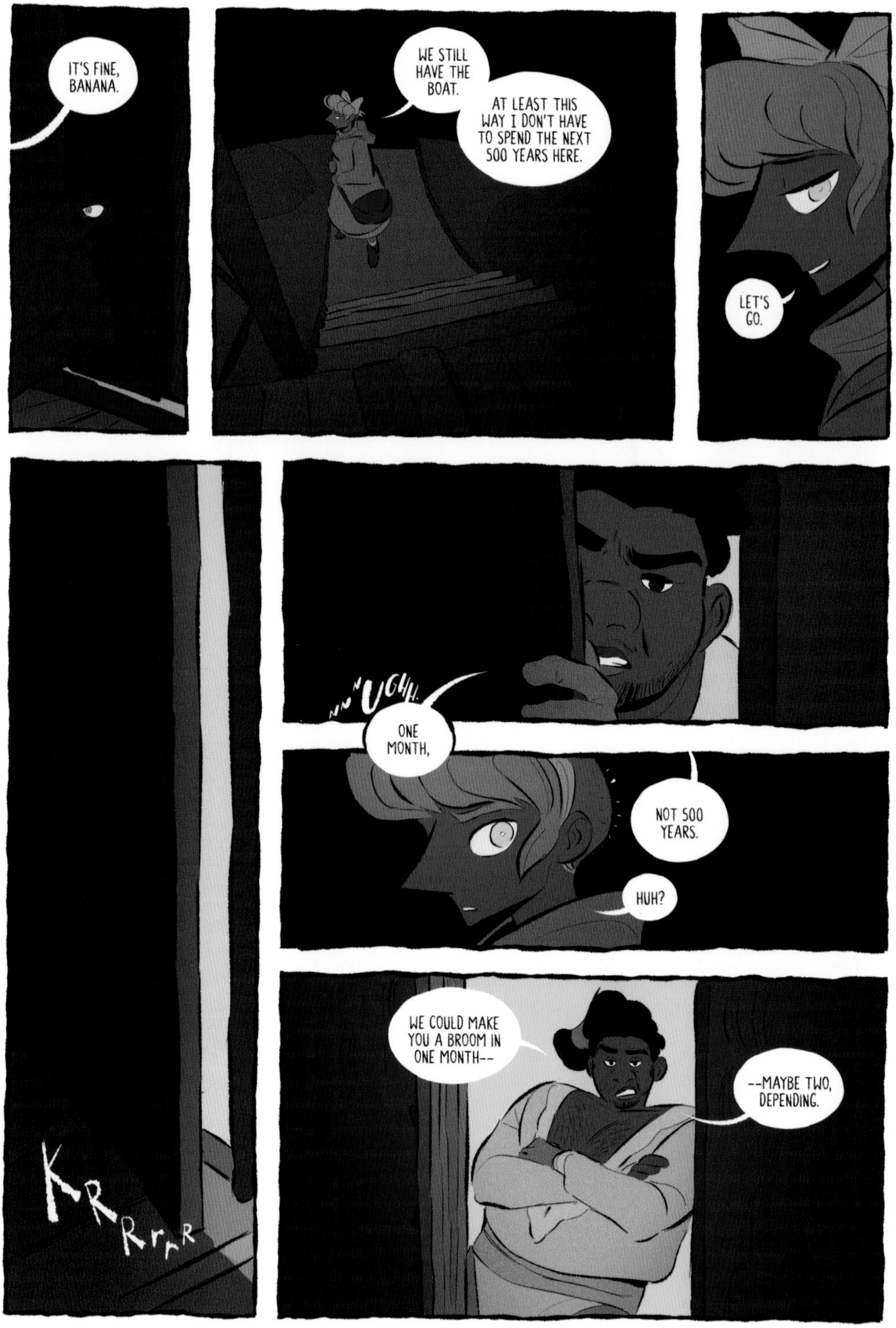
IT'S FINE, BANANA.
WE STILL HAVE THE BOAT.
AT LEAST THIS WAY I DON'T HAVE TO SPEND THE NEXT 500 YEARS HERE.
LET'S GO.
KRRrrR
NNN UGHH.
ONE MONTH,
NOT 500 YEARS.
HUH?
WE COULD MAKE YOU A BROOM IN ONE MONTH--
--MAYBE TWO, DEPENDING.

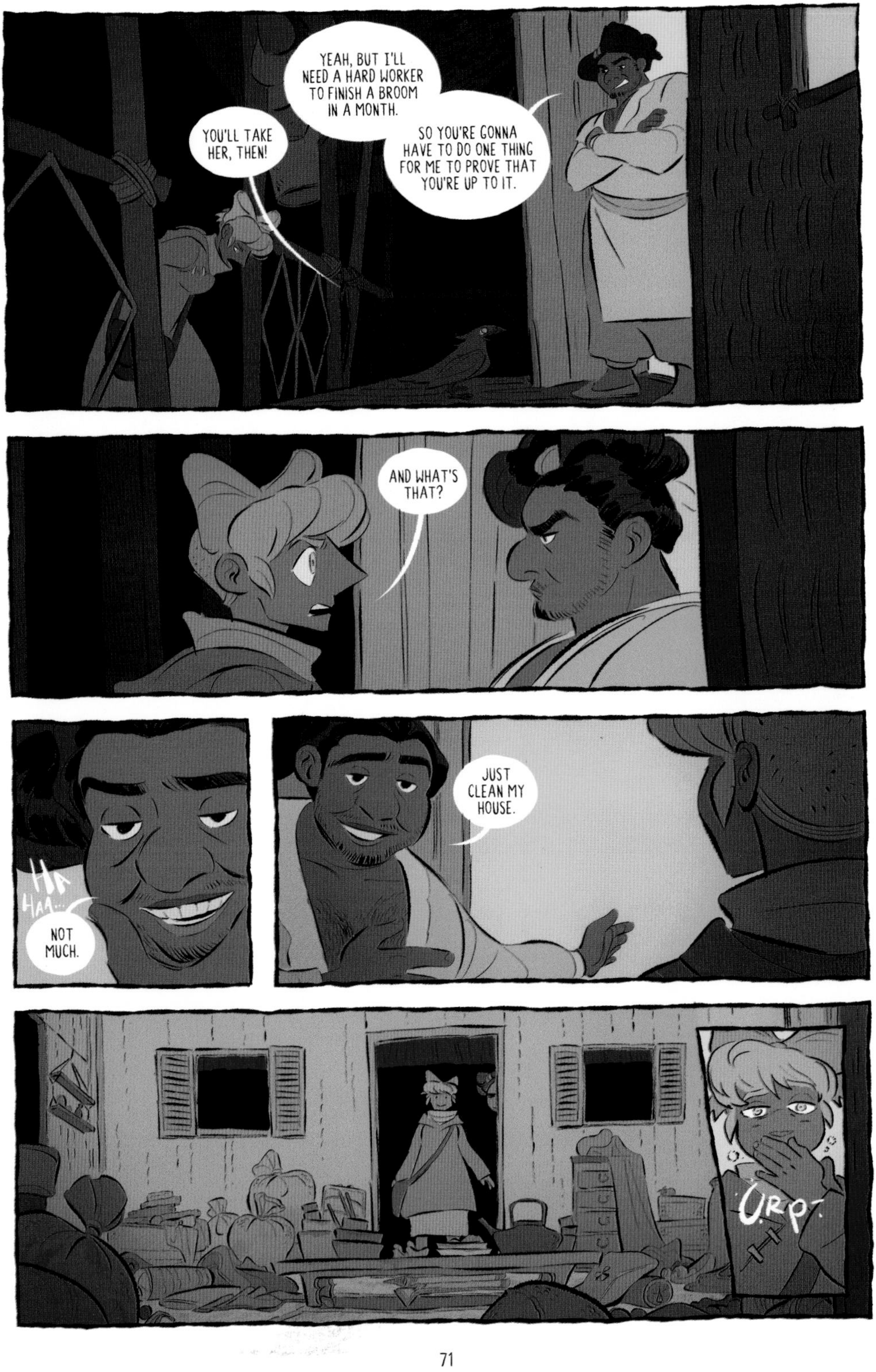
YOU'LL TAKE HER, THEN!
YEAH, BUT I'LL NEED A HARD WORKER TO FINISH A BROOM IN A MONTH.
SO YOU'RE GONNA HAVE TO DO ONE THING FOR ME TO PROVE THAT YOU'RE UP TO IT.
AND WHAT'S THAT?
HA HAA...
NOT MUCH.
JUST CLEAN MY HOUSE.
URP

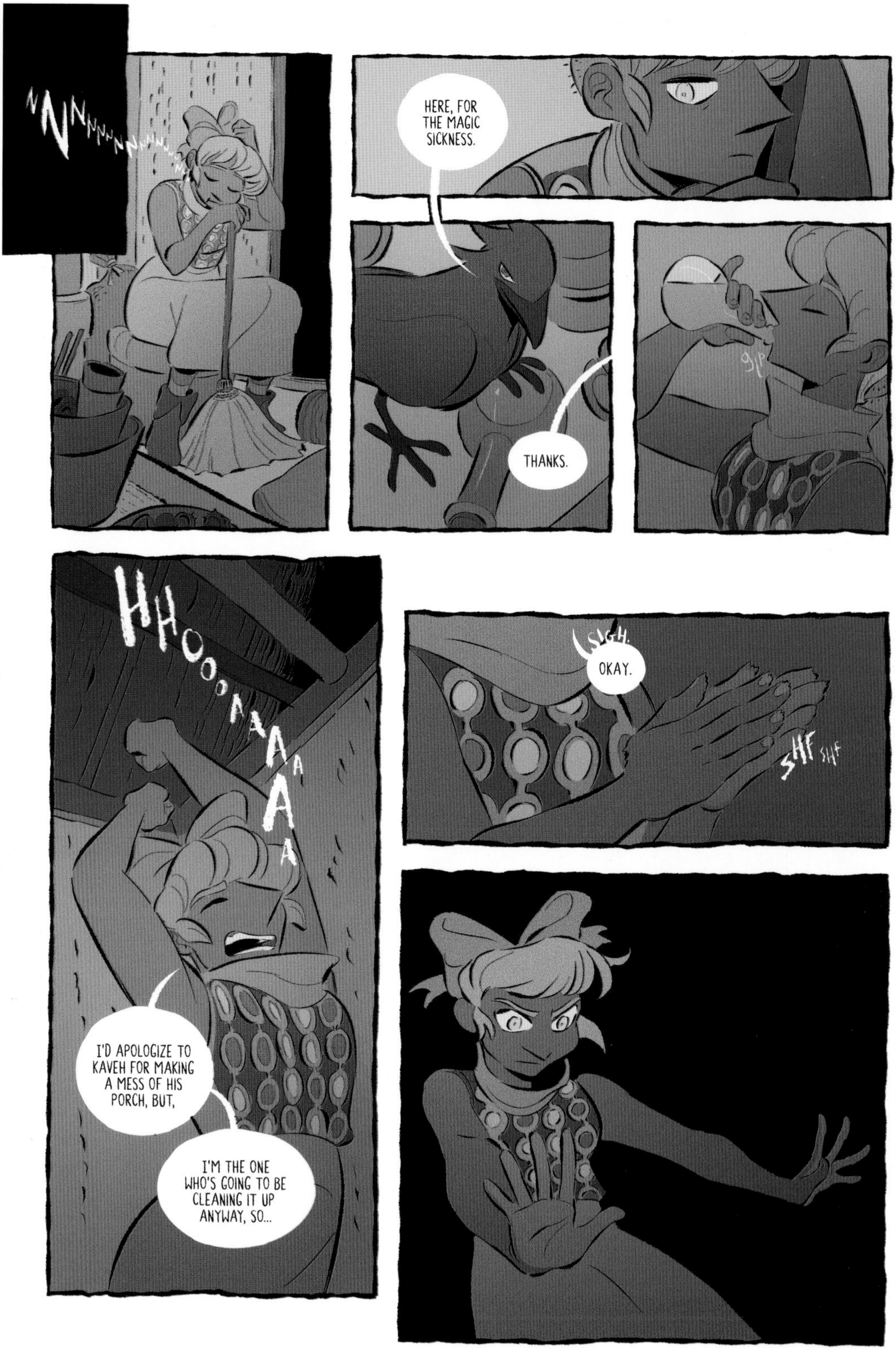

NNNNNNNNNNNNNNNN
HERE, FOR THE MAGIC SICKNESS.
THANKS.
GLIP
HHOOOAAAAAAA
I'D APOLOGIZE TO KAVEH FOR MAKING A MESS OF HIS PORCH, BUT,
I'M THE ONE WHO'S GOING TO BE CLEANING IT UP ANYWAY, SO...
SIGH.
OKAY.
SHF SHF

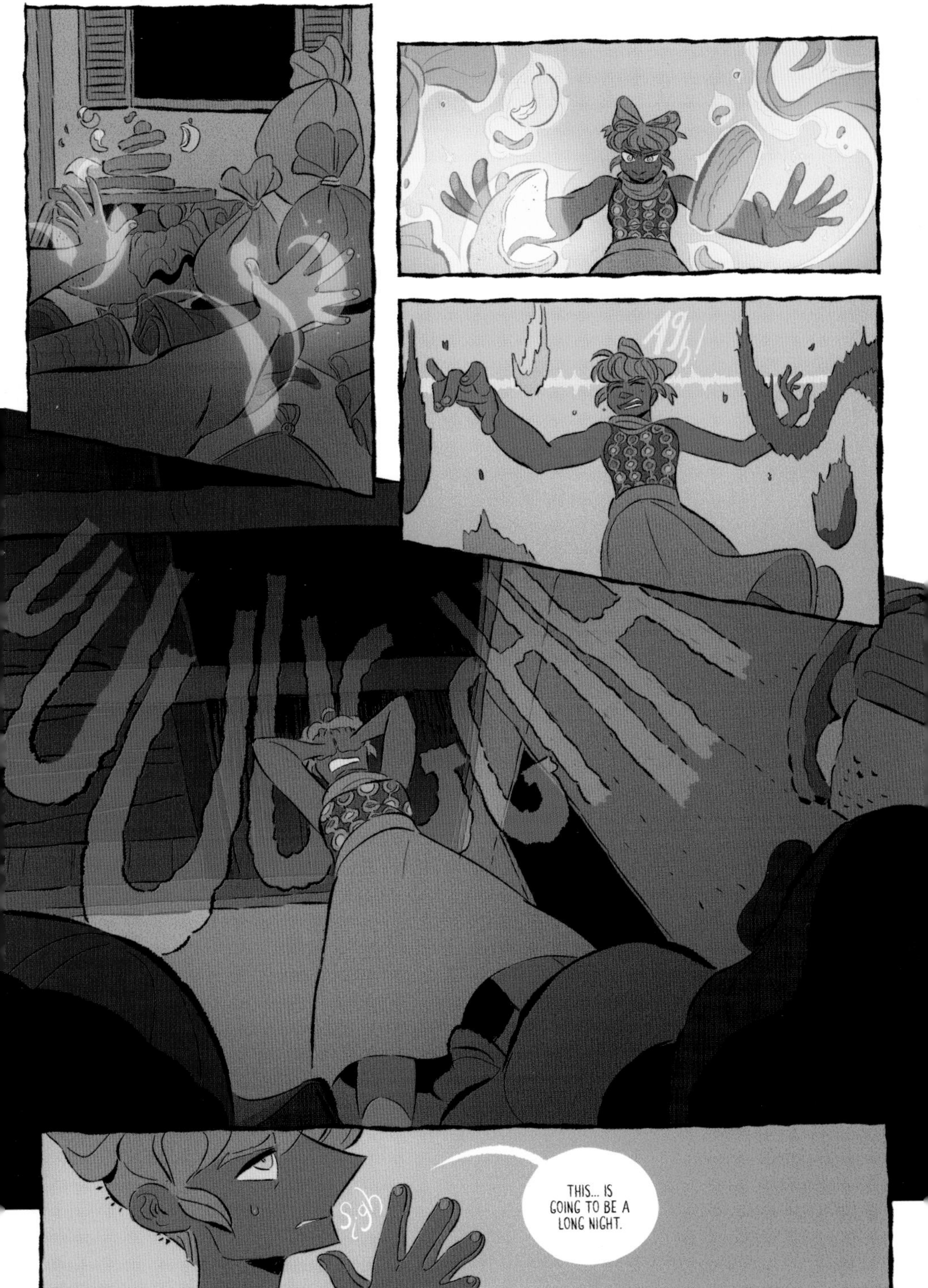
Agh!
Sigh
THIS... IS GOING TO BE A LONG NIGHT.

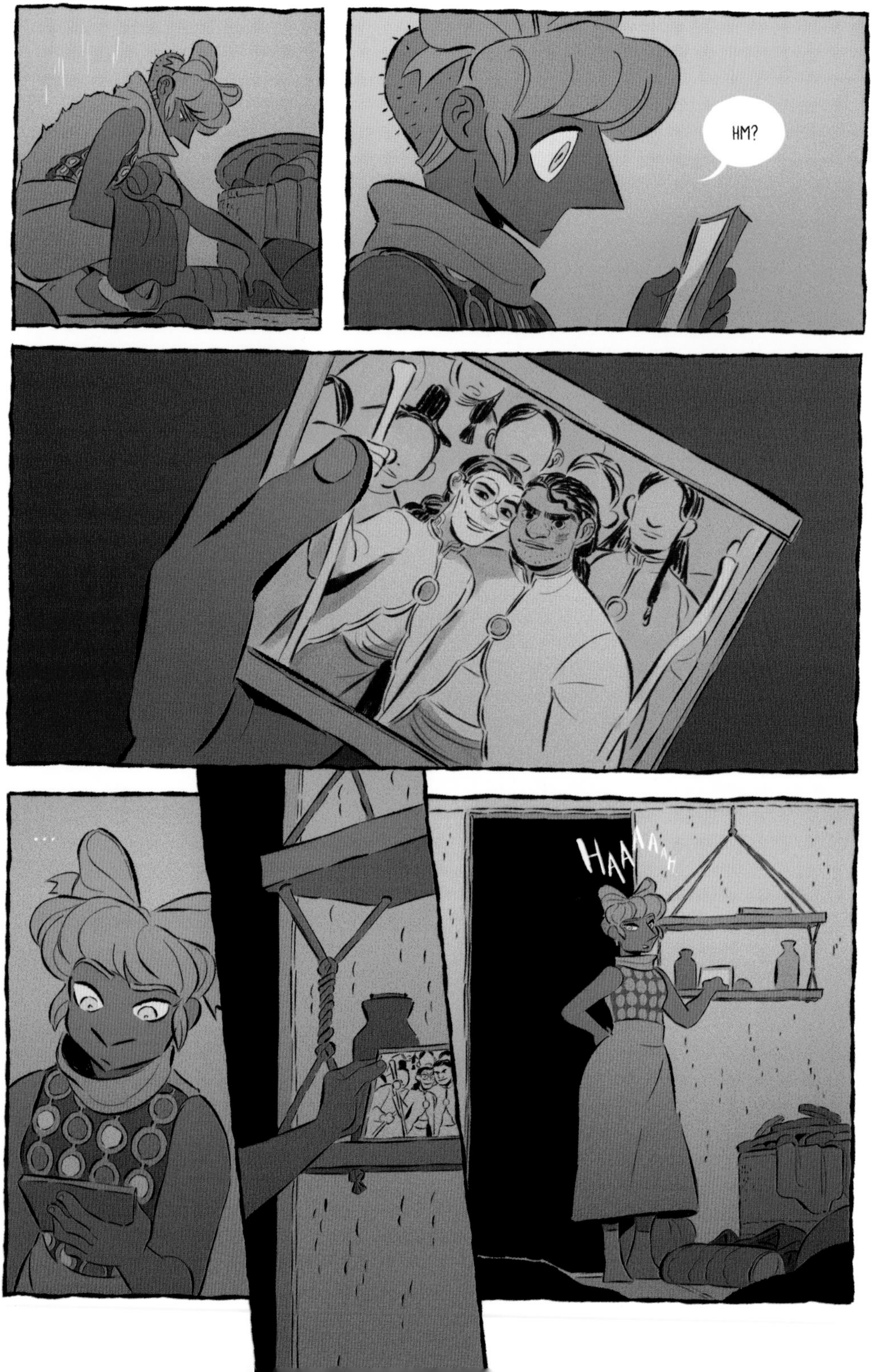
HM?
...
HAAAAAH.

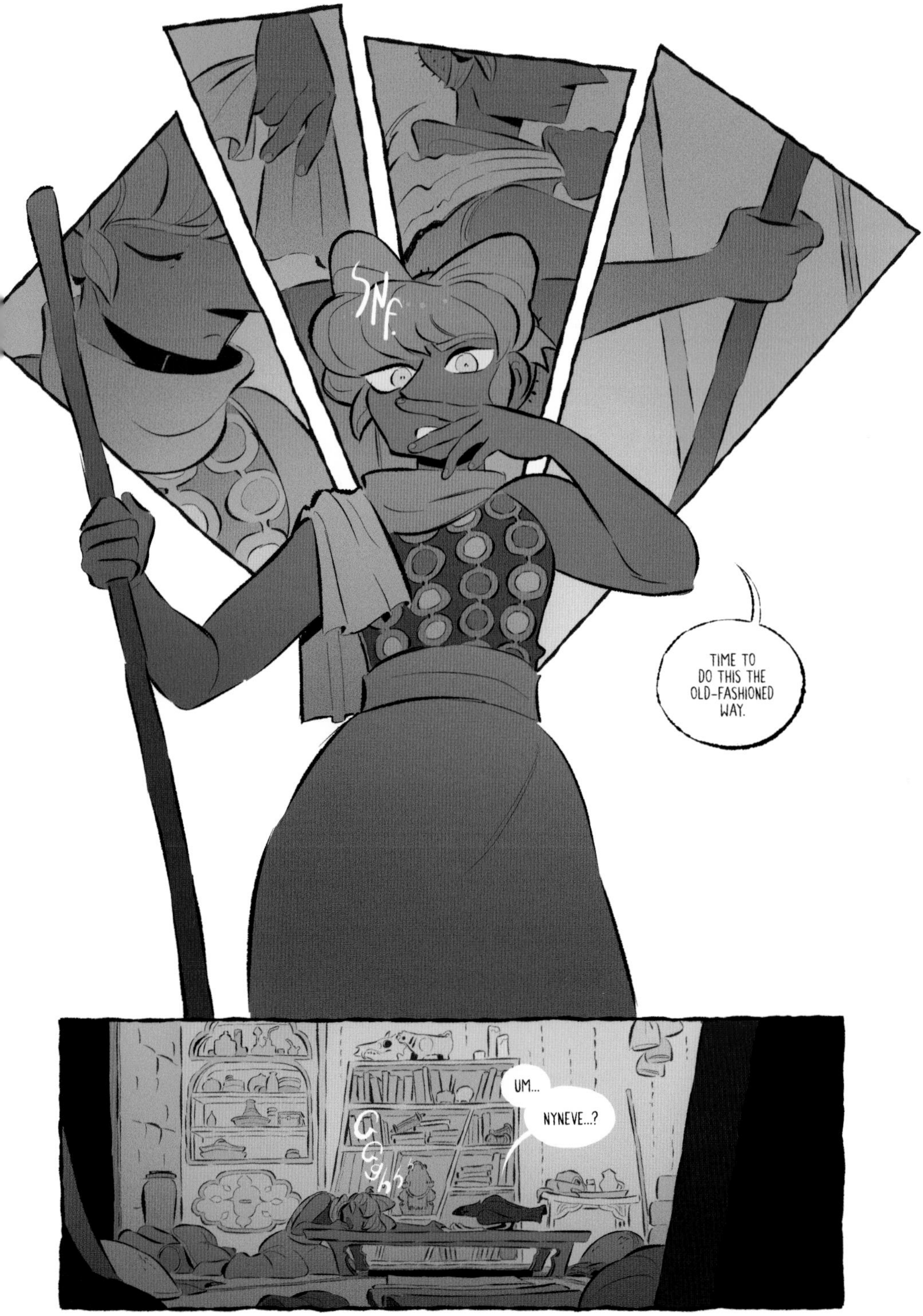
SNF.
TIME TO DO THIS THE OLD-FASHIONED WAY.
UM...
NYNEVE...?
GGghh

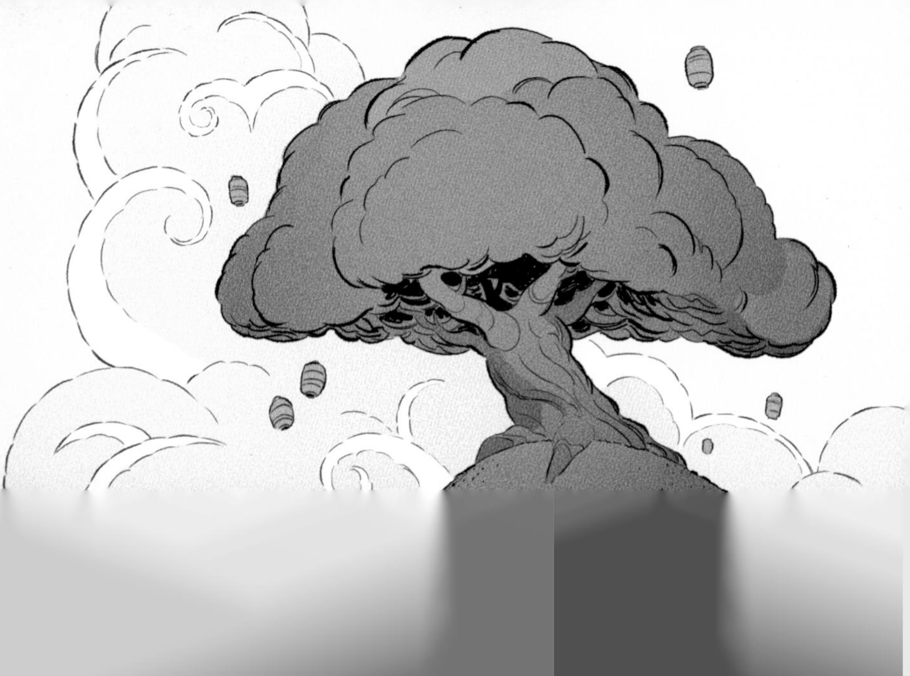

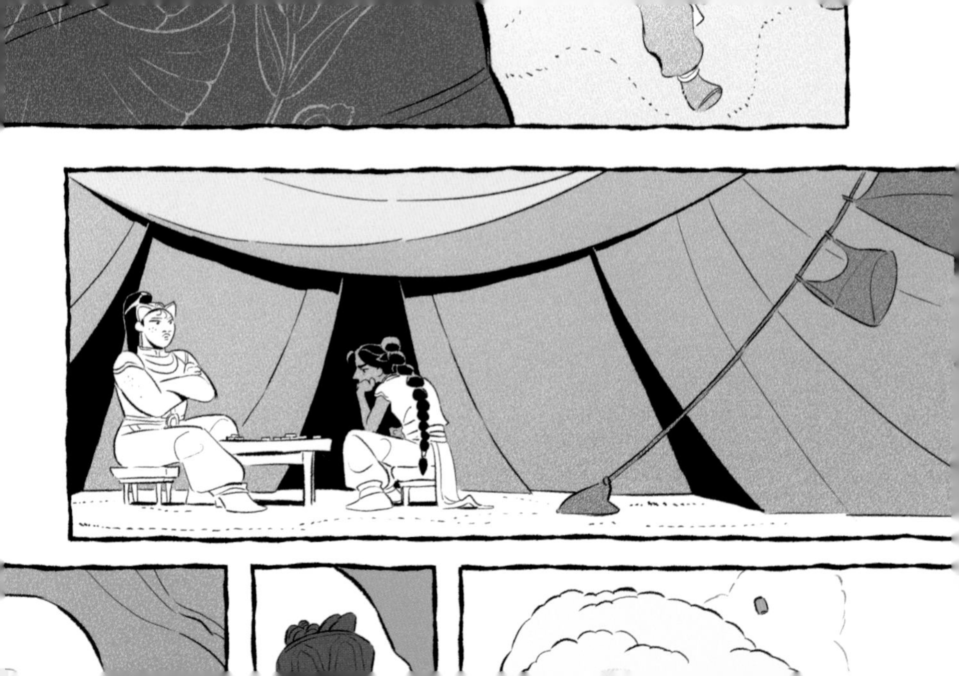

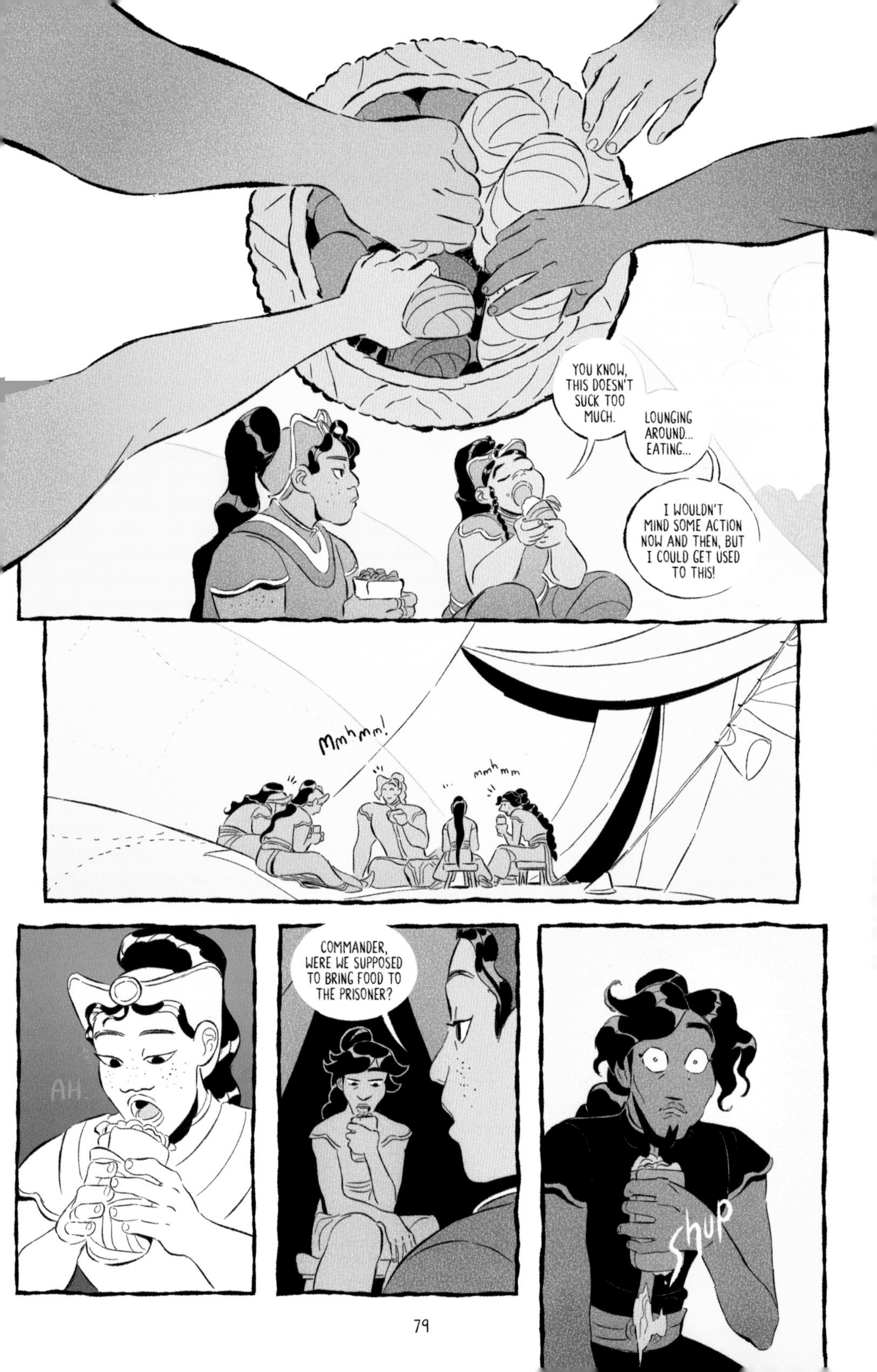
YOU KNOW, THIS DOESN'T SUCK TOO MUCH.
LOUNGING AROUND... EATING...
I WOULDN'T MIND SOME ACTION NOW AND THEN, BUT I COULD GET USED TO THIS!
Mmhmm!
mmhmm
AH.
COMMANDER, WERE WE SUPPOSED TO BRING FOOD TO THE PRISONER?
SHUP

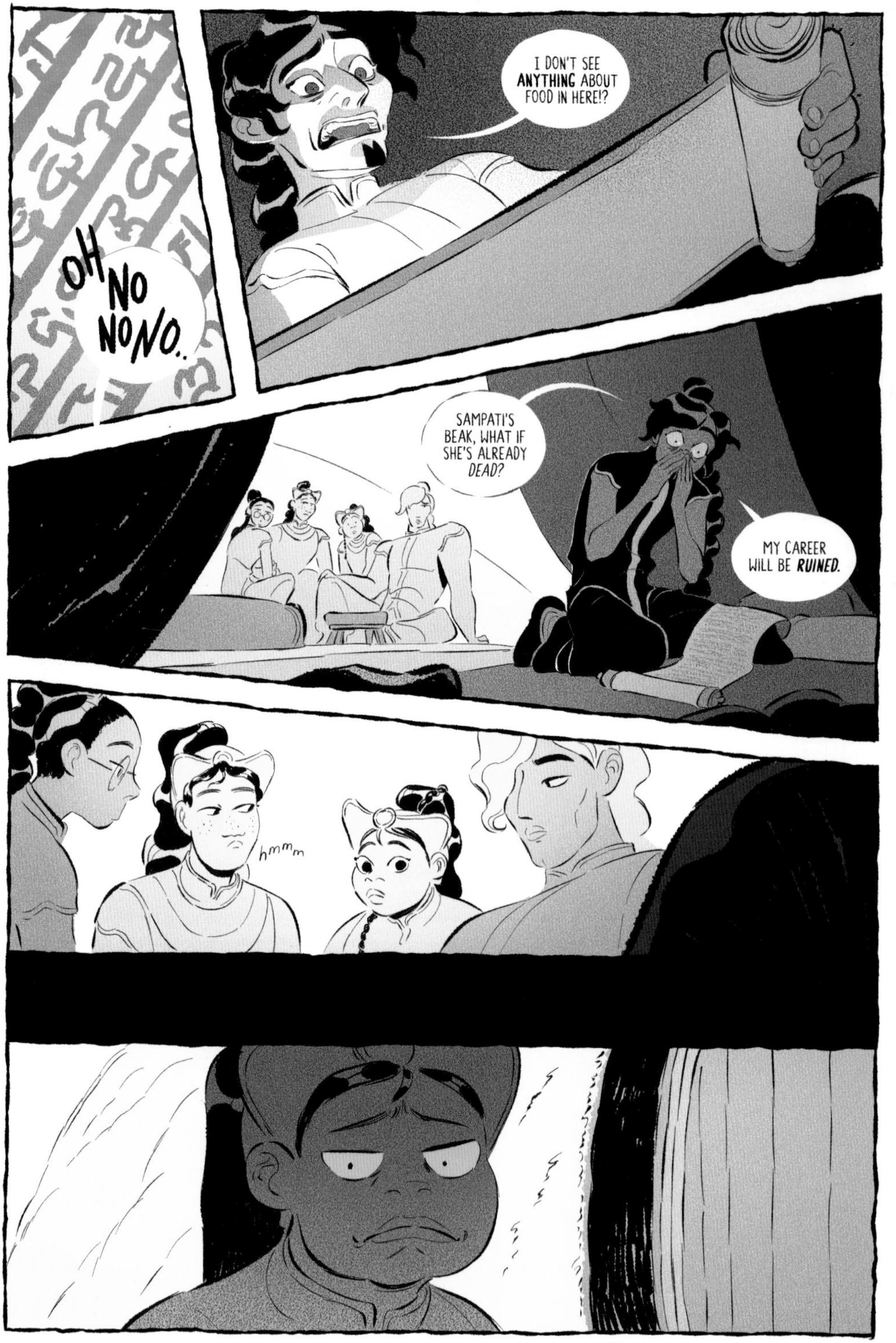
I DON'T SEE **ANYTHING** ABOUT FOOD IN HERE!?
OH NO NO NO NO..
SAMPATI'S BEAK, WHAT IF SHE'S ALREADY *DEAD?*
MY CAREER WILL BE **RUINED.**
hmmm

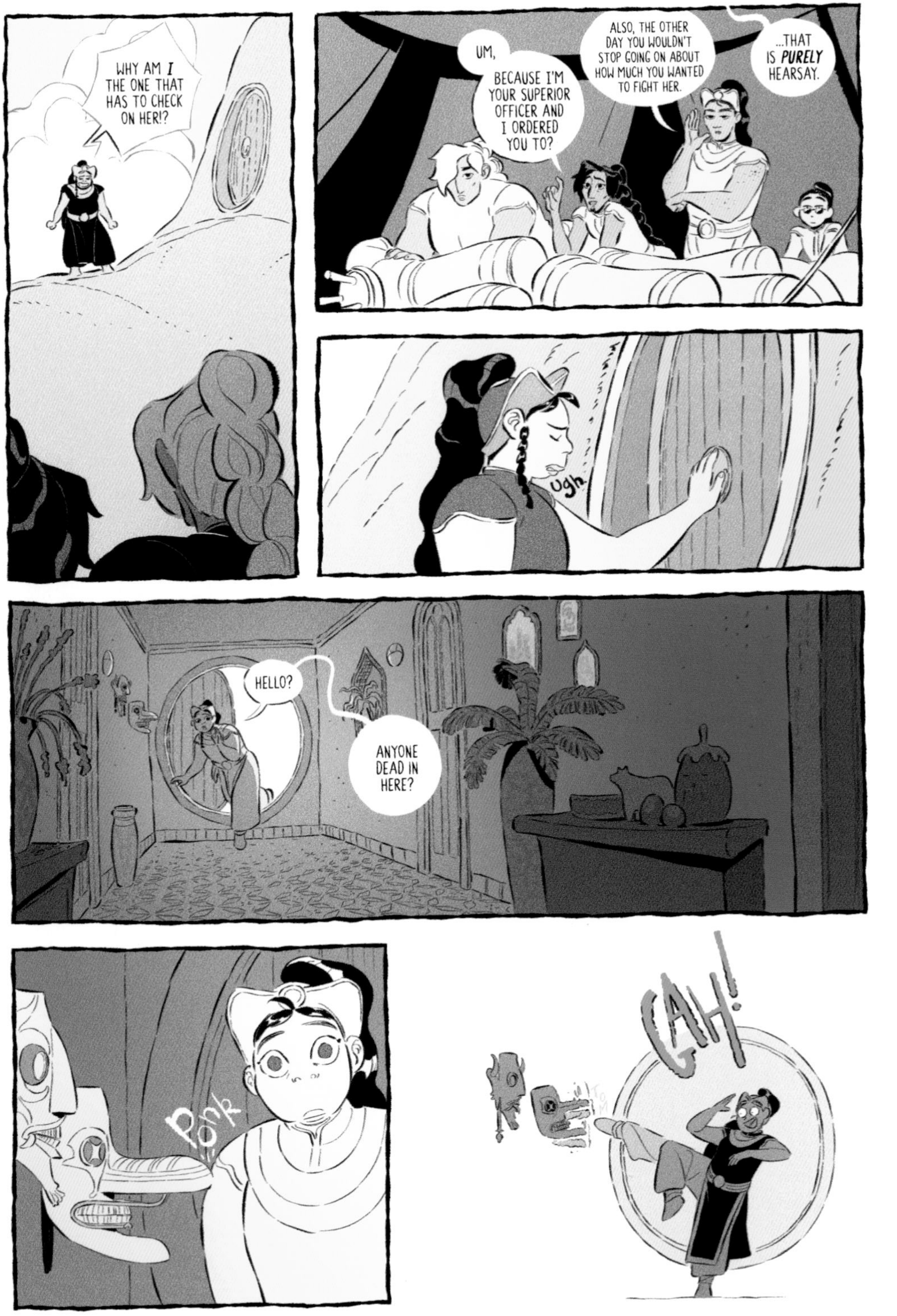
WHY AM *I* THE ONE THAT HAS TO CHECK ON HER!?
UM,
BECAUSE I'M YOUR SUPERIOR OFFICER AND I ORDERED YOU TO?
ALSO, THE OTHER DAY YOU WOULDN'T STOP GOING ON ABOUT HOW MUCH YOU WANTED TO FIGHT HER.
...THAT IS ***PURELY*** HEARSAY.
Ugh
HELLO?
ANYONE DEAD IN HERE?
PONK
GAH!

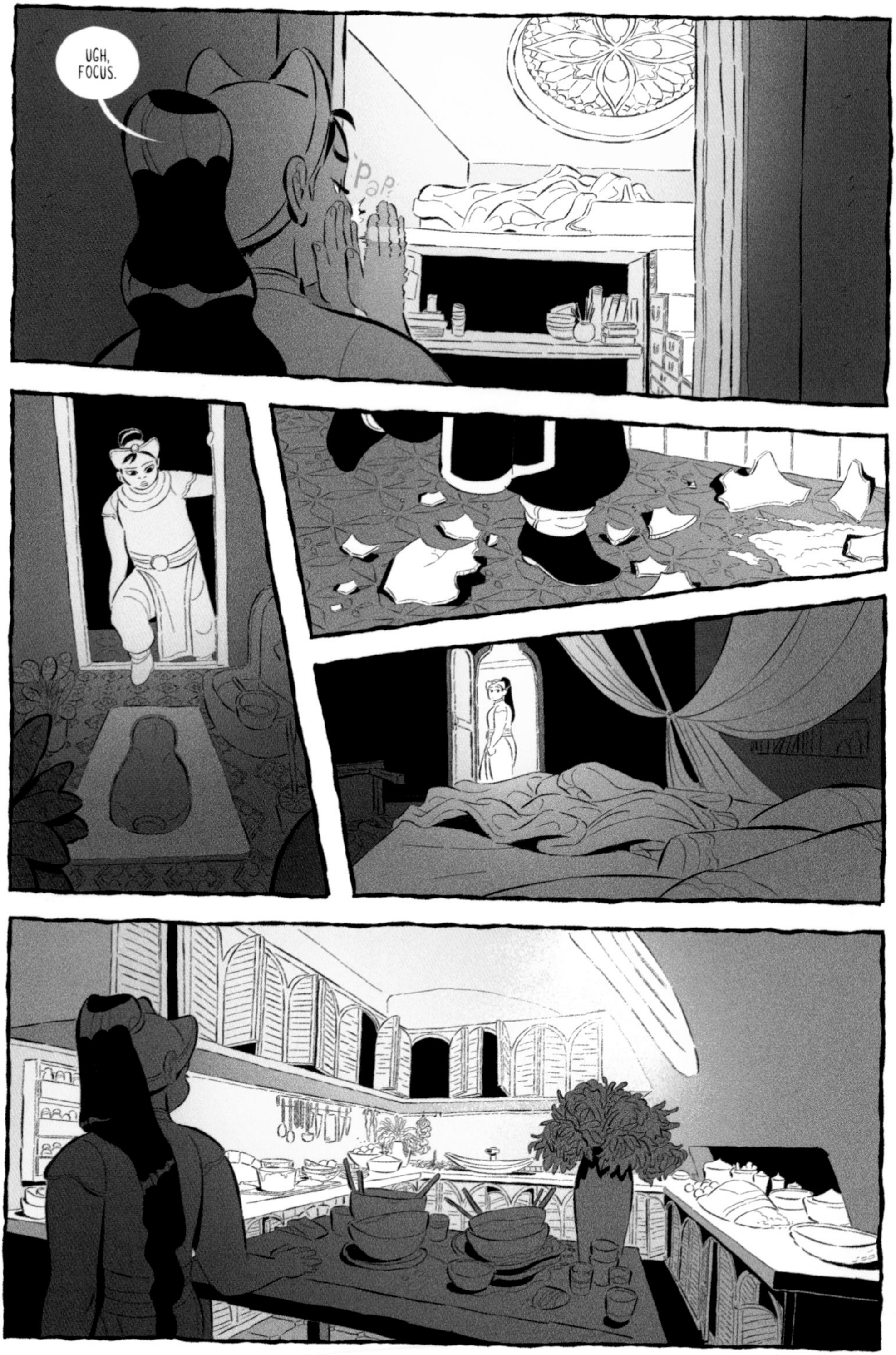
UGH, FOCUS.
PAP

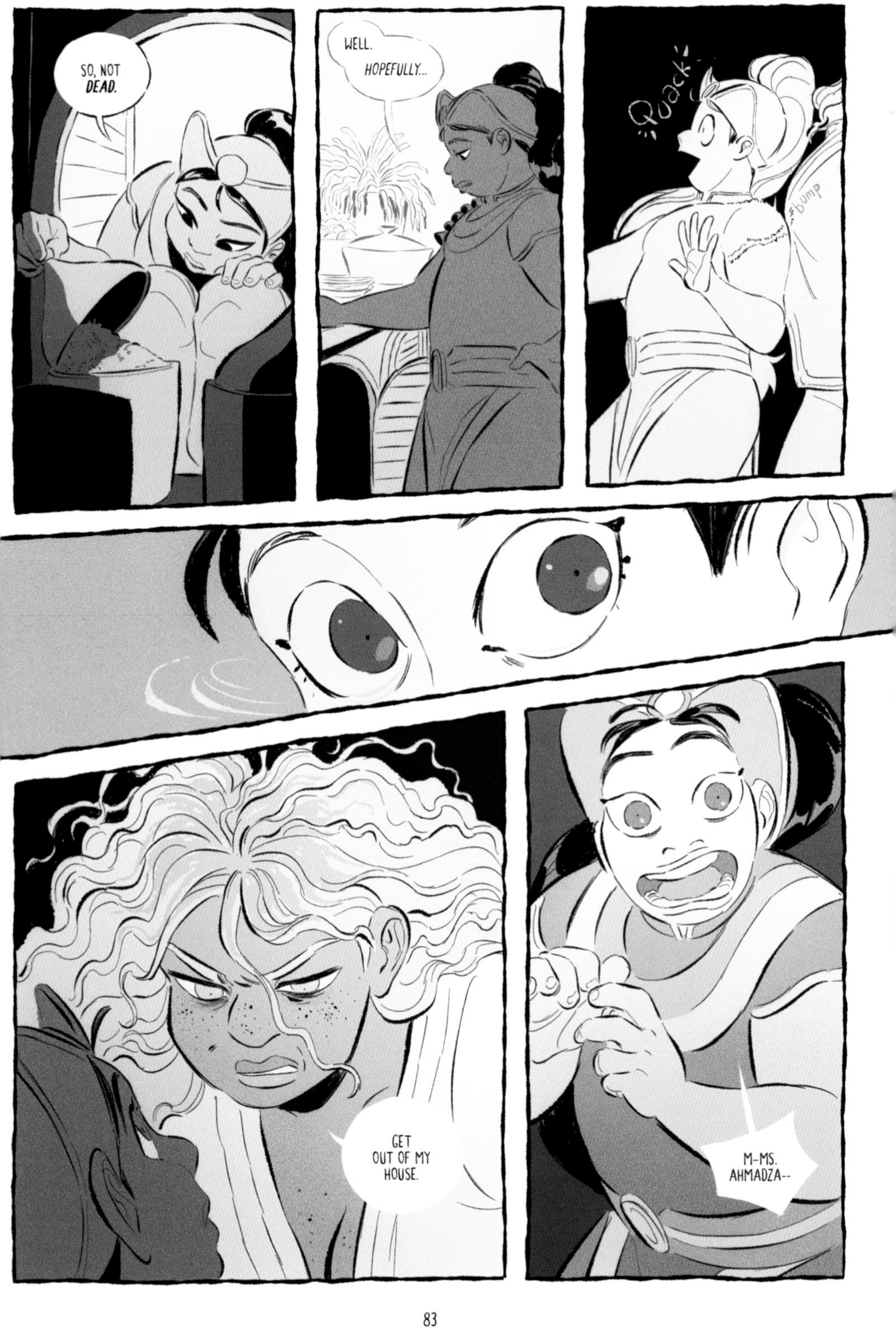
SO, NOT DEAD.
WELL.
HOPEFULLY...
QUACK
BUMP
GET OUT OF MY HOUSE.
M-MS. AHMADZA--

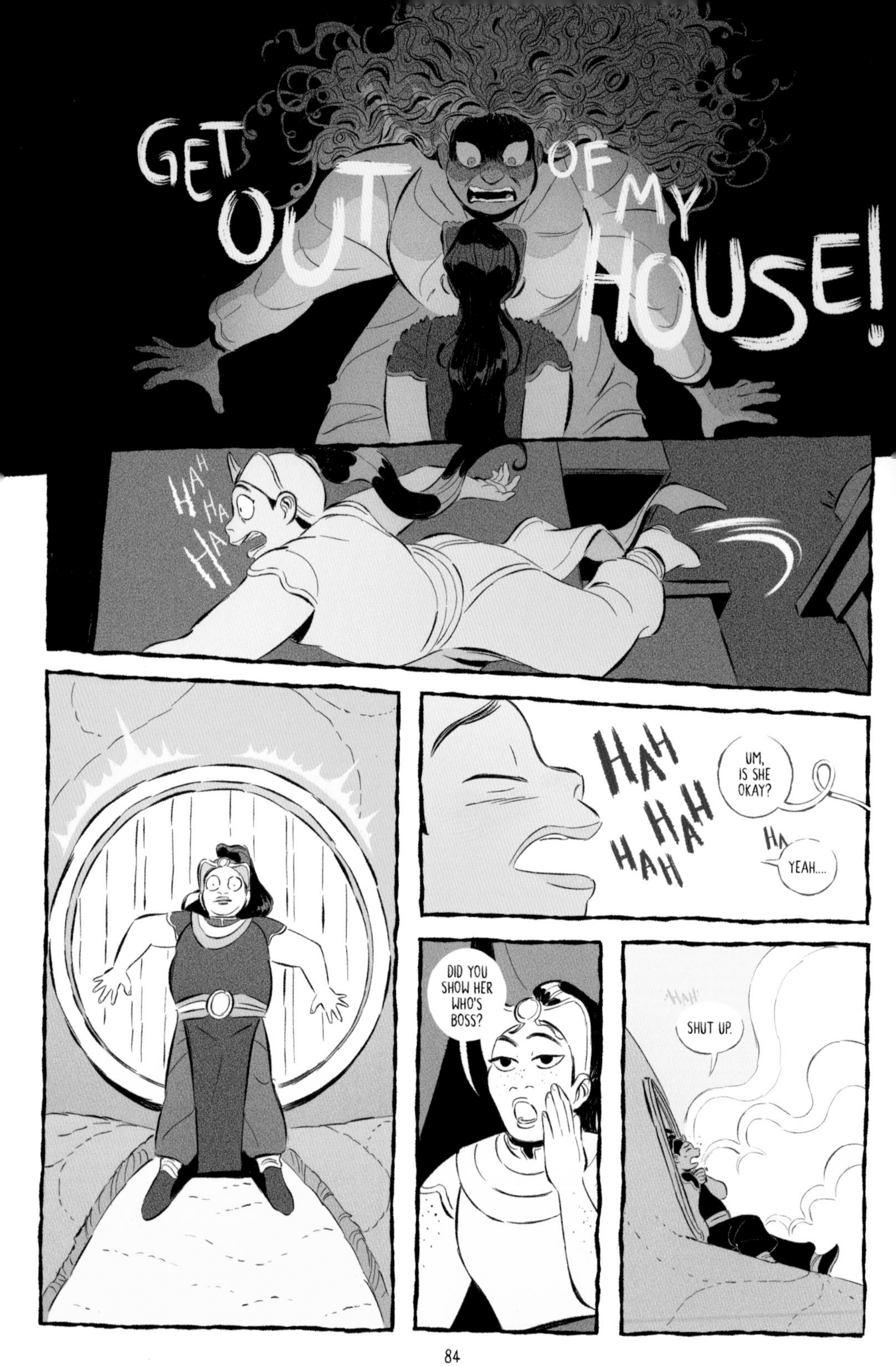
GET OUT OF MY HOUSE!
HAH HA HA HA
HAH HAH HAH HAH
UM, IS SHE OKAY?
HA
YEAH....
DID YOU SHOW HER WHO'S BOSS?
HAH
SHUT UP.

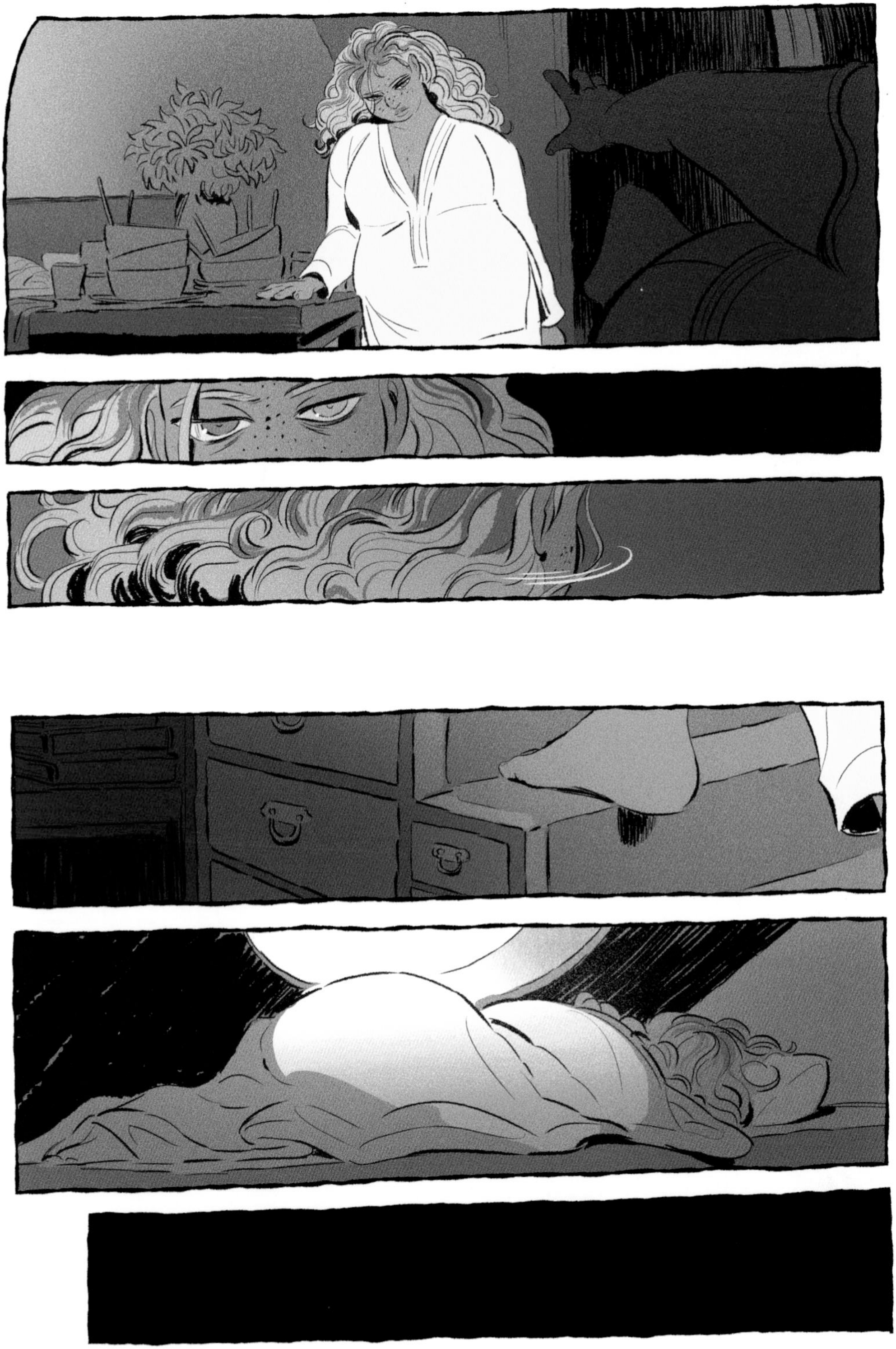

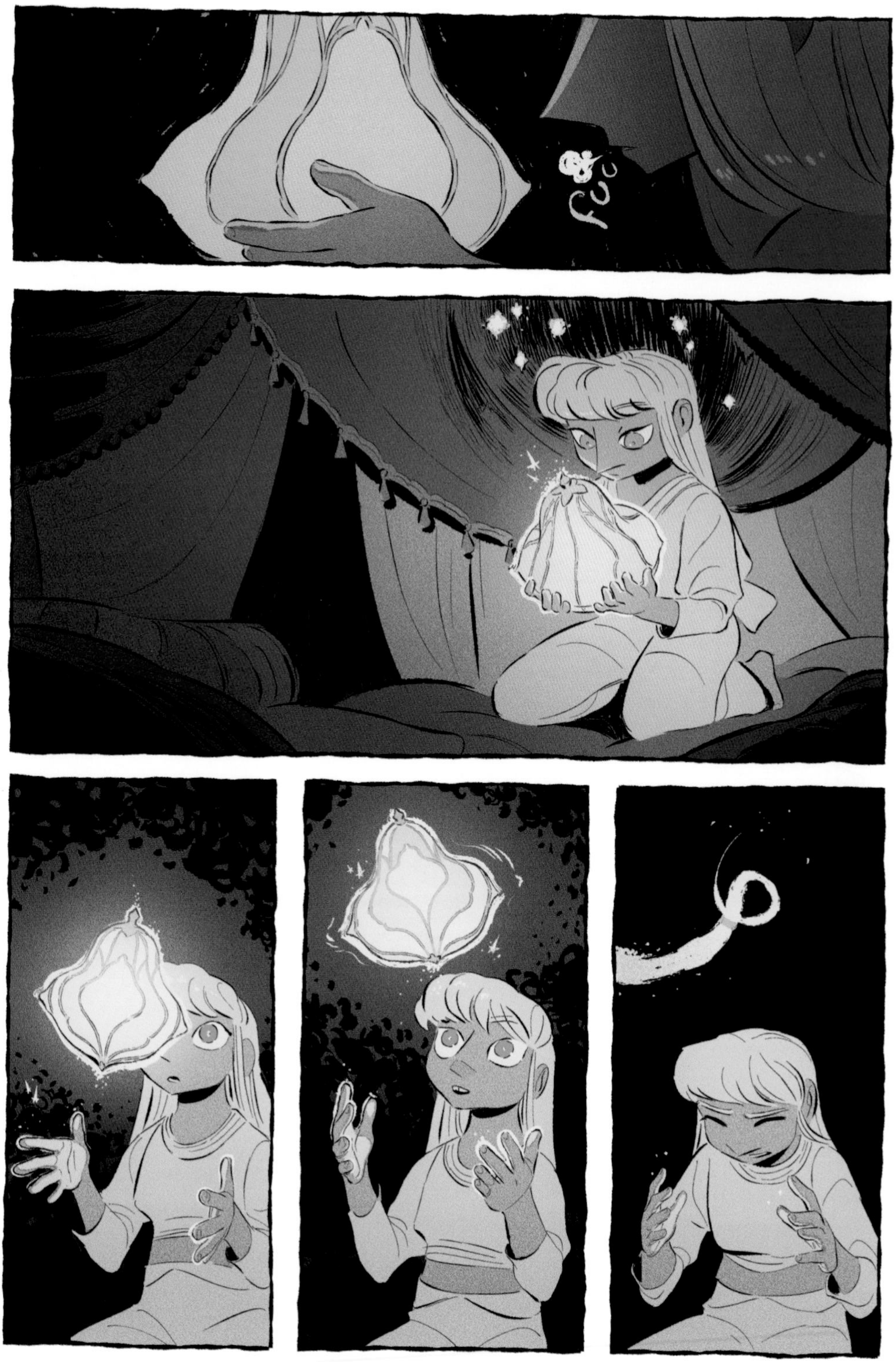

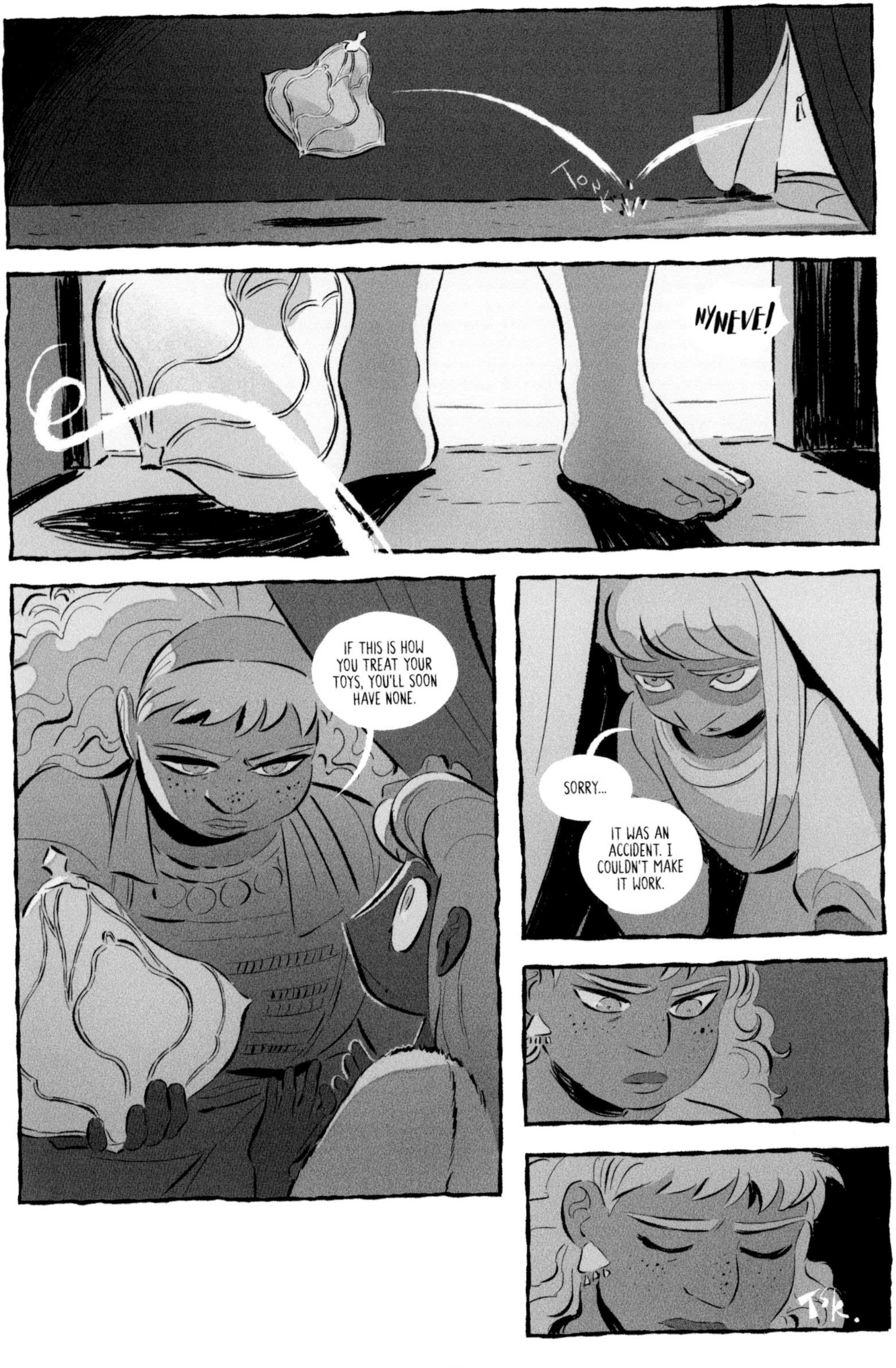
TONK
NYNEVE!
IF THIS IS HOW YOU TREAT YOUR TOYS, YOU'LL SOON HAVE NONE.
SORRY...
IT WAS AN ACCIDENT. I COULDN'T MAKE IT WORK.
TSK.

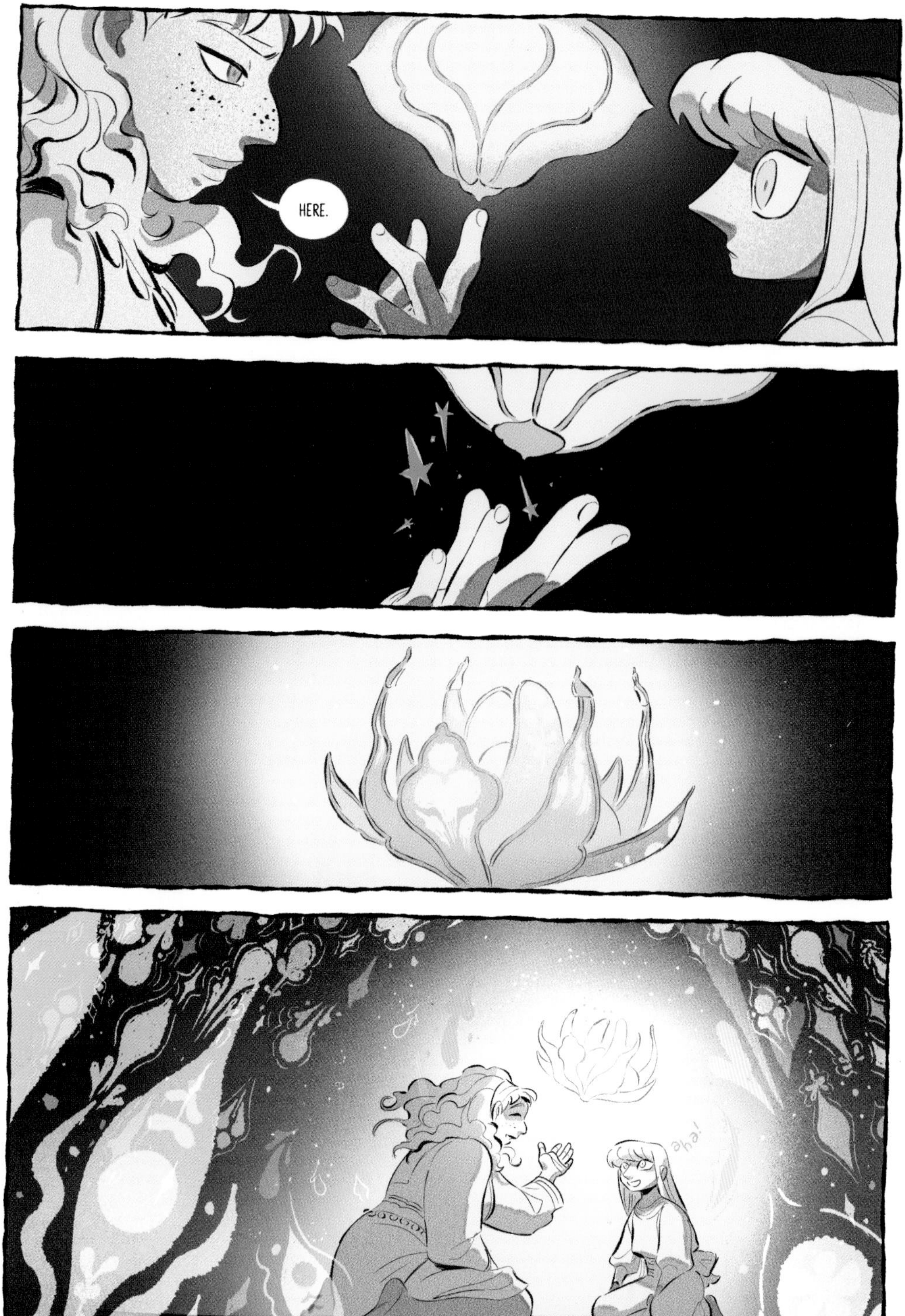
HERE.
aha!

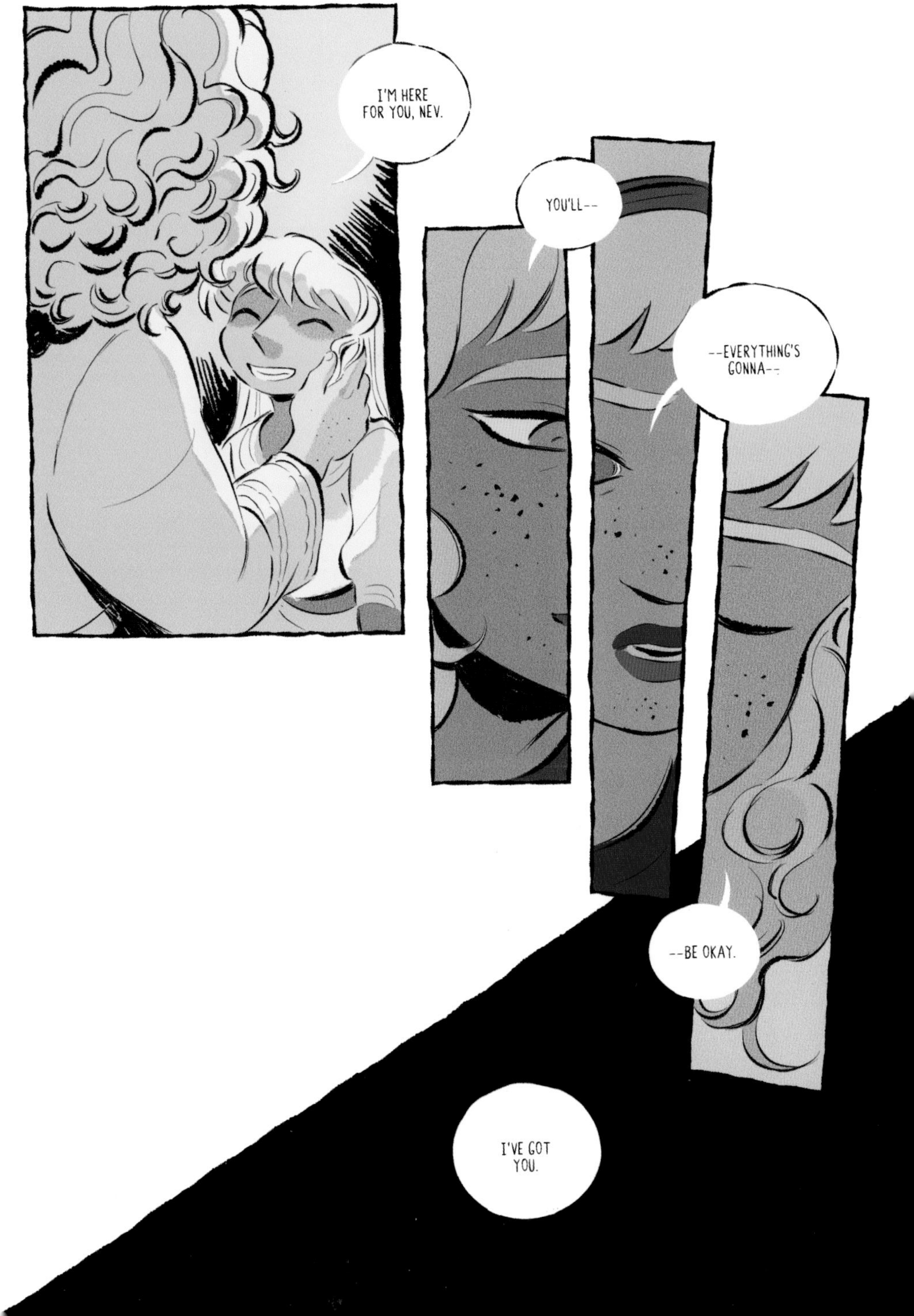
I'M HERE FOR YOU, NEV.
YOU'LL--
--EVERYTHING'S GONNA--
--BE OKAY.
I'VE GOT YOU.

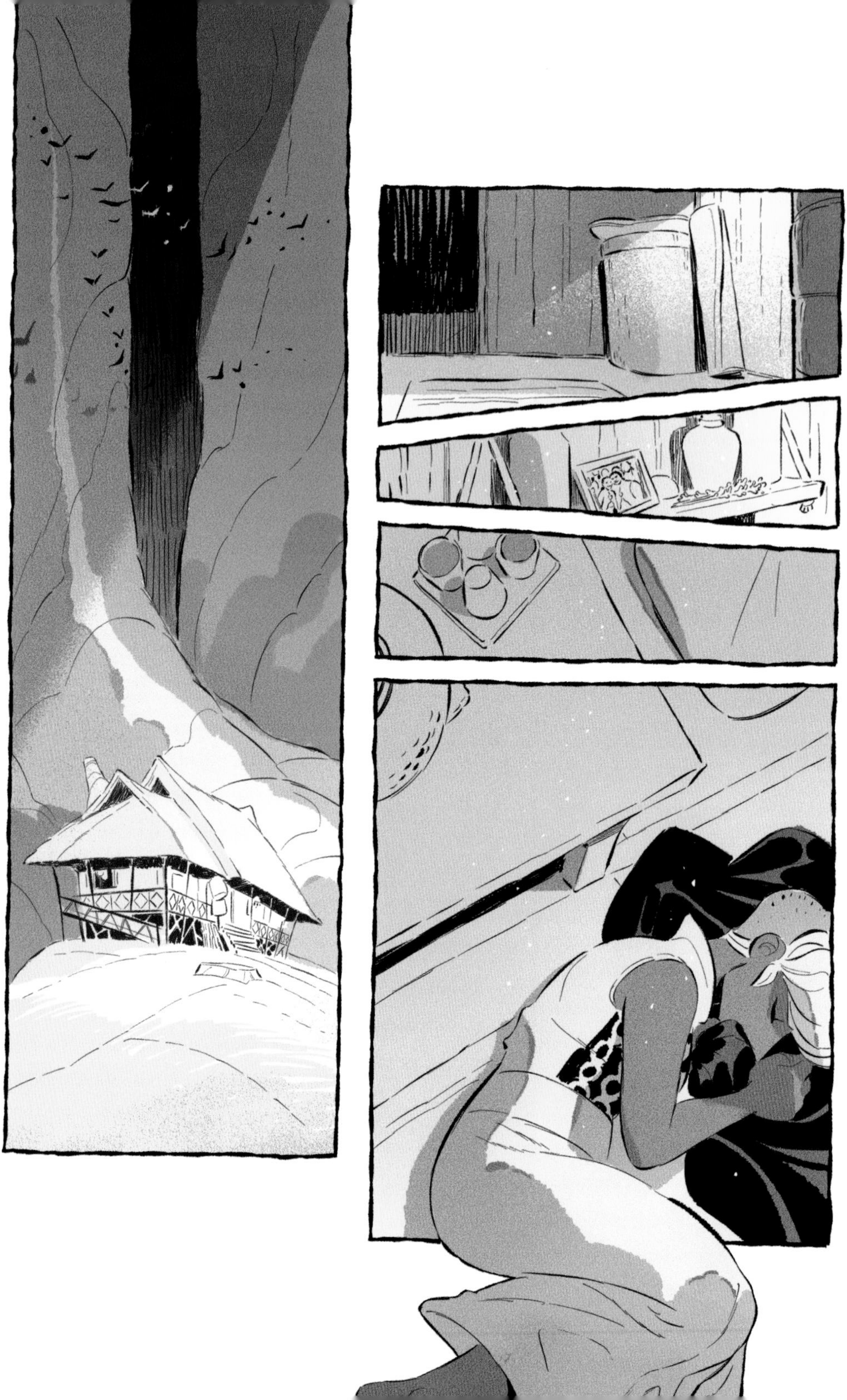

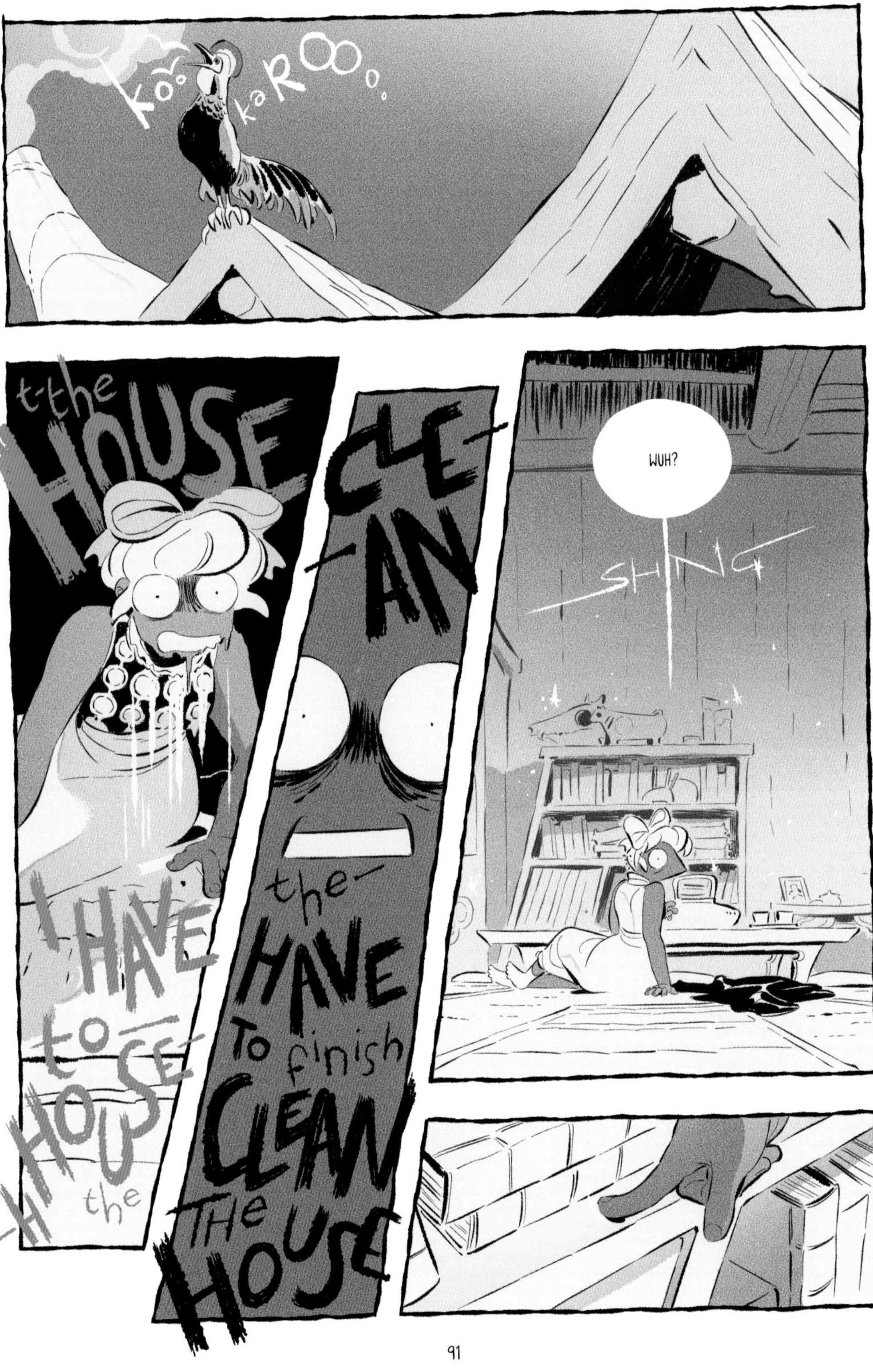
KOO KAROOOo
t-the HOUSE
CLE-AN
I HAVE to HOUSE the
the- HAVE TO finish CLEAN THE HOUSE
WUH?
SHING

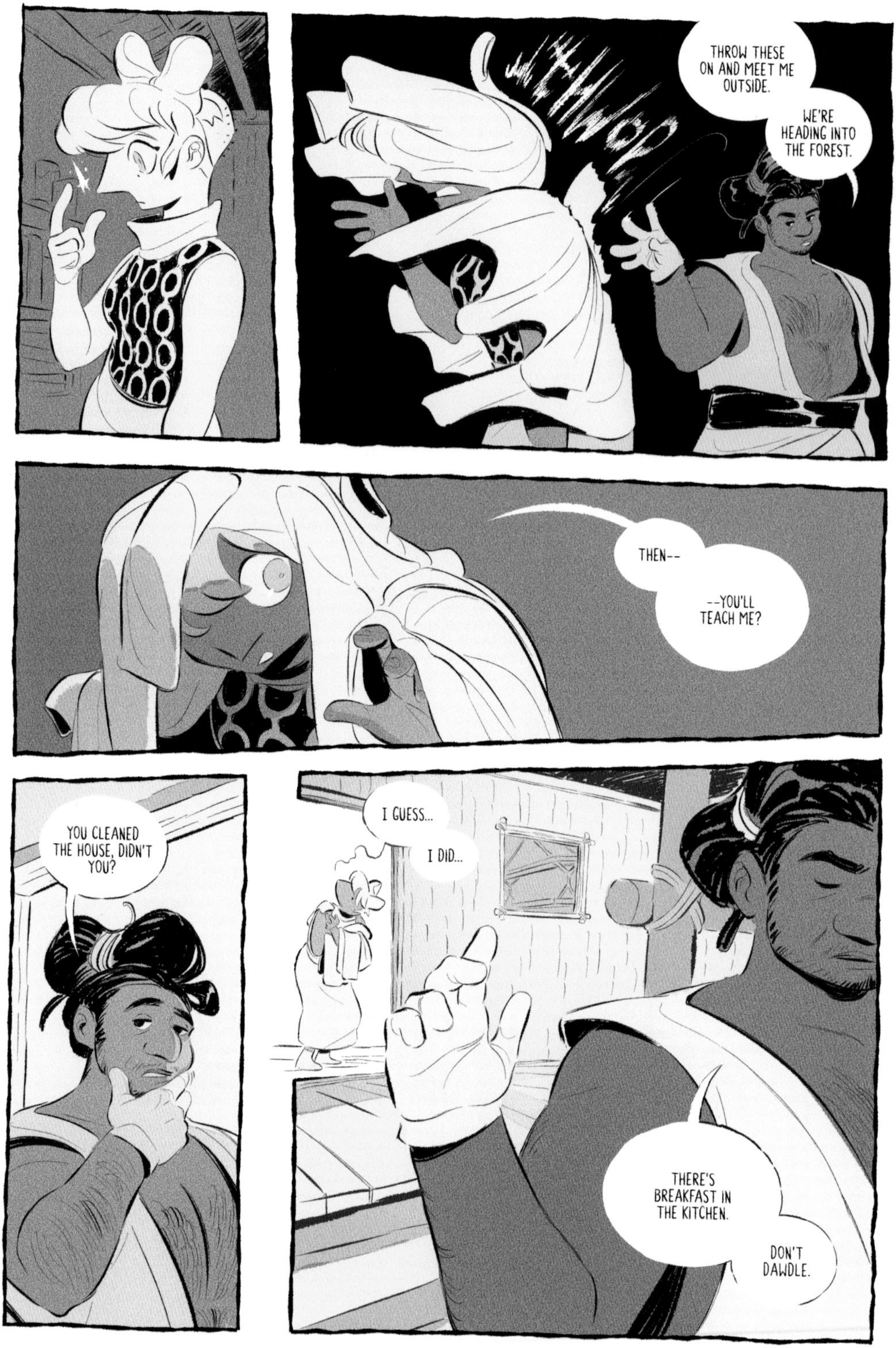
THROW THESE ON AND MEET ME OUTSIDE.
WE'RE HEADING INTO THE FOREST.
THEN--
--YOU'LL TEACH ME?
YOU CLEANED THE HOUSE, DIDN'T YOU?
I GUESS...
I DID...
THERE'S BREAKFAST IN THE KITCHEN.
DON'T DAWDLE.

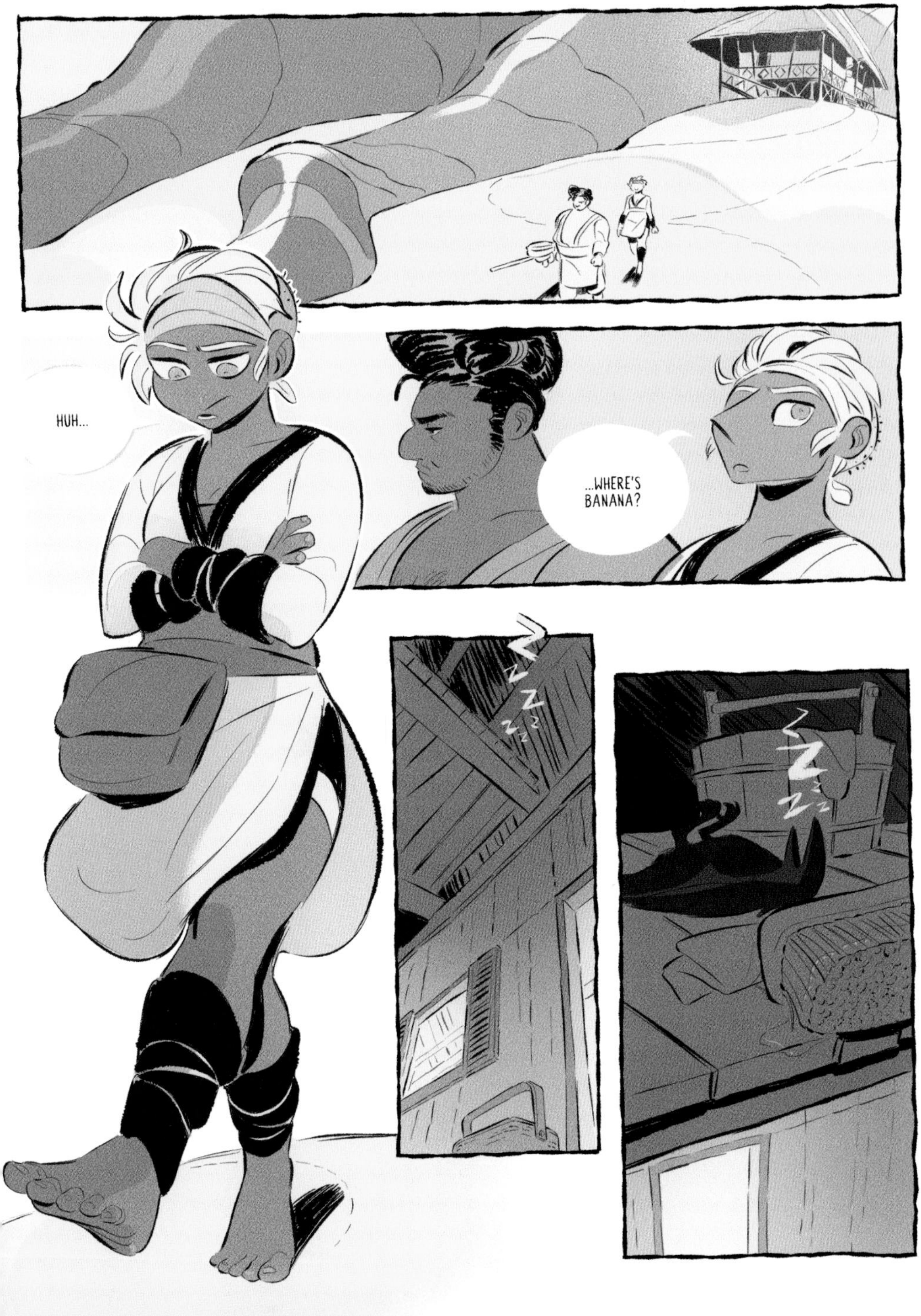
HUH...
...WHERE'S BANANA?
ZZZ

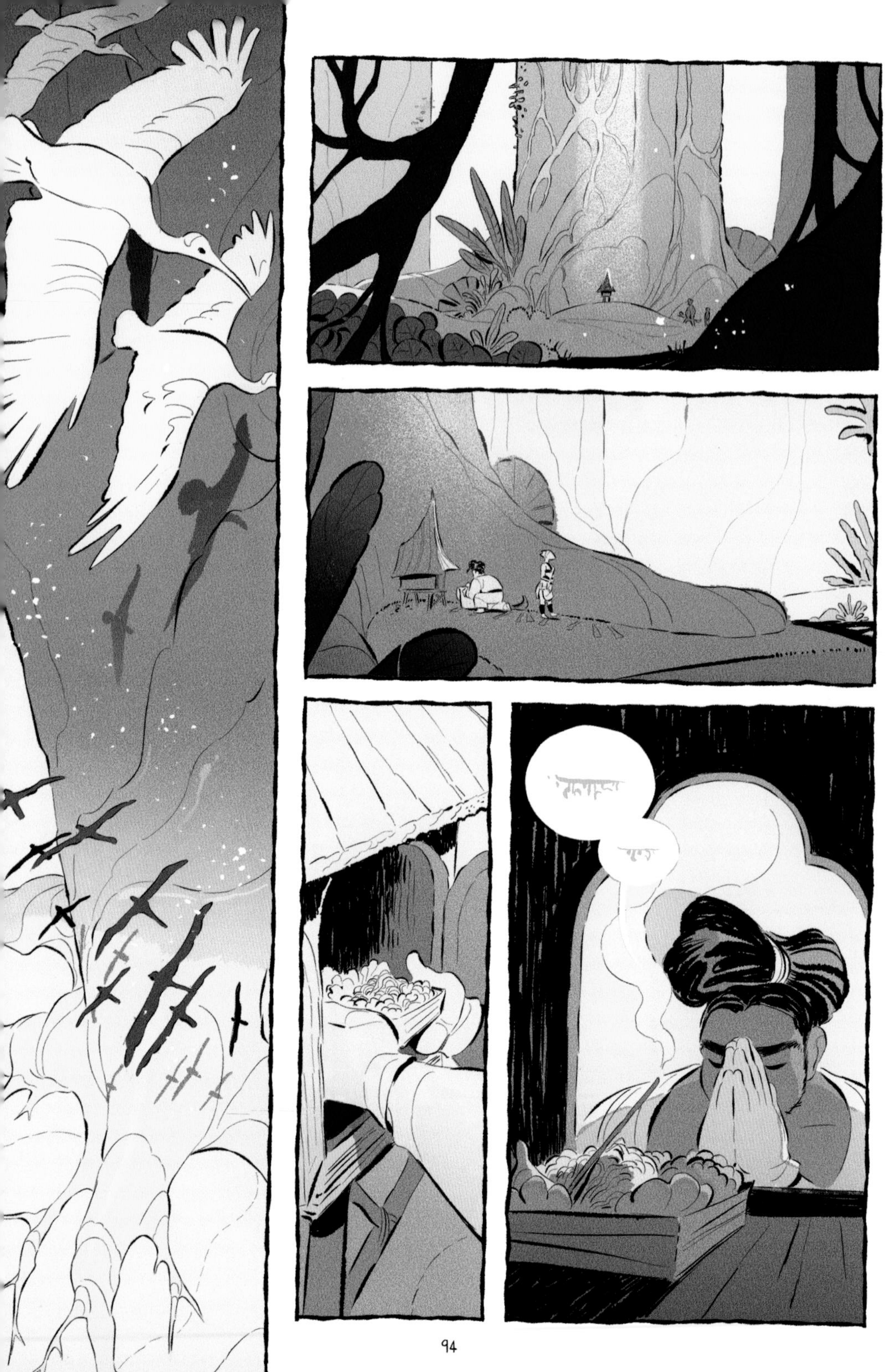

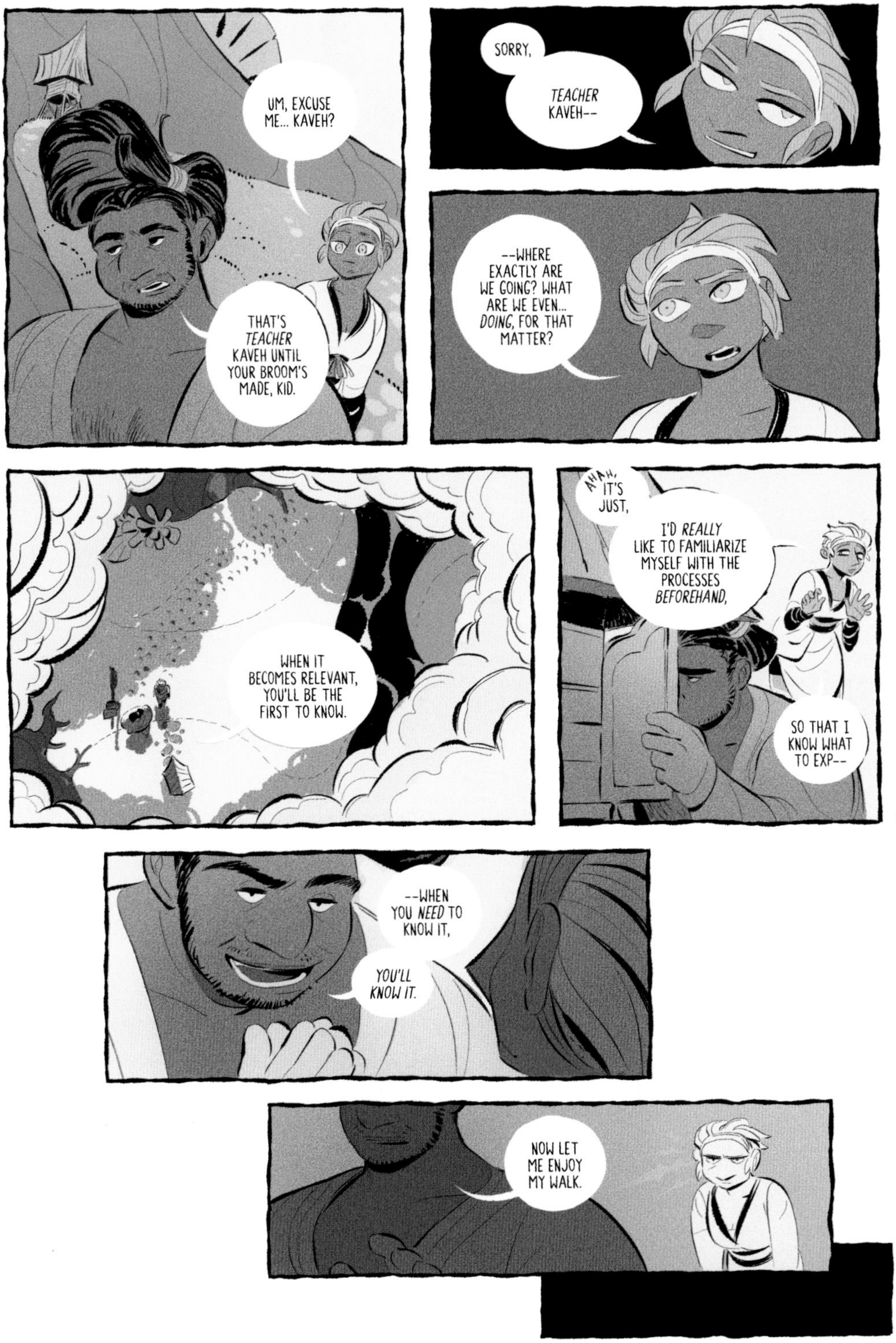
UM, EXCUSE ME... KAVEH?
THAT'S *TEACHER* KAVEH UNTIL YOUR BROOM'S MADE, KID.
SORRY,
TEACHER KAVEH--
--WHERE EXACTLY ARE WE GOING? WHAT ARE WE EVEN... *DOING*, FOR THAT MATTER?
WHEN IT BECOMES RELEVANT, YOU'LL BE THE FIRST TO KNOW.
AHAH, IT'S JUST,
I'D *REALLY* LIKE TO FAMILIARIZE MYSELF WITH THE PROCESSES *BEFOREHAND*,
SO THAT I KNOW WHAT TO EXP--
--WHEN YOU *NEED* TO KNOW IT,
YOU'LL KNOW IT.
NOW LET ME ENJOY MY WALK.

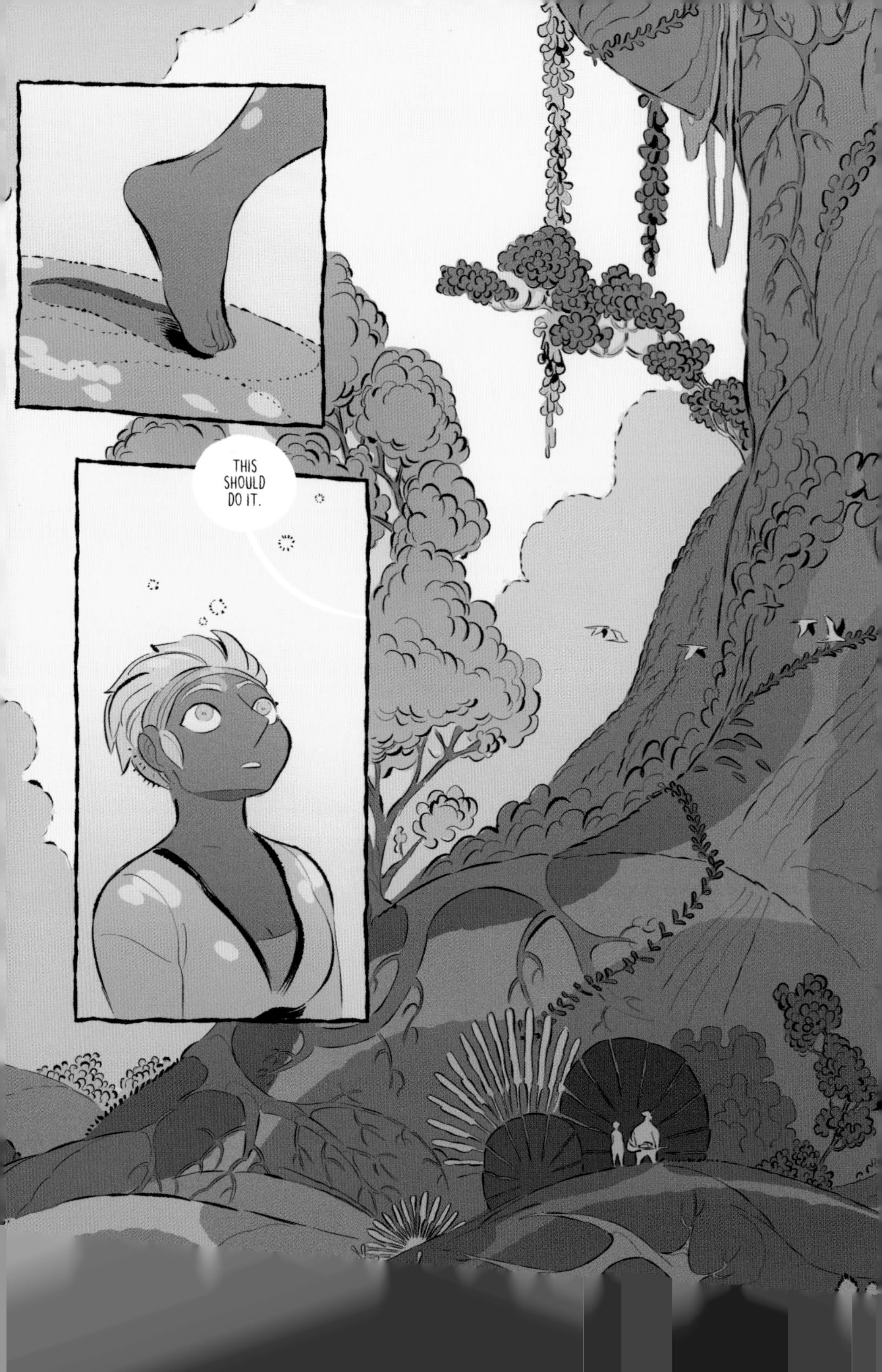
THIS SHOULD DO IT.

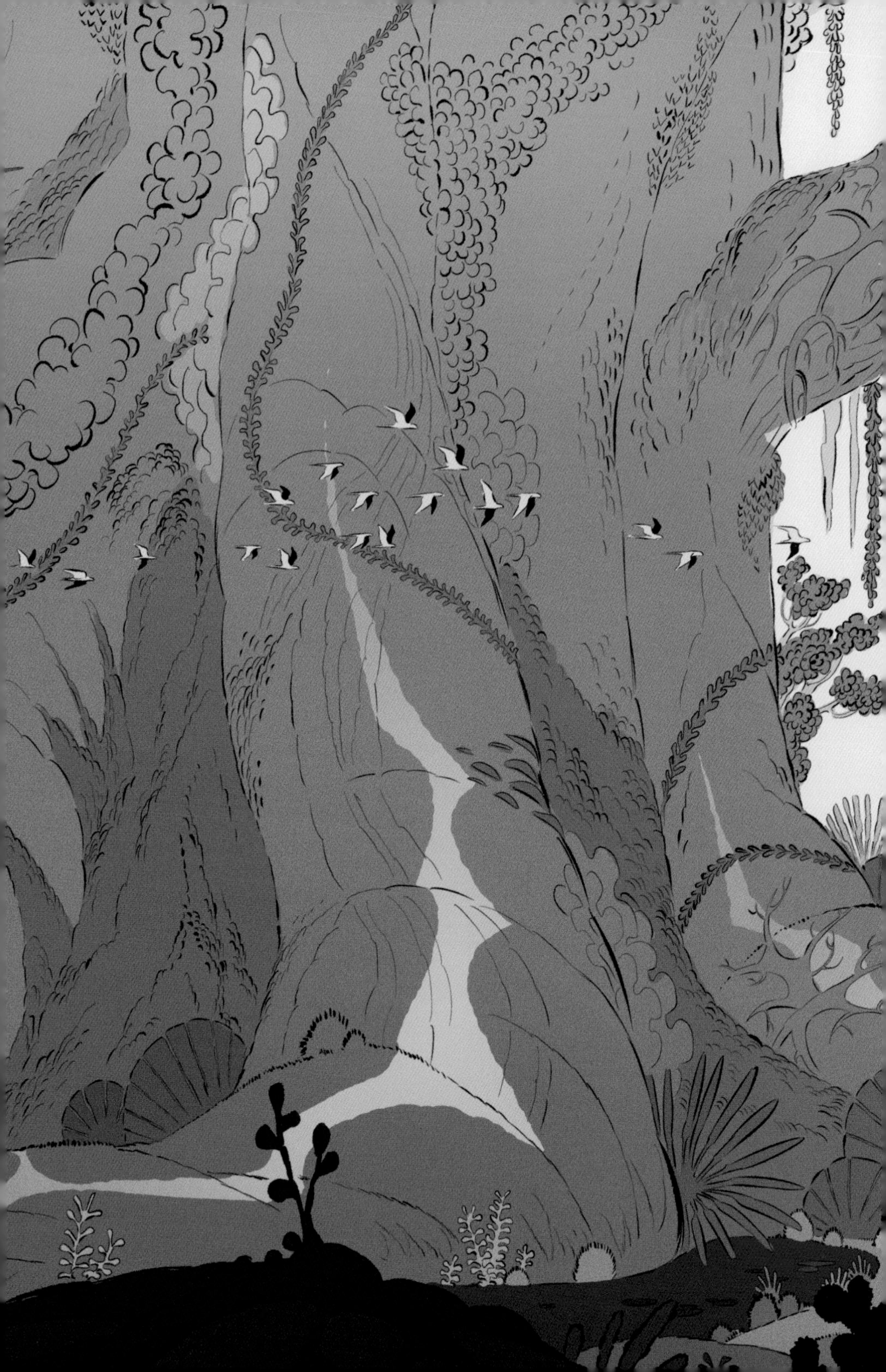

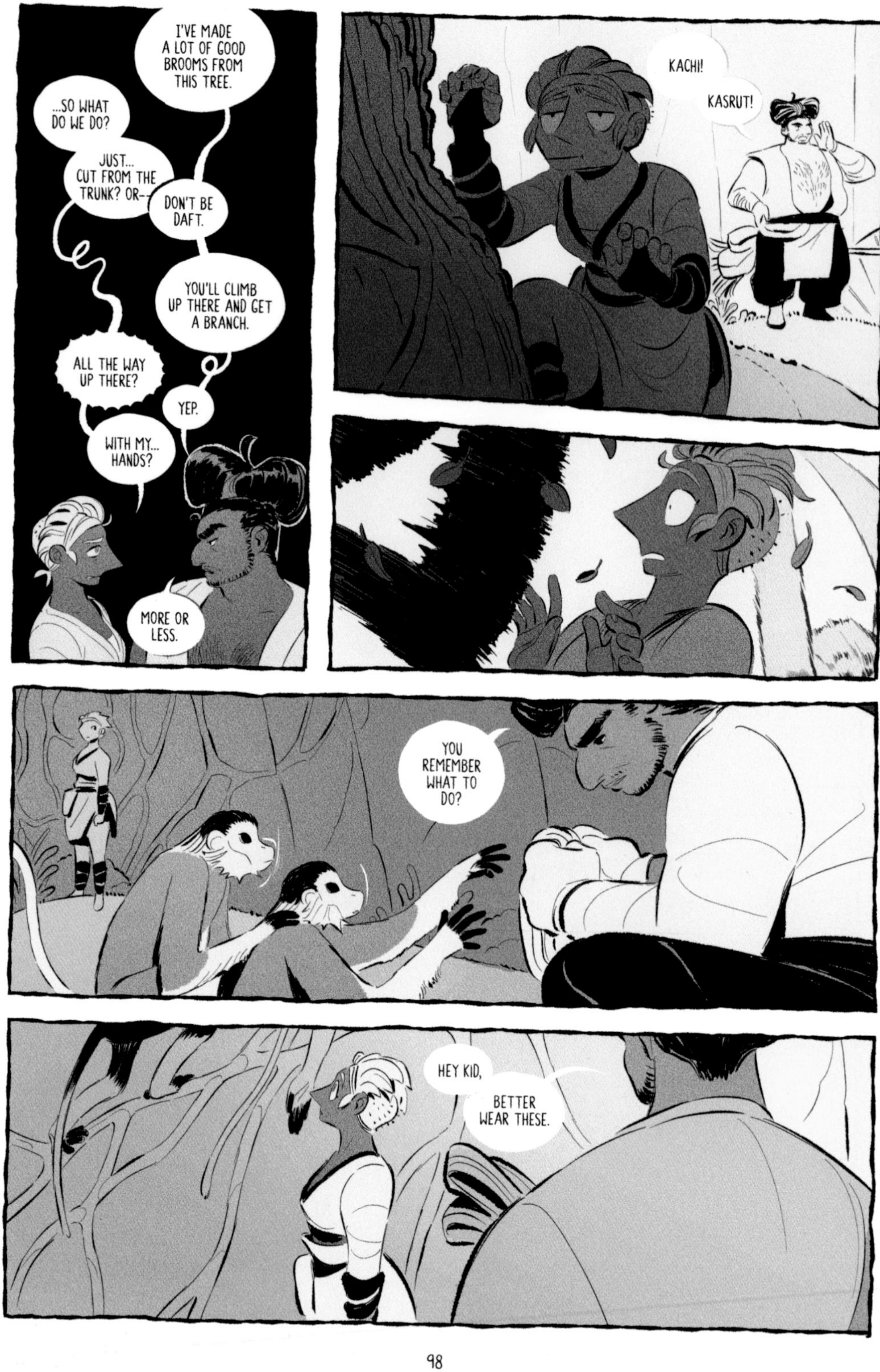
...SO WHAT DO WE DO?
I'VE MADE A LOT OF GOOD BROOMS FROM THIS TREE.
JUST... CUT FROM THE TRUNK? OR--
DON'T BE DAFT.
YOU'LL CLIMB UP THERE AND GET A BRANCH.
ALL THE WAY UP THERE?
YEP.
WITH MY... HANDS?
MORE OR LESS.
KACHI!
KASRUT!
YOU REMEMBER WHAT TO DO?
HEY KID,
BETTER WEAR THESE.

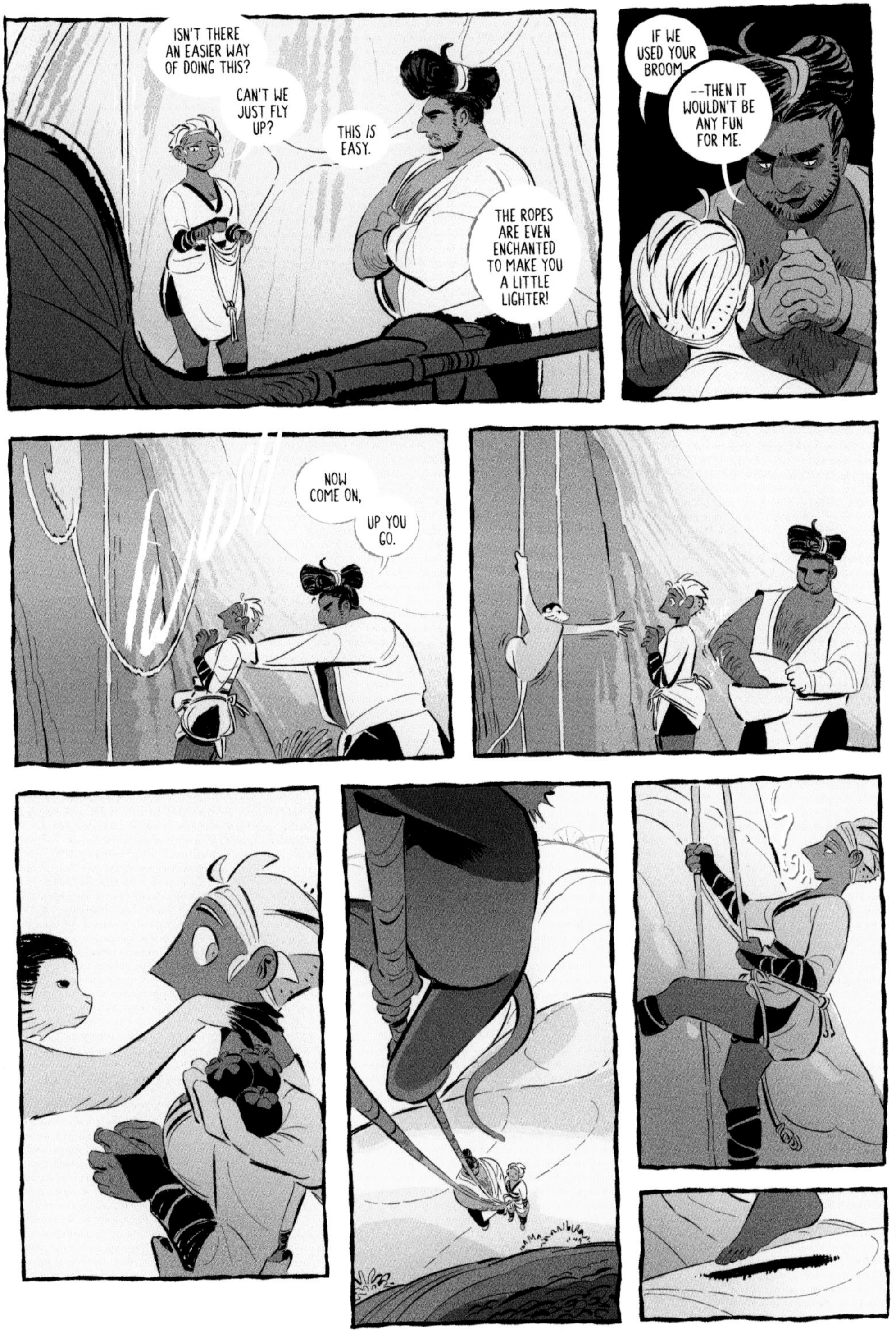
ISN'T THERE AN EASIER WAY OF DOING THIS?
CAN'T WE JUST FLY UP?
THIS *IS* EASY.
THE ROPES ARE EVEN ENCHANTED TO MAKE YOU A LITTLE LIGHTER!
IF WE USED YOUR BROOM—
--THEN IT WOULDN'T BE ANY FUN FOR ME.
NOW COME ON,
UP YOU GO.

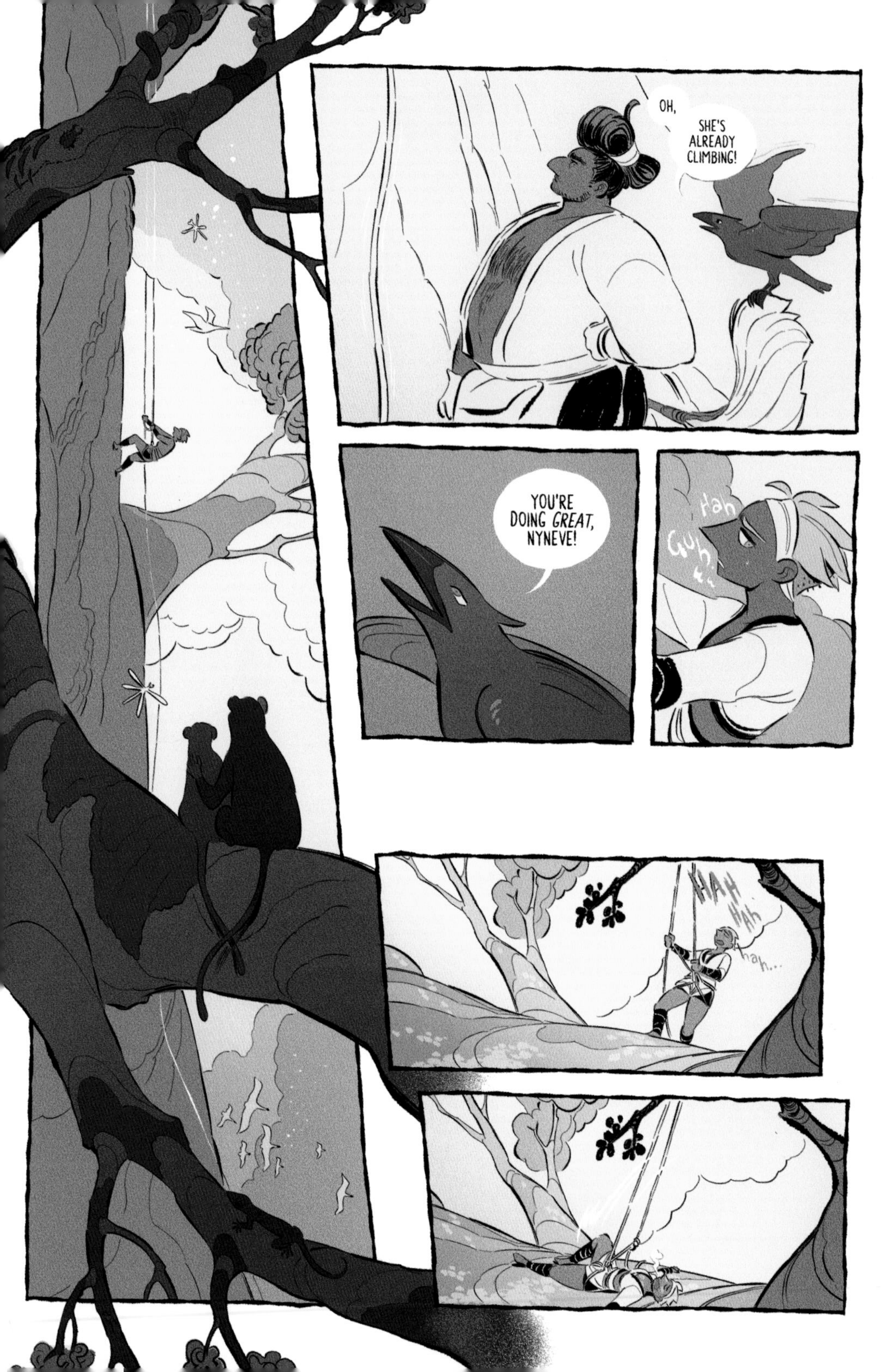
OH,
SHE'S ALREADY CLIMBING!
YOU'RE DOING GREAT, NYNEVE!
Hah
Guh
HAH
Hah
hah...

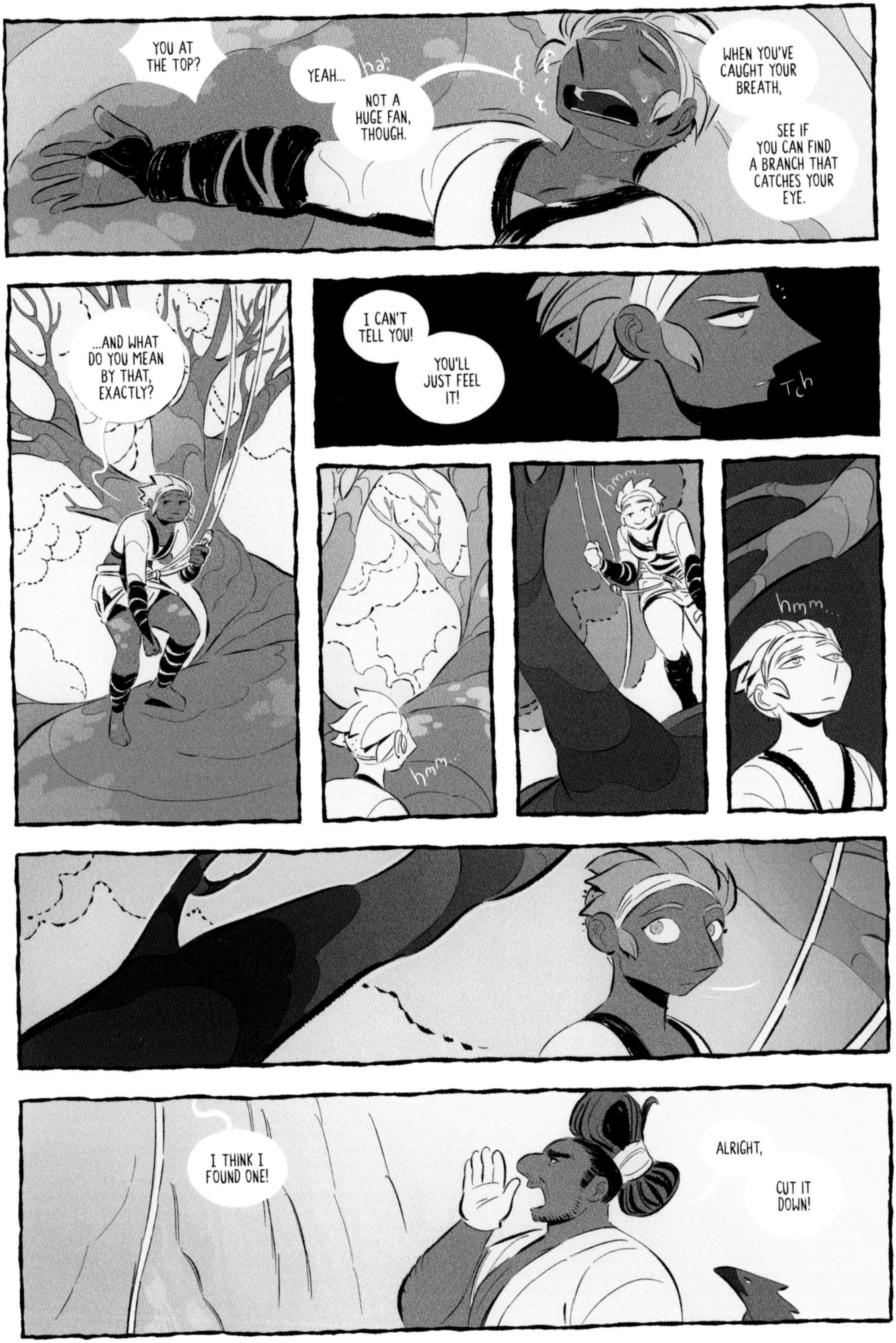
YOU AT THE TOP?
YEAH...
hah
NOT A HUGE FAN, THOUGH.
WHEN YOU'VE CAUGHT YOUR BREATH,
SEE IF YOU CAN FIND A BRANCH THAT CATCHES YOUR EYE.
...AND WHAT DO YOU MEAN BY THAT, EXACTLY?
I CAN'T TELL YOU!
YOU'LL JUST FEEL IT!
Tch
hmm...
hmm...
hmm...
I THINK I FOUND ONE!
ALRIGHT,
CUT IT DOWN!

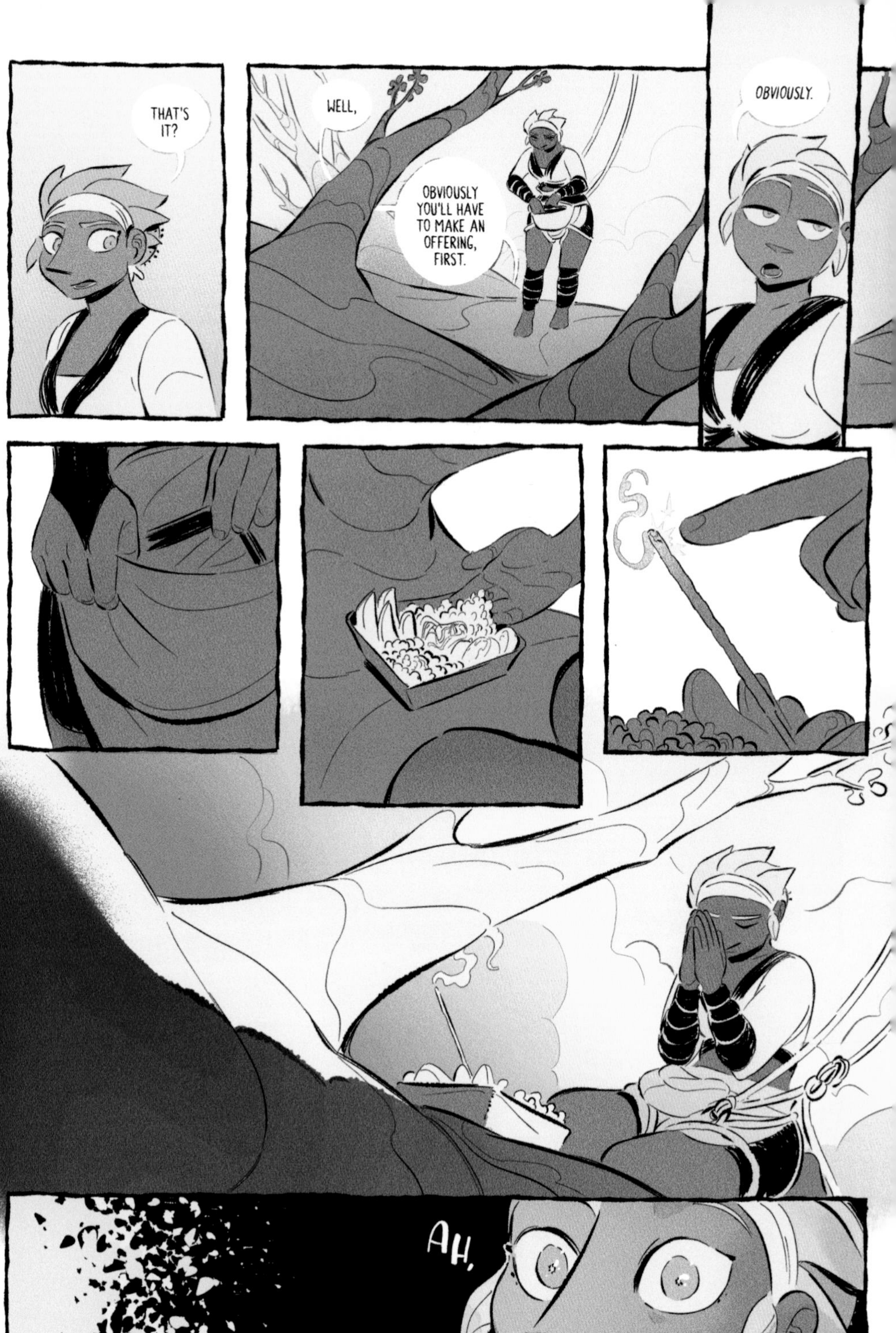

THAT'S IT?
WELL,
OBVIOUSLY YOU'LL HAVE TO MAKE AN OFFERING, FIRST.
OBVIOUSLY.
AH,

I'M SORRY... WILL YOU LET ME TAKE YOUR BRANCH?

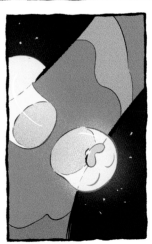

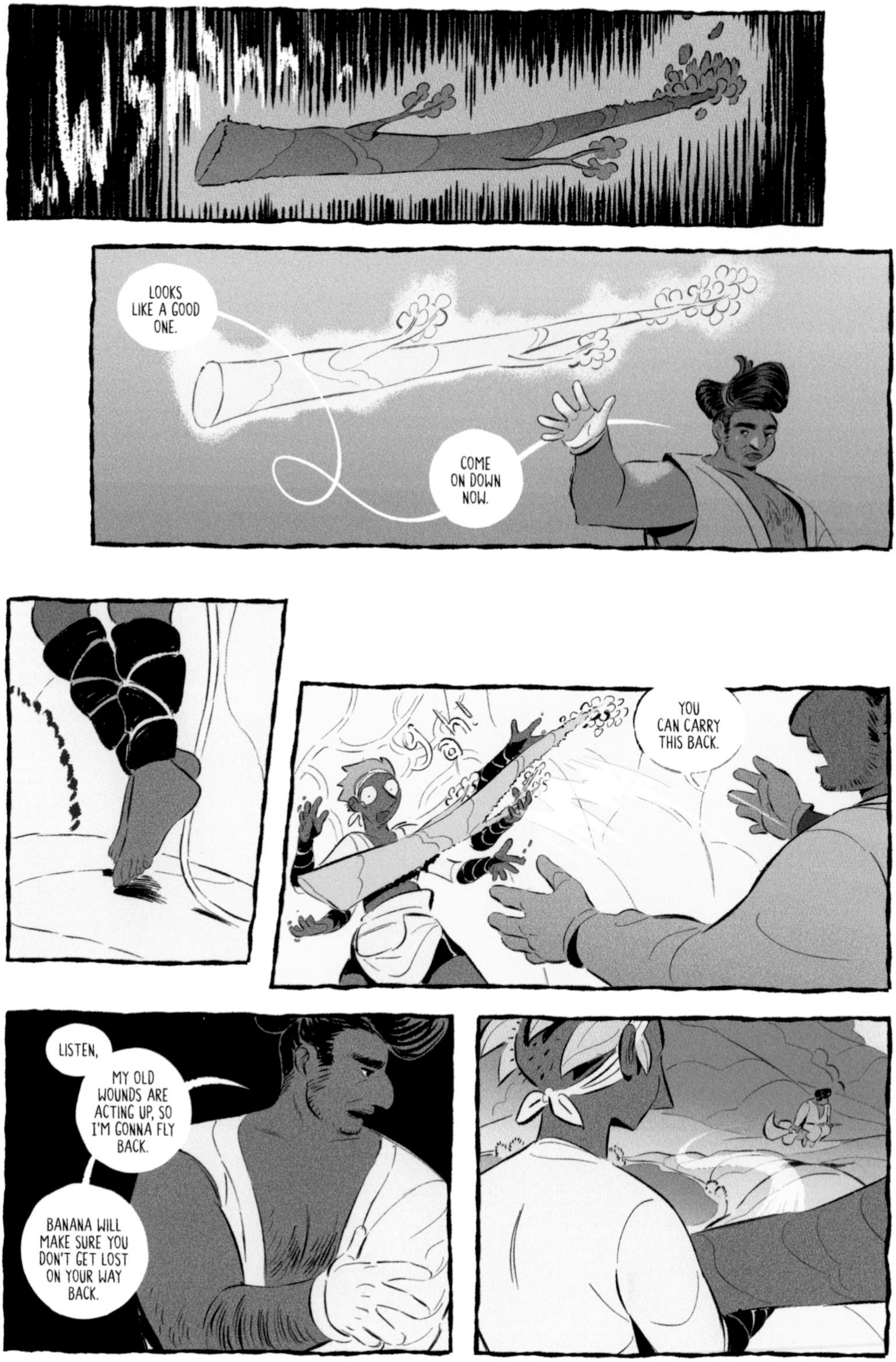
LOOKS LIKE A GOOD ONE.
COME ON DOWN NOW.
YOU CAN CARRY THIS BACK.
LISTEN,
MY OLD WOUNDS ARE ACTING UP, SO I'M GONNA FLY BACK.
BANANA WILL MAKE SURE YOU DON'T GET LOST ON YOUR WAY BACK.

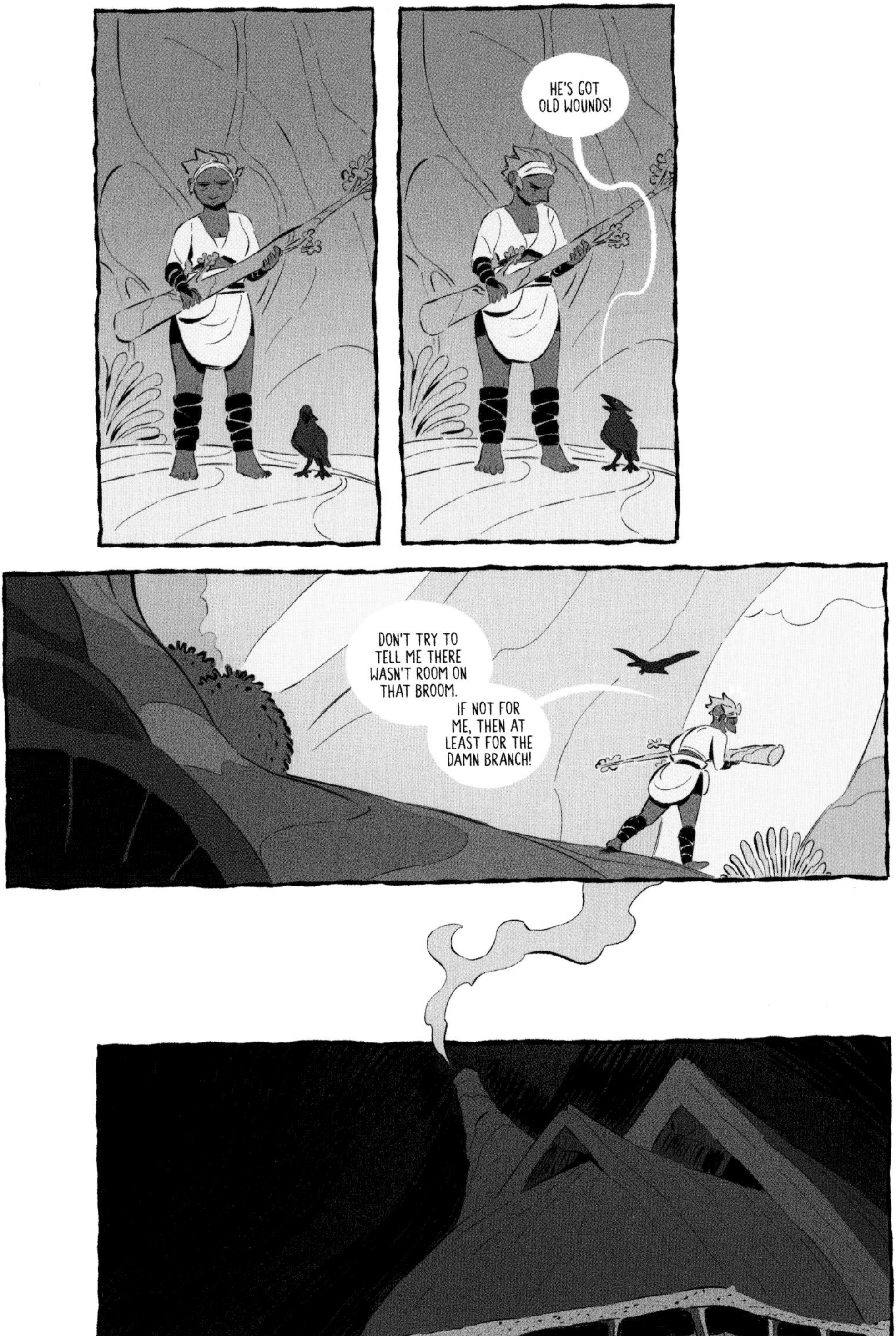
HE'S GOT OLD WOUNDS!
DON'T TRY TO TELL ME THERE WASN'T ROOM ON THAT BROOM.
IF NOT FOR ME, THEN AT LEAST FOR THE DAMN BRANCH!

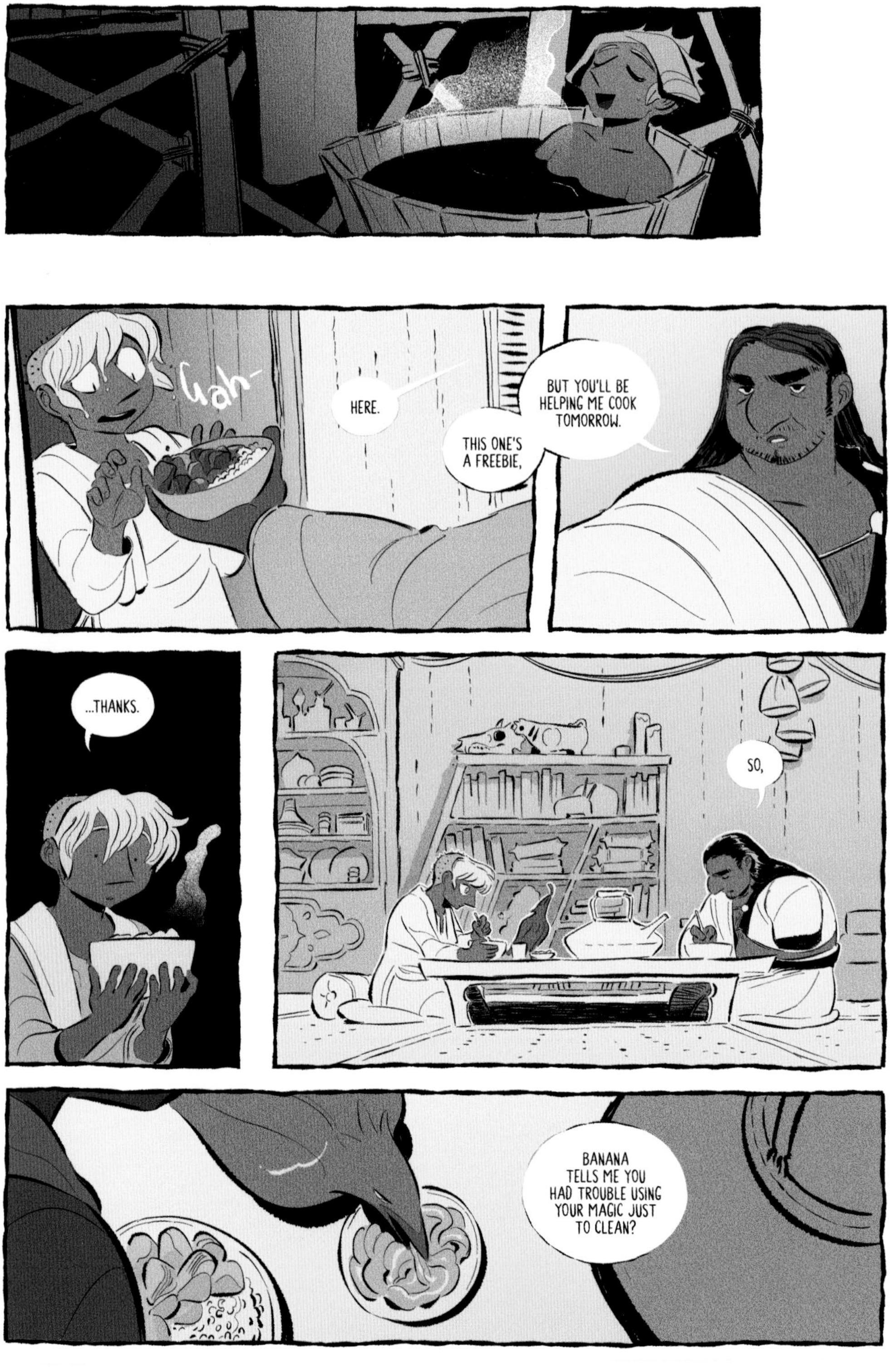
Gah-
HERE.
THIS ONE'S A FREEBIE,
BUT YOU'LL BE HELPING ME COOK TOMORROW.
...THANKS.
SO,
BANANA TELLS ME YOU HAD TROUBLE USING YOUR MAGIC JUST TO CLEAN?

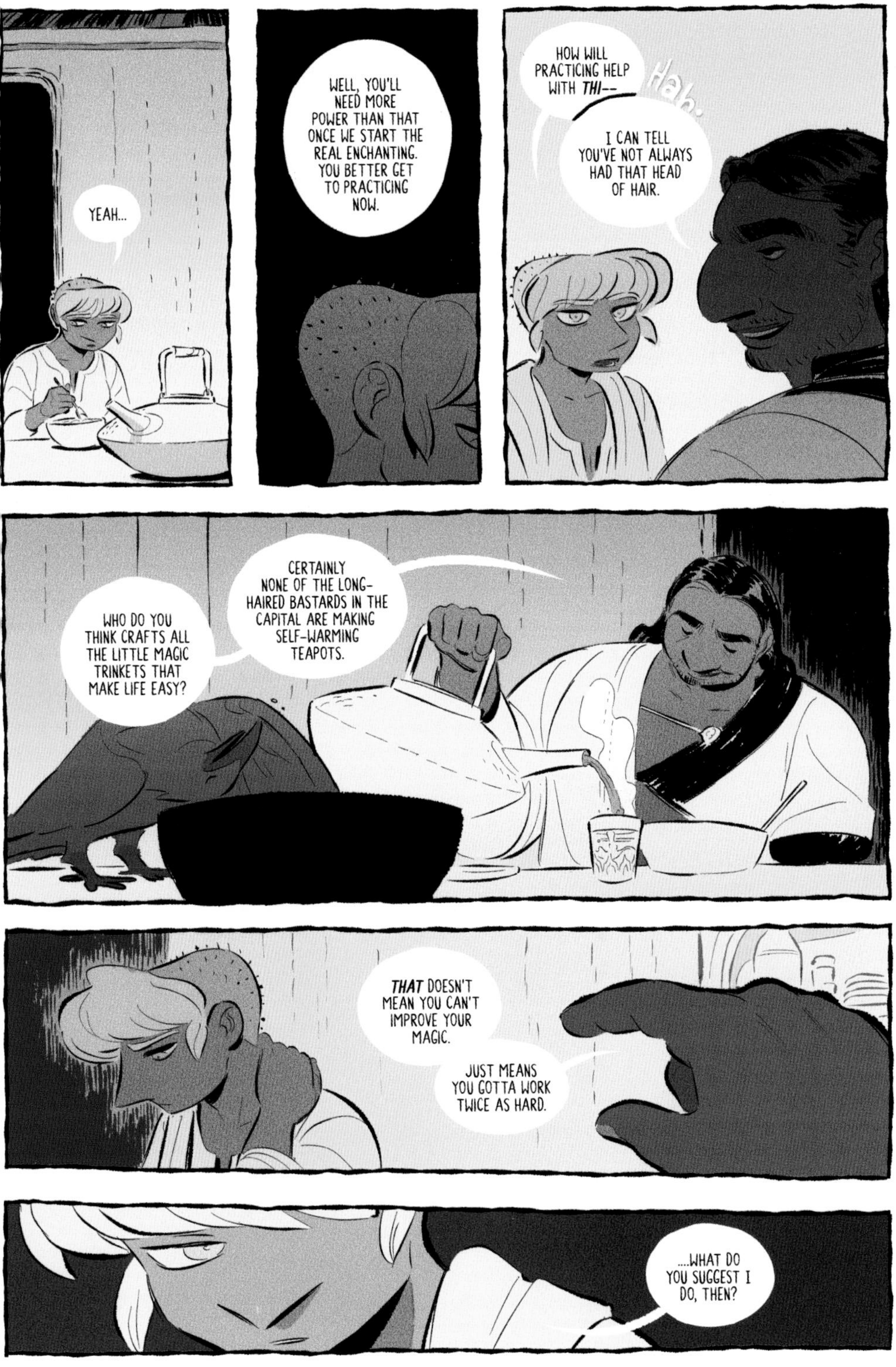
YEAH...
WELL, YOU'LL NEED MORE POWER THAN THAT ONCE WE START THE REAL ENCHANTING. YOU BETTER GET TO PRACTICING NOW.
HOW WILL PRACTICING HELP WITH ***THI***--
Hah.
I CAN TELL YOU'VE NOT ALWAYS HAD THAT HEAD OF HAIR.
WHO DO YOU THINK CRAFTS ALL THE LITTLE MAGIC TRINKETS THAT MAKE LIFE EASY?
CERTAINLY NONE OF THE LONG-HAIRED BASTARDS IN THE CAPITAL ARE MAKING SELF-WARMING TEAPOTS.
THAT DOESN'T MEAN YOU CAN'T IMPROVE YOUR MAGIC.
JUST MEANS YOU GOTTA WORK TWICE AS HARD.
....WHAT DO YOU SUGGEST I DO, THEN?

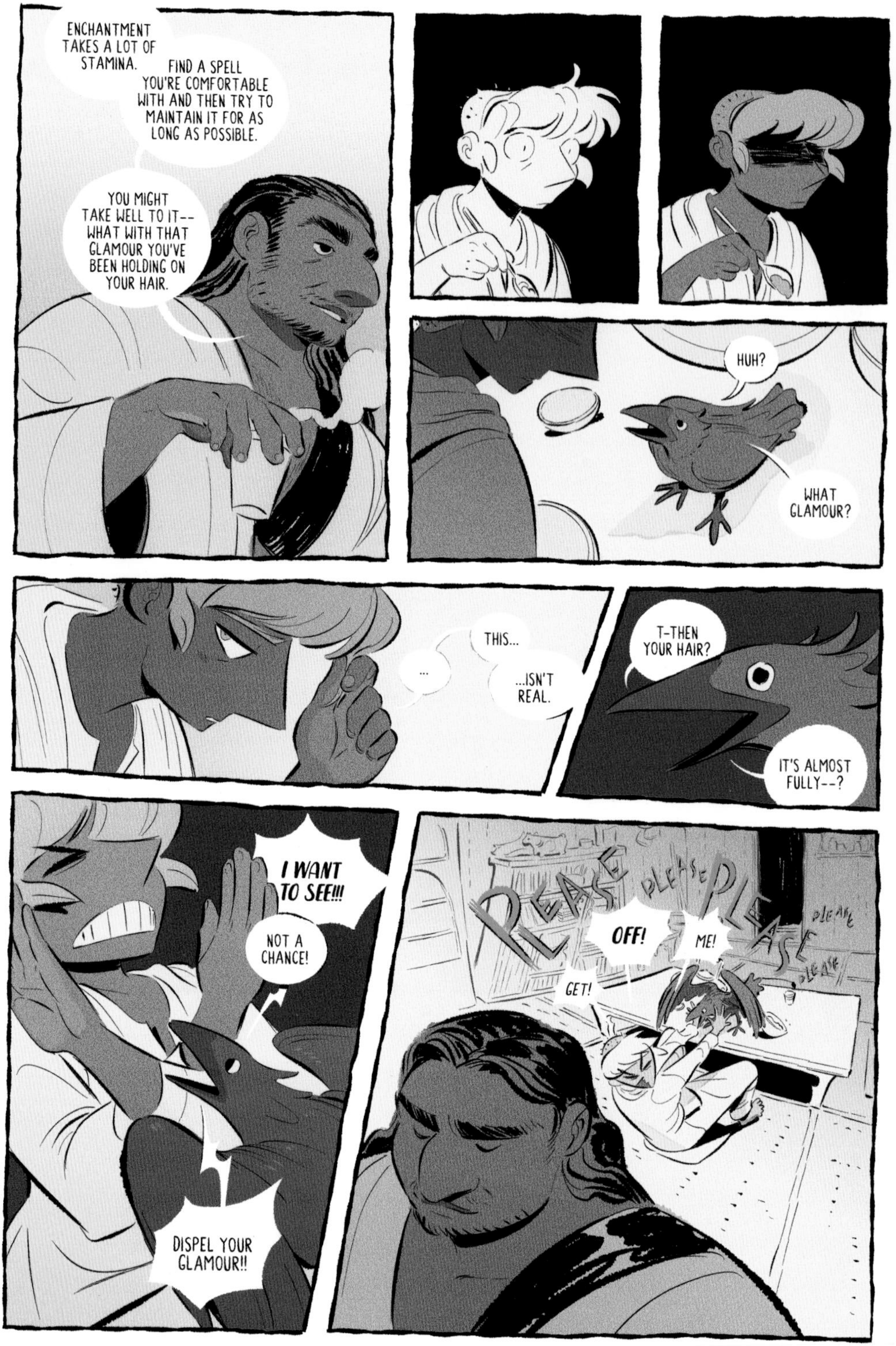
ENCHANTMENT TAKES A LOT OF STAMINA.
FIND A SPELL YOU'RE COMFORTABLE WITH AND THEN TRY TO MAINTAIN IT FOR AS LONG AS POSSIBLE.
YOU MIGHT TAKE WELL TO IT-- WHAT WITH THAT GLAMOUR YOU'VE BEEN HOLDING ON YOUR HAIR.
HUH?
WHAT GLAMOUR?
...
THIS...
...ISN'T REAL.
T-THEN YOUR HAIR?
IT'S ALMOST FULLY--?
I WANT TO SEE!!!
NOT A CHANCE!
DISPEL YOUR GLAMOUR!!
PLEASE
PLEASE
PLEASE
PLEASE
PLEASE
PLEASE
GET!
OFF!
ME!

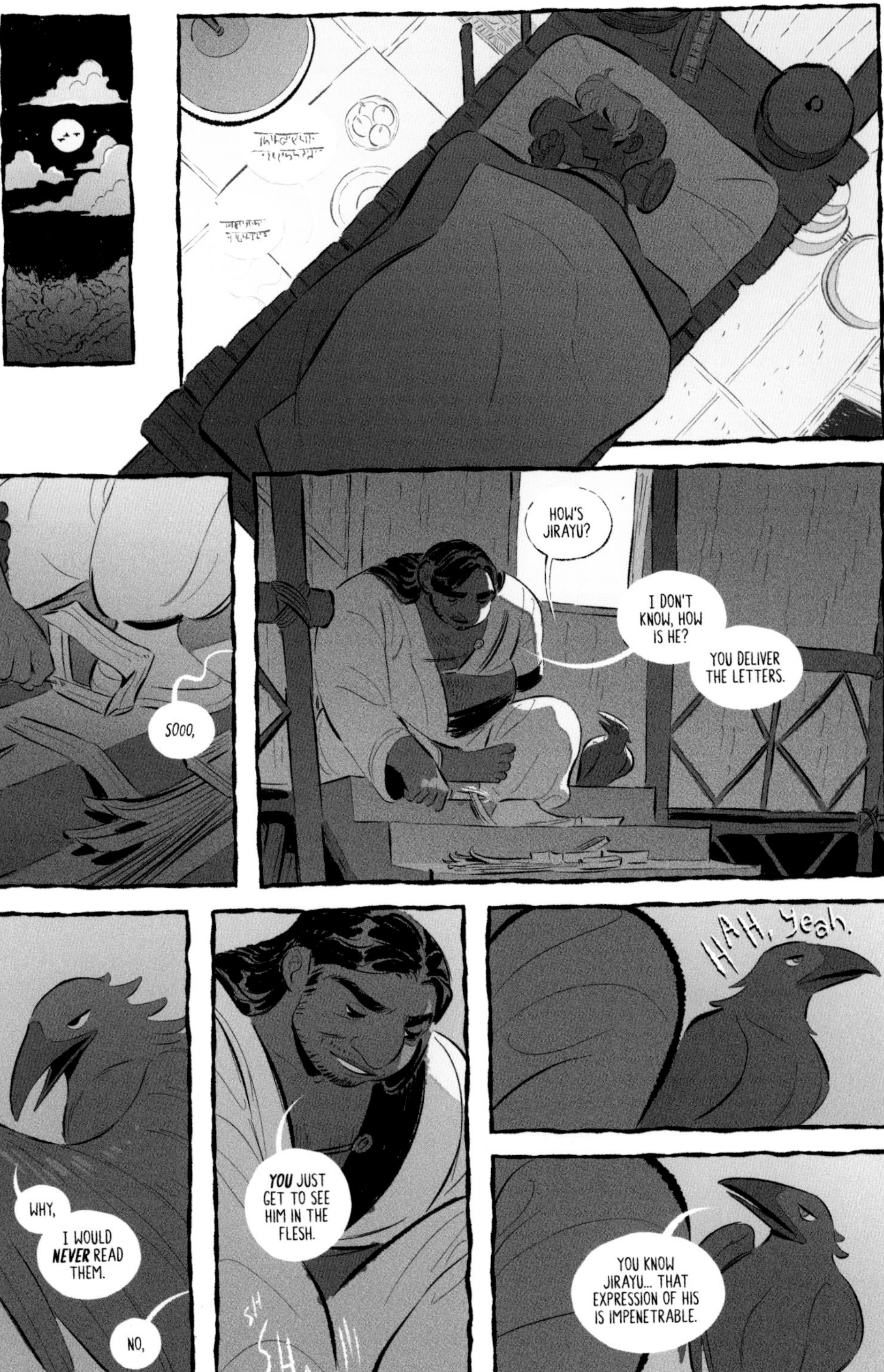
SOOO,
HOW'S JIRAYU?
I DON'T KNOW, HOW IS HE?
YOU DELIVER THE LETTERS.
WHY,
I WOULD **NEVER** READ THEM.
NO,
YOU JUST GET TO SEE HIM IN THE FLESH.
SH SHA
HAH. Yeah.
YOU KNOW JIRAYU... THAT EXPRESSION OF HIS IS IMPENETRABLE.

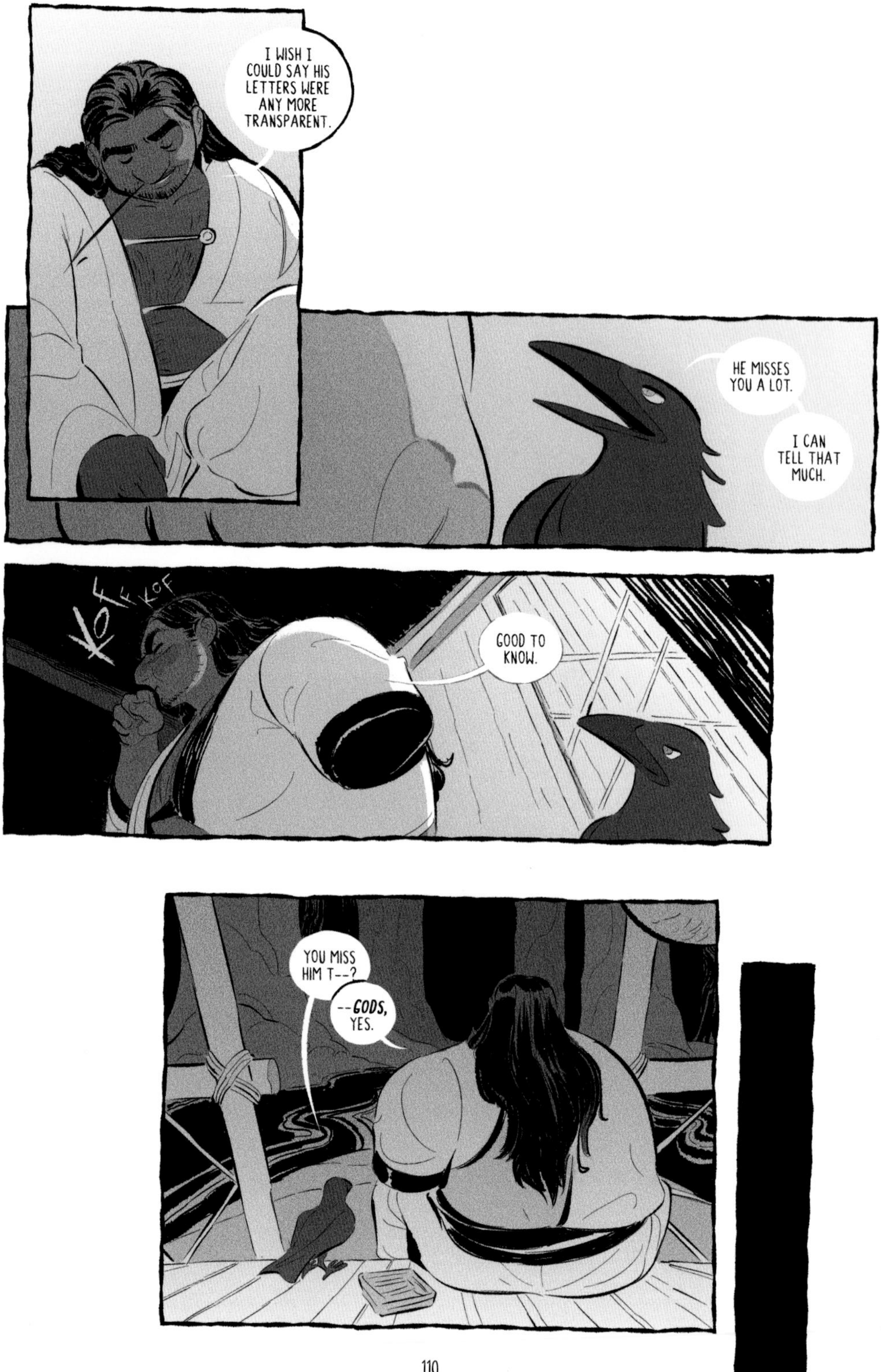
I WISH I COULD SAY HIS LETTERS WERE ANY MORE TRANSPARENT.
HE MISSES YOU A LOT.
I CAN TELL THAT MUCH.
KOF KOF KOF
GOOD TO KNOW.
YOU MISS HIM T--?
--GODS, YES.

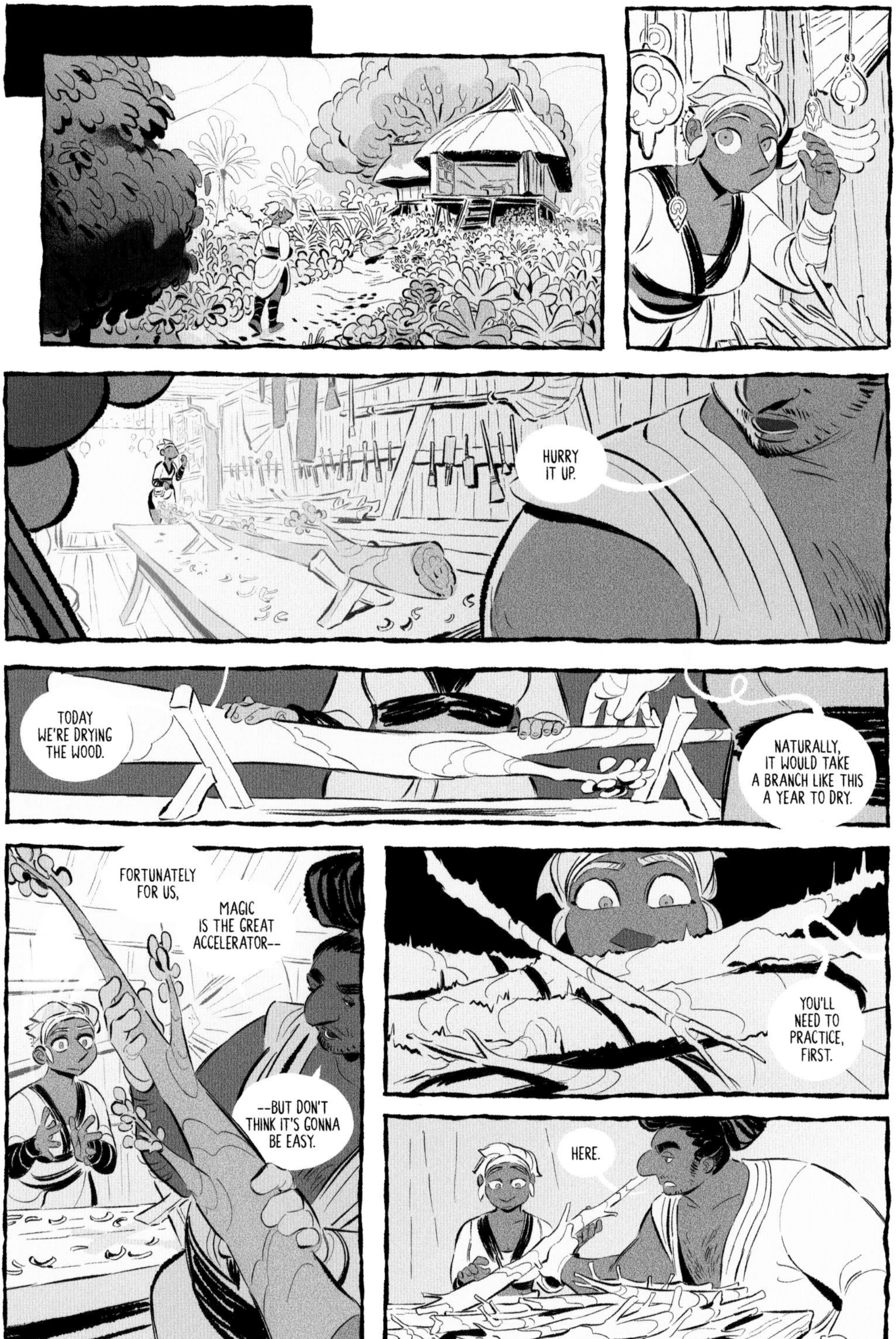
HURRY IT UP.
TODAY WE'RE DRYING THE WOOD.
NATURALLY, IT WOULD TAKE A BRANCH LIKE THIS A YEAR TO DRY.
FORTUNATELY FOR US,
MAGIC IS THE GREAT ACCELERATOR--
--BUT DON'T THINK IT'S GONNA BE EASY.
YOU'LL NEED TO PRACTICE, FIRST.
HERE.

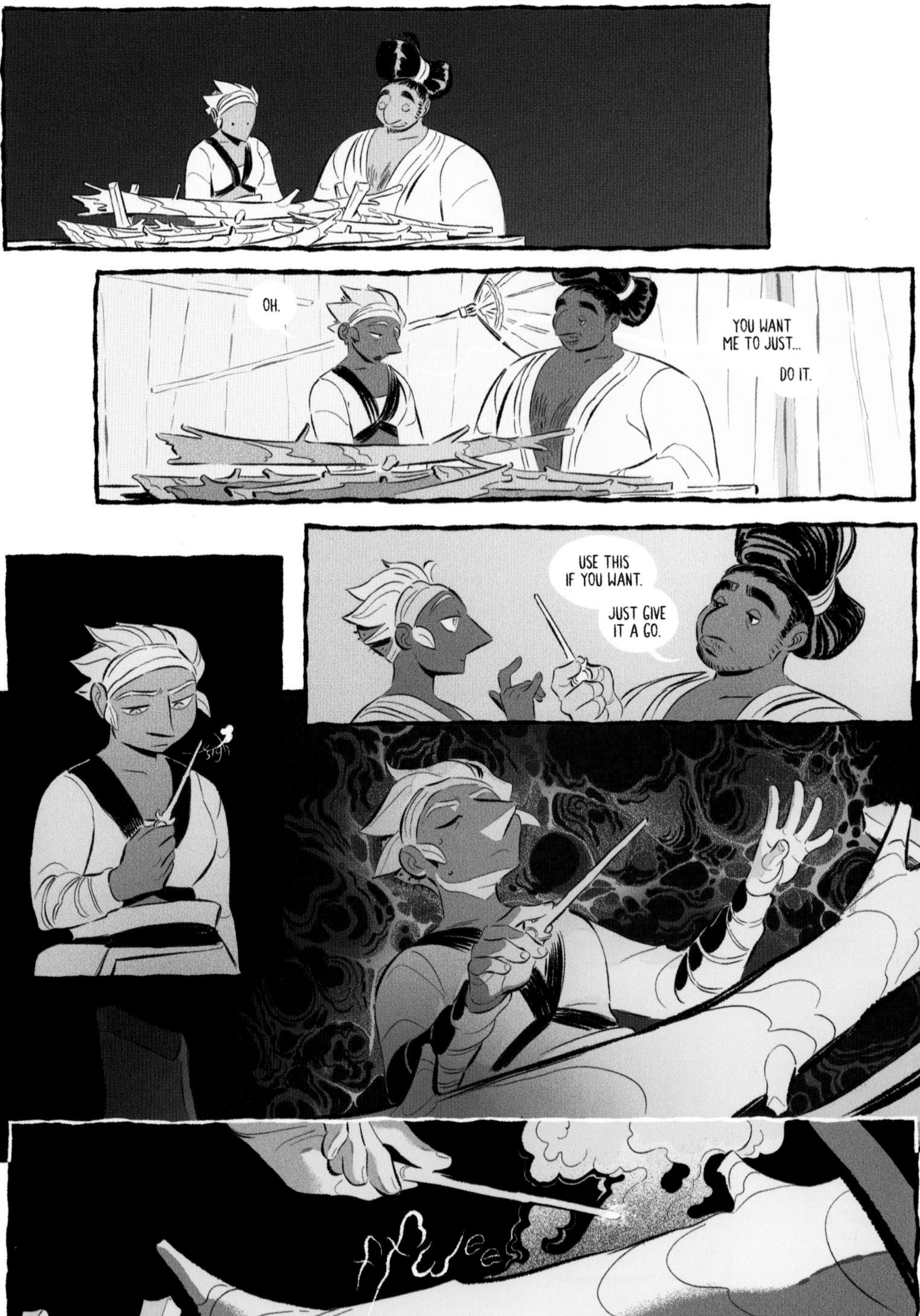
OH.
YOU WANT ME TO JUST...
DO IT.
USE THIS IF YOU WANT.
JUST GIVE IT A GO.

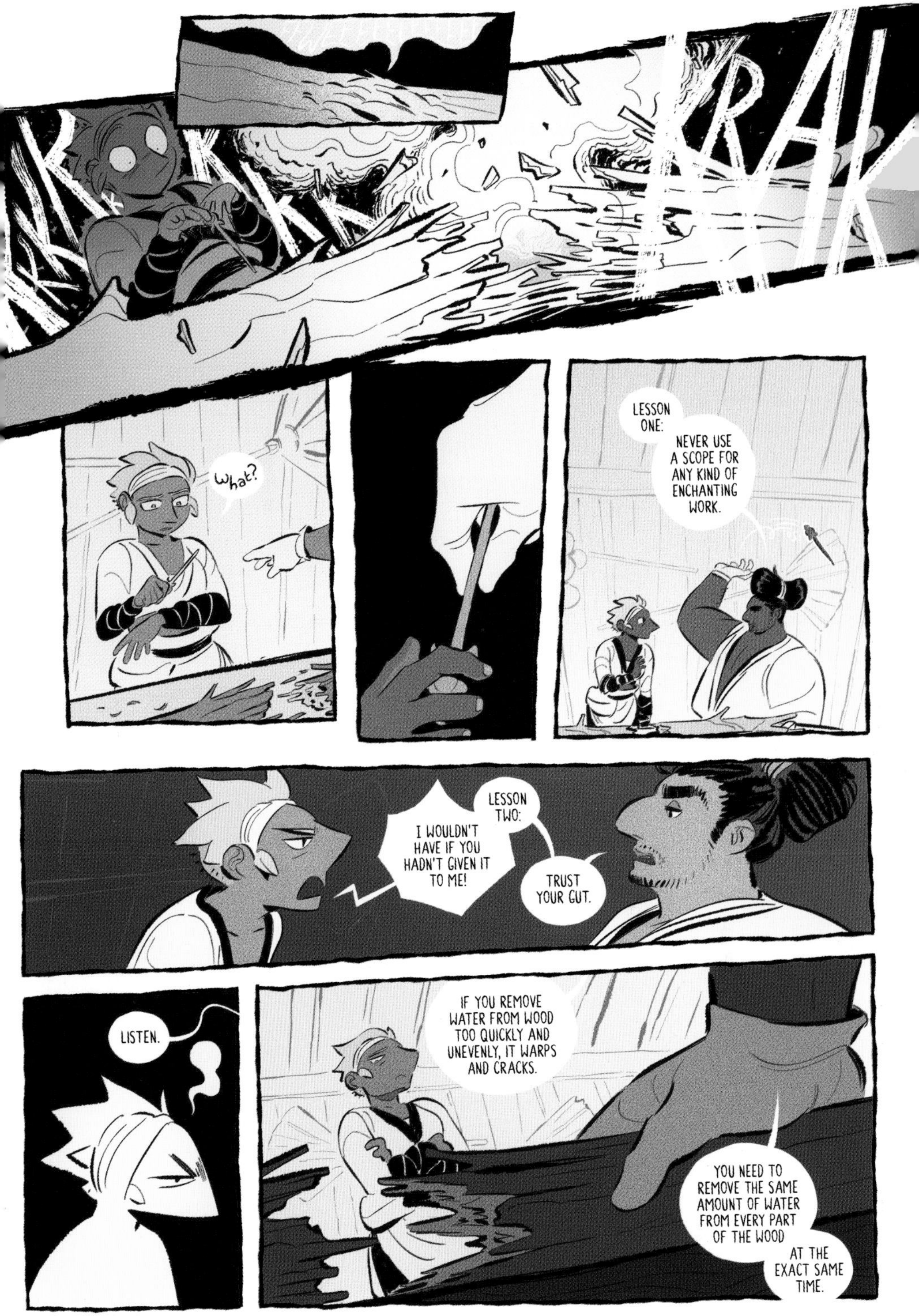
KRAK
What?
LESSON ONE:
NEVER USE A SCOPE FOR ANY KIND OF ENCHANTING WORK.
I WOULDN'T HAVE IF YOU HADN'T GIVEN IT TO ME!
LESSON TWO:
TRUST YOUR GUT.
LISTEN.
IF YOU REMOVE WATER FROM WOOD TOO QUICKLY AND UNEVENLY, IT WARPS AND CRACKS.
YOU NEED TO REMOVE THE SAME AMOUNT OF WATER FROM EVERY PART OF THE WOOD
AT THE EXACT SAME TIME.

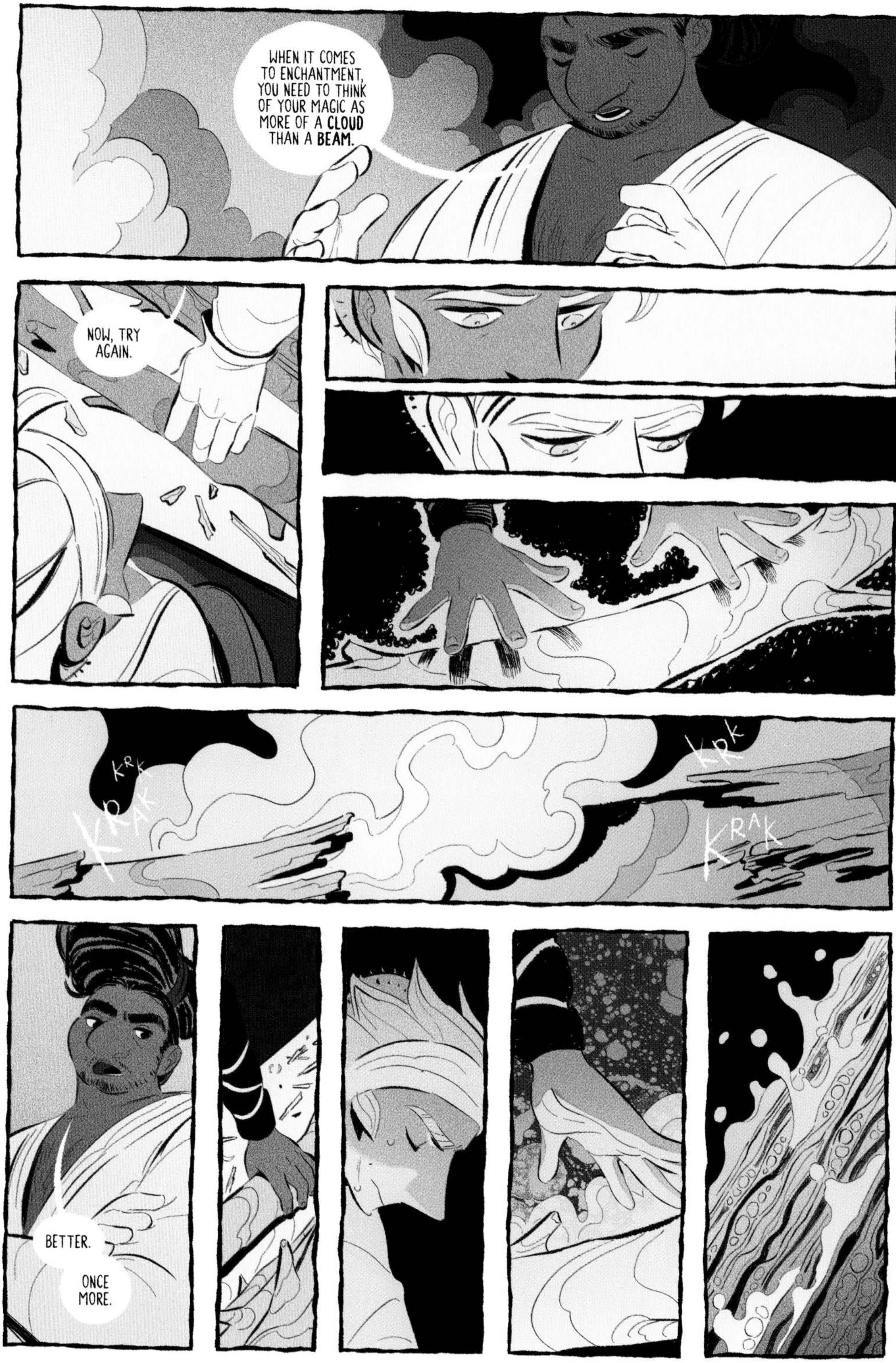
WHEN IT COMES TO ENCHANTMENT, YOU NEED TO THINK OF YOUR MAGIC AS MORE OF A **CLOUD** THAN A **BEAM.**
NOW, TRY AGAIN.
KRK
KRAK
KRK
KRAK
BETTER.
ONCE MORE.

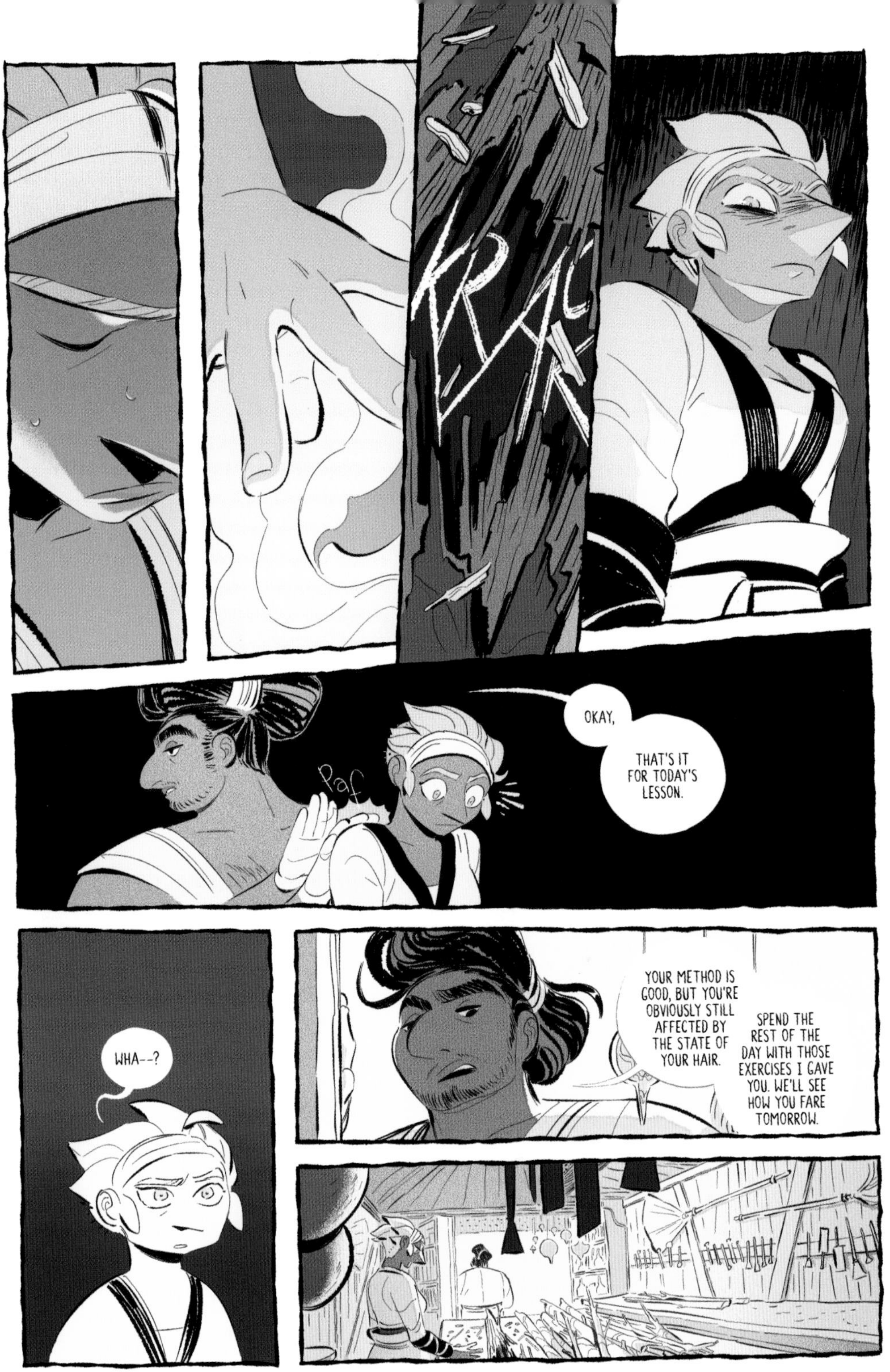
KRACK
OKAY,
THAT'S IT FOR TODAY'S LESSON.
Paf
WHA--?
YOUR METHOD IS GOOD, BUT YOU'RE OBVIOUSLY STILL AFFECTED BY THE STATE OF YOUR HAIR.
SPEND THE REST OF THE DAY WITH THOSE EXERCISES I GAVE YOU. WE'LL SEE HOW YOU FARE TOMORROW.

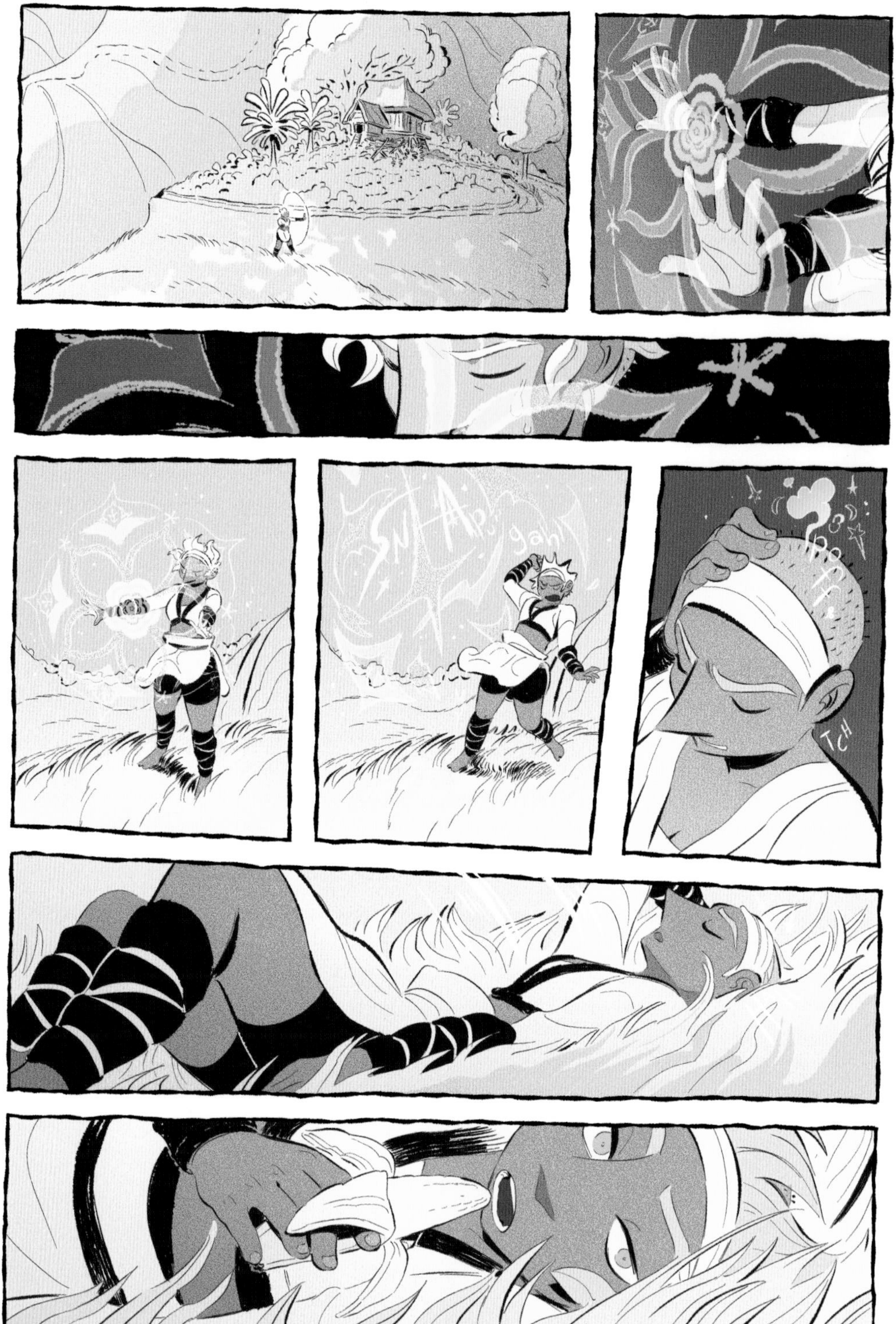
SNAP
gah!
poff
TCH

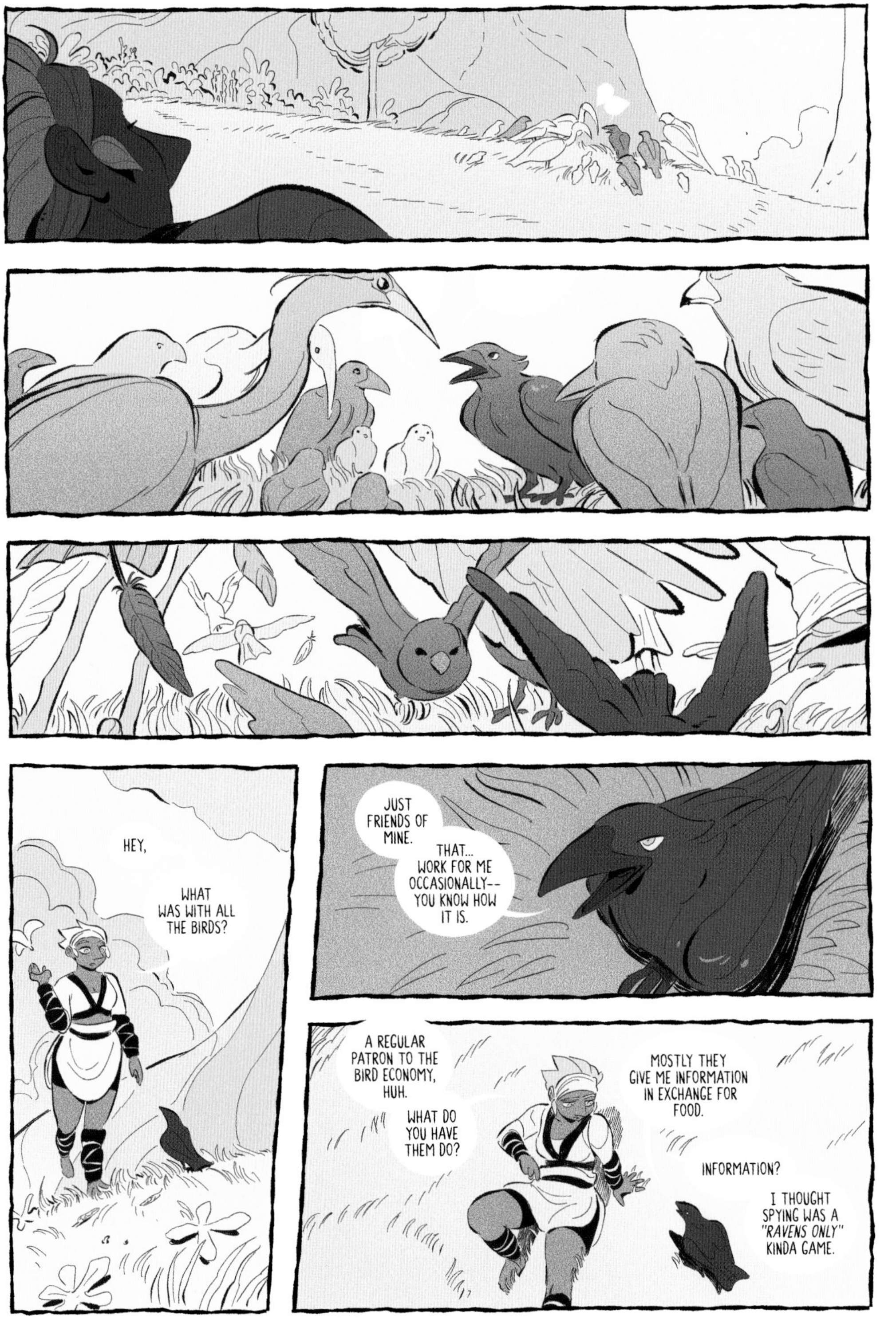
HEY,
WHAT WAS WITH ALL THE BIRDS?
JUST FRIENDS OF MINE.
THAT... WORK FOR ME OCCASIONALLY-- YOU KNOW HOW IT IS.
A REGULAR PATRON TO THE BIRD ECONOMY, HUH.
WHAT DO YOU HAVE THEM DO?
MOSTLY THEY GIVE ME INFORMATION IN EXCHANGE FOR FOOD.
INFORMATION?
I THOUGHT SPYING WAS A *"RAVENS ONLY"* KINDA GAME.

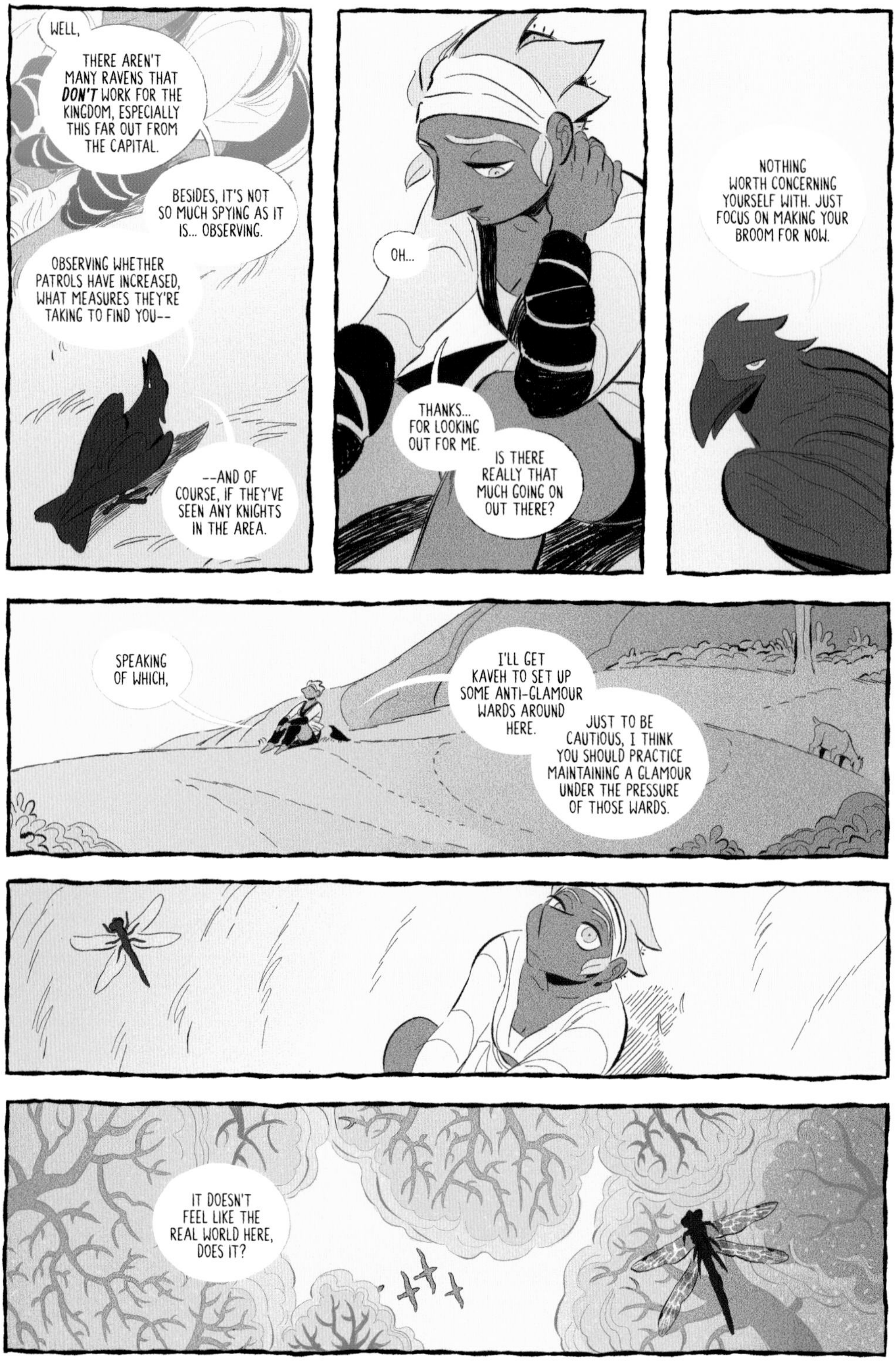

WELL,
THERE AREN'T MANY RAVENS THAT **DON'T** WORK FOR THE KINGDOM, ESPECIALLY THIS FAR OUT FROM THE CAPITAL.
BESIDES, IT'S NOT SO MUCH SPYING AS IT IS... OBSERVING.
OBSERVING WHETHER PATROLS HAVE INCREASED, WHAT MEASURES THEY'RE TAKING TO FIND YOU--
--AND OF COURSE, IF THEY'VE SEEN ANY KNIGHTS IN THE AREA.
OH...
THANKS... FOR LOOKING OUT FOR ME.
IS THERE REALLY THAT MUCH GOING ON OUT THERE?
NOTHING WORTH CONCERNING YOURSELF WITH. JUST FOCUS ON MAKING YOUR BROOM FOR NOW.
SPEAKING OF WHICH,
I'LL GET KAVEH TO SET UP SOME ANTI-GLAMOUR WARDS AROUND HERE.
JUST TO BE CAUTIOUS, I THINK YOU SHOULD PRACTICE MAINTAINING A GLAMOUR UNDER THE PRESSURE OF THOSE WARDS.
IT DOESN'T FEEL LIKE THE REAL WORLD HERE, DOES IT?

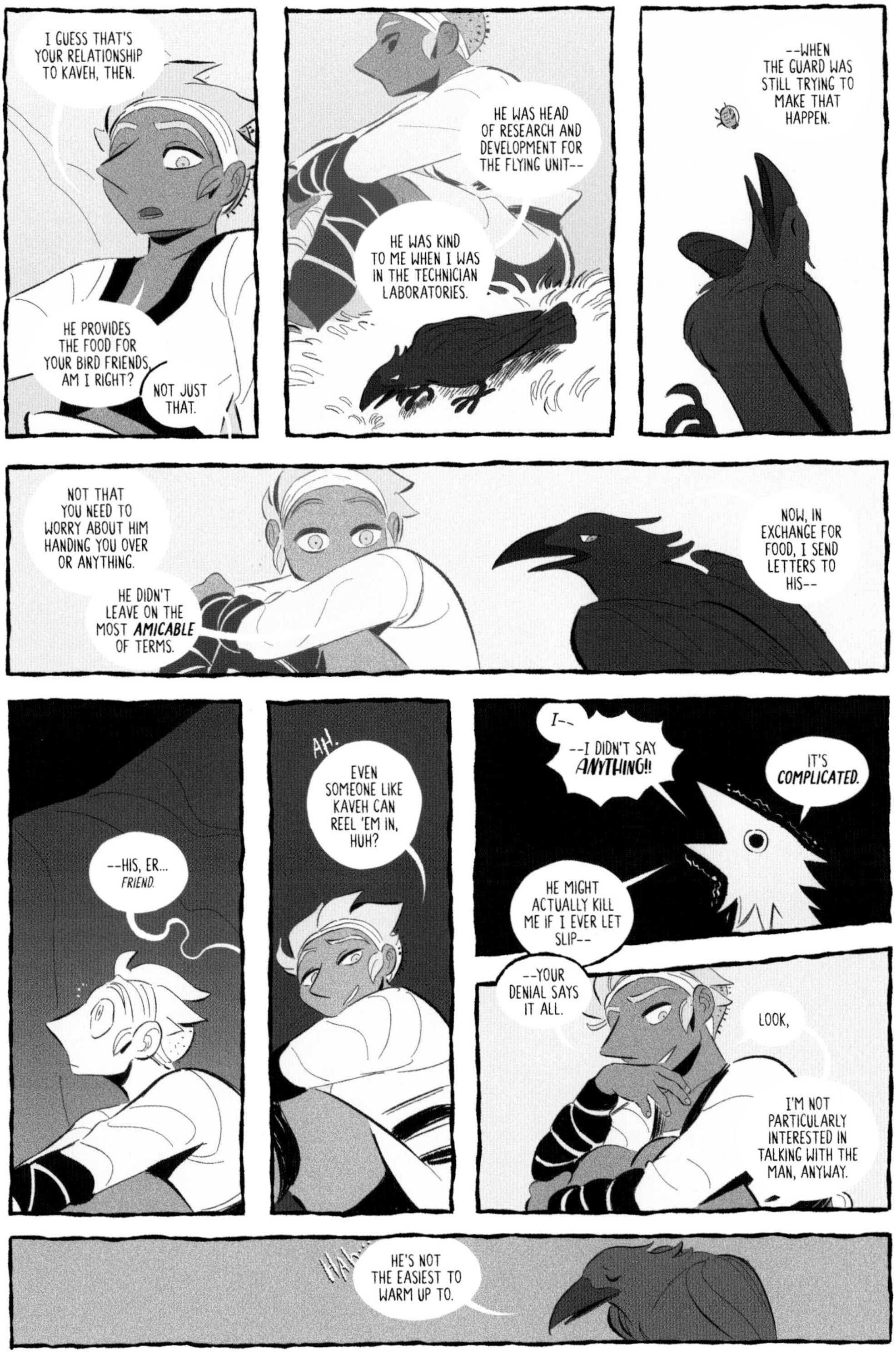
I GUESS THAT'S YOUR RELATIONSHIP TO KAVEH, THEN.
HE PROVIDES THE FOOD FOR YOUR BIRD FRIENDS, AM I RIGHT?
NOT JUST THAT.
HE WAS HEAD OF RESEARCH AND DEVELOPMENT FOR THE FLYING UNIT--
HE WAS KIND TO ME WHEN I WAS IN THE TECHNICIAN LABORATORIES.
--WHEN THE GUARD WAS STILL TRYING TO MAKE THAT HAPPEN.
NOT THAT YOU NEED TO WORRY ABOUT HIM HANDING YOU OVER OR ANYTHING.
HE DIDN'T LEAVE ON THE MOST AMICABLE OF TERMS.
NOW, IN EXCHANGE FOR FOOD, I SEND LETTERS TO HIS--
--HIS, ER... FRIEND.
AH.
EVEN SOMEONE LIKE KAVEH CAN REEL 'EM IN, HUH?
I--
--I DIDN'T SAY ANYTHING!!
IT'S COMPLICATED.
HE MIGHT ACTUALLY KILL ME IF I EVER LET SLIP--
--YOUR DENIAL SAYS IT ALL.
LOOK,
I'M NOT PARTICULARLY INTERESTED IN TALKING WITH THE MAN, ANYWAY.
HE'S NOT THE EASIEST TO WARM UP TO.

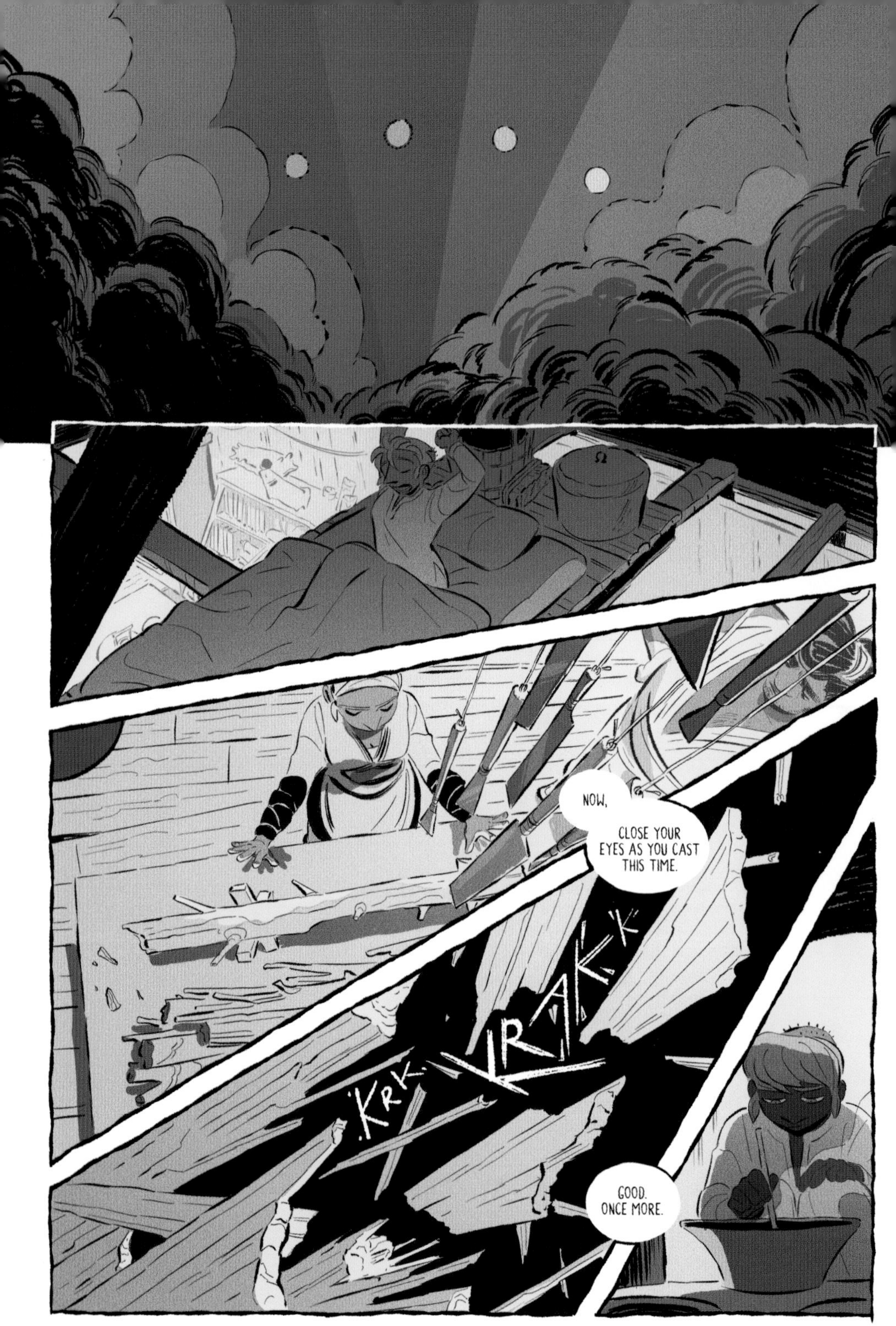
NOW,
CLOSE YOUR EYES AS YOU CAST THIS TIME.
KRK KRAKK
GOOD. ONCE MORE.

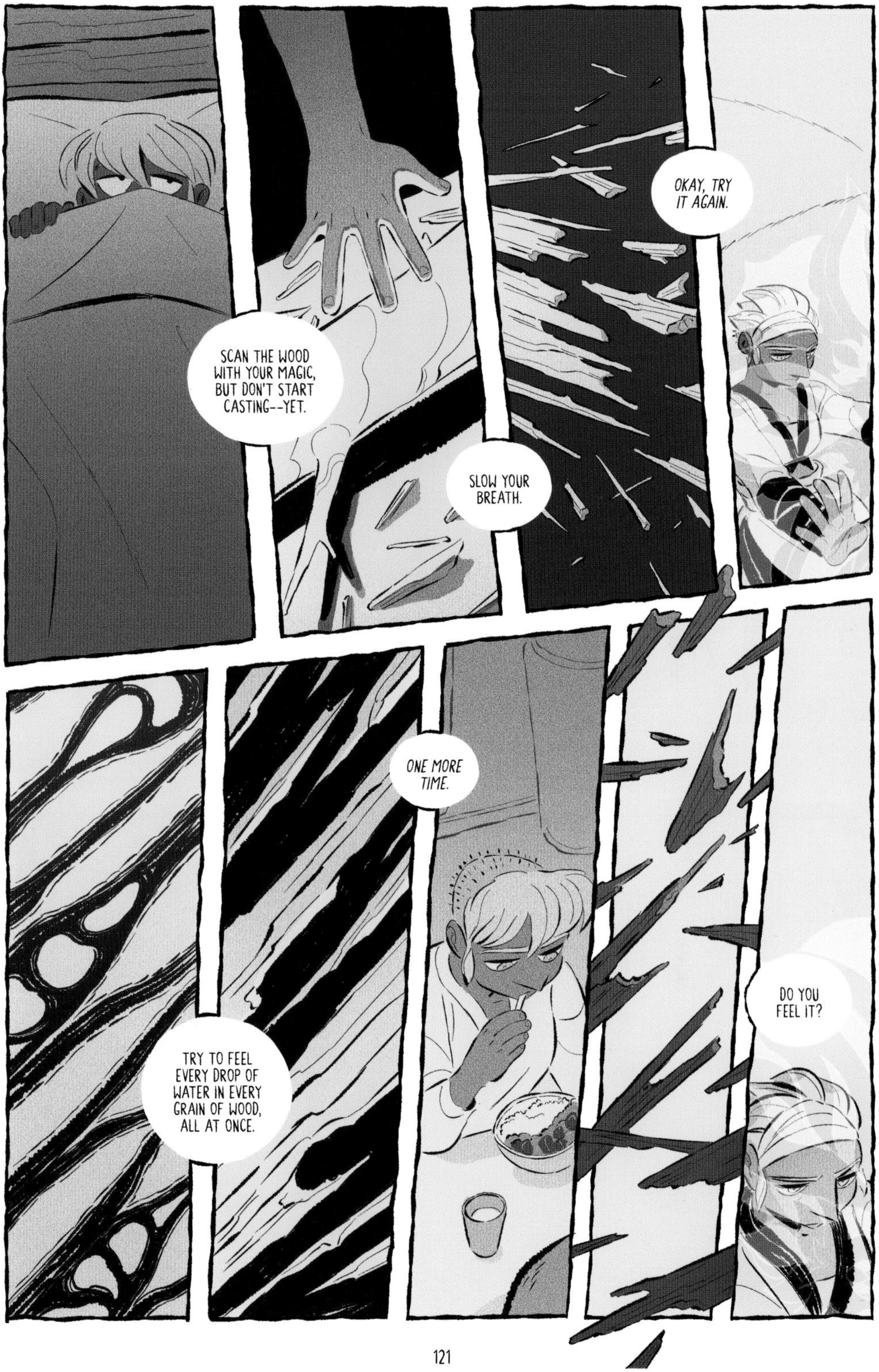
SCAN THE WOOD WITH YOUR MAGIC, BUT DON'T START CASTING--YET.
SLOW YOUR BREATH.
OKAY, TRY IT AGAIN.
TRY TO FEEL EVERY DROP OF WATER IN EVERY GRAIN OF WOOD, ALL AT ONCE.
ONE MORE TIME.
DO YOU FEEL IT?

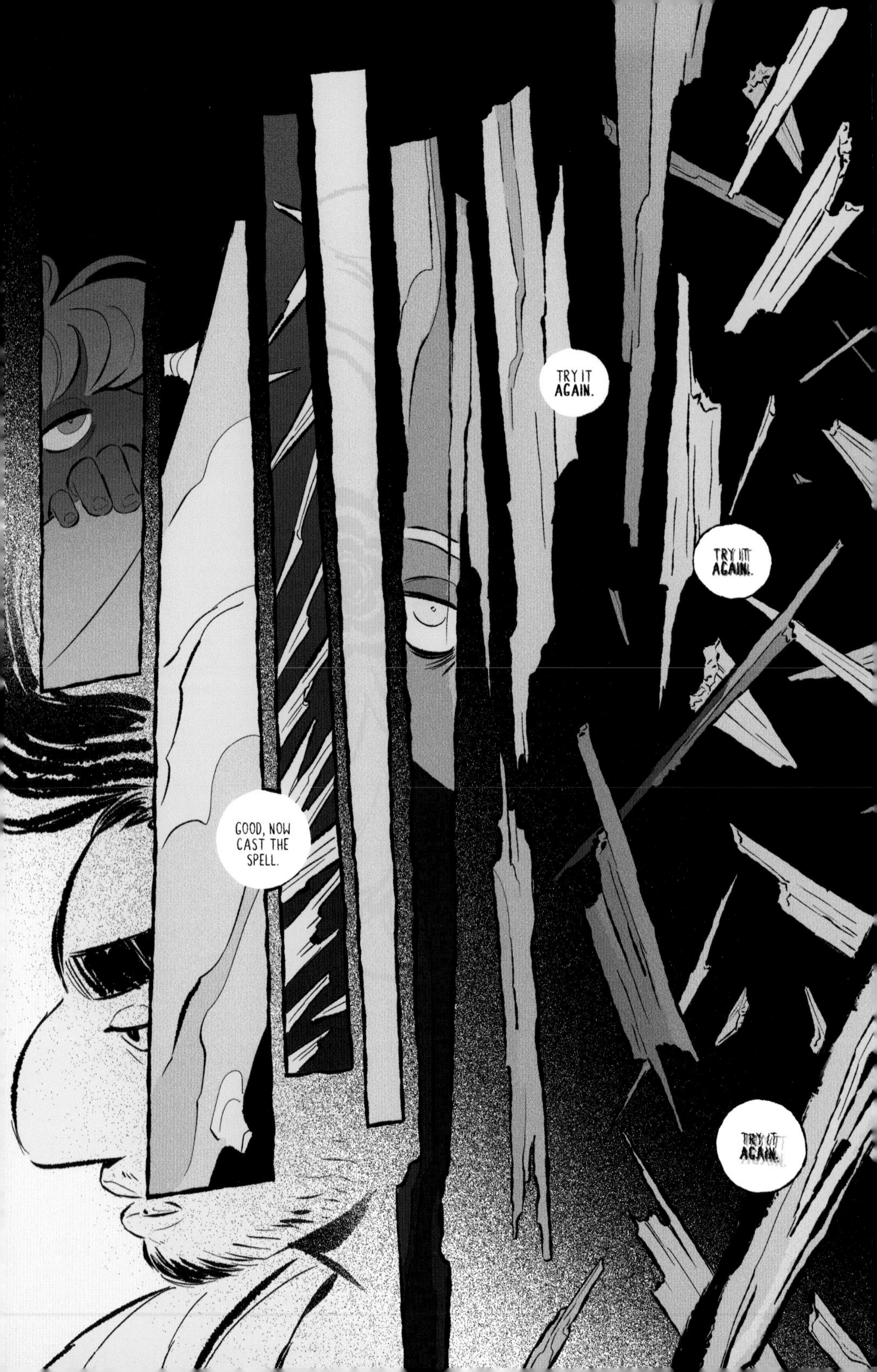

TRY IT AGAIN.
TRY IT AGAIN.
GOOD, NOW CAST THE SPELL.
TRY IT AGAIN.

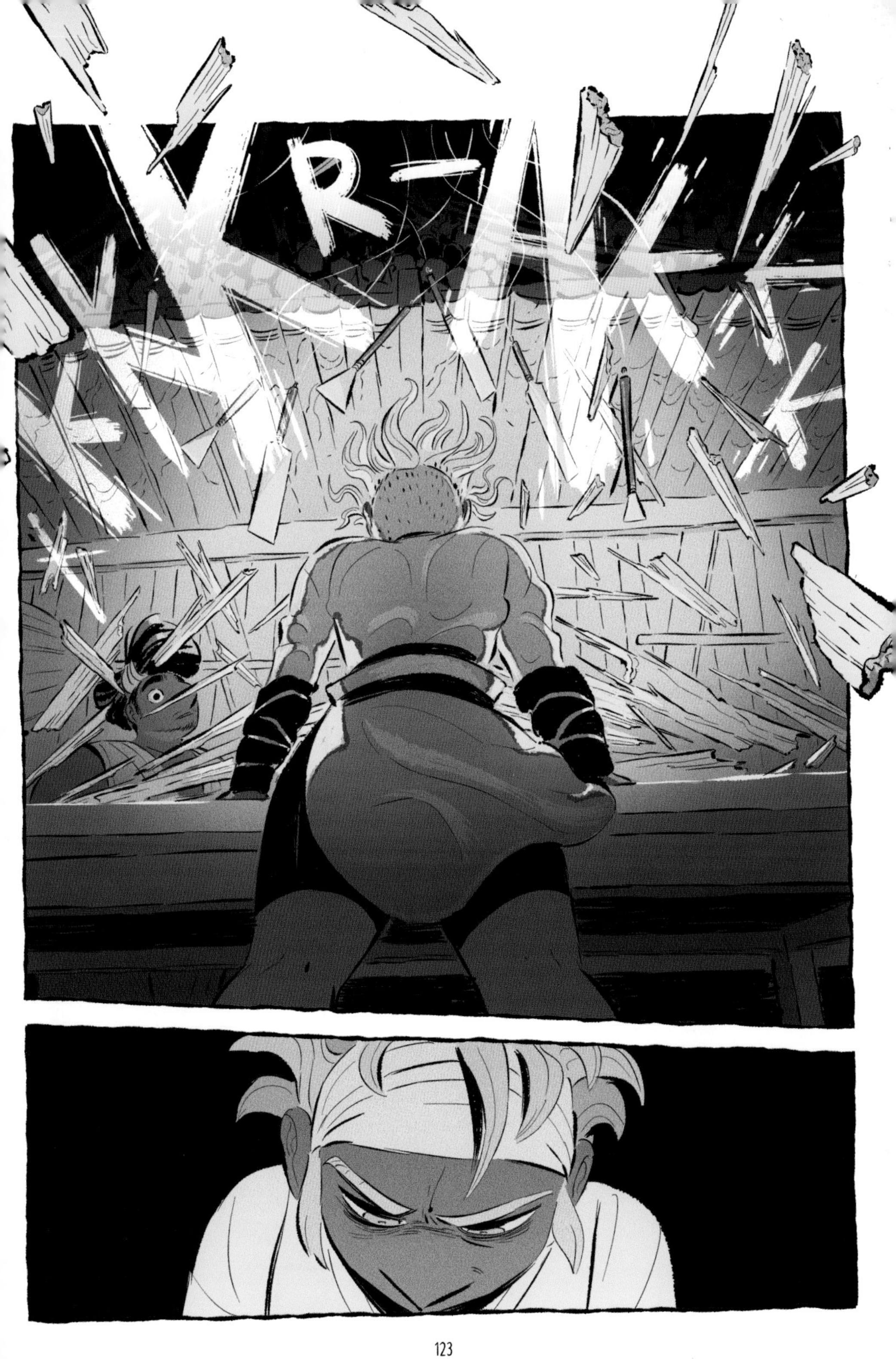
KR-AKK

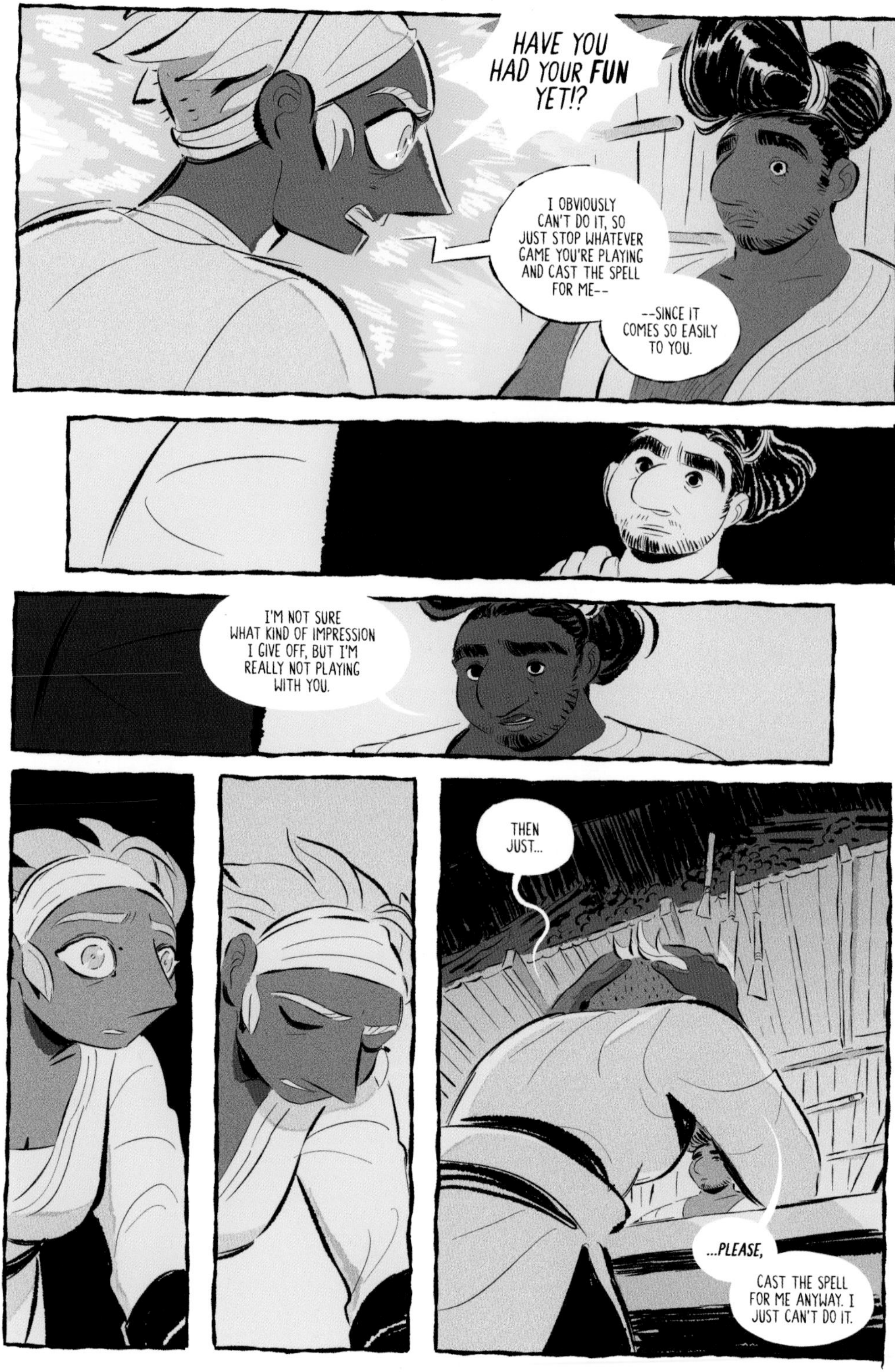
HAVE YOU HAD YOUR **FUN** YET!?
I OBVIOUSLY CAN'T DO IT, SO JUST STOP WHATEVER GAME YOU'RE PLAYING AND CAST THE SPELL FOR ME--
--SINCE IT COMES SO EASILY TO YOU.
I'M NOT SURE WHAT KIND OF IMPRESSION I GIVE OFF, BUT I'M REALLY NOT PLAYING WITH YOU.
THEN JUST...
...PLEASE,
CAST THE SPELL FOR ME ANYWAY. I JUST CAN'T DO IT.

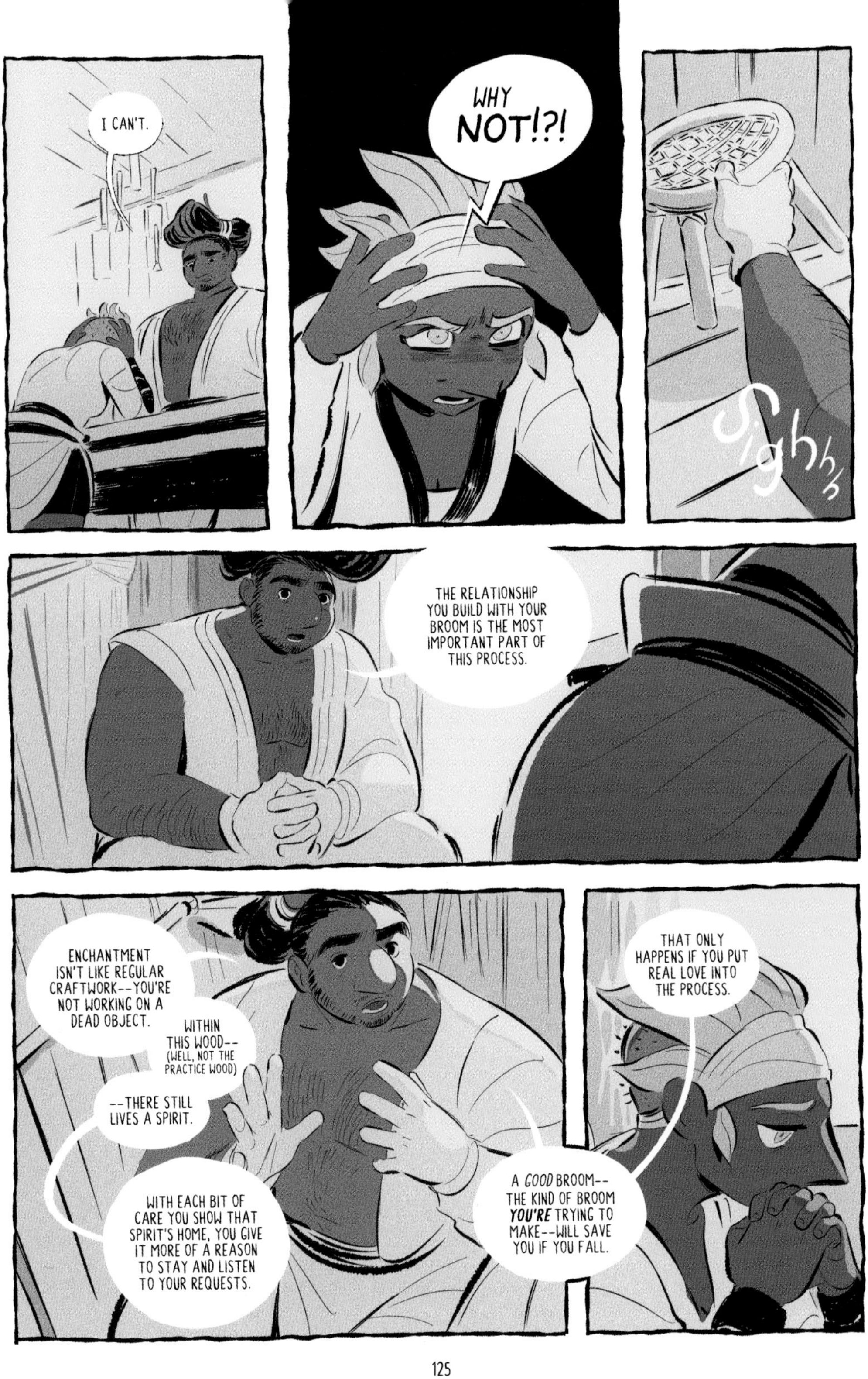

I CAN'T.
WHY NOT!?!
Sighhh
THE RELATIONSHIP YOU BUILD WITH YOUR BROOM IS THE MOST IMPORTANT PART OF THIS PROCESS.
ENCHANTMENT ISN'T LIKE REGULAR CRAFTWORK--YOU'RE NOT WORKING ON A DEAD OBJECT.
WITHIN THIS WOOD--
(WELL, NOT THE PRACTICE WOOD)
--THERE STILL LIVES A SPIRIT.
WITH EACH BIT OF CARE YOU SHOW THAT SPIRIT'S HOME, YOU GIVE IT MORE OF A REASON TO STAY AND LISTEN TO YOUR REQUESTS.
A *GOOD* BROOM--THE KIND OF BROOM ***YOU'RE*** TRYING TO MAKE--WILL SAVE YOU IF YOU FALL.
THAT ONLY HAPPENS IF YOU PUT REAL LOVE INTO THE PROCESS.

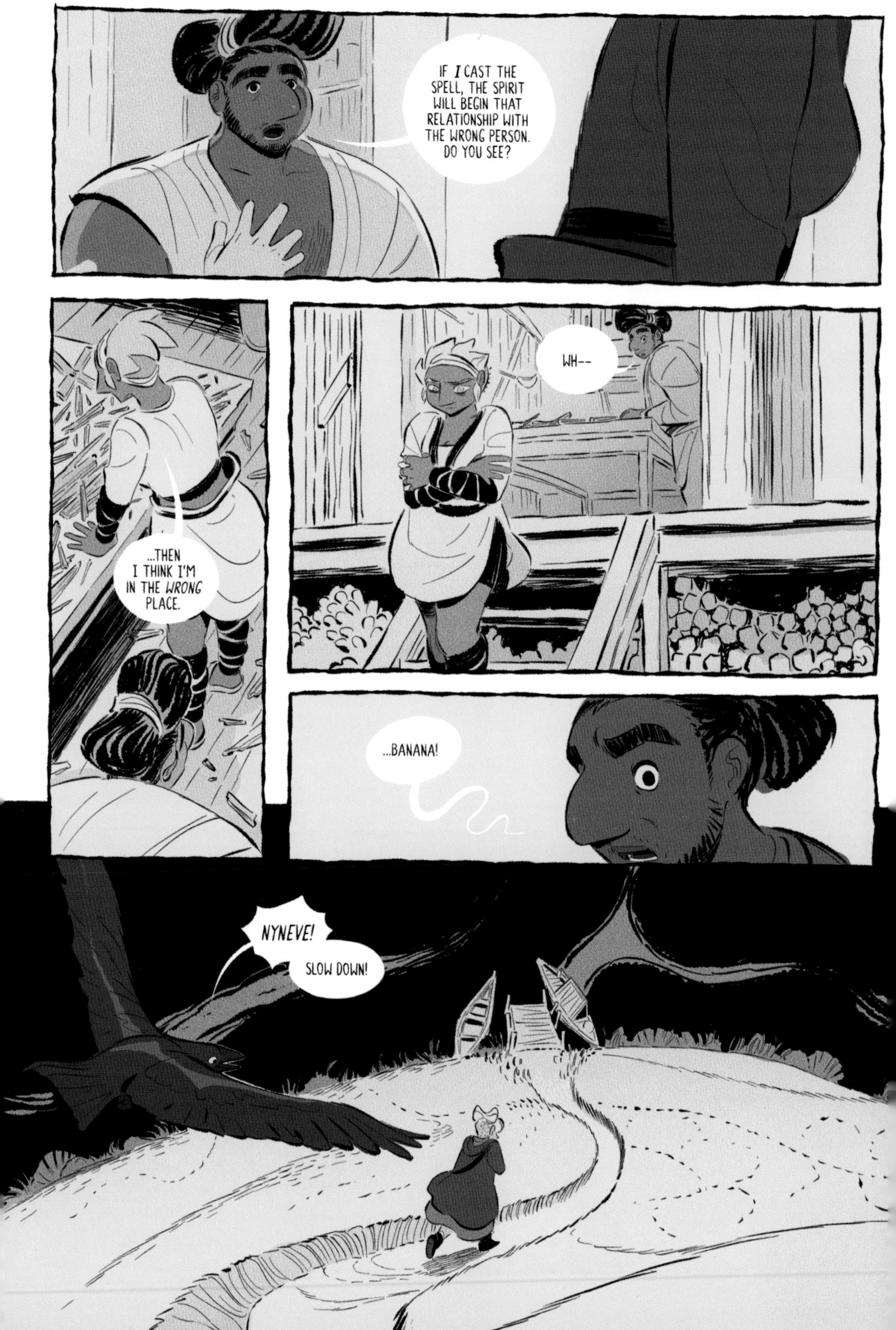
IF *I* CAST THE SPELL, THE SPIRIT WILL BEGIN THAT RELATIONSHIP WITH THE WRONG PERSON. DO YOU SEE?
...THEN I THINK I'M IN THE *WRONG* PLACE.
WH--
...BANANA!
NYNEVE!
SLOW DOWN!

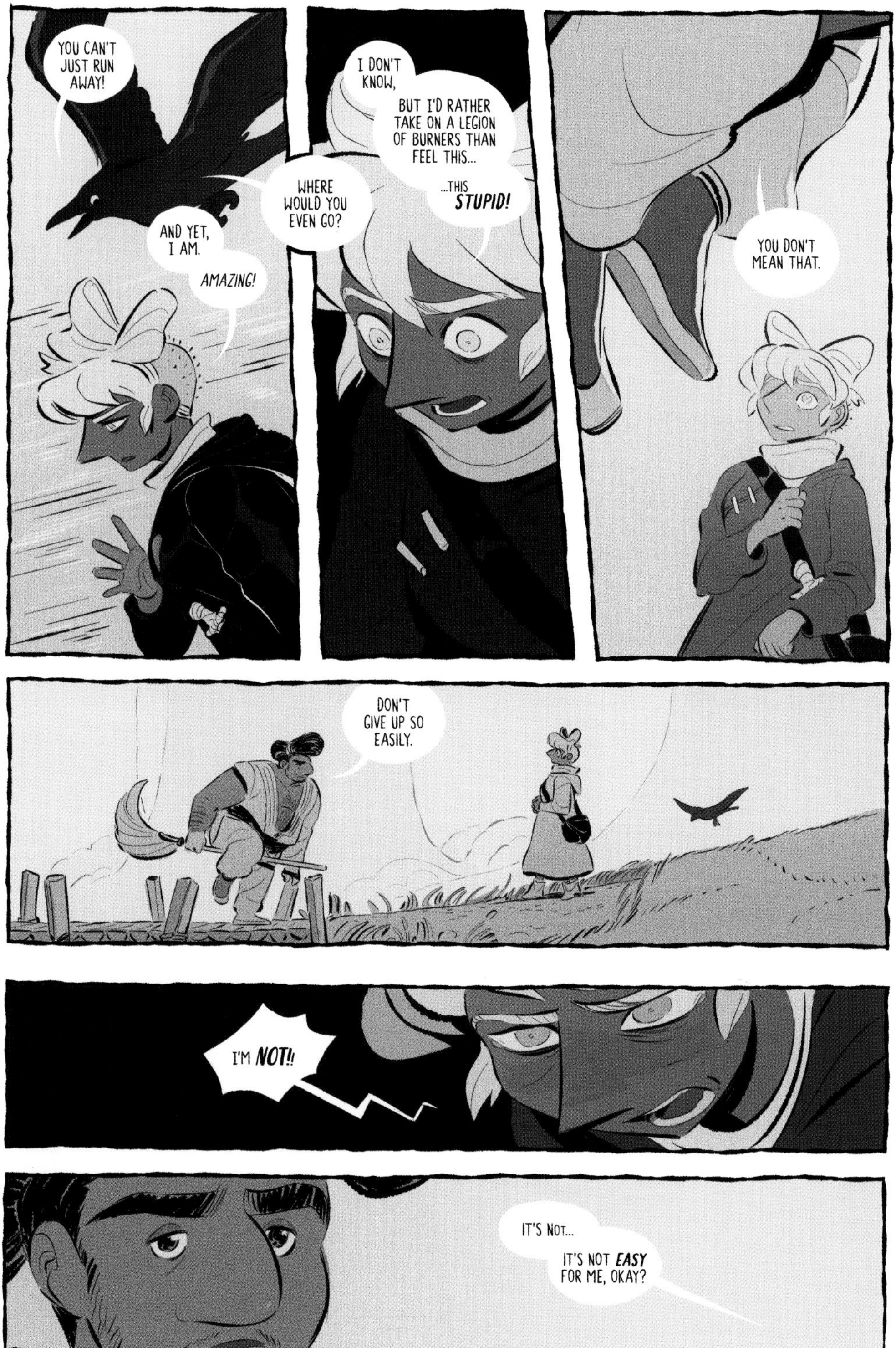
YOU CAN'T JUST RUN AWAY!
AND YET, I AM.
AMAZING!
WHERE WOULD YOU EVEN GO?
I DON'T KNOW,
BUT I'D RATHER TAKE ON A LEGION OF BURNERS THAN FEEL THIS...
...THIS STUPID!
YOU DON'T MEAN THAT.
DON'T GIVE UP SO EASILY.
I'M NOT!!
IT'S NOT...
IT'S NOT EASY FOR ME, OKAY?

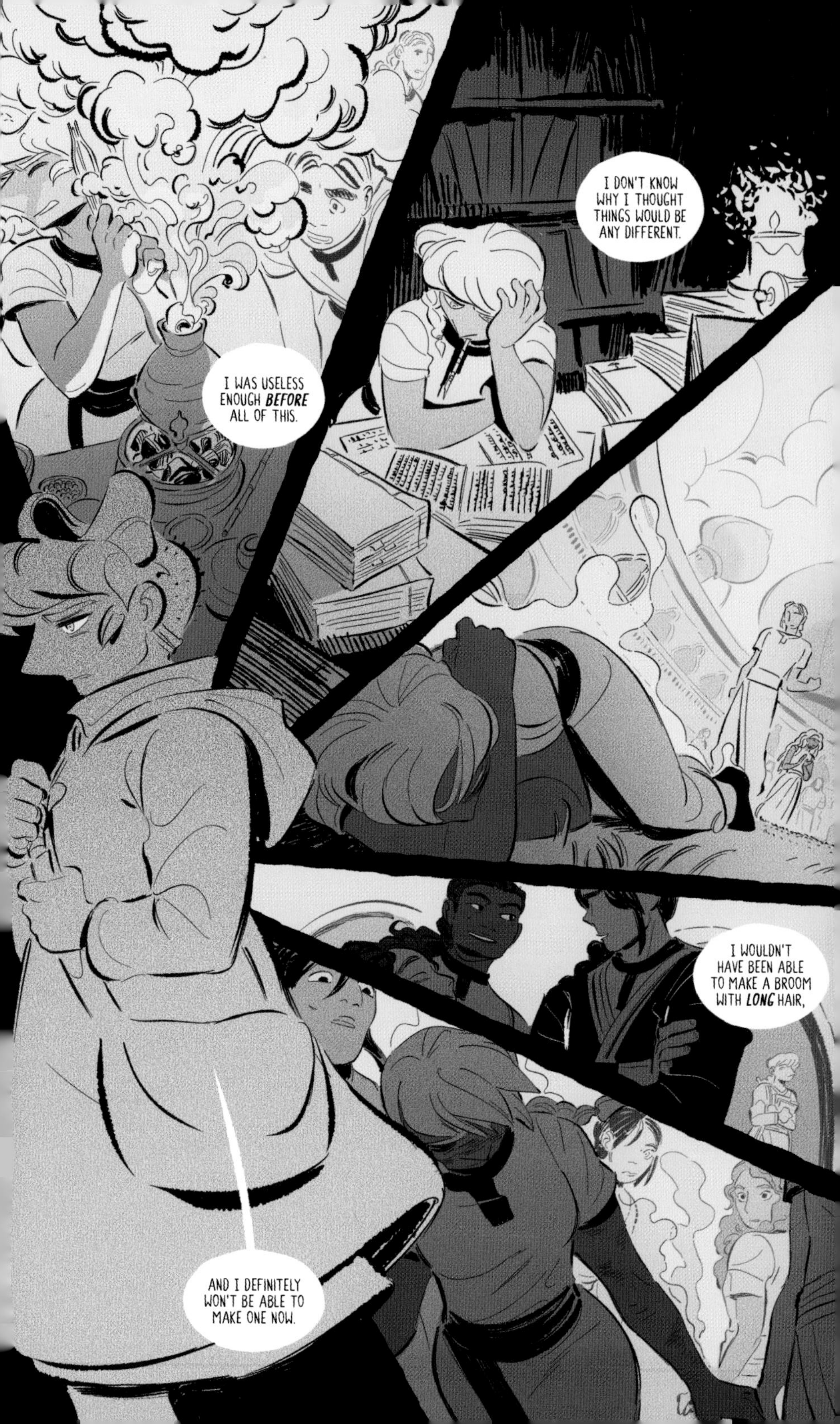
I WAS USELESS ENOUGH BEFORE ALL OF THIS.
I DON'T KNOW WHY I THOUGHT THINGS WOULD BE ANY DIFFERENT.
I WOULDN'T HAVE BEEN ABLE TO MAKE A BROOM WITH LONG HAIR,
AND I DEFINITELY WON'T BE ABLE TO MAKE ONE NOW.

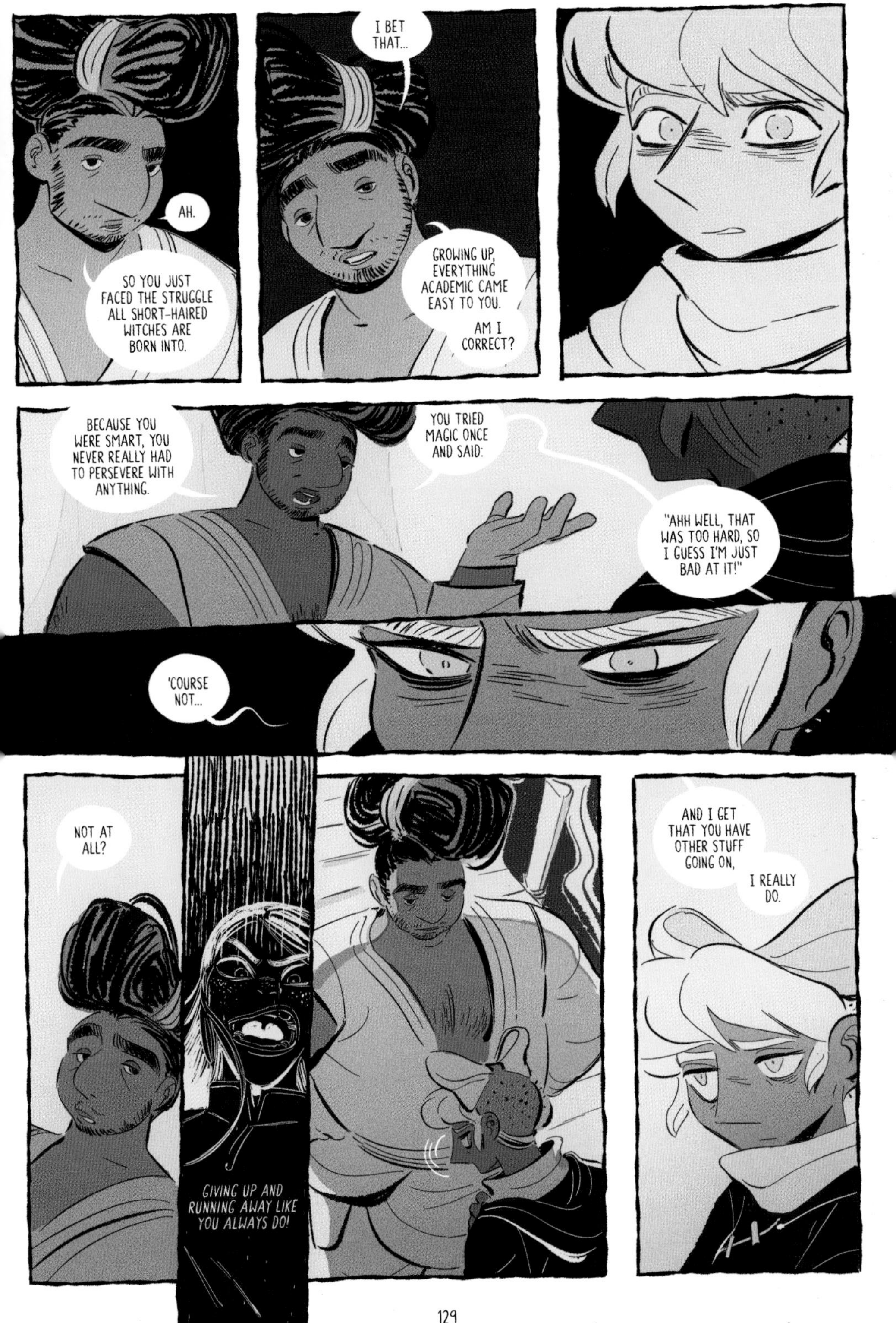
AH.
SO YOU JUST FACED THE STRUGGLE ALL SHORT-HAIRED WITCHES ARE BORN INTO.
I BET THAT...
GROWING UP, EVERYTHING ACADEMIC CAME EASY TO YOU.
AM I CORRECT?
BECAUSE YOU WERE SMART, YOU NEVER REALLY HAD TO PERSEVERE WITH ANYTHING.
YOU TRIED MAGIC ONCE AND SAID:
"AHH WELL, THAT WAS TOO HARD, SO I GUESS I'M JUST BAD AT IT!"
'COURSE NOT...
NOT AT ALL?
GIVING UP AND RUNNING AWAY LIKE YOU ALWAYS DO!
AND I GET THAT YOU HAVE OTHER STUFF GOING ON,
I REALLY DO.

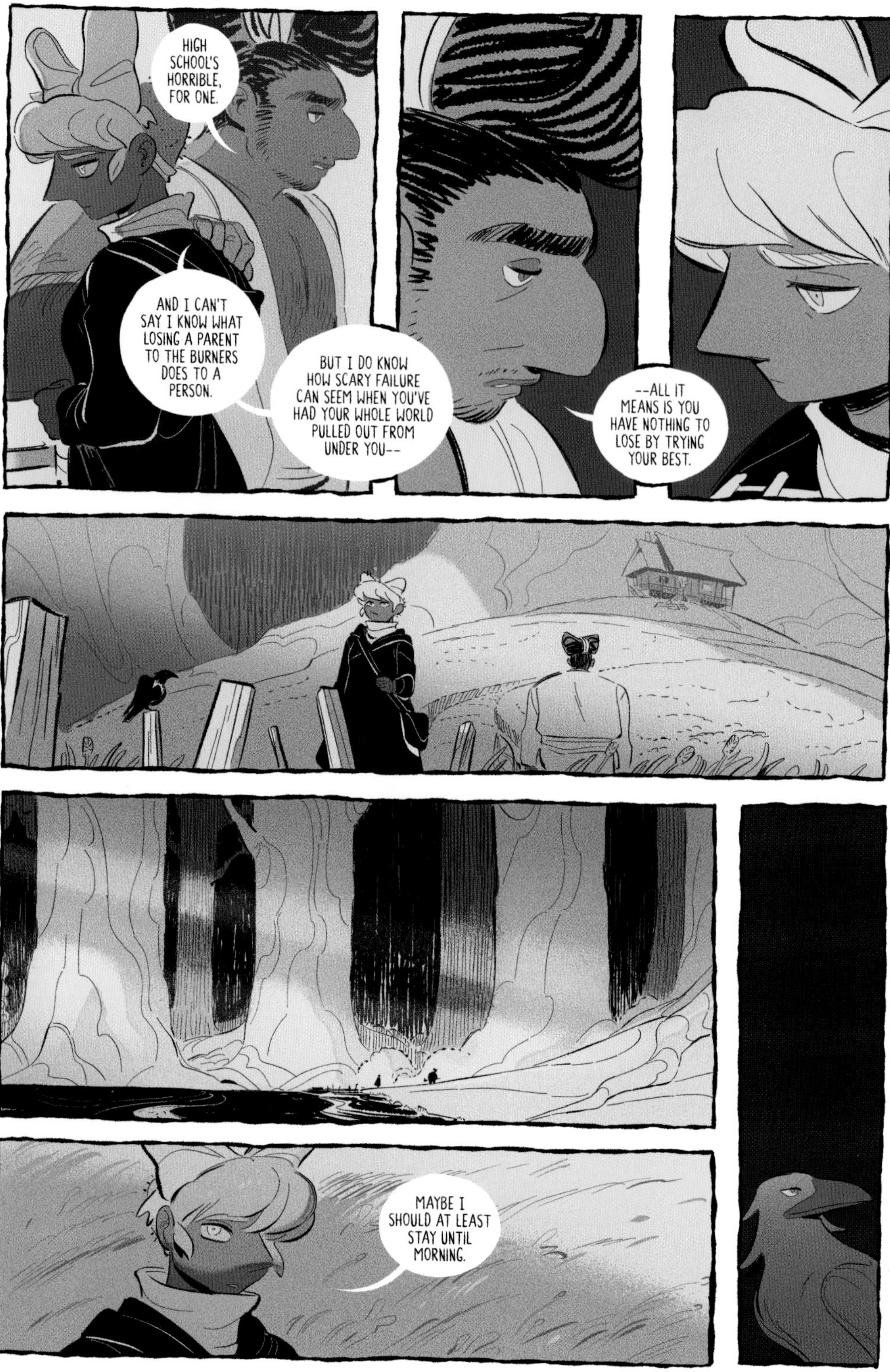

HIGH SCHOOL'S HORRIBLE, FOR ONE.
AND I CAN'T SAY I KNOW WHAT LOSING A PARENT TO THE BURNERS DOES TO A PERSON.
BUT I DO KNOW HOW SCARY FAILURE CAN SEEM WHEN YOU'VE HAD YOUR WHOLE WORLD PULLED OUT FROM UNDER YOU--
--ALL IT MEANS IS YOU HAVE NOTHING TO LOSE BY TRYING YOUR BEST.
MAYBE I SHOULD AT LEAST STAY UNTIL MORNING.

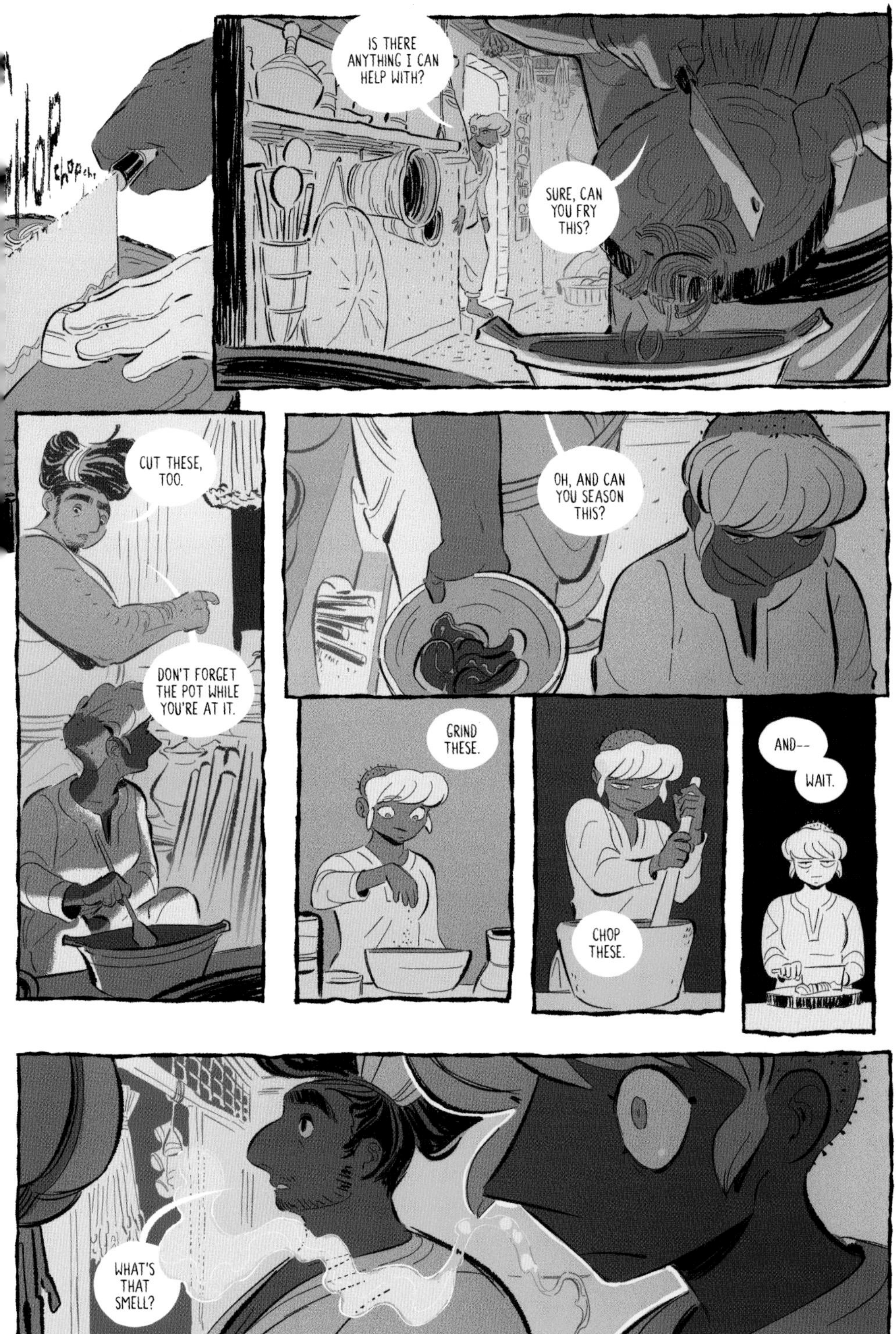
CHOP chop ch
IS THERE ANYTHING I CAN HELP WITH?
SURE, CAN YOU FRY THIS?
CUT THESE, TOO.
DON'T FORGET THE POT WHILE YOU'RE AT IT.
OH, AND CAN YOU SEASON THIS?
GRIND THESE.
CHOP THESE.
AND--
WAIT.
WHAT'S THAT SMELL?

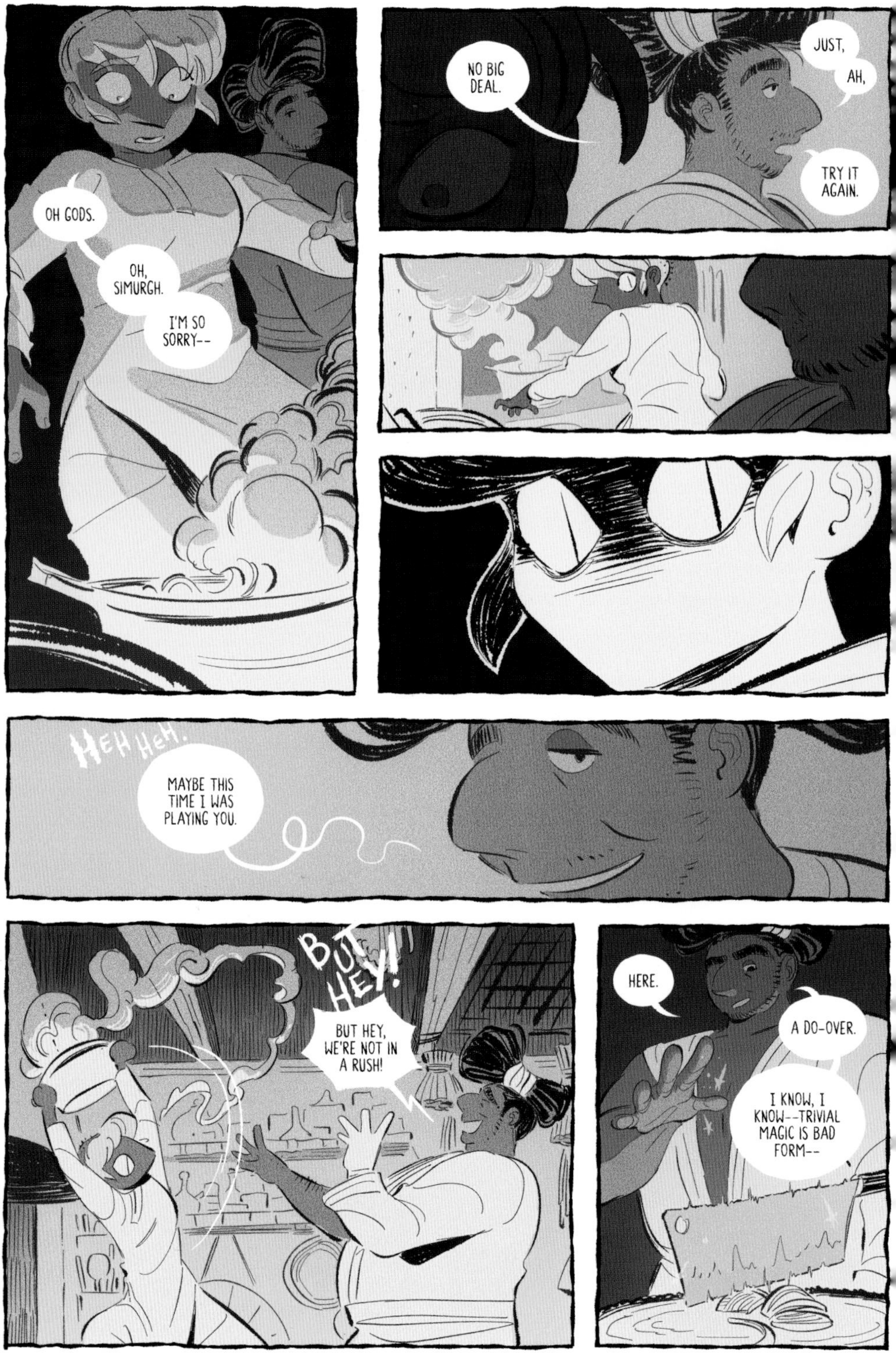
OH GODS.
OH, SIMURGH.
I'M SO SORRY--
NO BIG DEAL.
JUST,
AH,
TRY IT AGAIN.
HEH HEH.
MAYBE THIS TIME I WAS PLAYING YOU.
BUT HEY!
BUT HEY, WE'RE NOT IN A RUSH!
HERE.
A DO-OVER.
I KNOW, I KNOW--TRIVIAL MAGIC IS BAD FORM--

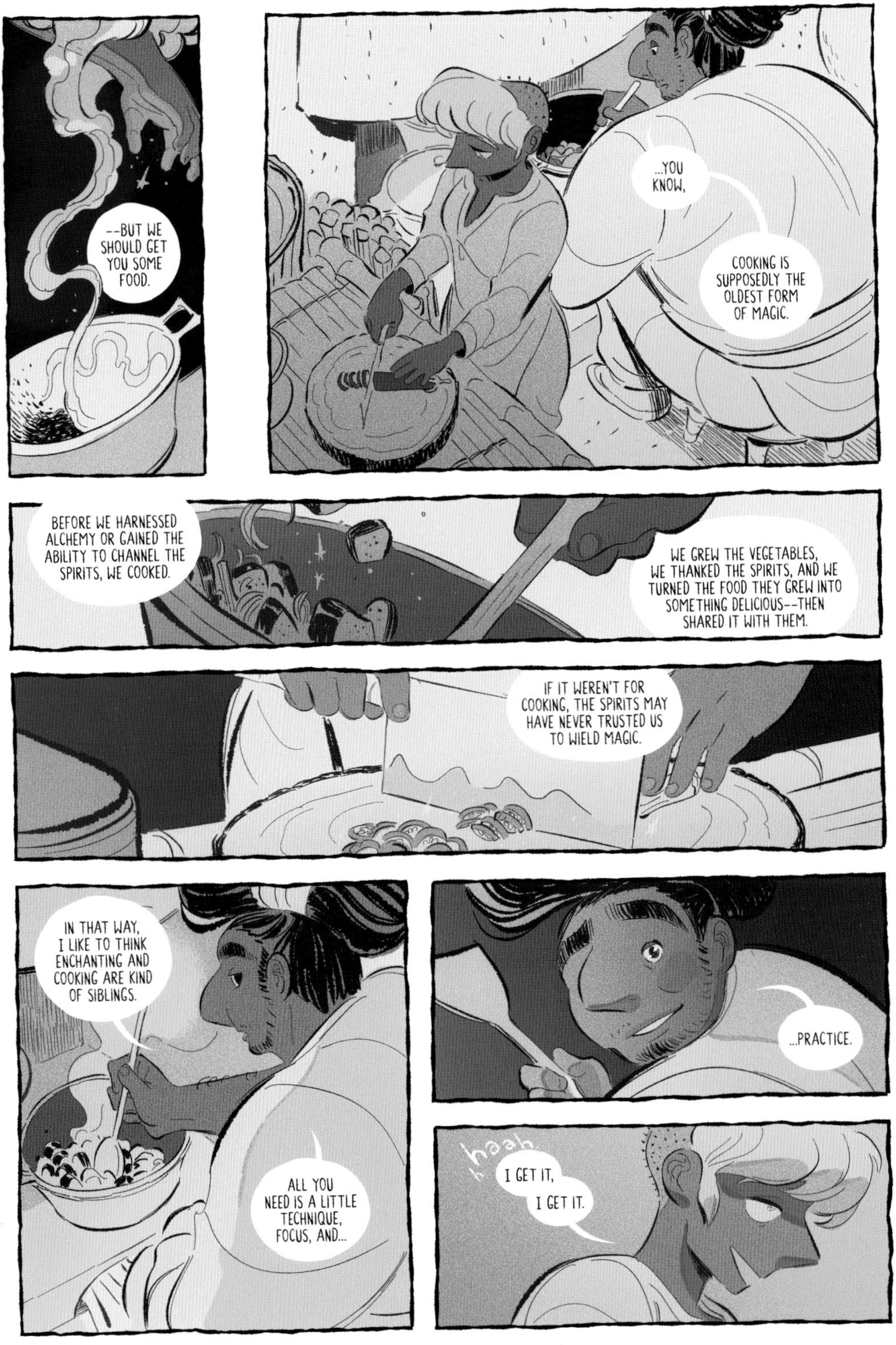
--BUT WE SHOULD GET YOU SOME FOOD.
...YOU KNOW,
COOKING IS SUPPOSEDLY THE OLDEST FORM OF MAGIC.
BEFORE WE HARNESSED ALCHEMY OR GAINED THE ABILITY TO CHANNEL THE SPIRITS, WE COOKED.
WE GREW THE VEGETABLES, WE THANKED THE SPIRITS, AND WE TURNED THE FOOD THEY GREW INTO SOMETHING DELICIOUS--THEN SHARED IT WITH THEM.
IF IT WEREN'T FOR COOKING, THE SPIRITS MAY HAVE NEVER TRUSTED US TO WIELD MAGIC.
IN THAT WAY, I LIKE TO THINK ENCHANTING AND COOKING ARE KIND OF SIBLINGS.
ALL YOU NEED IS A LITTLE TECHNIQUE, FOCUS, AND...
...PRACTICE.
haah.
I GET IT,
I GET IT.

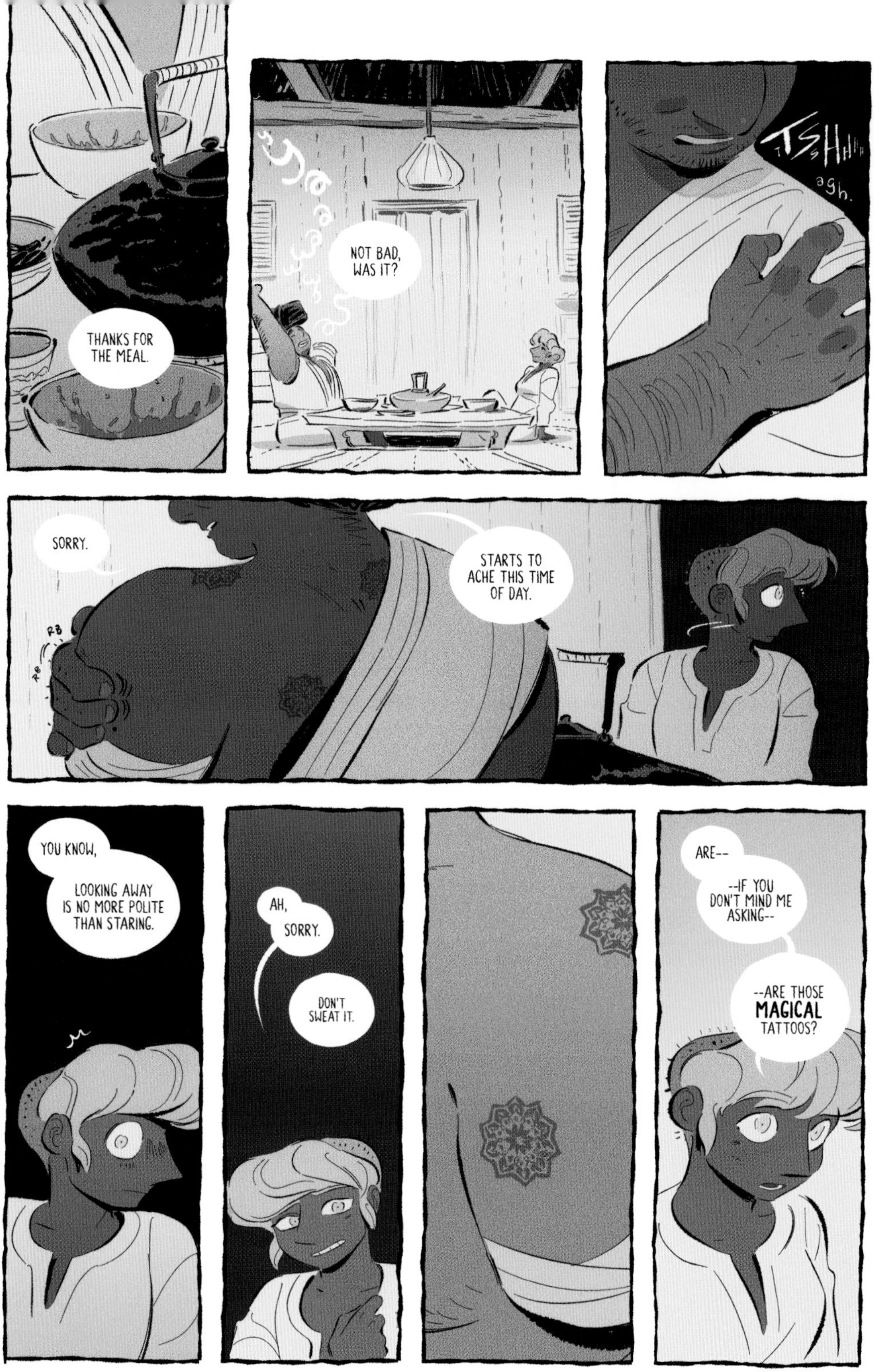
THANKS FOR THE MEAL.
NOT BAD, WAS IT?
TSH
agh.
SORRY.
STARTS TO ACHE THIS TIME OF DAY.
YOU KNOW,
LOOKING AWAY IS NO MORE POLITE THAN STARING.
AH,
SORRY.
DON'T SWEAT IT.
ARE--
--IF YOU DON'T MIND ME ASKING--
--ARE THOSE **MAGICAL** TATTOOS?

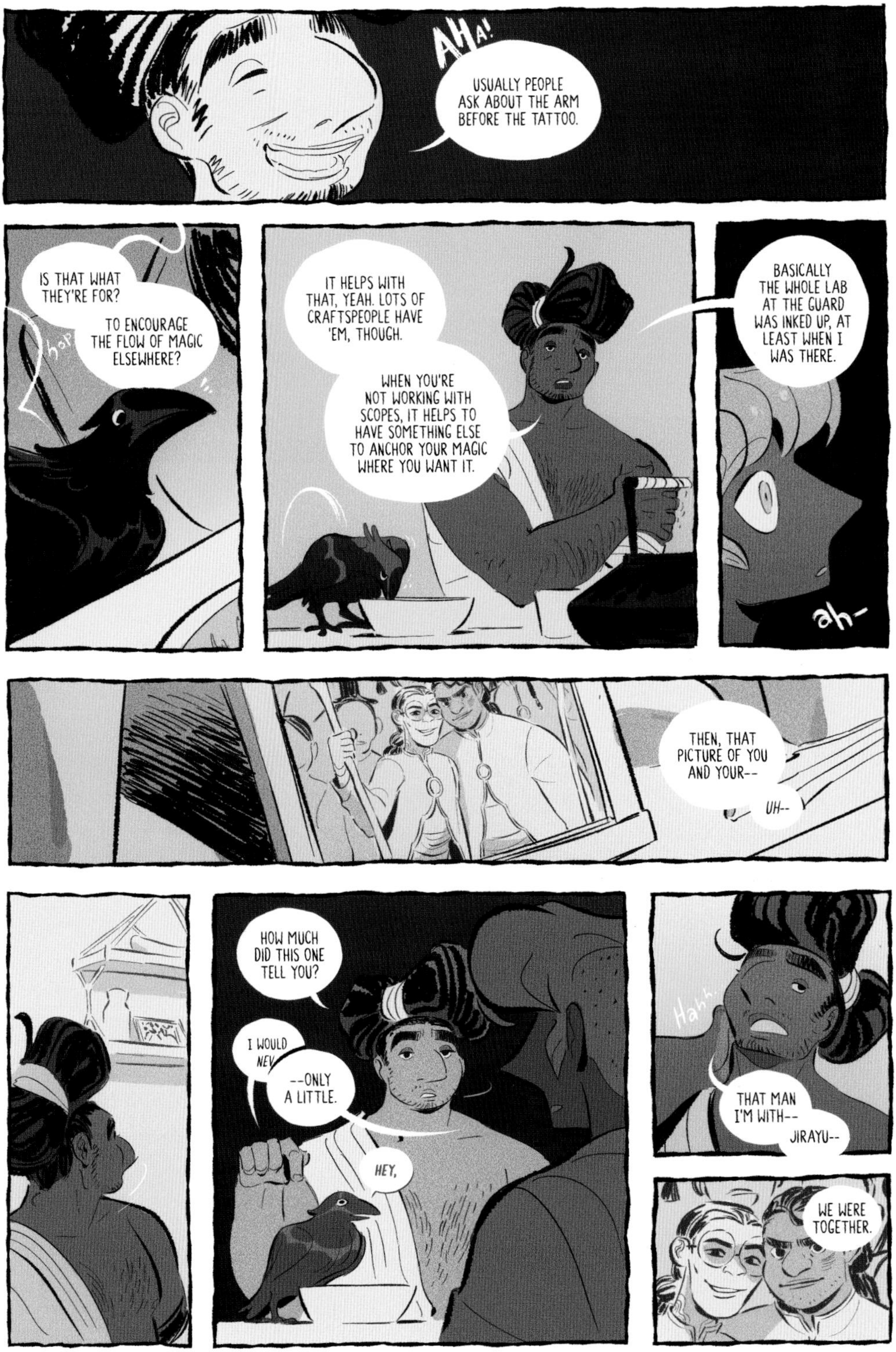
AHA!
USUALLY PEOPLE ASK ABOUT THE ARM BEFORE THE TATTOO.
IS THAT WHAT THEY'RE FOR?
TO ENCOURAGE THE FLOW OF MAGIC ELSEWHERE?
IT HELPS WITH THAT, YEAH. LOTS OF CRAFTSPEOPLE HAVE 'EM, THOUGH.
WHEN YOU'RE NOT WORKING WITH SCOPES, IT HELPS TO HAVE SOMETHING ELSE TO ANCHOR YOUR MAGIC WHERE YOU WANT IT.
BASICALLY THE WHOLE LAB AT THE GUARD WAS INKED UP, AT LEAST WHEN I WAS THERE.
ah-
THEN, THAT PICTURE OF YOU AND YOUR--
UH--
HOW MUCH DID THIS ONE TELL YOU?
I WOULD NEV
--ONLY A LITTLE.
HEY,
Hahh.
THAT MAN I'M WITH--
JIRAYU--
WE WERE TOGETHER.

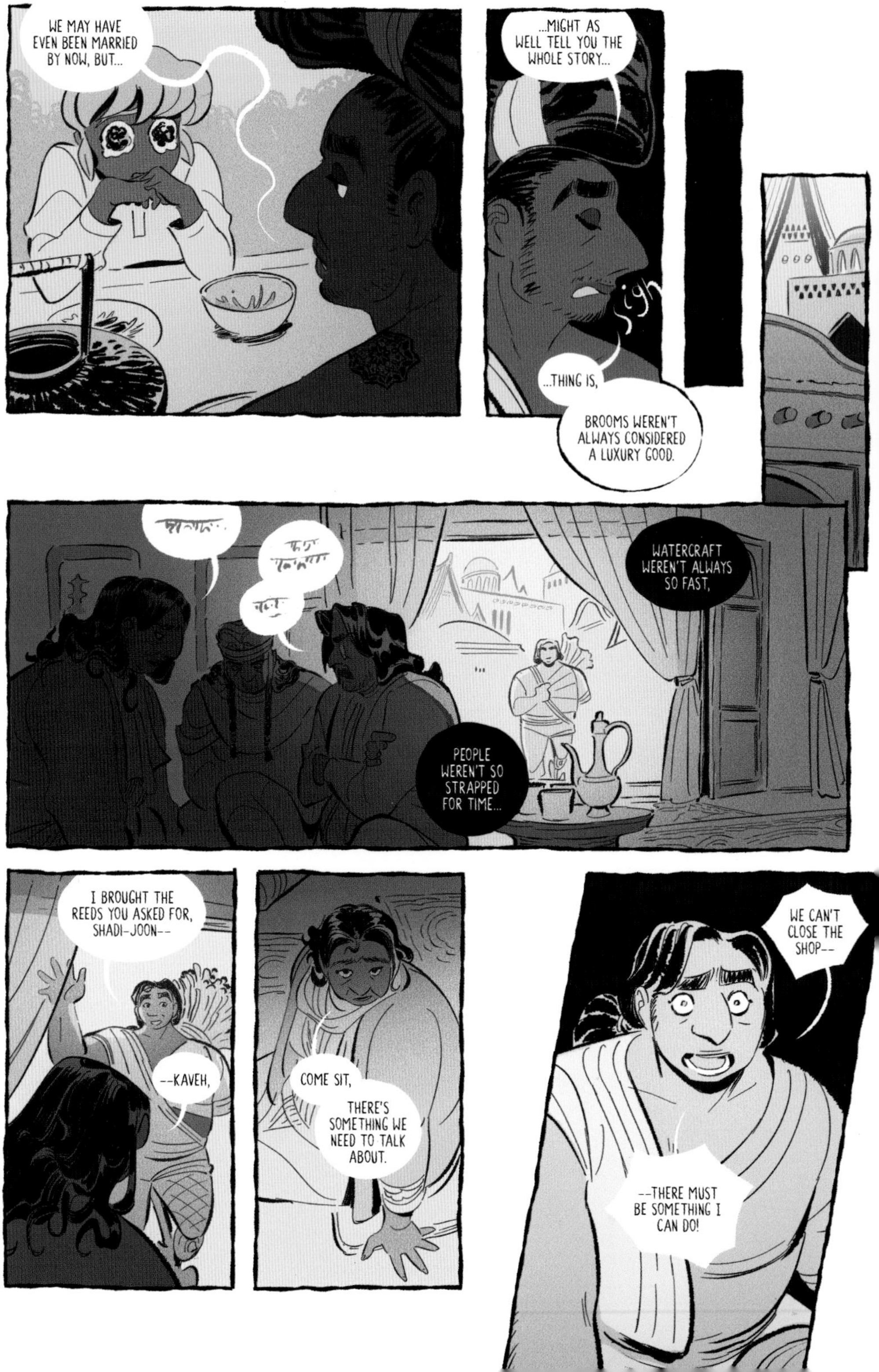
WE MAY HAVE EVEN BEEN MARRIED BY NOW, BUT...
...MIGHT AS WELL TELL YOU THE WHOLE STORY...
sigh
...THING IS,
BROOMS WEREN'T ALWAYS CONSIDERED A LUXURY GOOD.
WATERCRAFT WEREN'T ALWAYS SO FAST,
...
PEOPLE WEREN'T SO STRAPPED FOR TIME...
I BROUGHT THE REEDS YOU ASKED FOR, SHADI-JOON--
--KAVEH,
COME SIT,
THERE'S SOMETHING WE NEED TO TALK ABOUT.
WE CAN'T CLOSE THE SHOP--
--THERE MUST BE SOMETHING I CAN DO!

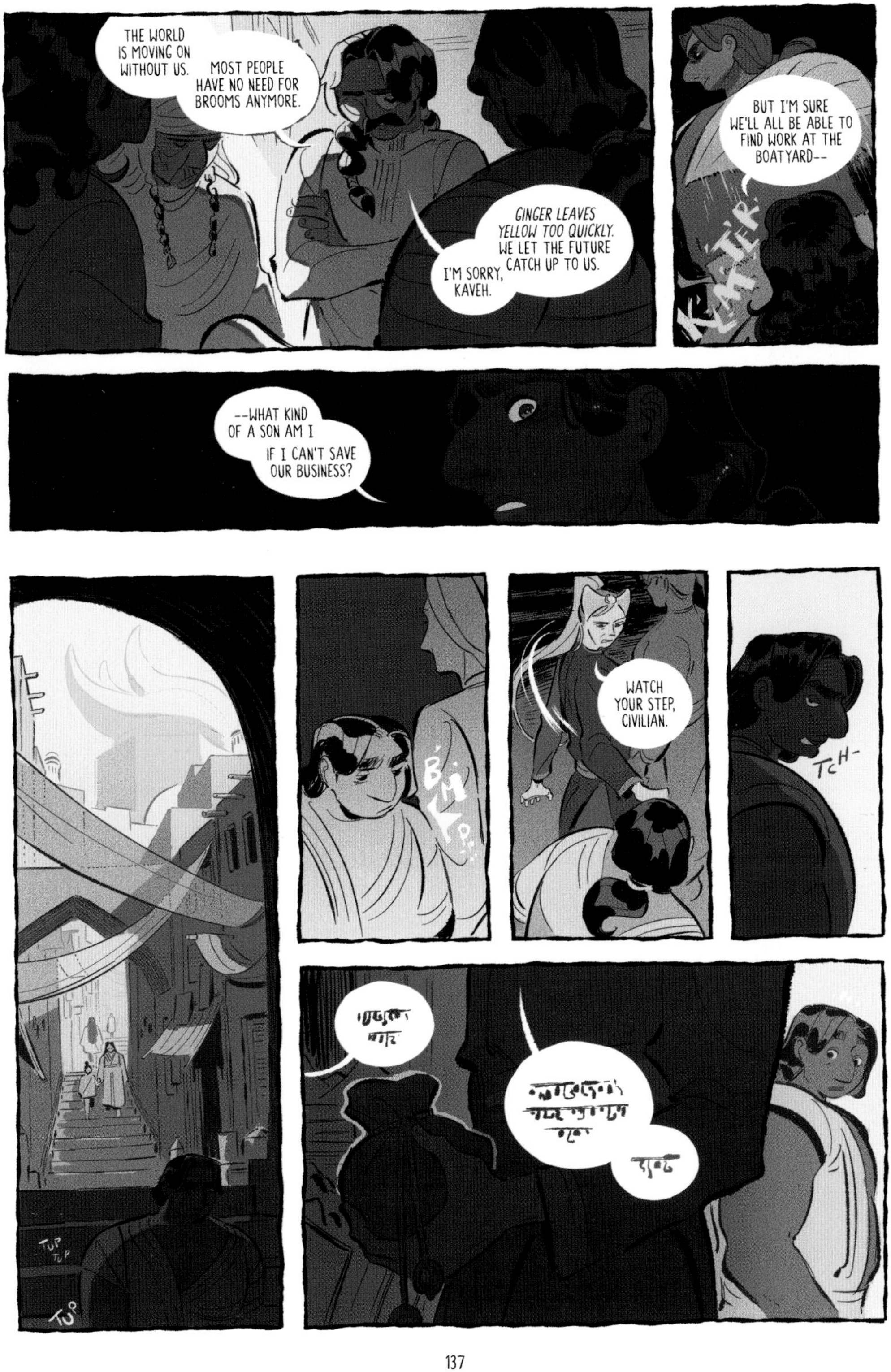
THE WORLD IS MOVING ON WITHOUT US.
MOST PEOPLE HAVE NO NEED FOR BROOMS ANYMORE.
GINGER LEAVES YELLOW TOO QUICKLY. WE LET THE FUTURE CATCH UP TO US.
I'M SORRY, KAVEH.
BUT I'M SURE WE'LL ALL BE ABLE TO FIND WORK AT THE BOATYARD--
--WHAT KIND OF A SON AM I
IF I CAN'T SAVE OUR BUSINESS?
TUP TUP
TUP
WATCH YOUR STEP, CIVILIAN.
TCH-

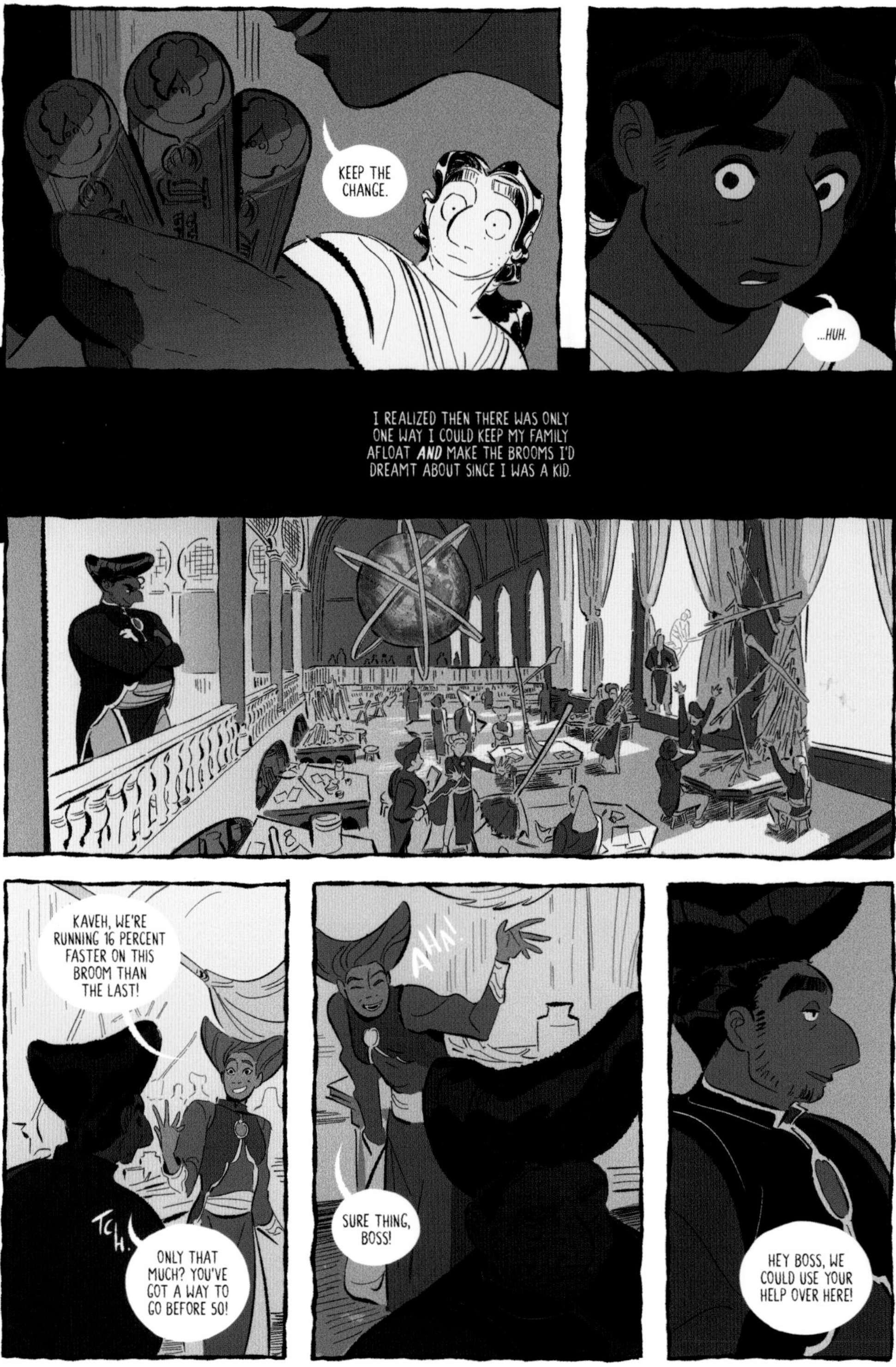
KEEP THE CHANGE.
...HUH.
I REALIZED THEN THERE WAS ONLY ONE WAY I COULD KEEP MY FAMILY AFLOAT AND MAKE THE BROOMS I'D DREAMT ABOUT SINCE I WAS A KID.
KAVEH, WE'RE RUNNING 16 PERCENT FASTER ON THIS BROOM THAN THE LAST!
TCH.
ONLY THAT MUCH? YOU'VE GOT A WAY TO GO BEFORE 50!
AHH!
SURE THING, BOSS!
HEY BOSS, WE COULD USE YOUR HELP OVER HERE!

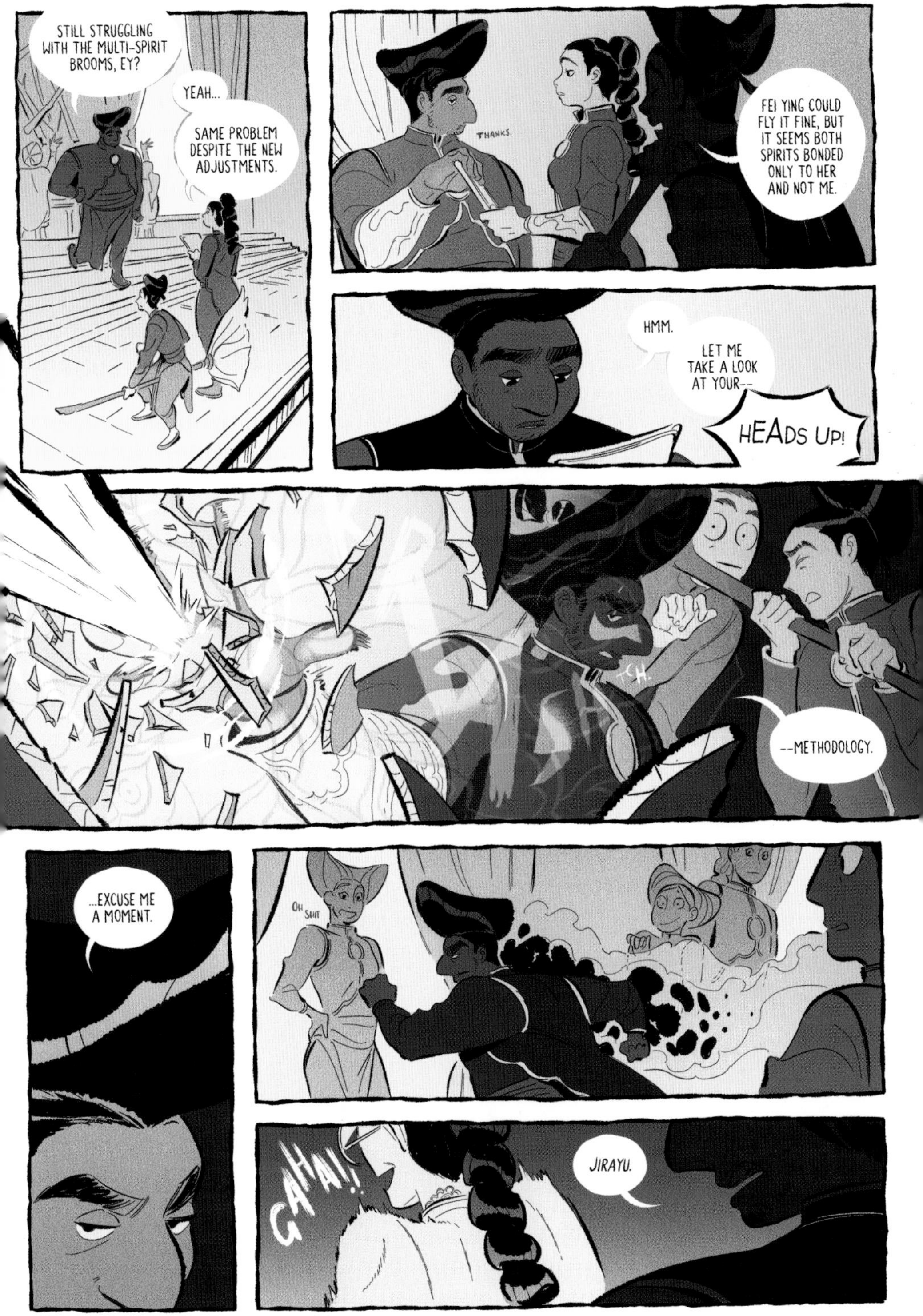
STILL STRUGGLING WITH THE MULTI-SPIRIT BROOMS, EY?
YEAH...
SAME PROBLEM DESPITE THE NEW ADJUSTMENTS.
THANKS.
FEI YING COULD FLY IT FINE, BUT IT SEEMS BOTH SPIRITS BONDED ONLY TO HER AND NOT ME.
HMM.
LET ME TAKE A LOOK AT YOUR--
HEADS UP!
TCH.
--METHODOLOGY.
...EXCUSE ME A MOMENT.
OH SHIT
GAHA!!
JIRAYU.

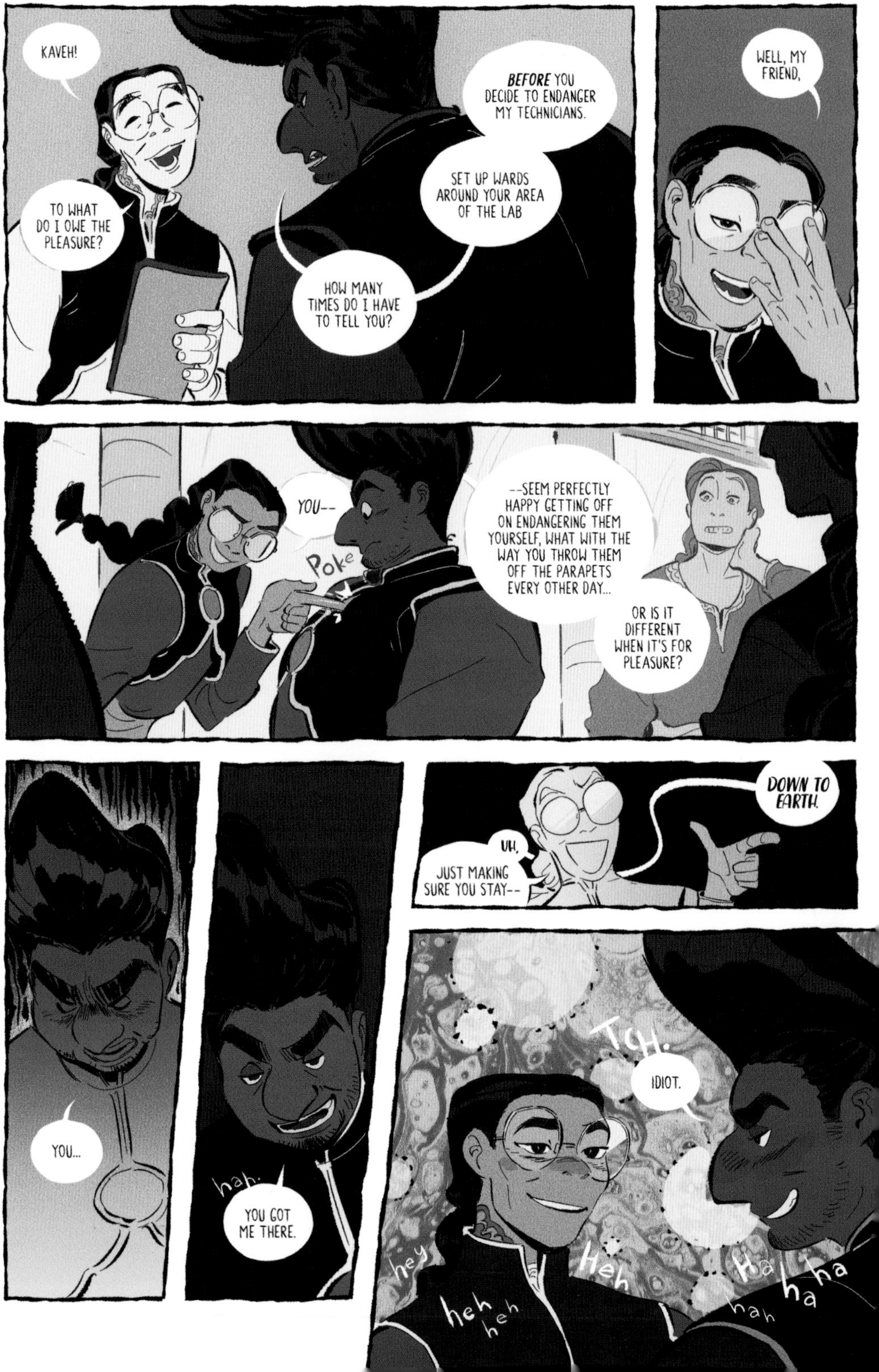
KAVEH!
TO WHAT DO I OWE THE PLEASURE?
HOW MANY TIMES DO I HAVE TO TELL YOU?
SET UP WARDS AROUND YOUR AREA OF THE LAB
BEFORE YOU DECIDE TO ENDANGER MY TECHNICIANS.
WELL, MY FRIEND,
YOU--
POKE
--SEEM PERFECTLY HAPPY GETTING OFF ON ENDANGERING THEM YOURSELF, WHAT WITH THE WAY YOU THROW THEM OFF THE PARAPETS EVERY OTHER DAY...
OR IS IT DIFFERENT WHEN IT'S FOR PLEASURE?
UH,
JUST MAKING SURE YOU STAY--
DOWN TO EARTH.
YOU...
hah.
YOU GOT ME THERE.
TCH.
IDIOT.
hey
heh heh h
Heh
Ha ha ha
hah

THEY'RE AT IT AGAIN.

OH FOR--

OI!!!

IF THE REST OF US DON'T GET TO FRATERNIZE IN THE LABS, THEN NEITHER DO YOU!

SEEMS WE'VE BEEN BUSTED.

YEAH.

SORRY TO INTERRUPT YOU TWO, AH,

BUT, AH,

CAPTAIN JAWAHIR WANTS TO SEE YOU, KAVEH.

UGH.

SMOOCH

FINE.

NOW, JIRAYU, I'M CURIOUS TO SEE HOW YOUR PROJECT IS C̶ ̶L̶O̶N̶G̶. I THINK IT M̶ ̶ ̶S̶ ̶A̶ GREAT A̶ ̶

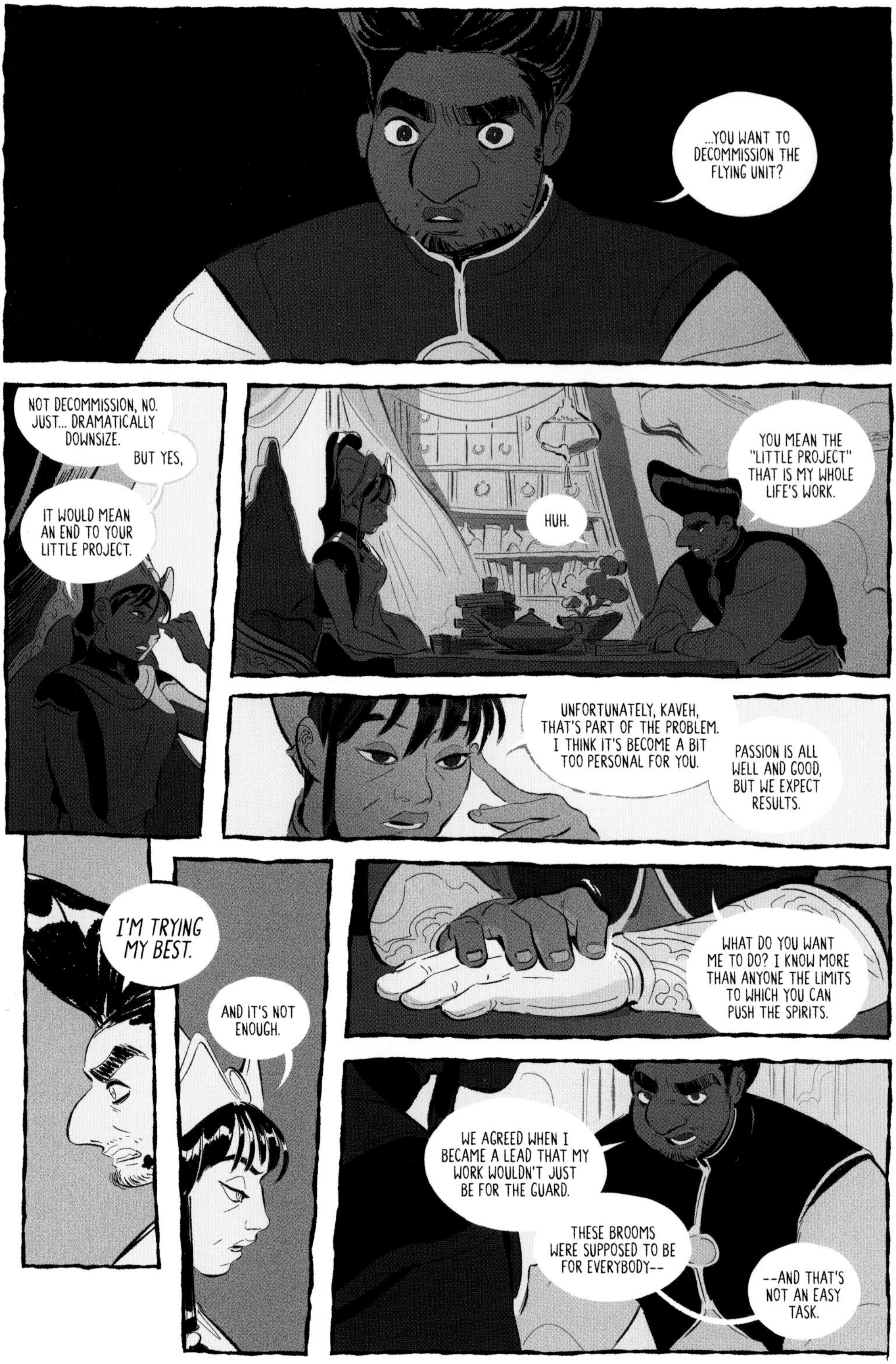
...YOU WANT TO DECOMMISSION THE FLYING UNIT?
NOT DECOMMISSION, NO. JUST... DRAMATICALLY DOWNSIZE.
BUT YES,
IT WOULD MEAN AN END TO YOUR LITTLE PROJECT.
HUH.
YOU MEAN THE "LITTLE PROJECT" THAT IS MY WHOLE LIFE'S WORK.
UNFORTUNATELY, KAVEH, THAT'S PART OF THE PROBLEM. I THINK IT'S BECOME A BIT TOO PERSONAL FOR YOU.
PASSION IS ALL WELL AND GOOD, BUT WE EXPECT RESULTS.
I'M TRYING MY BEST.
AND IT'S NOT ENOUGH.
WHAT DO YOU WANT ME TO DO? I KNOW MORE THAN ANYONE THE LIMITS TO WHICH YOU CAN PUSH THE SPIRITS.
WE AGREED WHEN I BECAME A LEAD THAT MY WORK WOULDN'T JUST BE FOR THE GUARD.
THESE BROOMS WERE SUPPOSED TO BE FOR EVERYBODY--
--AND THAT'S NOT AN EASY TASK.

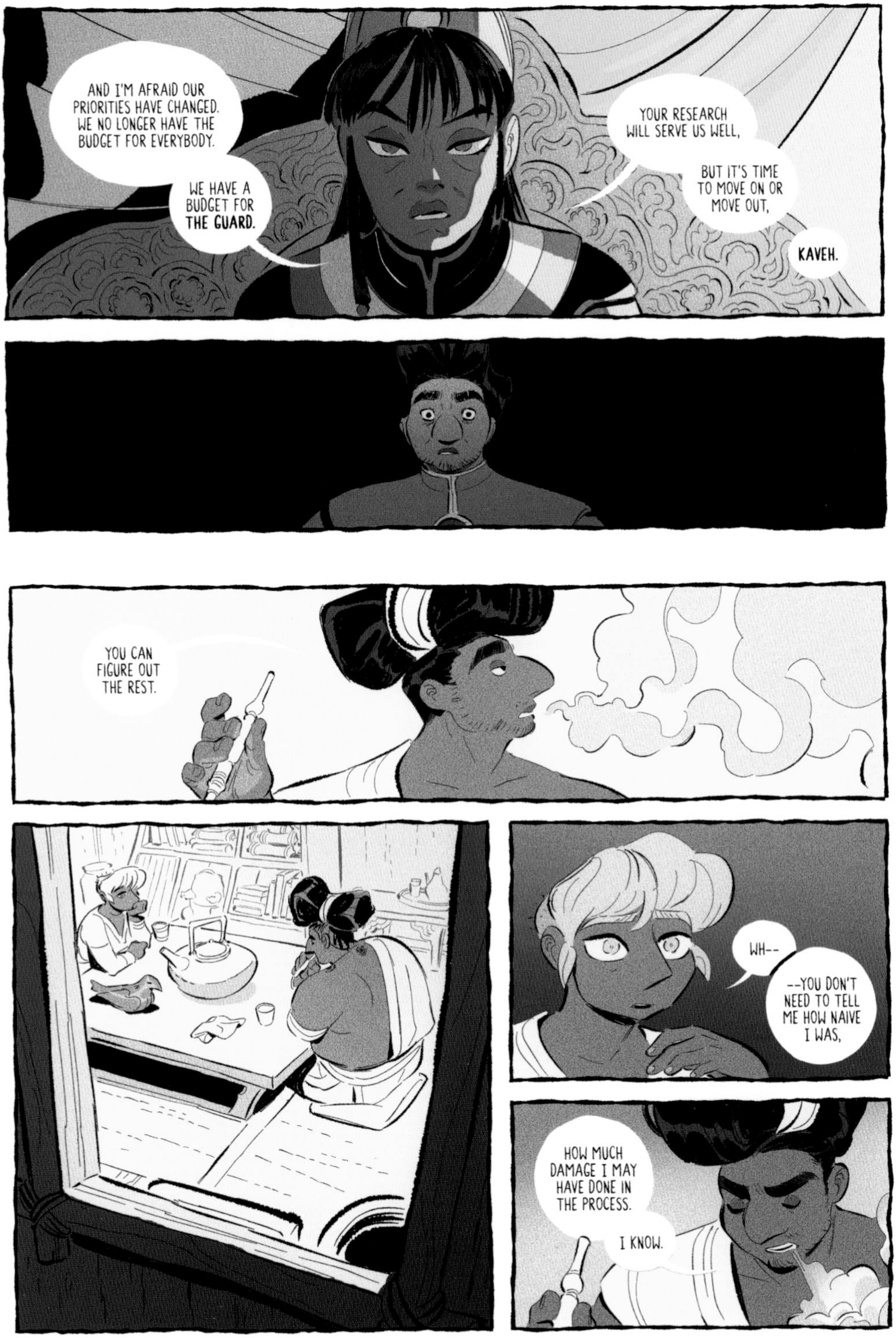
AND I'M AFRAID OUR PRIORITIES HAVE CHANGED. WE NO LONGER HAVE THE BUDGET FOR EVERYBODY.
WE HAVE A BUDGET FOR **THE GUARD.**
YOUR RESEARCH WILL SERVE US WELL,
BUT IT'S TIME TO MOVE ON OR MOVE OUT,
KAVEH.
YOU CAN FIGURE OUT THE REST.
WH--
--YOU DON'T NEED TO TELL ME HOW NAIVE I WAS,
HOW MUCH DAMAGE I MAY HAVE DONE IN THE PROCESS.
I KNOW.

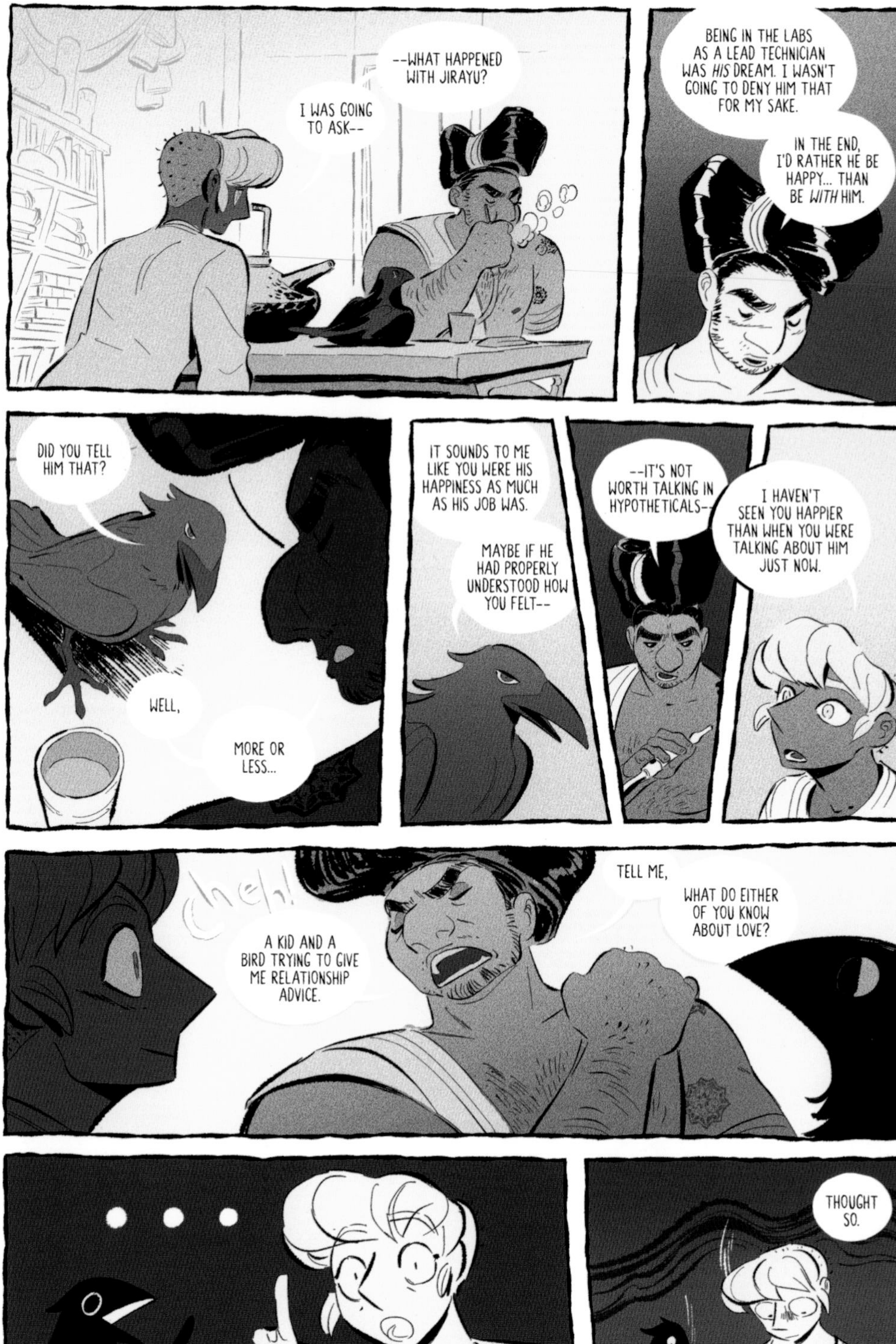
I WAS GOING TO ASK--
--WHAT HAPPENED WITH JIRAYU?
BEING IN THE LABS AS A LEAD TECHNICIAN WAS *HIS* DREAM. I WASN'T GOING TO DENY HIM THAT FOR MY SAKE.
IN THE END, I'D RATHER HE BE HAPPY... THAN BE *WITH* HIM.
DID YOU TELL HIM THAT?
WELL,
MORE OR LESS...
IT SOUNDS TO ME LIKE YOU WERE HIS HAPPINESS AS MUCH AS HIS JOB WAS.
MAYBE IF HE HAD PROPERLY UNDERSTOOD HOW YOU FELT--
--IT'S NOT WORTH TALKING IN HYPOTHETICALS--
I HAVEN'T SEEN YOU HAPPIER THAN WHEN YOU WERE TALKING ABOUT HIM JUST NOW.
Cheh!
A KID AND A BIRD TRYING TO GIVE ME RELATIONSHIP ADVICE.
TELL ME,
WHAT DO EITHER OF YOU KNOW ABOUT LOVE?
THOUGHT SO.

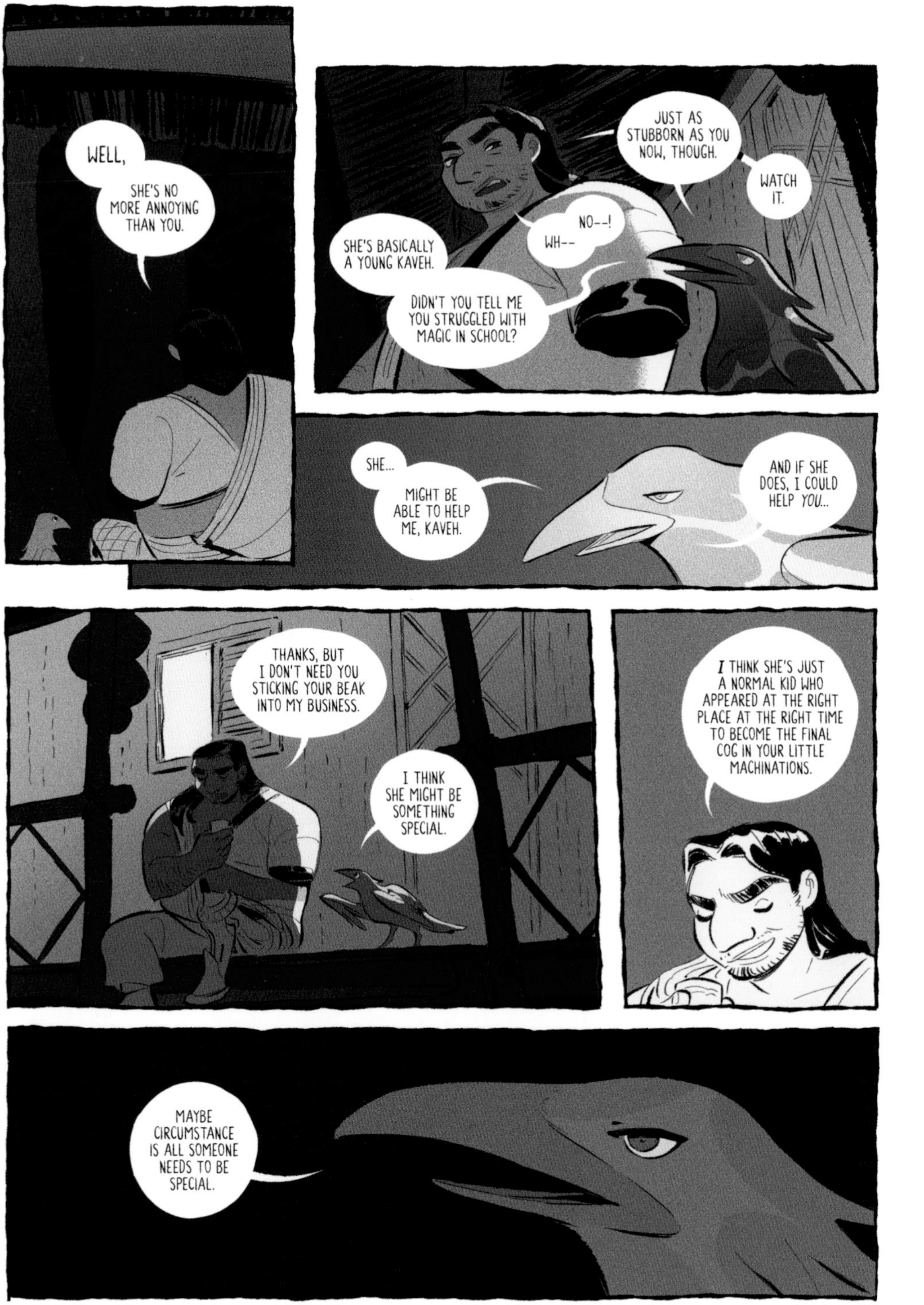
WELL,
SHE'S NO MORE ANNOYING THAN YOU.
SHE'S BASICALLY A YOUNG KAVEH.
DIDN'T YOU TELL ME YOU STRUGGLED WITH MAGIC IN SCHOOL?
WH--
NO--!
JUST AS STUBBORN AS YOU NOW, THOUGH.
WATCH IT.
SHE...
MIGHT BE ABLE TO HELP ME, KAVEH.
AND IF SHE DOES, I COULD HELP *YOU*...
THANKS, BUT I DON'T NEED YOU STICKING YOUR BEAK INTO MY BUSINESS.
I THINK SHE MIGHT BE SOMETHING SPECIAL.
I THINK SHE'S JUST A NORMAL KID WHO APPEARED AT THE RIGHT PLACE AT THE RIGHT TIME TO BECOME THE FINAL COG IN YOUR LITTLE MACHINATIONS.
MAYBE CIRCUMSTANCE IS ALL SOMEONE NEEDS TO BE SPECIAL.

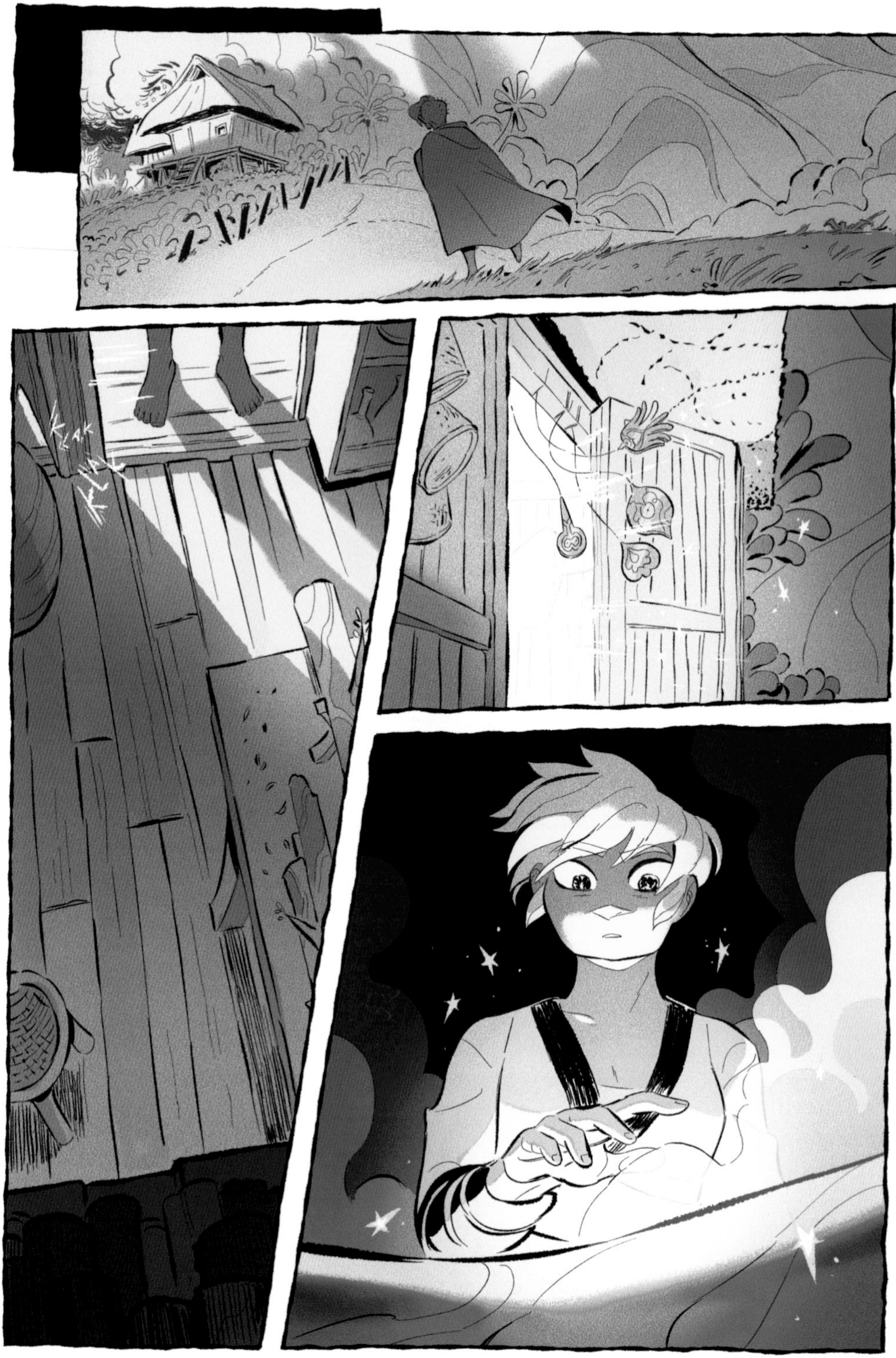
KLAK
KLAK

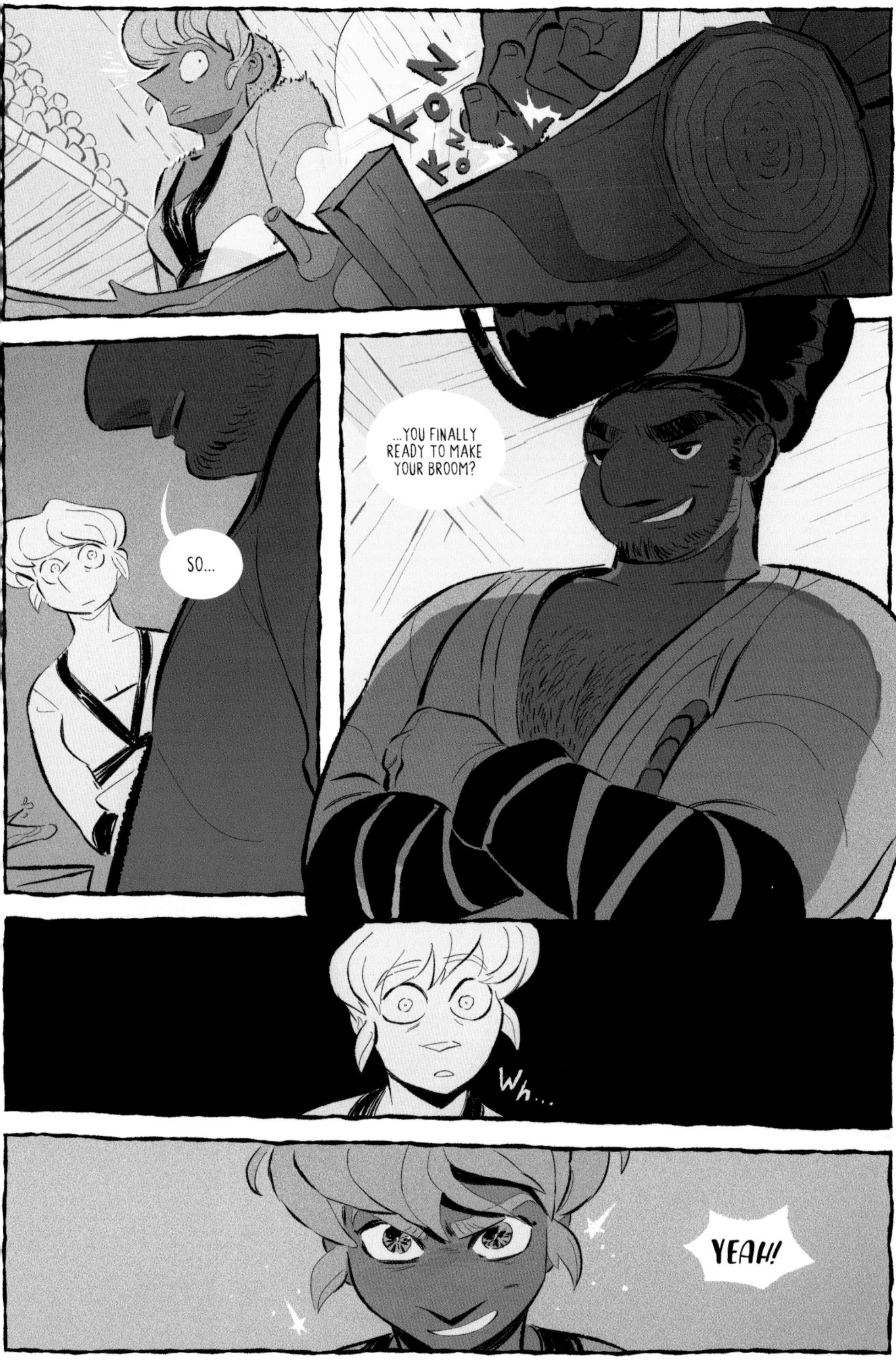
KONK KONK
SO...
...YOU FINALLY READY TO MAKE YOUR BROOM?
Wh...
YEAH!

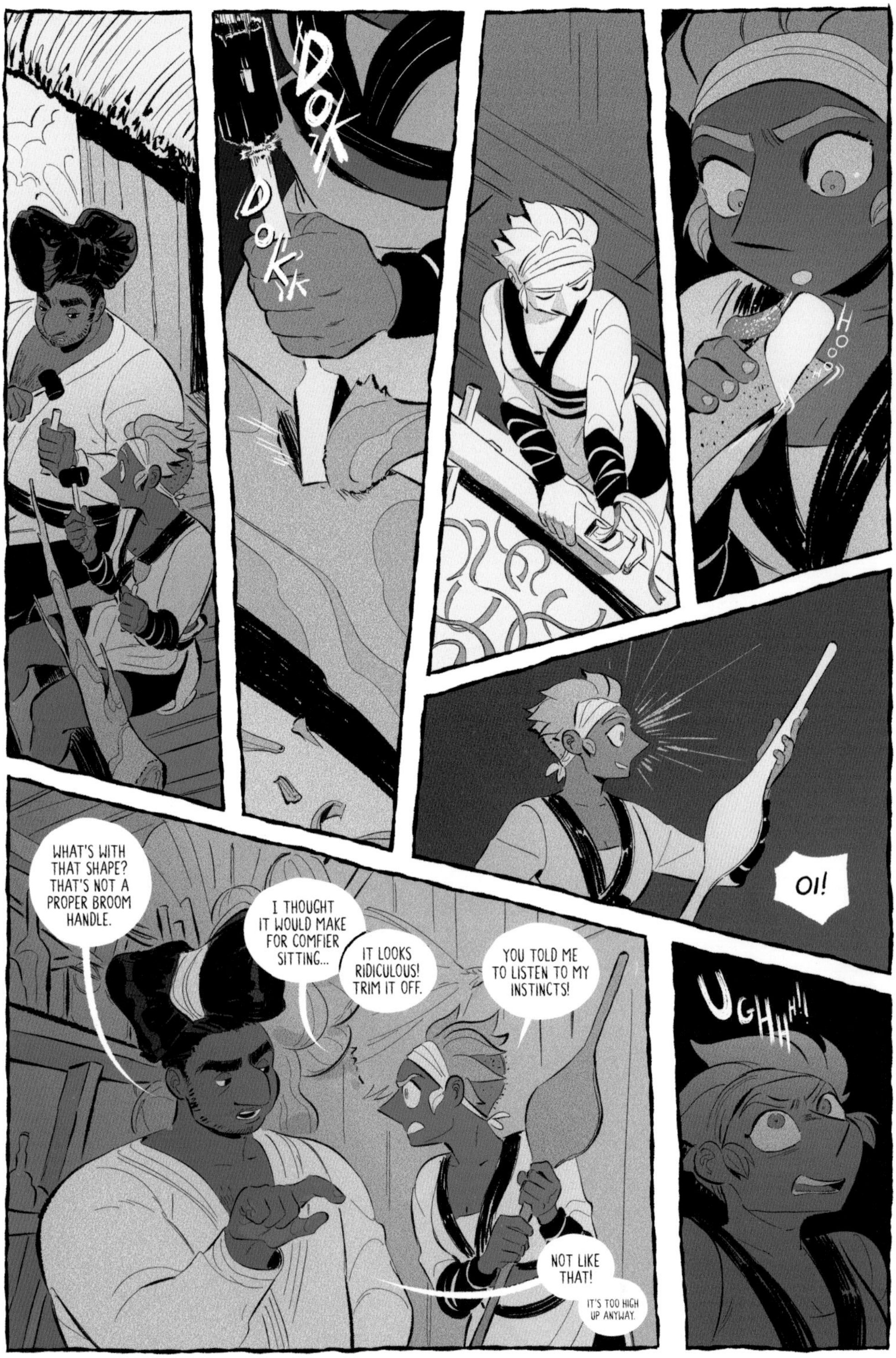
DOK
DOK
HOO
OI!
WHAT'S WITH THAT SHAPE? THAT'S NOT A PROPER BROOM HANDLE.
I THOUGHT IT WOULD MAKE FOR COMFIER SITTING...
IT LOOKS RIDICULOUS! TRIM IT OFF.
YOU TOLD ME TO LISTEN TO MY INSTINCTS!
NOT LIKE THAT!
IT'S TOO HIGH UP ANYWAY.
UGHH!!

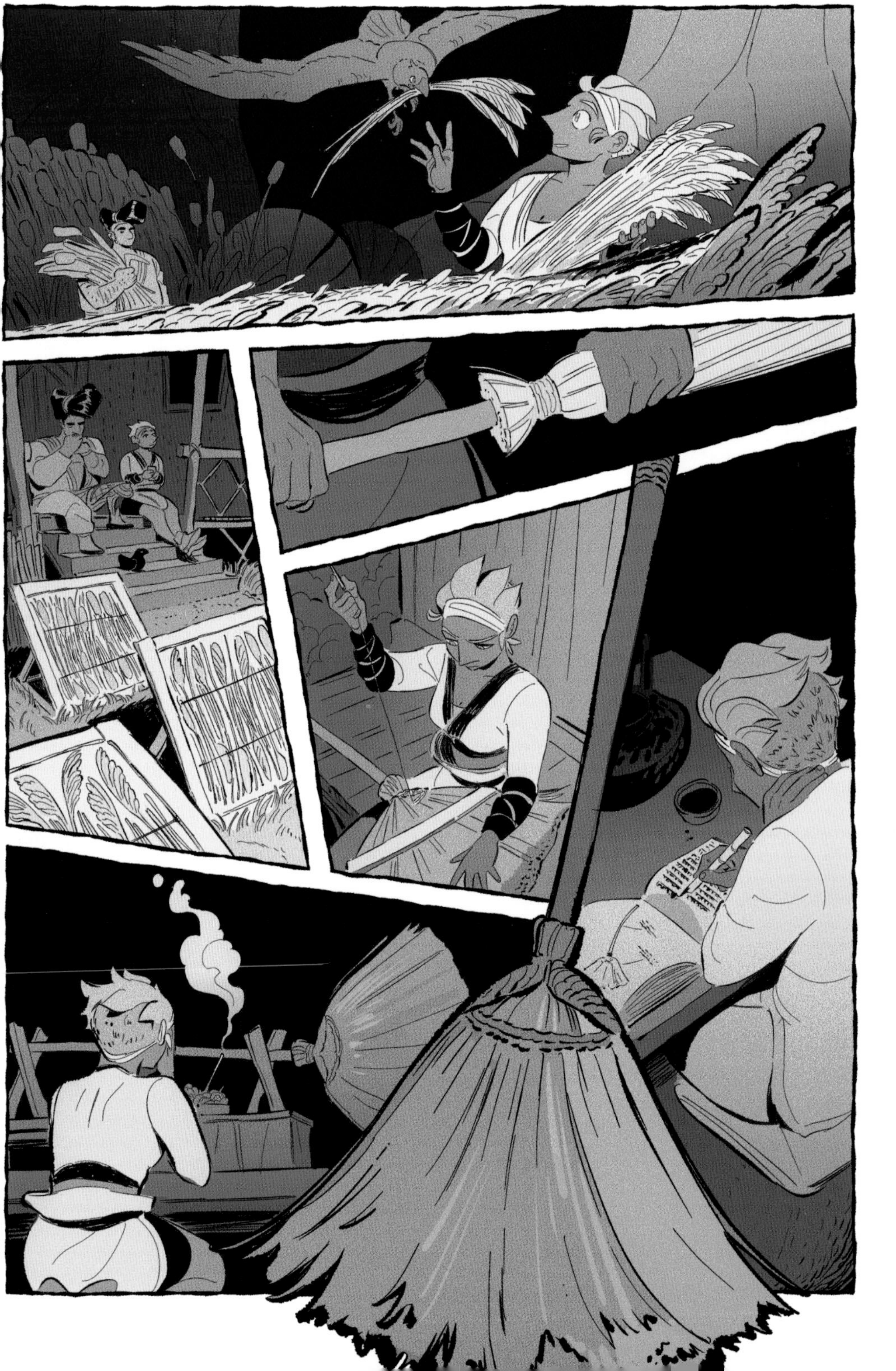

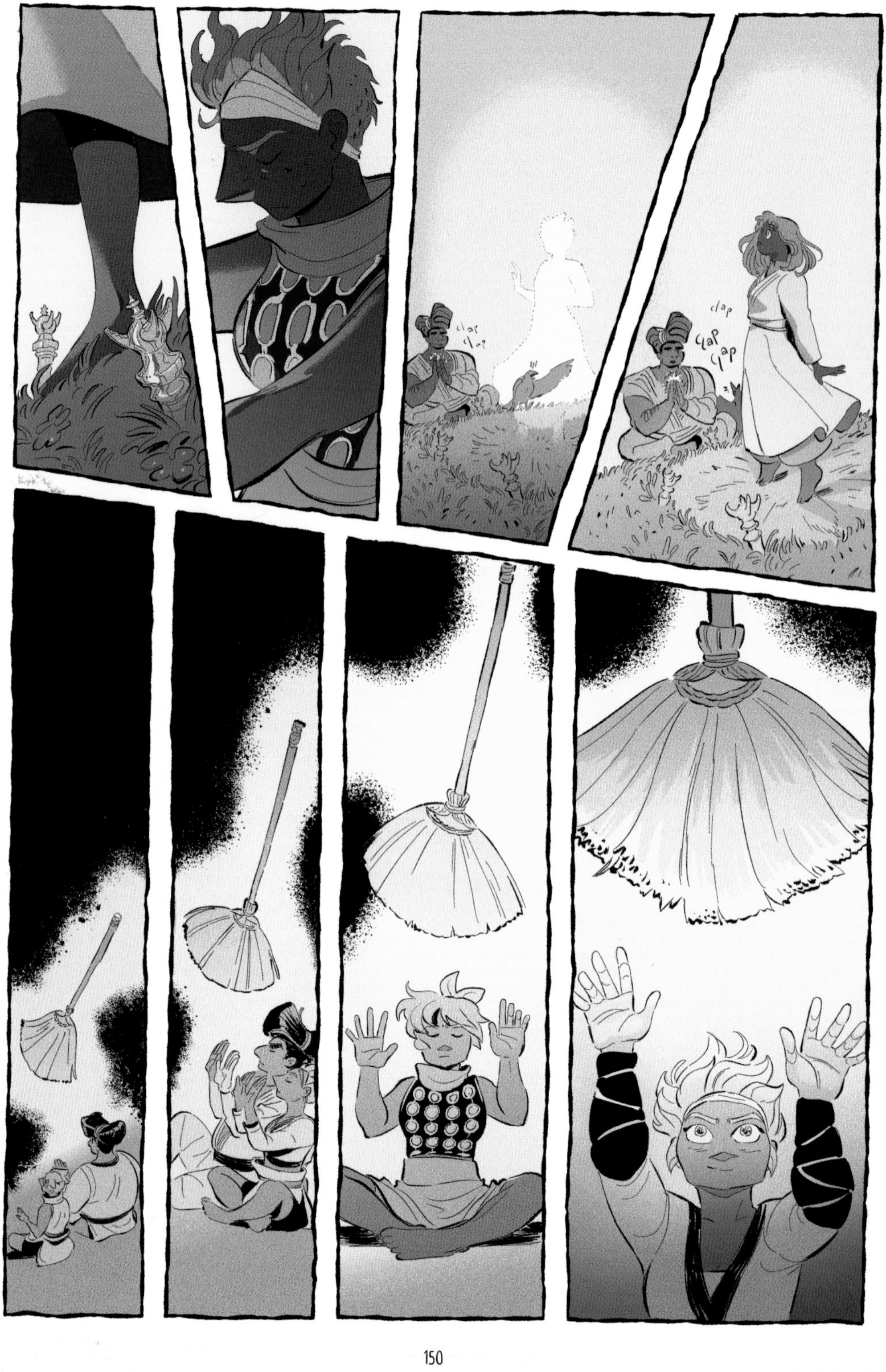
clap
clap
clap
clap
clap

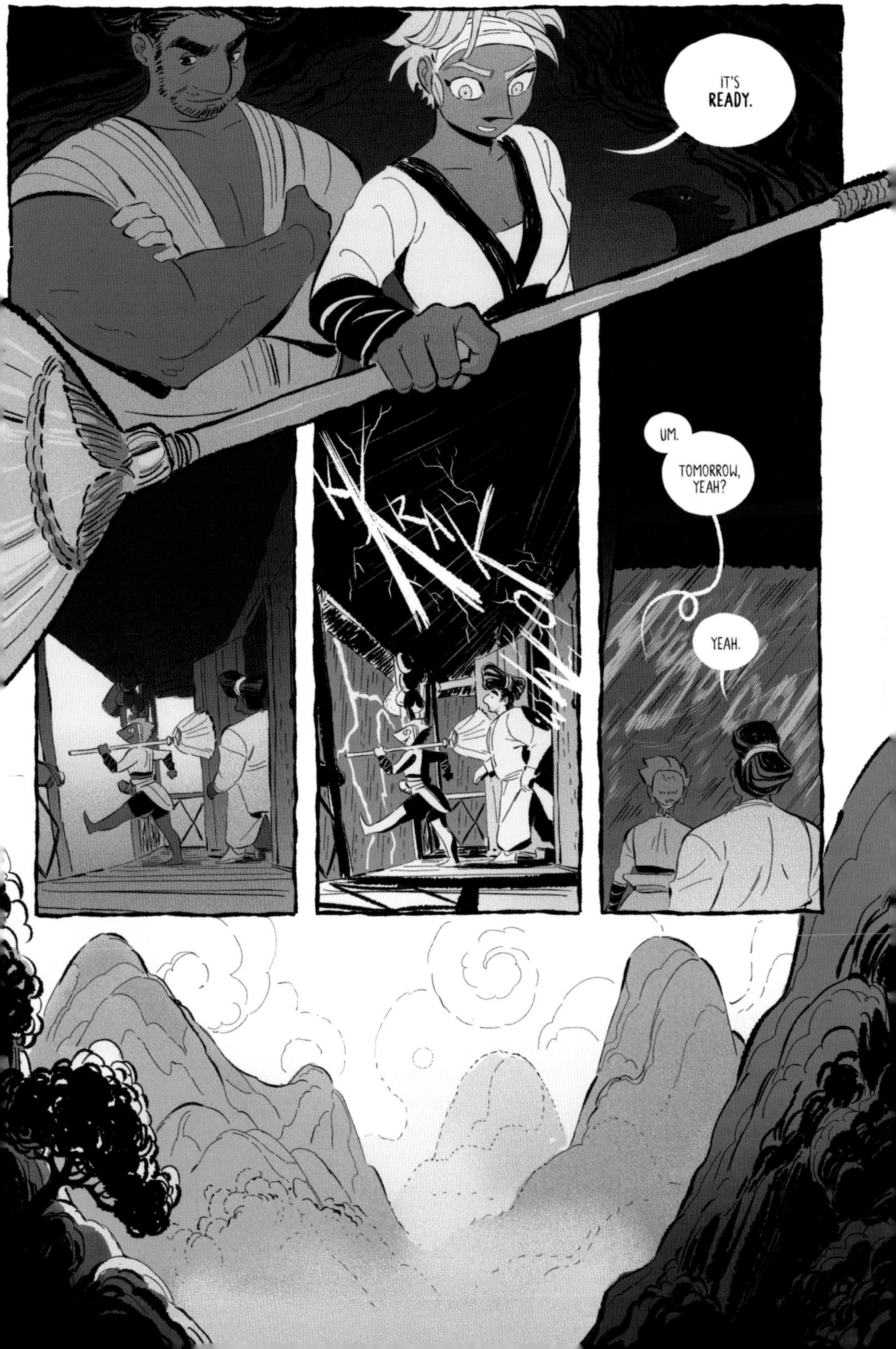
IT'S READY.
UM.
TOMORROW, YEAH?
YEAH.

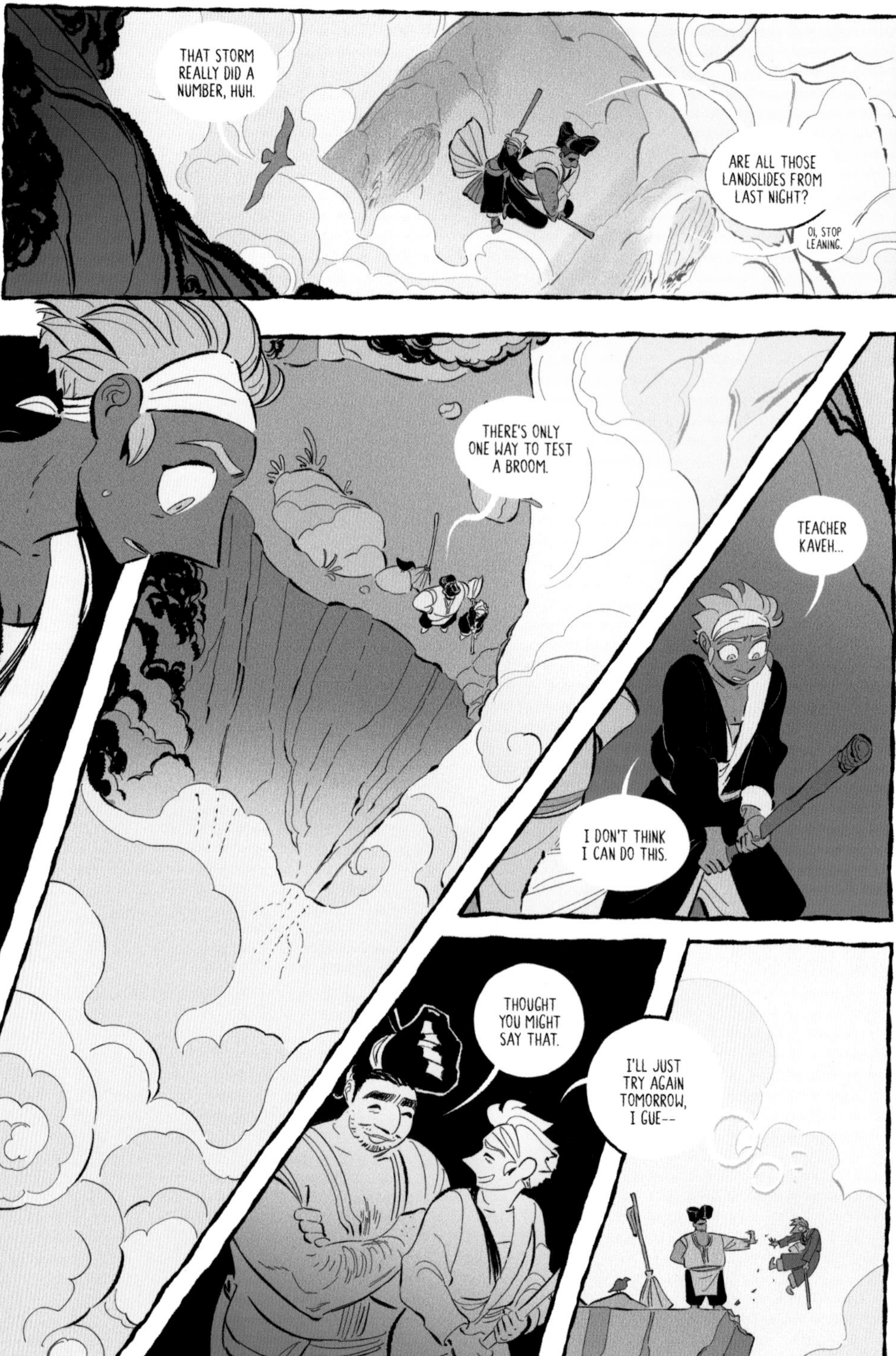
THAT STORM REALLY DID A NUMBER, HUH.
ARE ALL THOSE LANDSLIDES FROM LAST NIGHT?
OI, STOP LEANING.
THERE'S ONLY ONE WAY TO TEST A BROOM.
TEACHER KAVEH...
I DON'T THINK I CAN DO THIS.
THOUGHT YOU MIGHT SAY THAT.
I'LL JUST TRY AGAIN TOMORROW, I GUE--

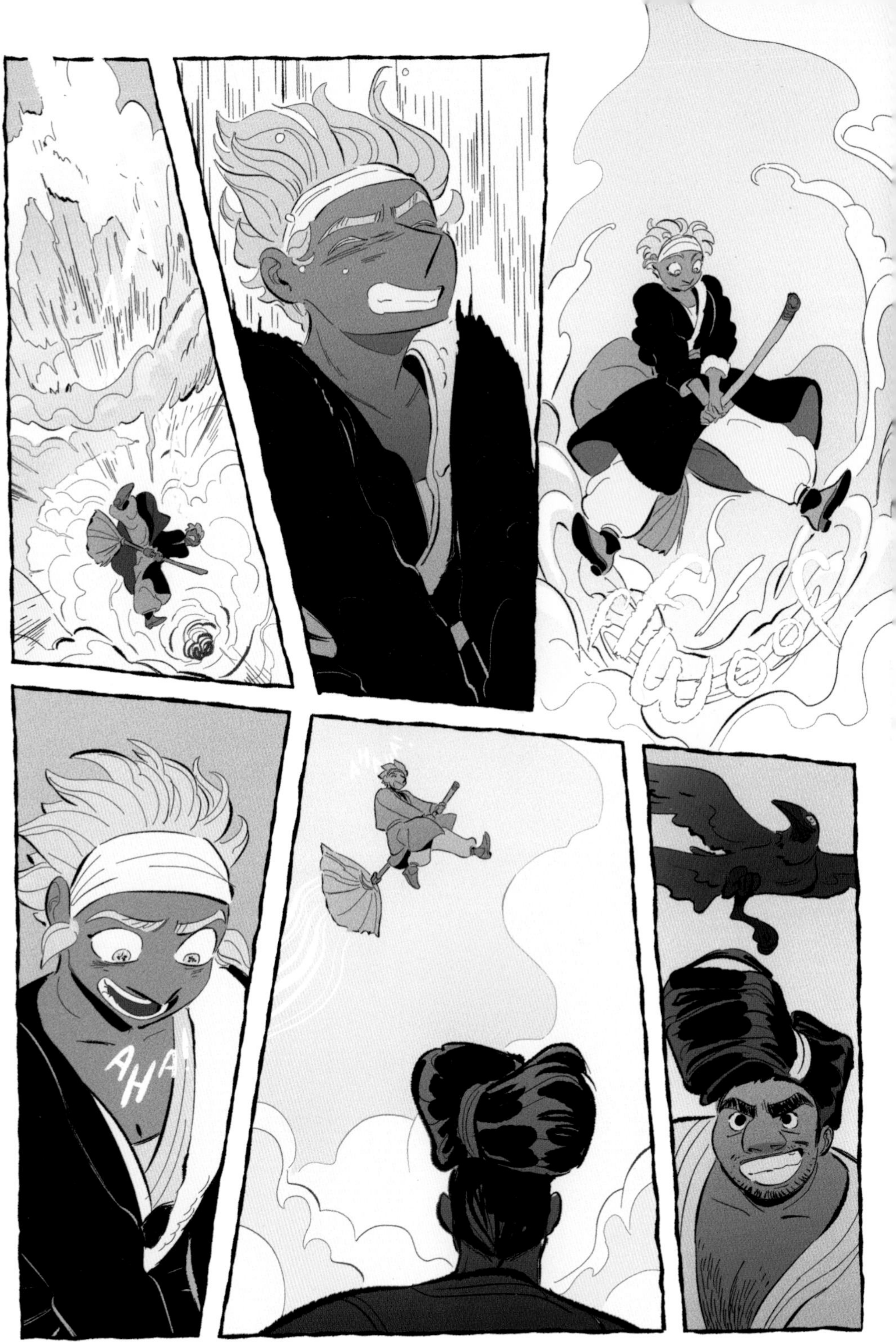
AHA!

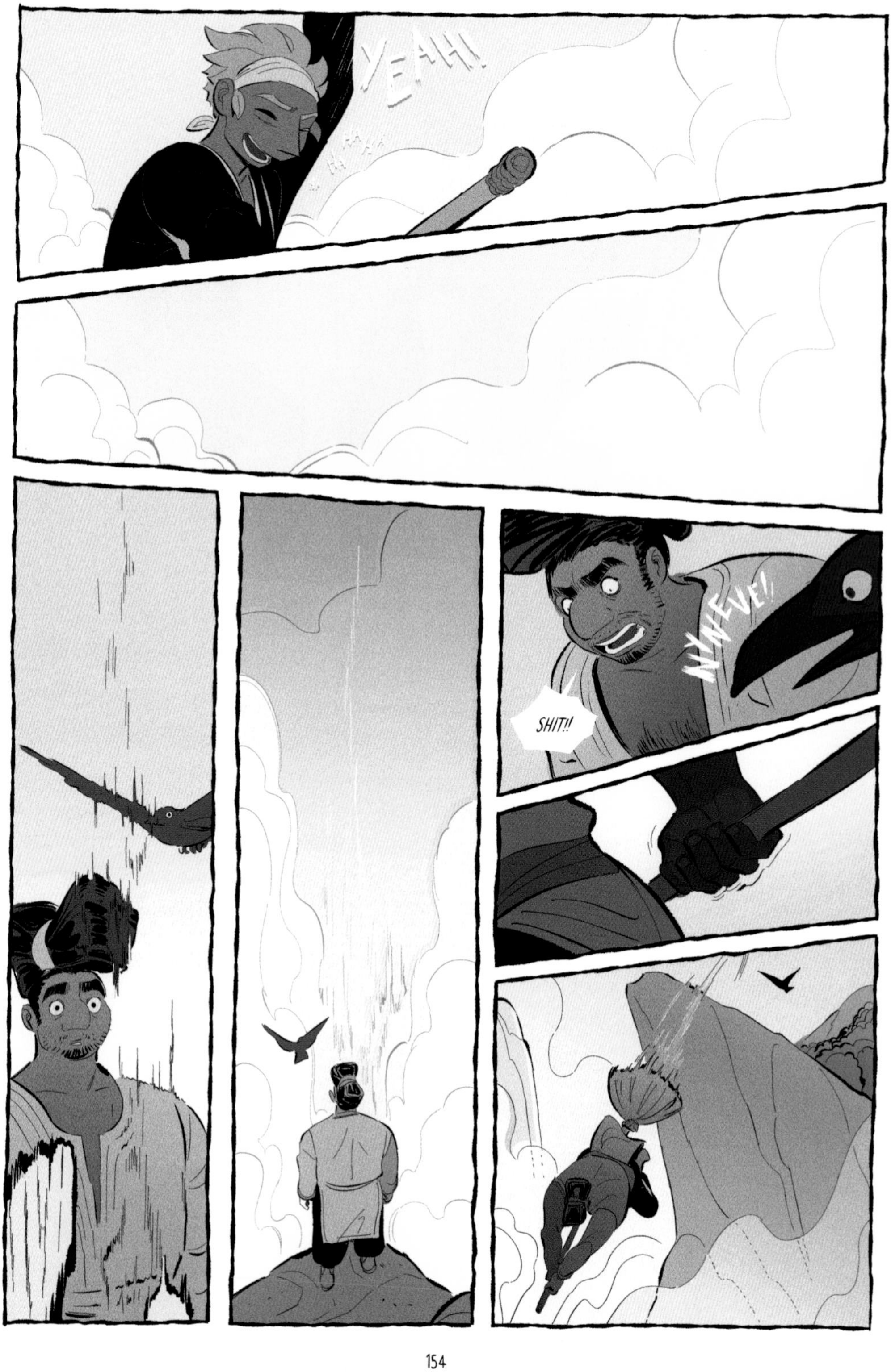
YEAH!
HA HA HA HA
NYNEVE!
SHIT!!

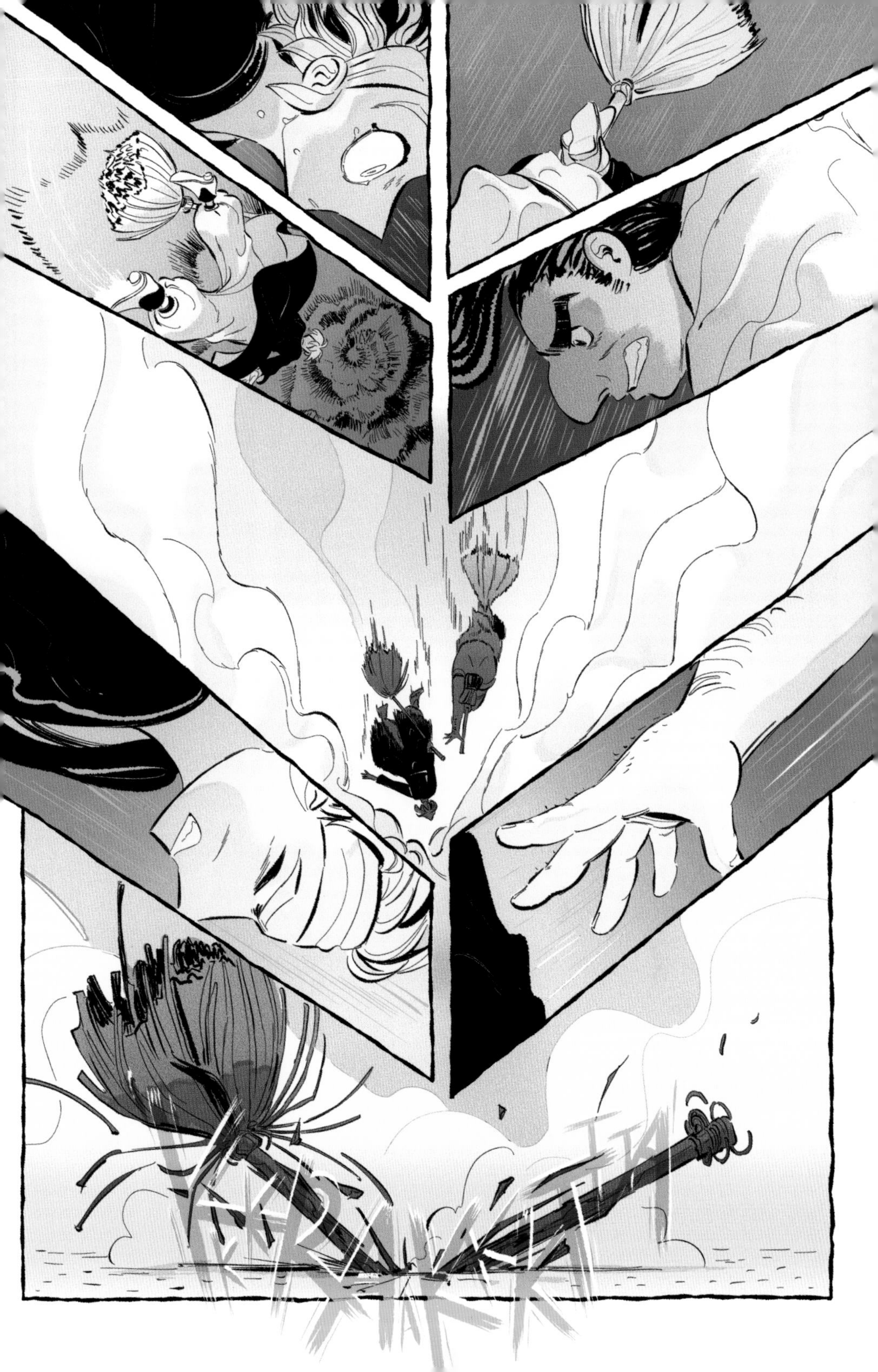

I'M SORRY, KID...

SOMETIMES THE ENCHANTMENT JUST DOESN'T TAKE.

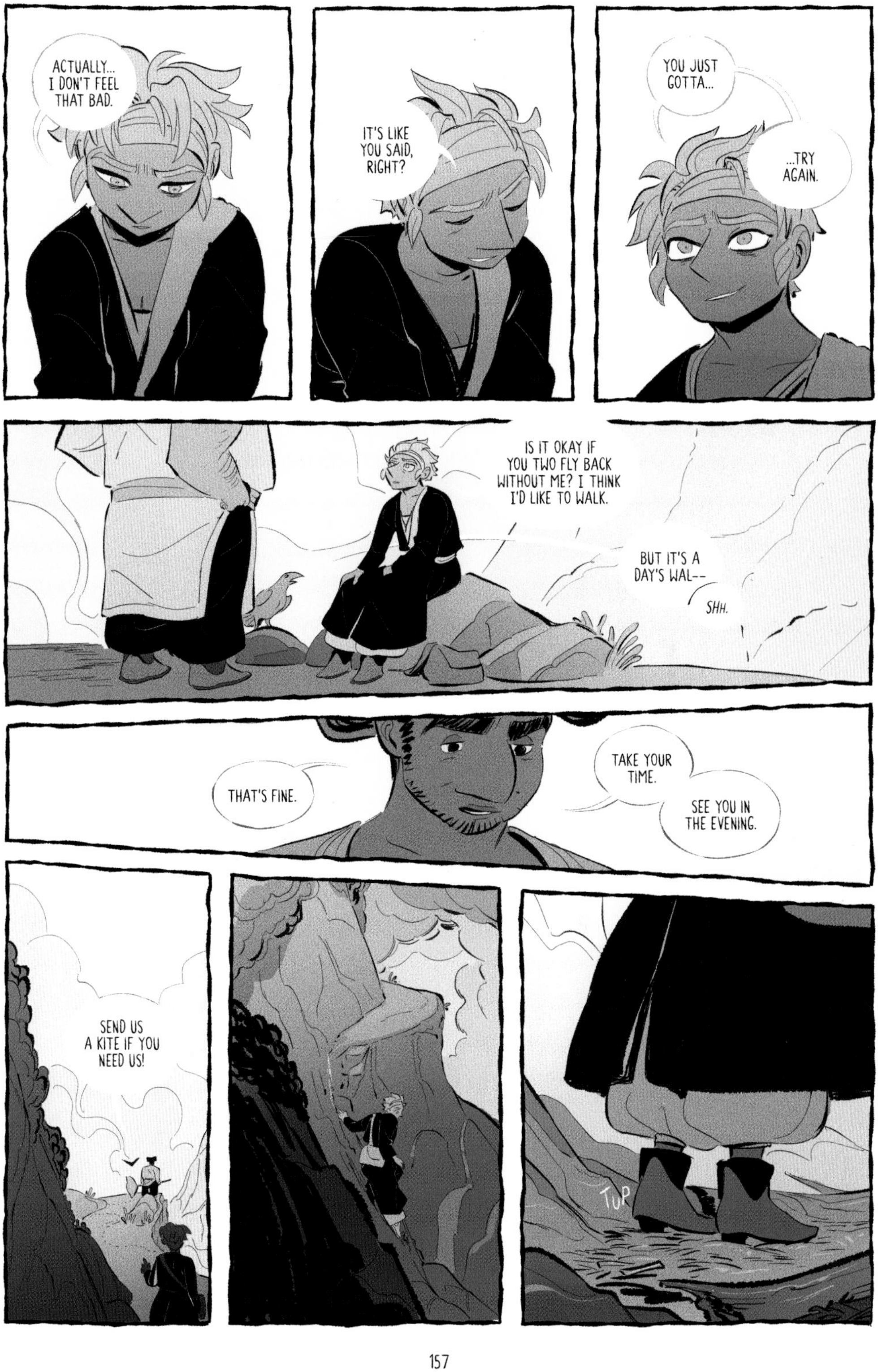
ACTUALLY... I DON'T FEEL THAT BAD.
IT'S LIKE YOU SAID, RIGHT?
YOU JUST GOTTA...
...TRY AGAIN.
IS IT OKAY IF YOU TWO FLY BACK WITHOUT ME? I THINK I'D LIKE TO WALK.
BUT IT'S A DAY'S WAL--
SHH.
THAT'S FINE.
TAKE YOUR TIME.
SEE YOU IN THE EVENING.
SEND US A KITE IF YOU NEED US!
TUP

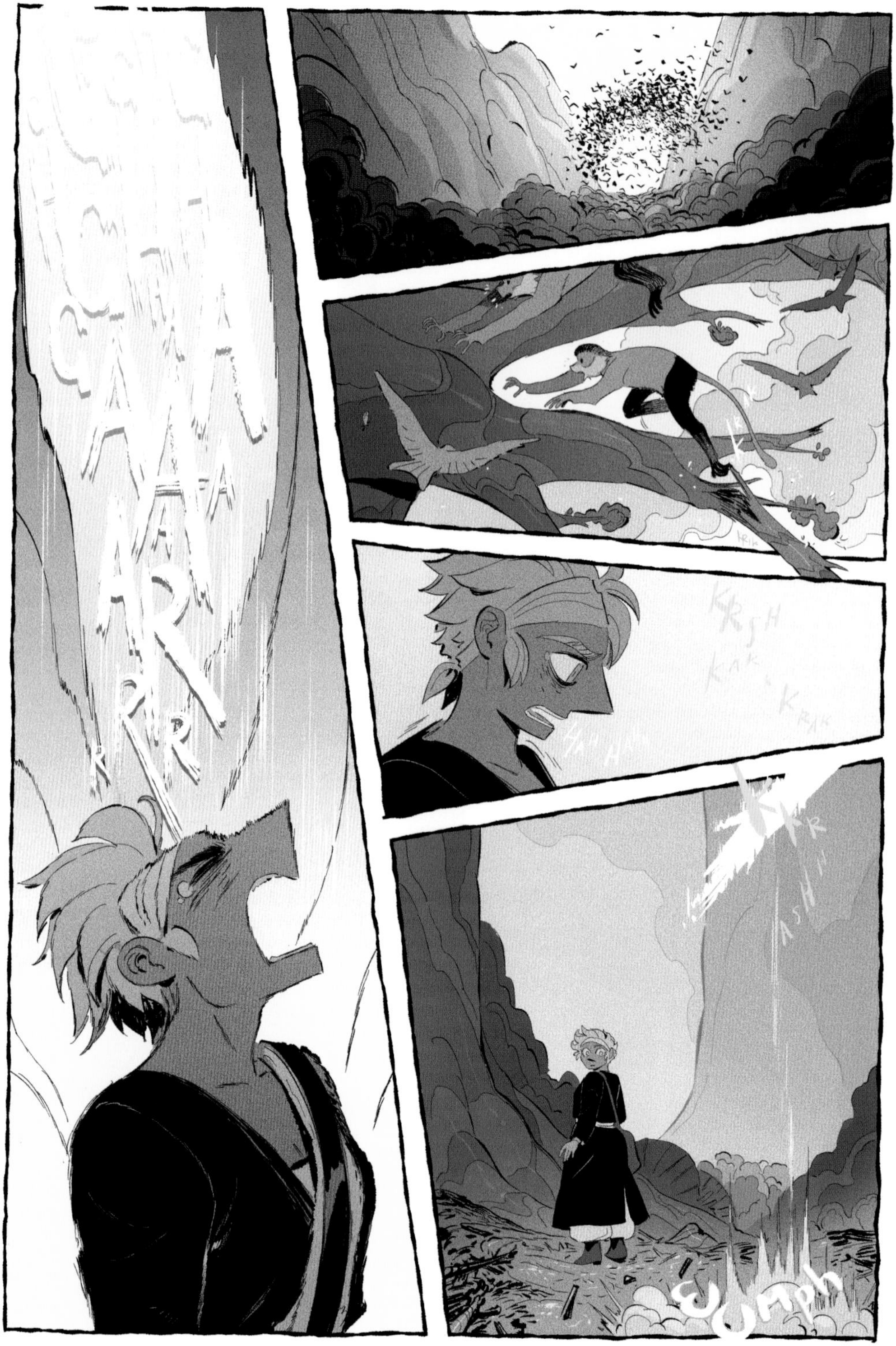
CAAAAAARRRR
KRIK
KRSH
KRAK
KRAK
HAH HAH
KRR
ASHH
WUMPH

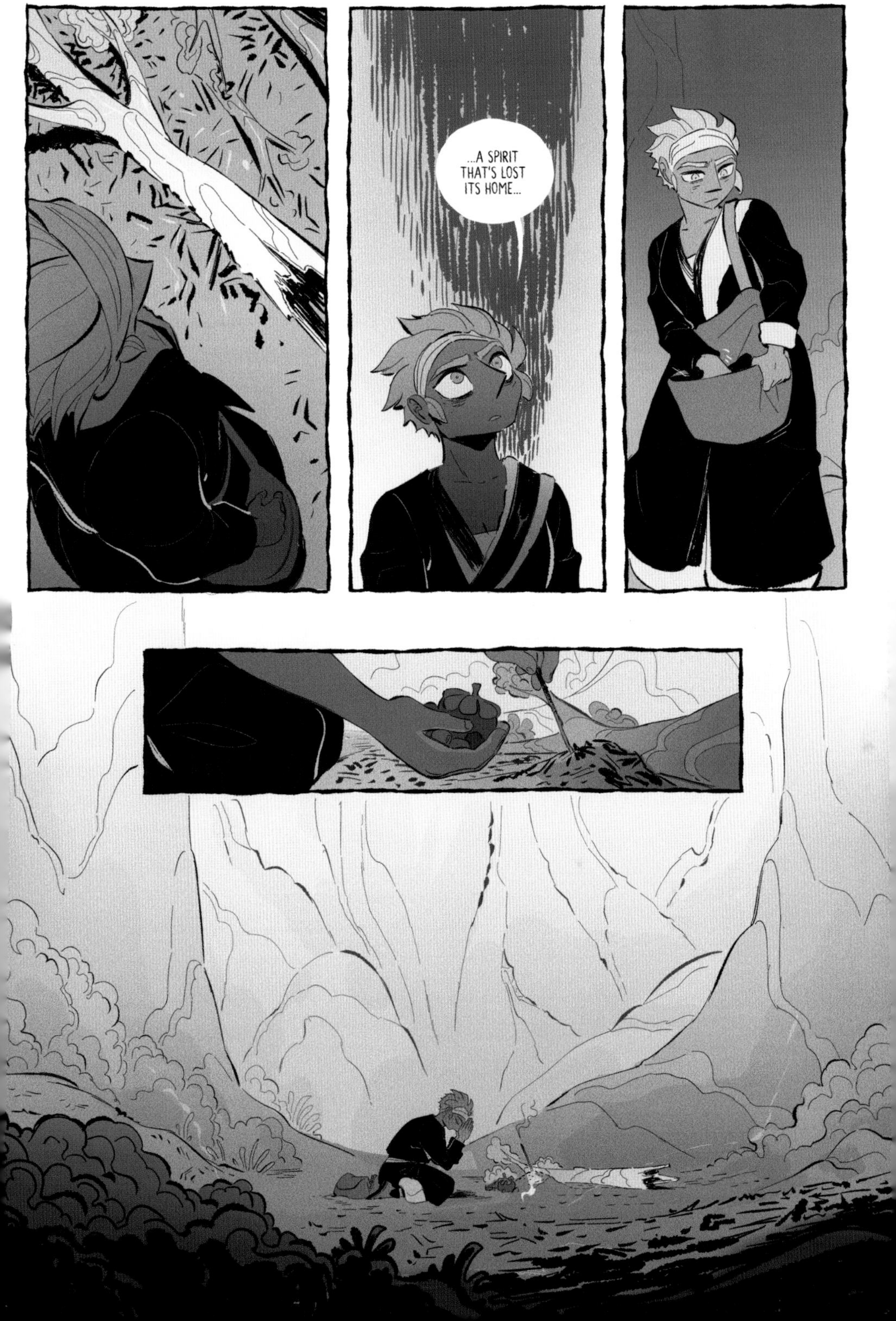
...A SPIRIT THAT'S LOST ITS HOME...

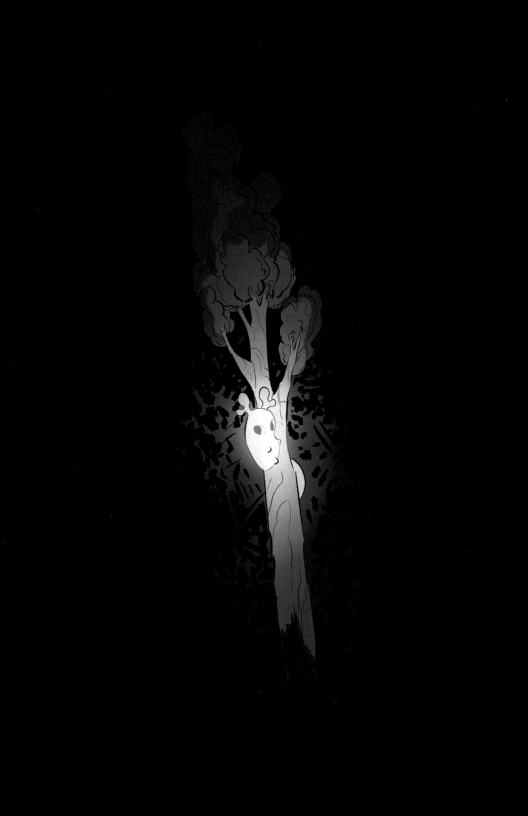

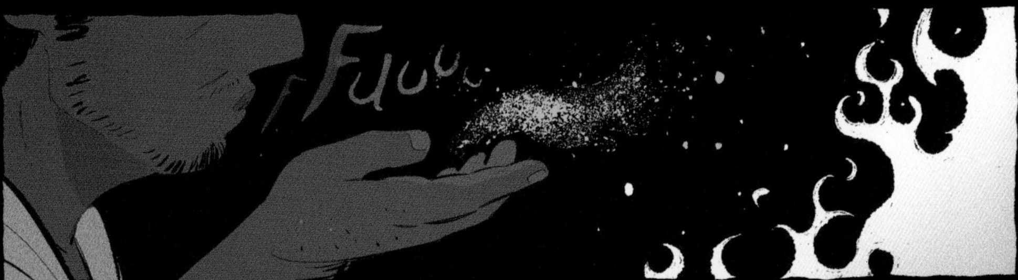
Fuuuu

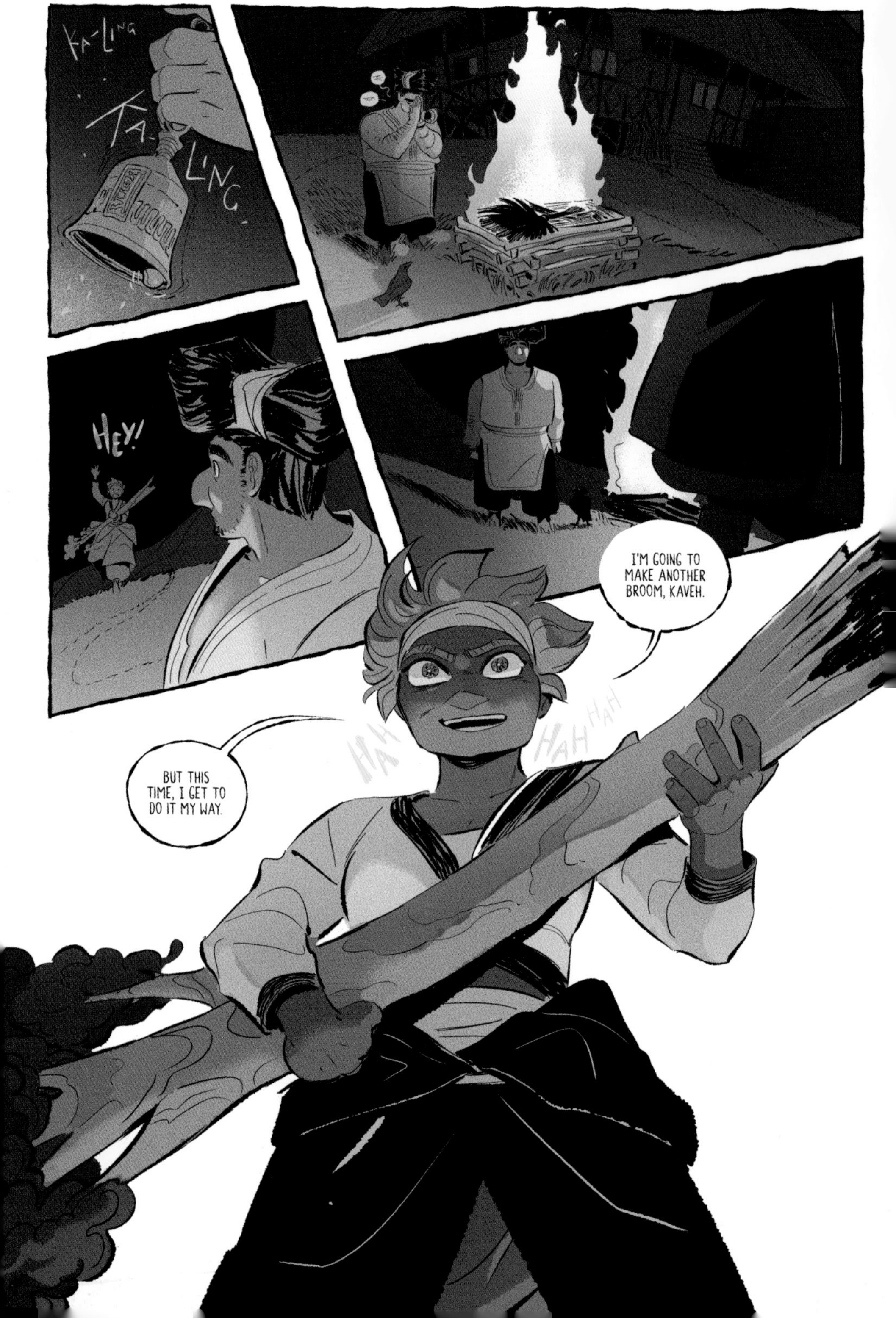
KA-LING
KA-LING.
HEY!
I'M GOING TO MAKE ANOTHER BROOM, KAVEH.
HAH HAH HAH
BUT THIS TIME, I GET TO DO IT MY WAY.

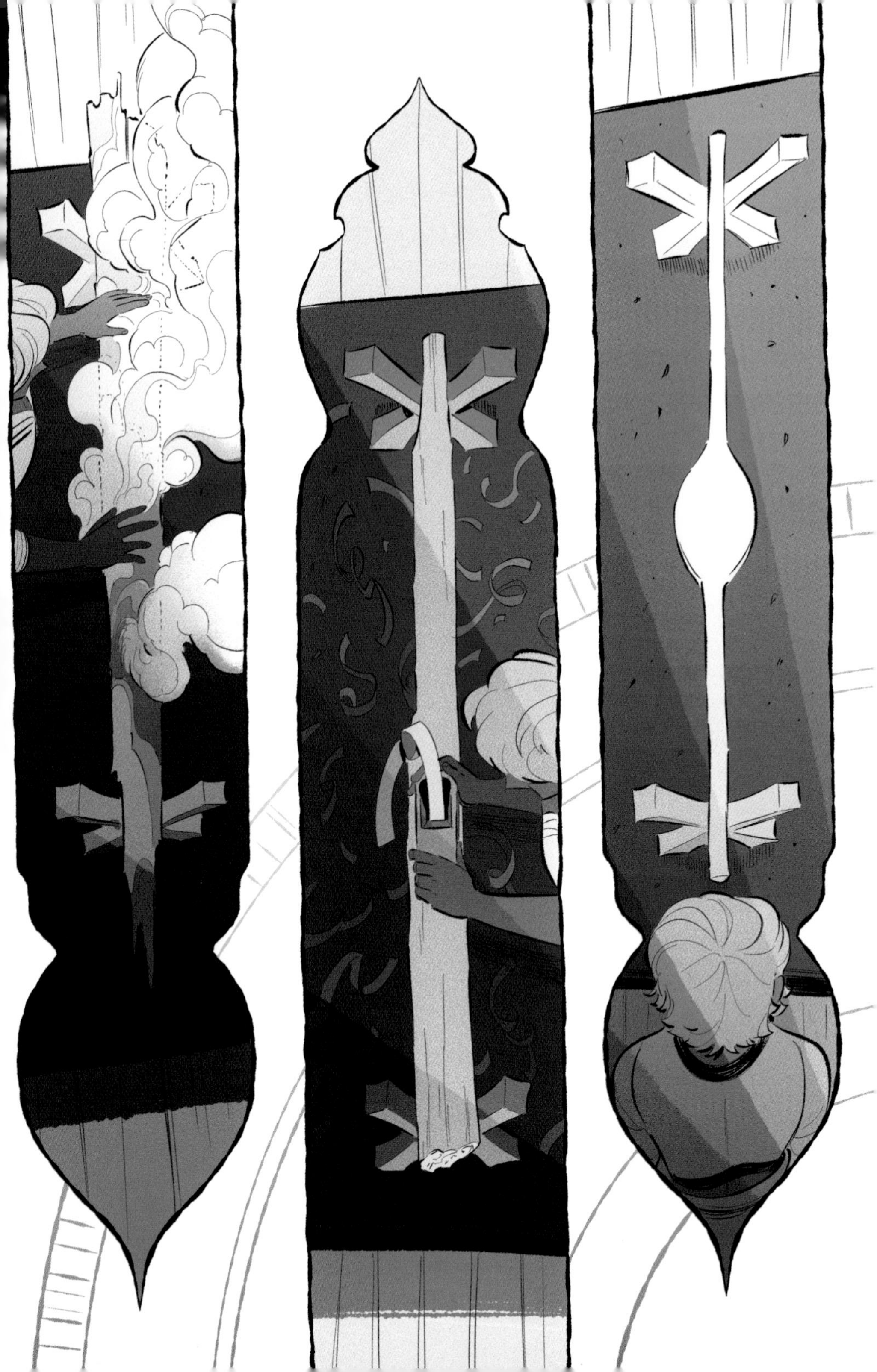

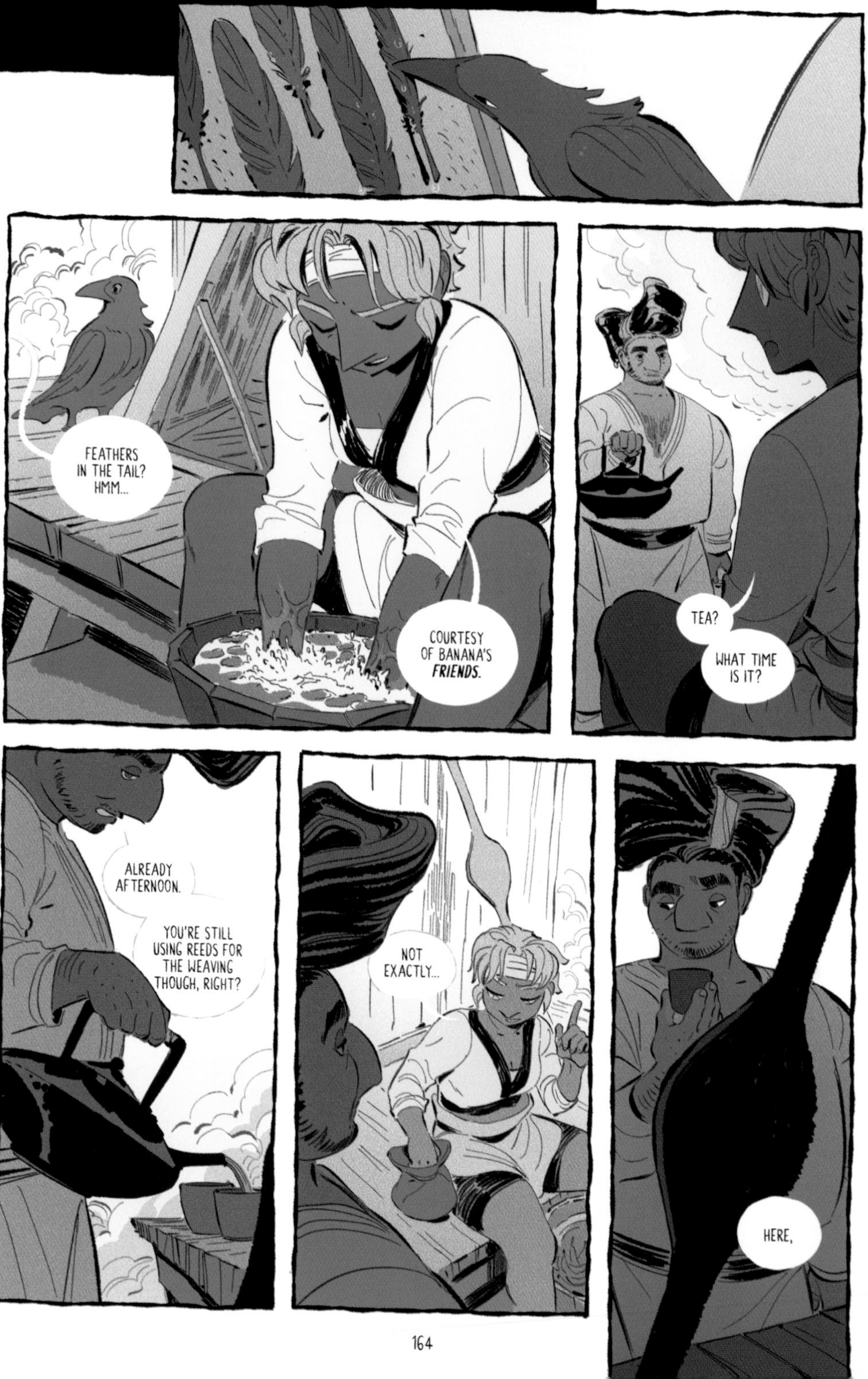
FEATHERS IN THE TAIL? HMM...
COURTESY OF BANANA'S **FRIENDS.**
TEA?
WHAT TIME IS IT?
ALREADY AFTERNOON.
YOU'RE STILL USING REEDS FOR THE WEAVING THOUGH, RIGHT?
NOT EXACTLY...
HERE,

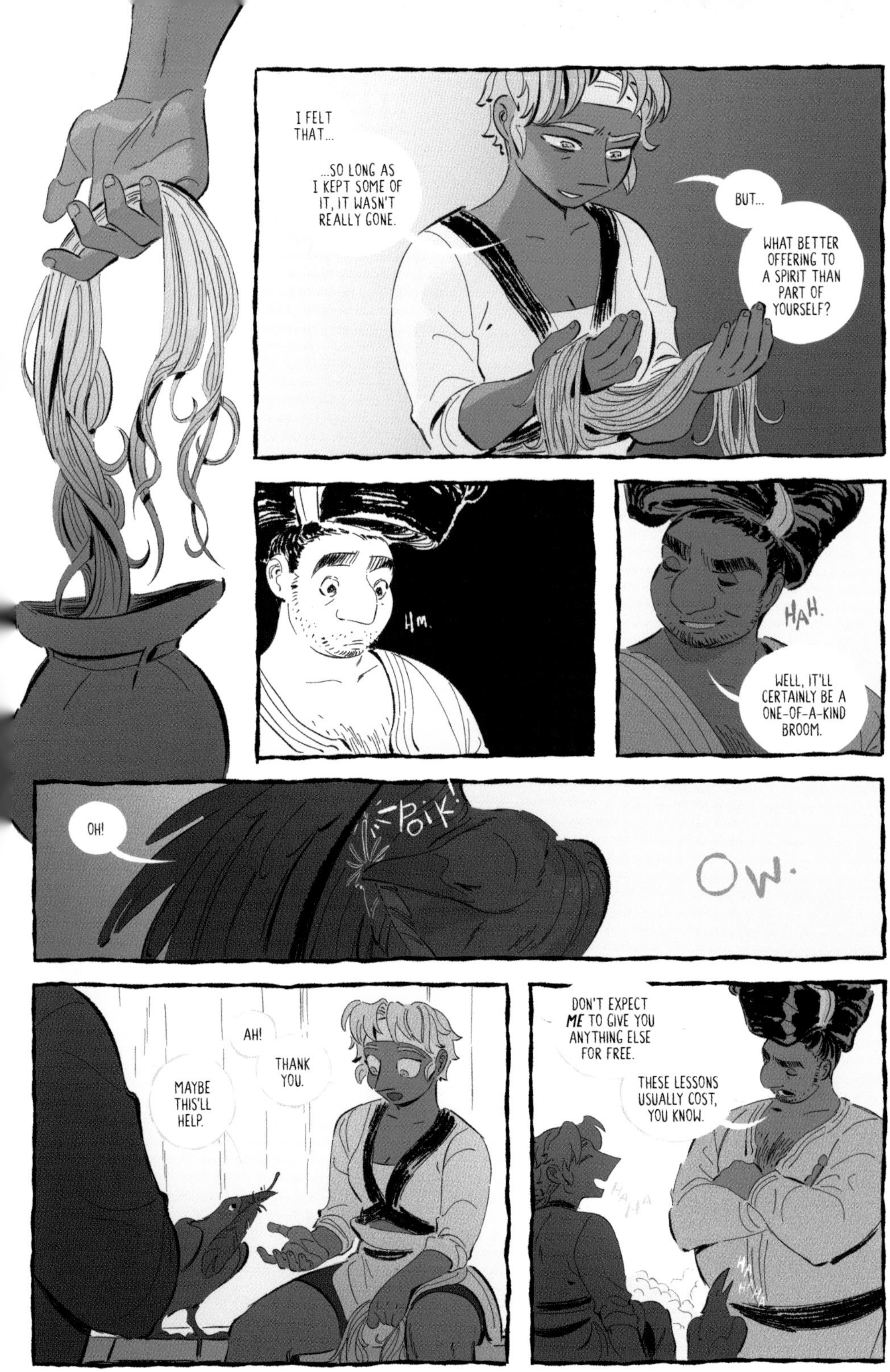
I FELT THAT...
...SO LONG AS I KEPT SOME OF IT, IT WASN'T REALLY GONE.
BUT...
WHAT BETTER OFFERING TO A SPIRIT THAN PART OF YOURSELF?
HM.
HAH.
WELL, IT'LL CERTAINLY BE A ONE-OF-A-KIND BROOM.
OH!
POIK!
OW.
MAYBE THIS'LL HELP.
AH!
THANK YOU.
DON'T EXPECT ME TO GIVE YOU ANYTHING ELSE FOR FREE.
THESE LESSONS USUALLY COST, YOU KNOW.
HAHA
HA HA HA

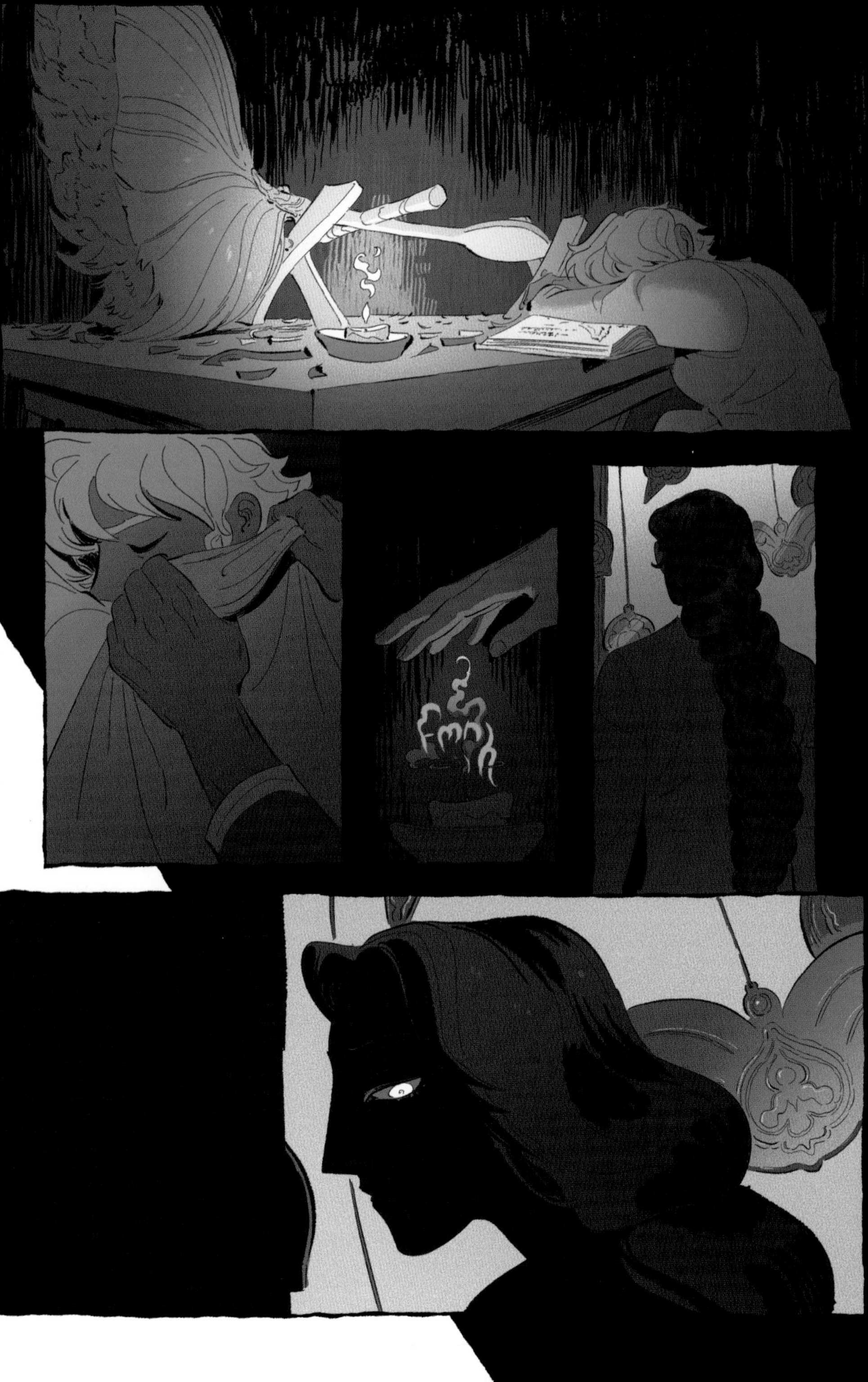

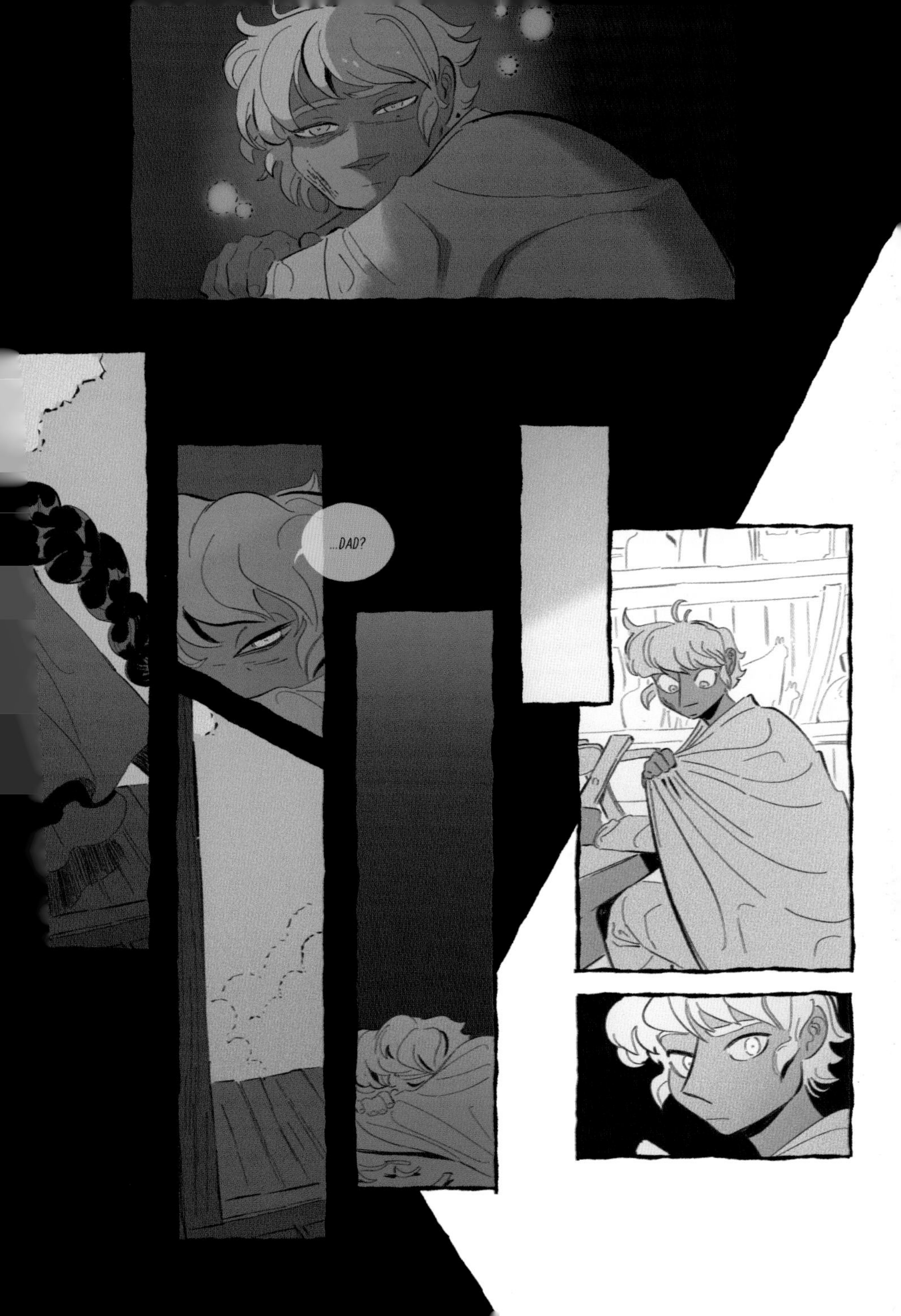
...DAD?

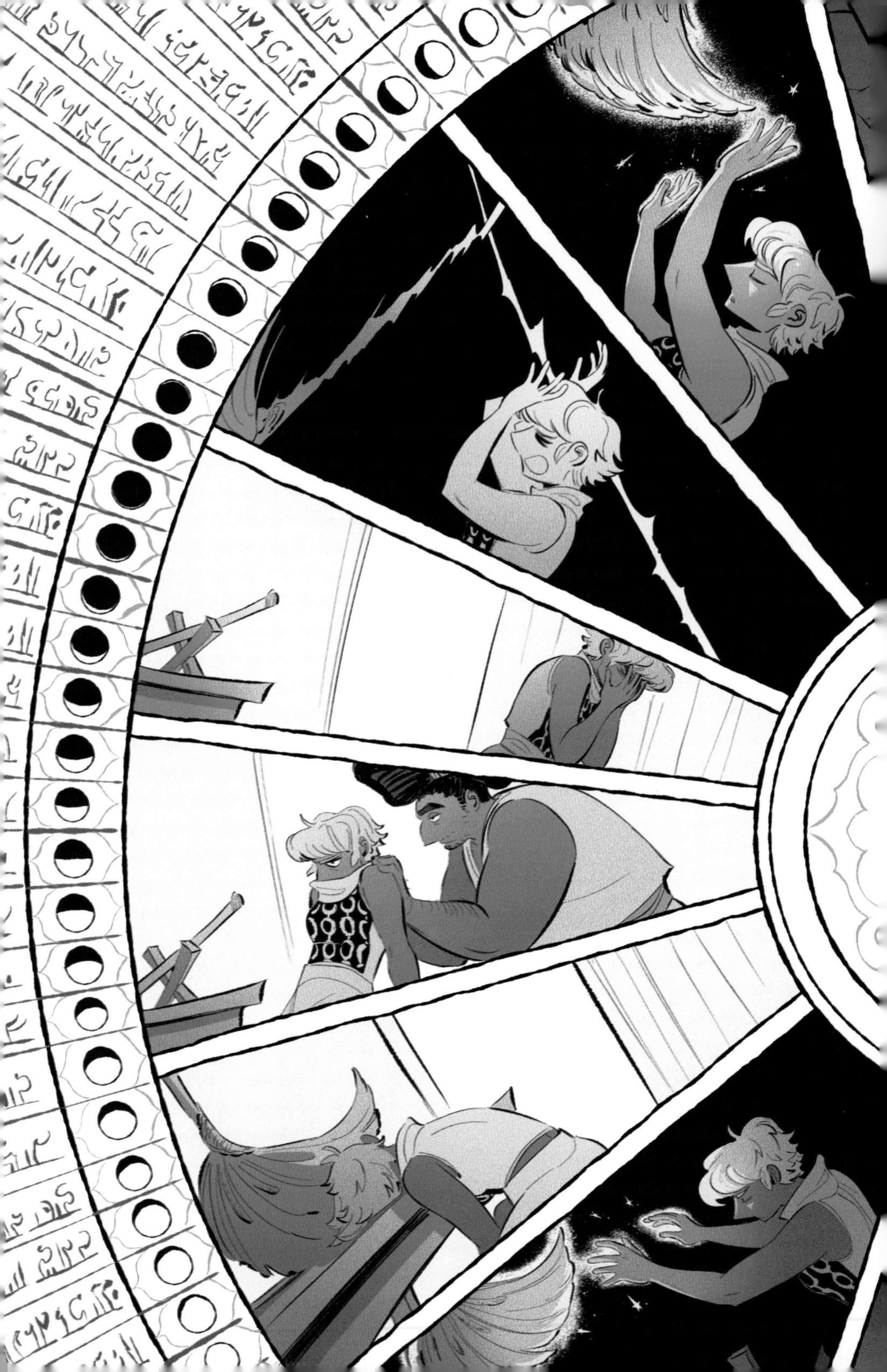

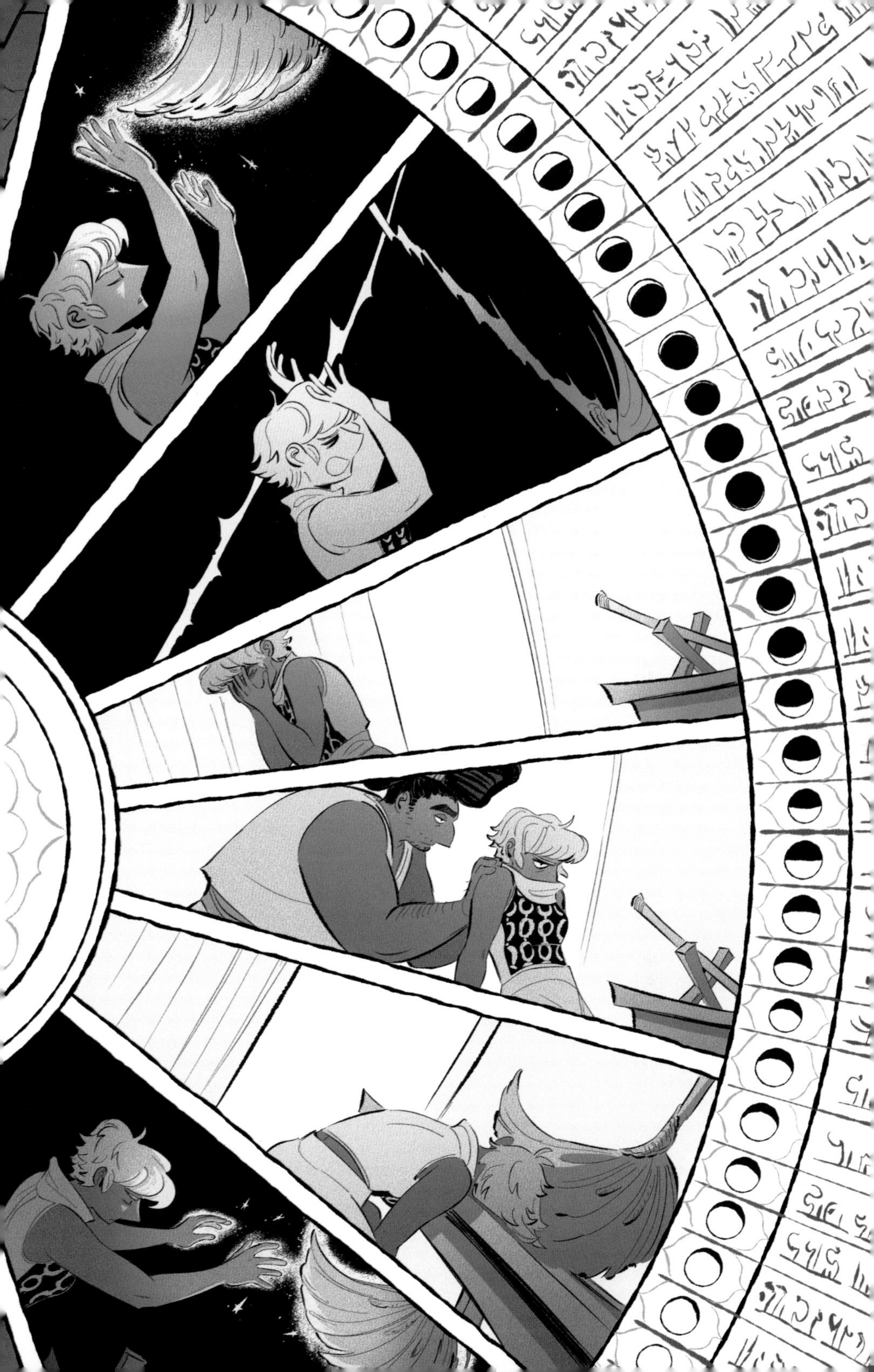

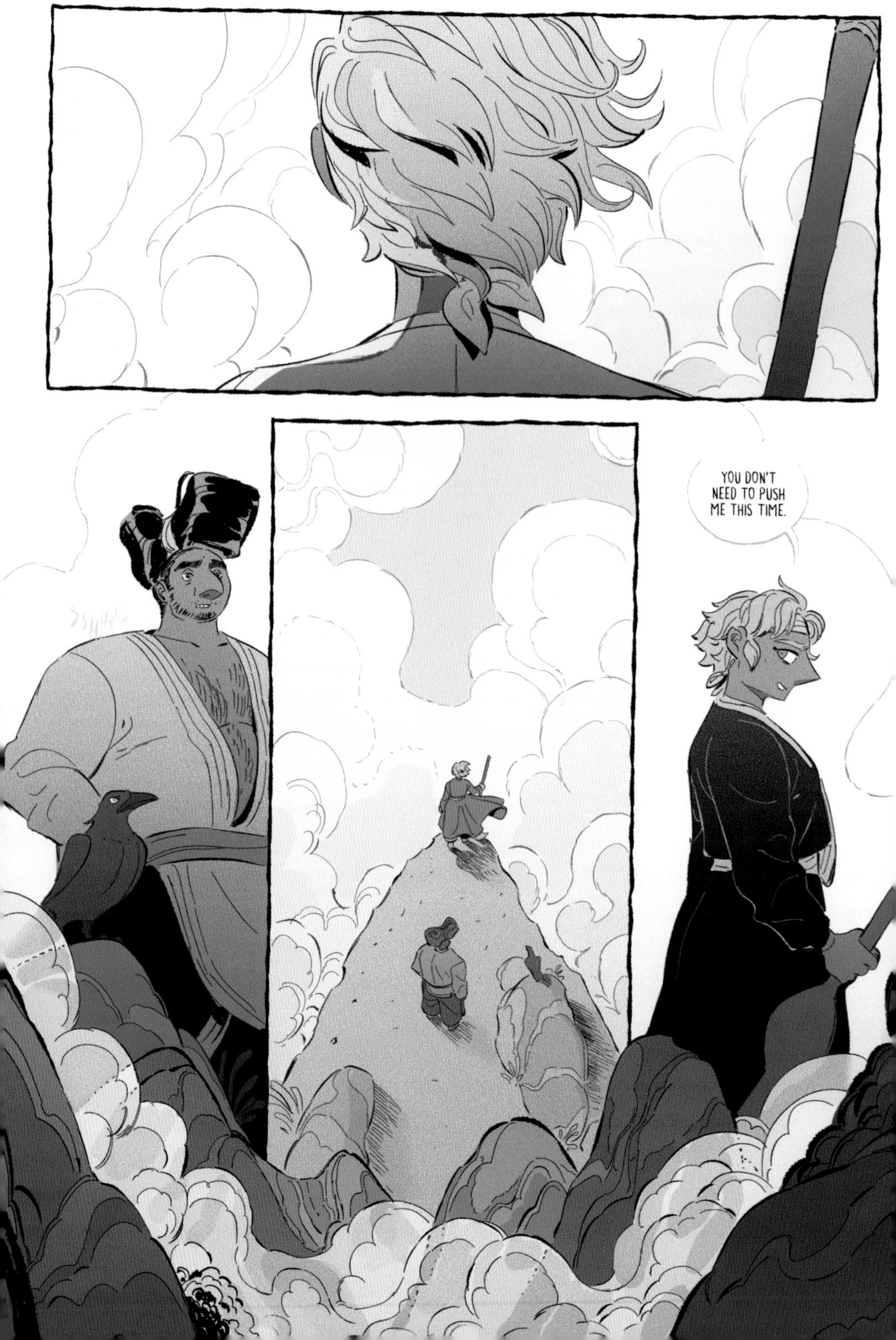
YOU DON'T NEED TO PUSH ME THIS TIME.

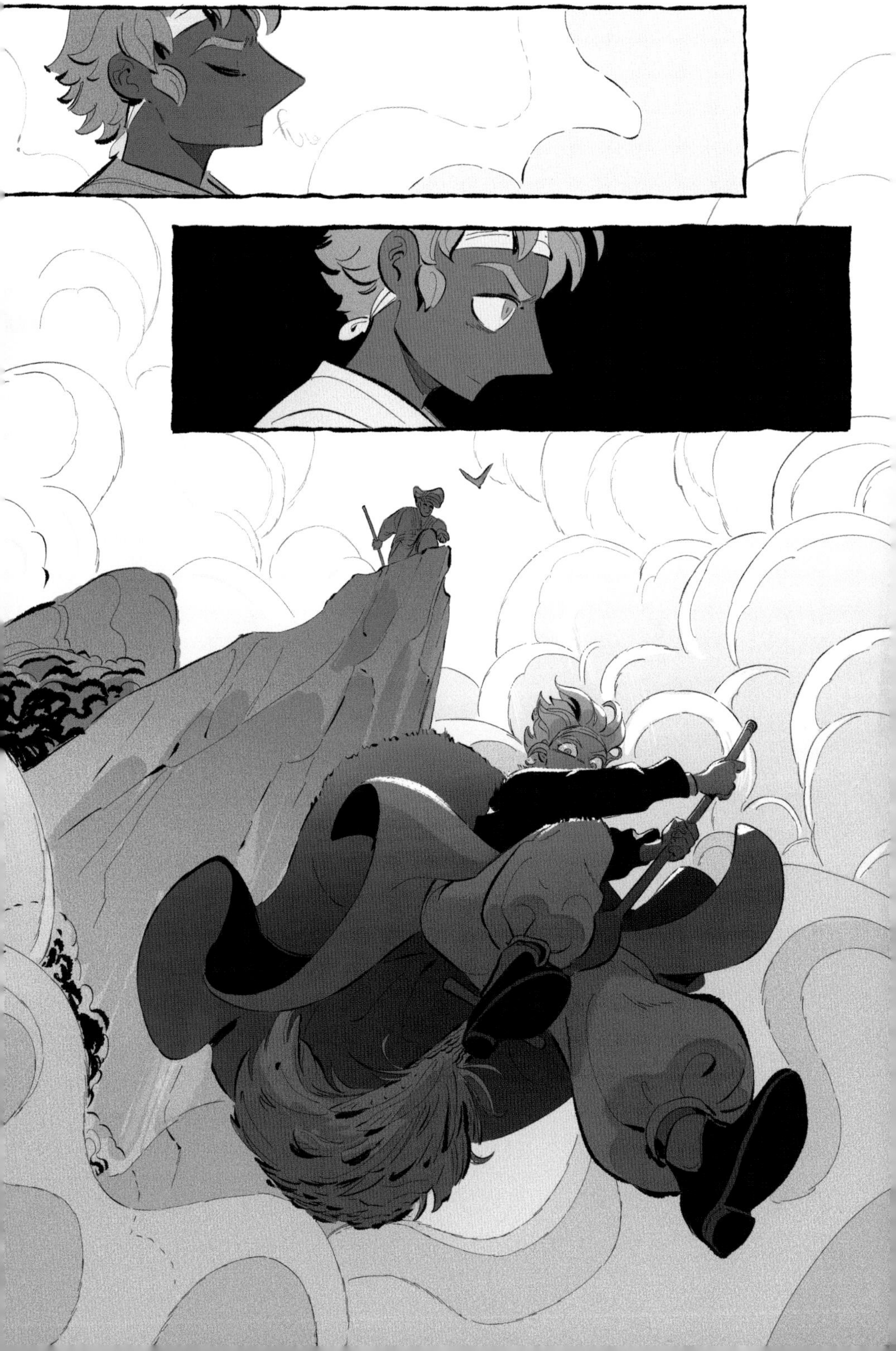
fuu

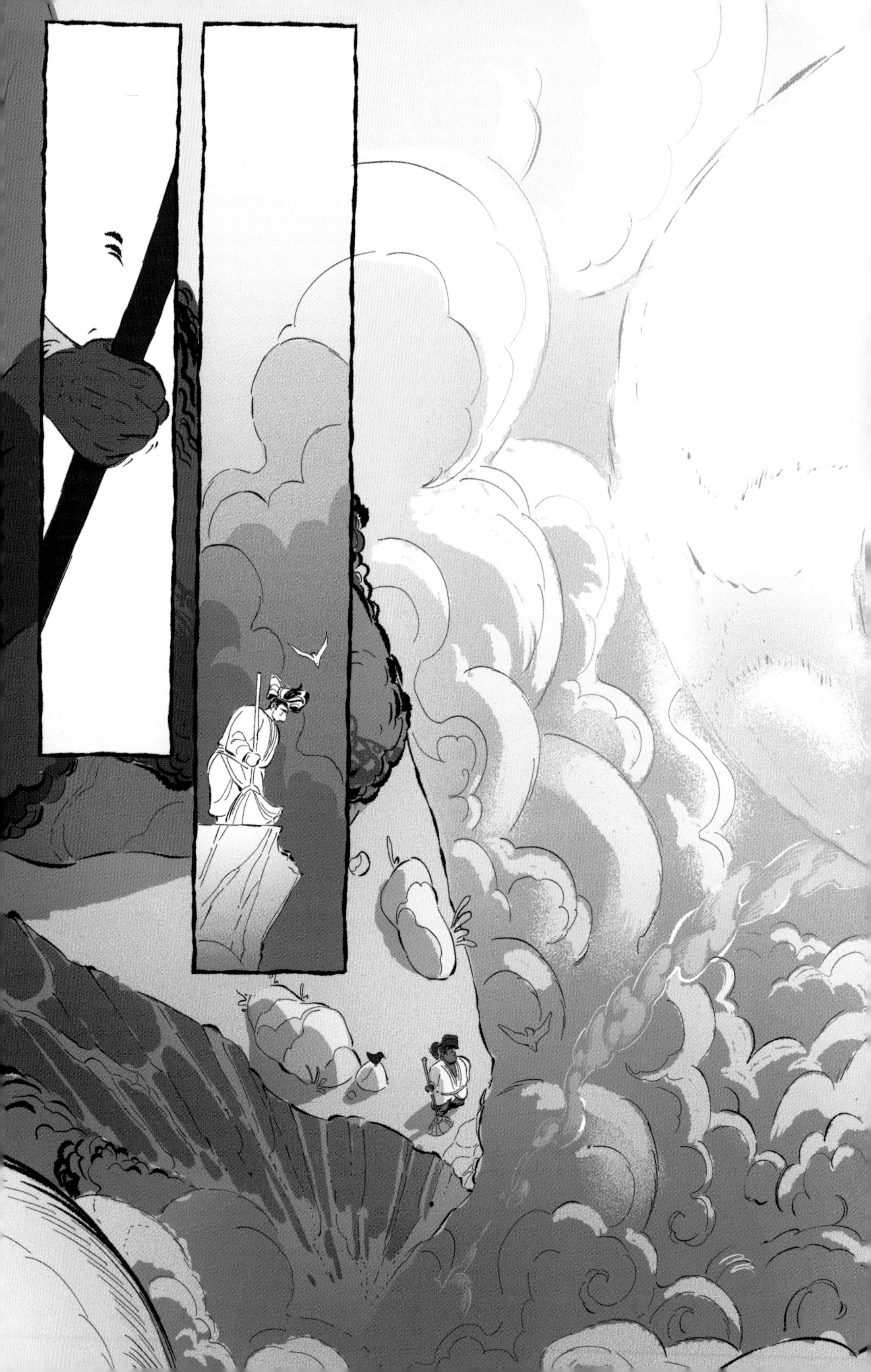

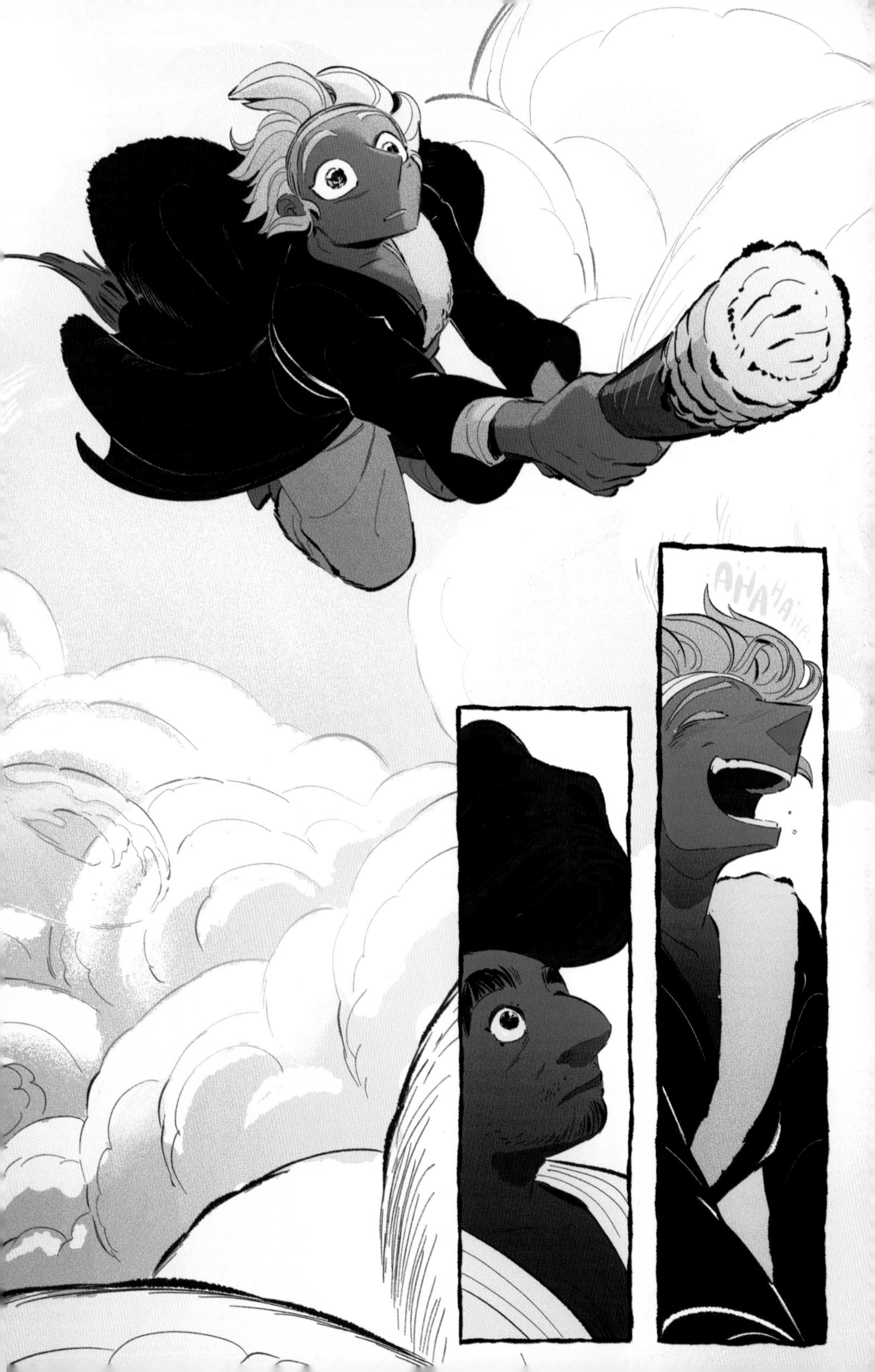
AHAHAHA.

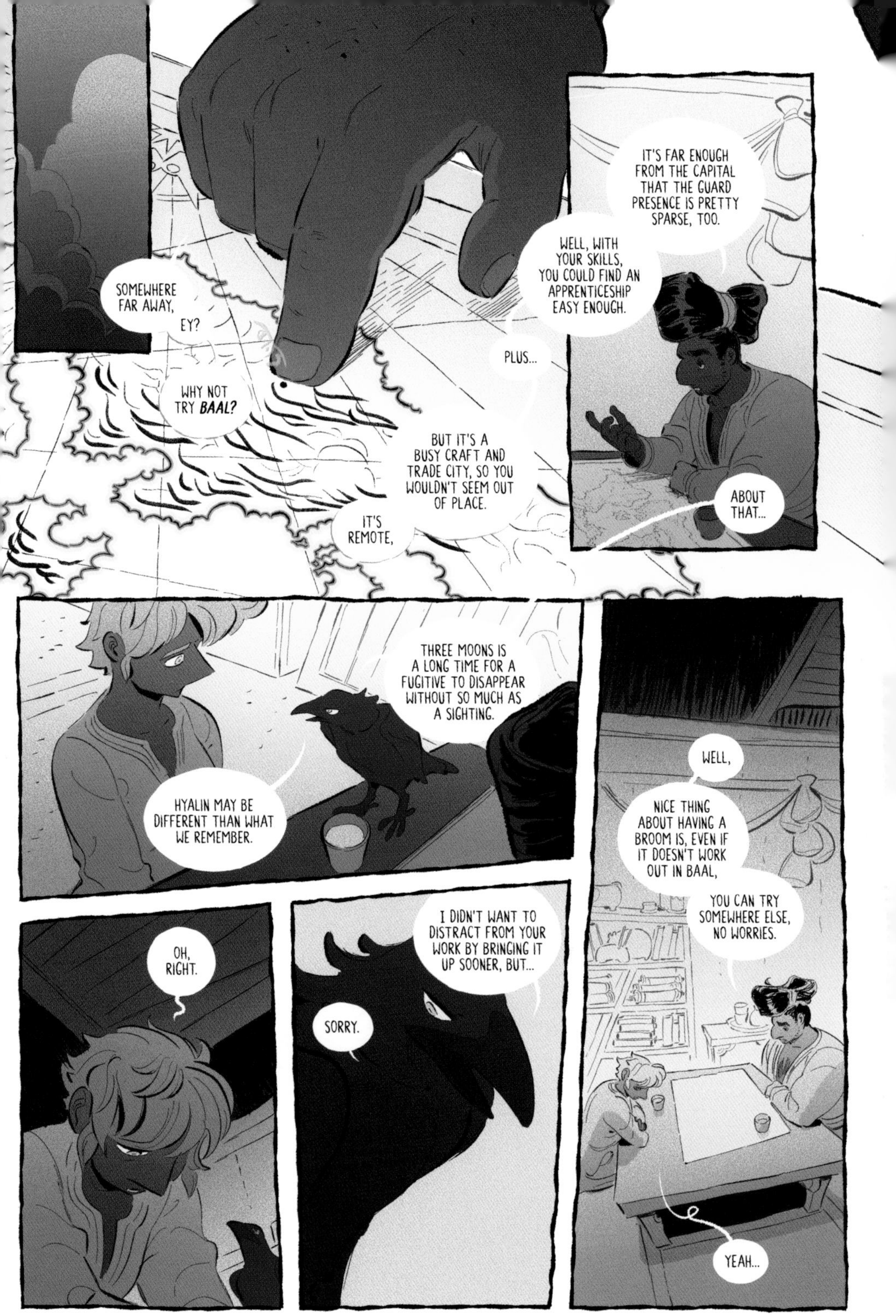

SOMEWHERE FAR AWAY, EY?
WHY NOT TRY ***BAAL?***
IT'S REMOTE,
BUT IT'S A BUSY CRAFT AND TRADE CITY, SO YOU WOULDN'T SEEM OUT OF PLACE.
IT'S FAR ENOUGH FROM THE CAPITAL THAT THE GUARD PRESENCE IS PRETTY SPARSE, TOO.
PLUS...
WELL, WITH YOUR SKILLS, YOU COULD FIND AN APPRENTICESHIP EASY ENOUGH.
ABOUT THAT...
THREE MOONS IS A LONG TIME FOR A FUGITIVE TO DISAPPEAR WITHOUT SO MUCH AS A SIGHTING.
HYALIN MAY BE DIFFERENT THAN WHAT WE REMEMBER.
OH, RIGHT.
I DIDN'T WANT TO DISTRACT FROM YOUR WORK BY BRINGING IT UP SOONER, BUT...
SORRY.
WELL,
NICE THING ABOUT HAVING A BROOM IS, EVEN IF IT DOESN'T WORK OUT IN BAAL,
YOU CAN TRY SOMEWHERE ELSE, NO WORRIES.
YEAH...

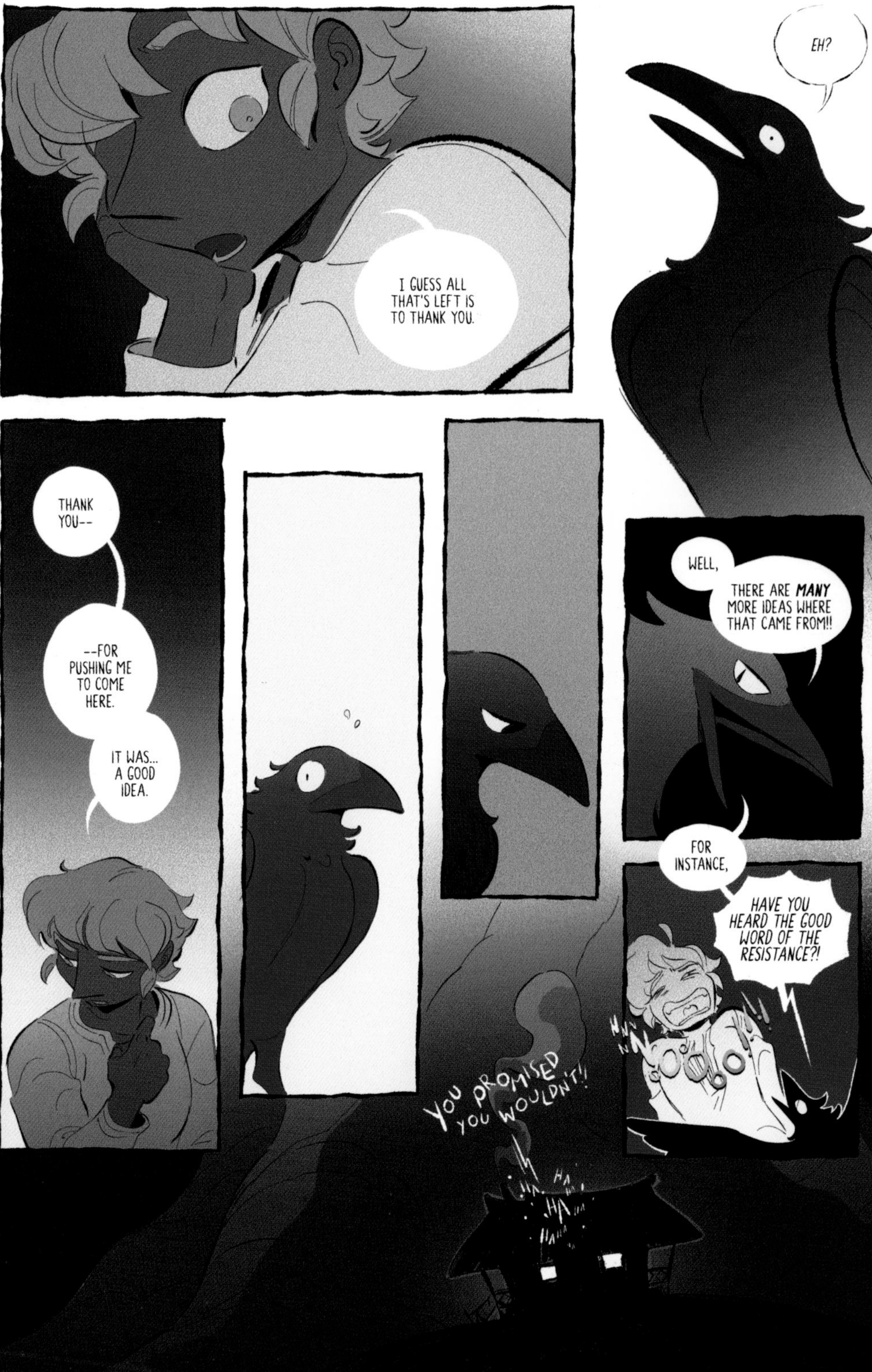
I GUESS ALL THAT'S LEFT IS TO THANK YOU.
EH?
THANK YOU--
--FOR PUSHING ME TO COME HERE.
IT WAS... A GOOD IDEA.
WELL,
THERE ARE **MANY** MORE IDEAS WHERE THAT CAME FROM!!
FOR INSTANCE,
HAVE YOU HEARD THE GOOD WORD OF THE RESISTANCE?!
YOU PROMISED YOU WOULDN'T!!

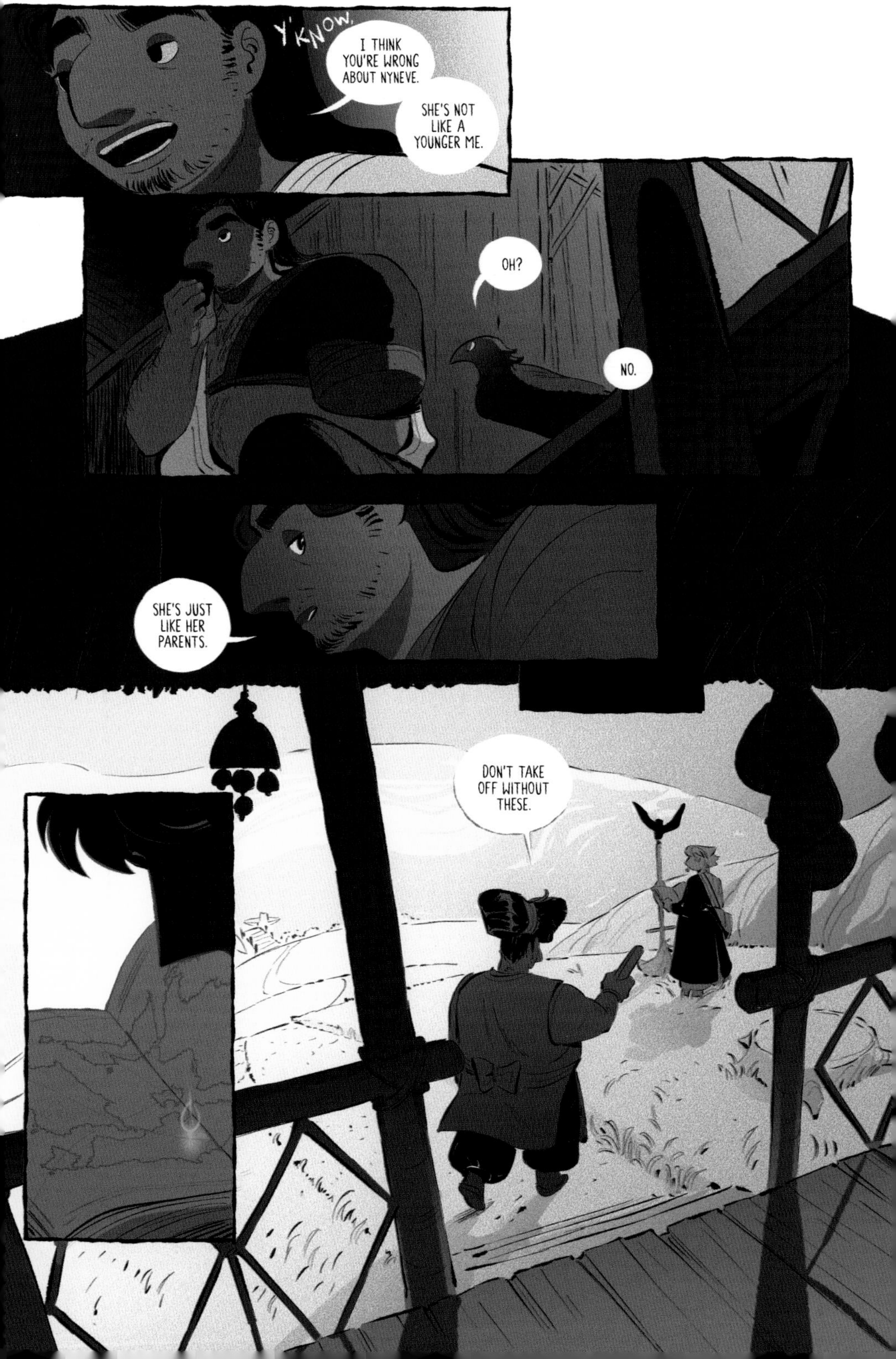

Y'KNOW,
I THINK YOU'RE WRONG ABOUT NYNEVE.
SHE'S NOT LIKE A YOUNGER ME.
OH?
NO.
SHE'S JUST LIKE HER PARENTS.
DON'T TAKE OFF WITHOUT THESE.

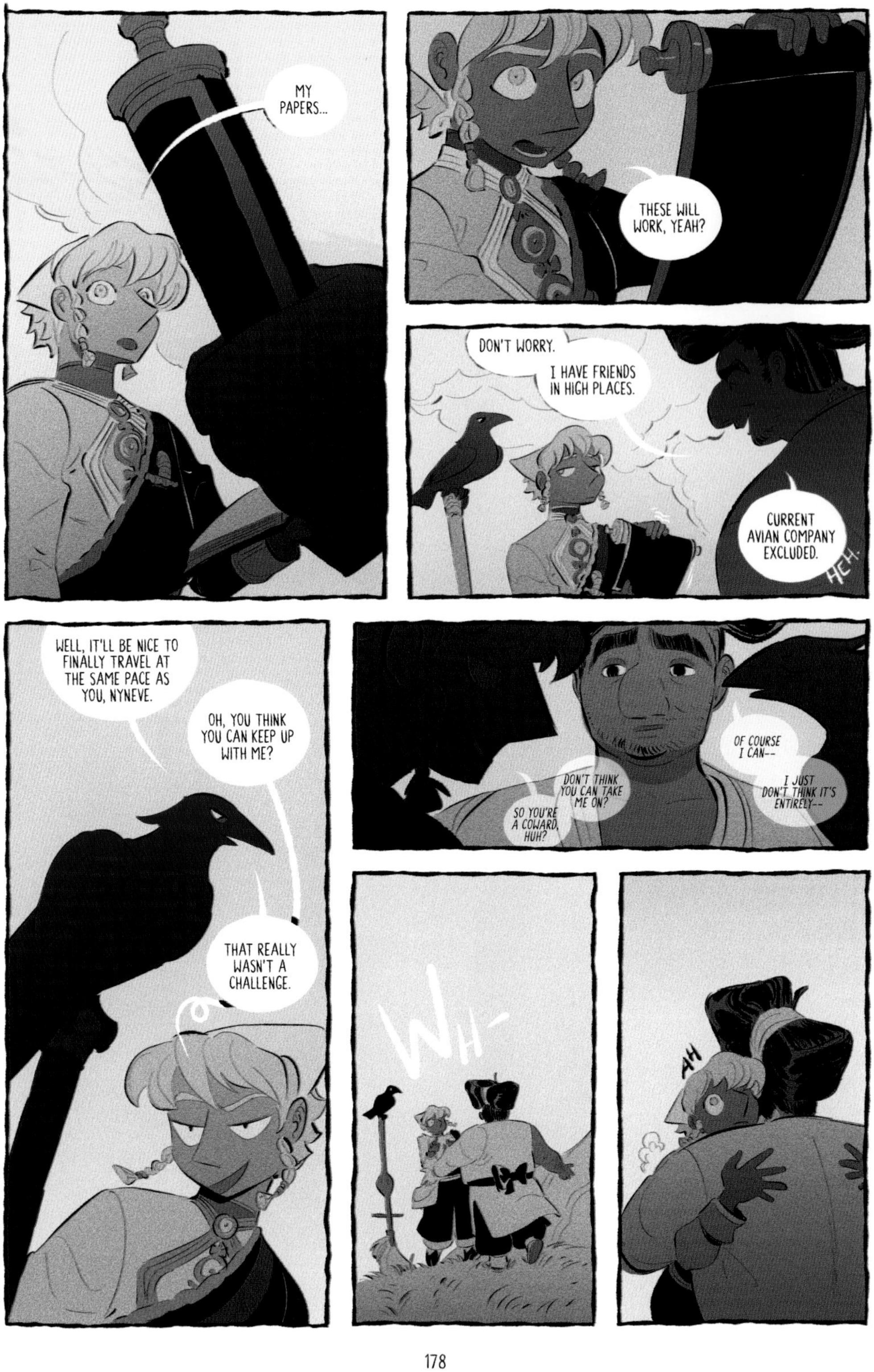
MY PAPERS...
THESE WILL WORK, YEAH?
DON'T WORRY.
I HAVE FRIENDS IN HIGH PLACES.
CURRENT AVIAN COMPANY EXCLUDED.
HEH.
WELL, IT'LL BE NICE TO FINALLY TRAVEL AT THE SAME PACE AS YOU, NYNEVE.
OH, YOU THINK YOU CAN KEEP UP WITH ME?
THAT REALLY WASN'T A CHALLENGE.
OF COURSE I CAN--
I JUST DON'T THINK IT'S ENTIRELY--
DON'T THINK YOU CAN TAKE ME ON?
SO YOU'RE A COWARD, HUH?
WH-
AH

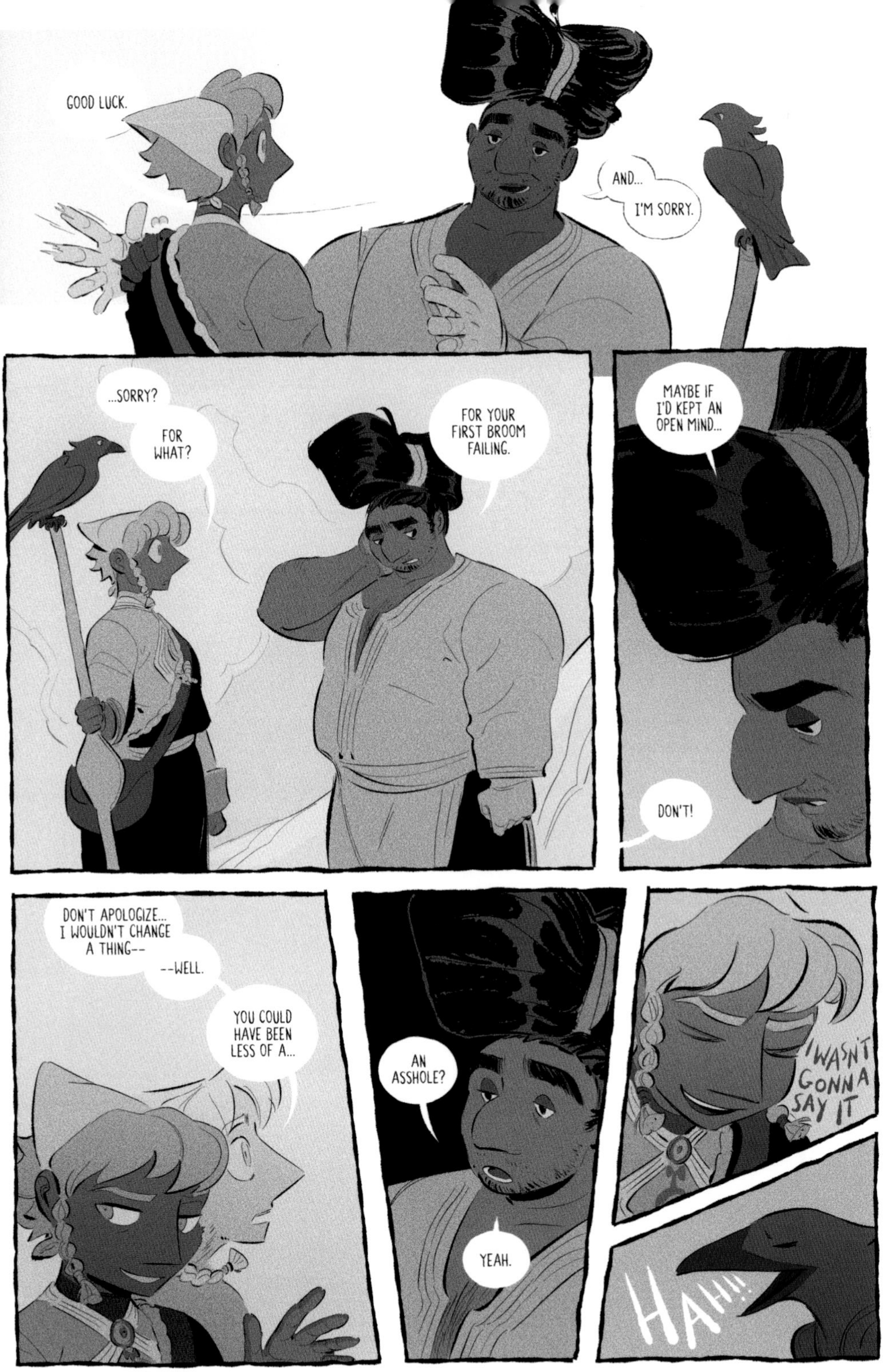
GOOD LUCK.
AND...
I'M SORRY.
...SORRY?
FOR WHAT?
FOR YOUR FIRST BROOM FAILING.
MAYBE IF I'D KEPT AN OPEN MIND...
DON'T!
DON'T APOLOGIZE... I WOULDN'T CHANGE A THING--
--WELL.
YOU COULD HAVE BEEN LESS OF A...
AN ASSHOLE?
YEAH.
I WASN'T GONNA SAY IT
HAH!!

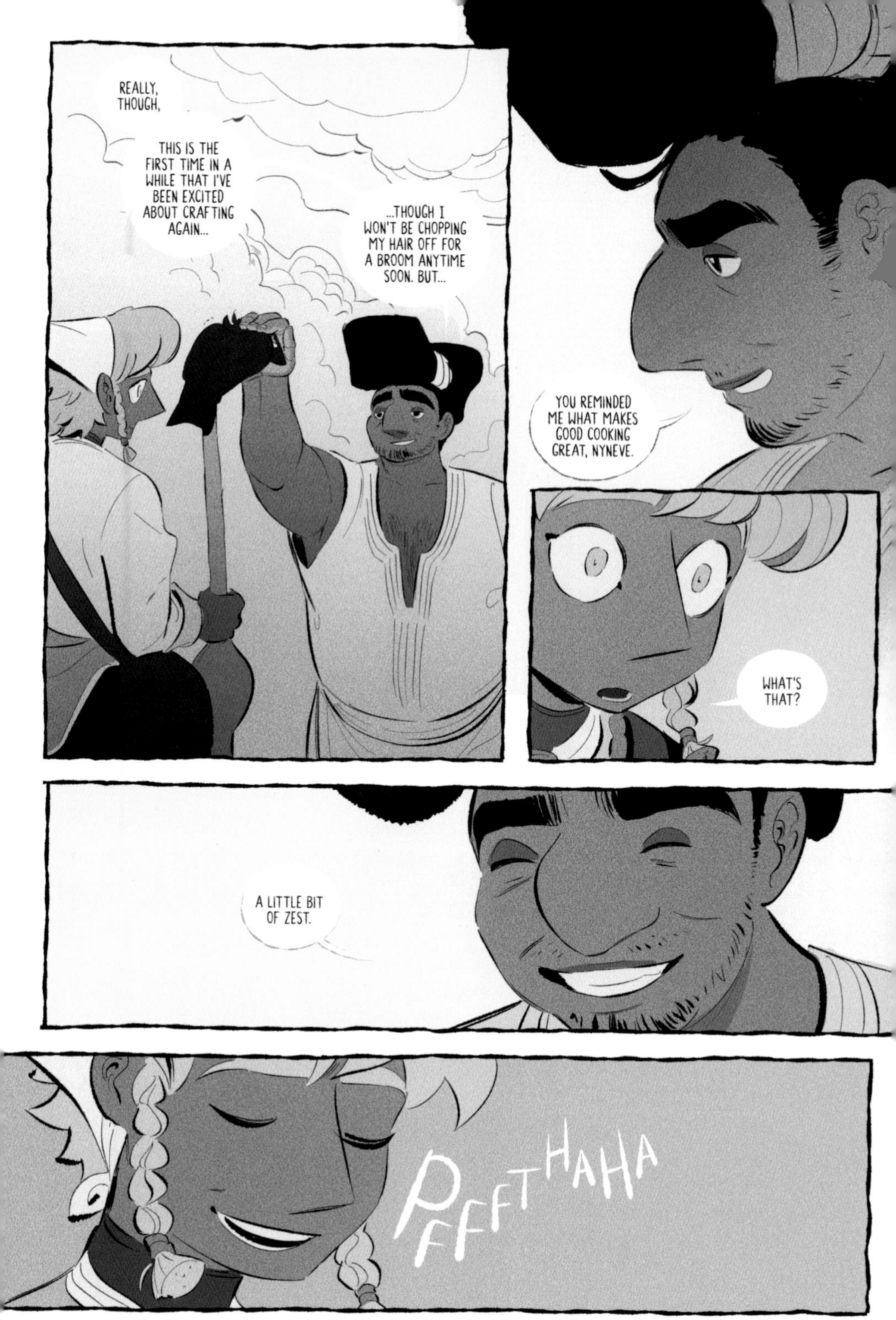
REALLY, THOUGH,
THIS IS THE FIRST TIME IN A WHILE THAT I'VE BEEN EXCITED ABOUT CRAFTING AGAIN...
...THOUGH I WON'T BE CHOPPING MY HAIR OFF FOR A BROOM ANYTIME SOON. BUT...
YOU REMINDED ME WHAT MAKES GOOD COOKING GREAT, NYNEVE.
WHAT'S THAT?
A LITTLE BIT OF ZEST.
PFFFTHAHA

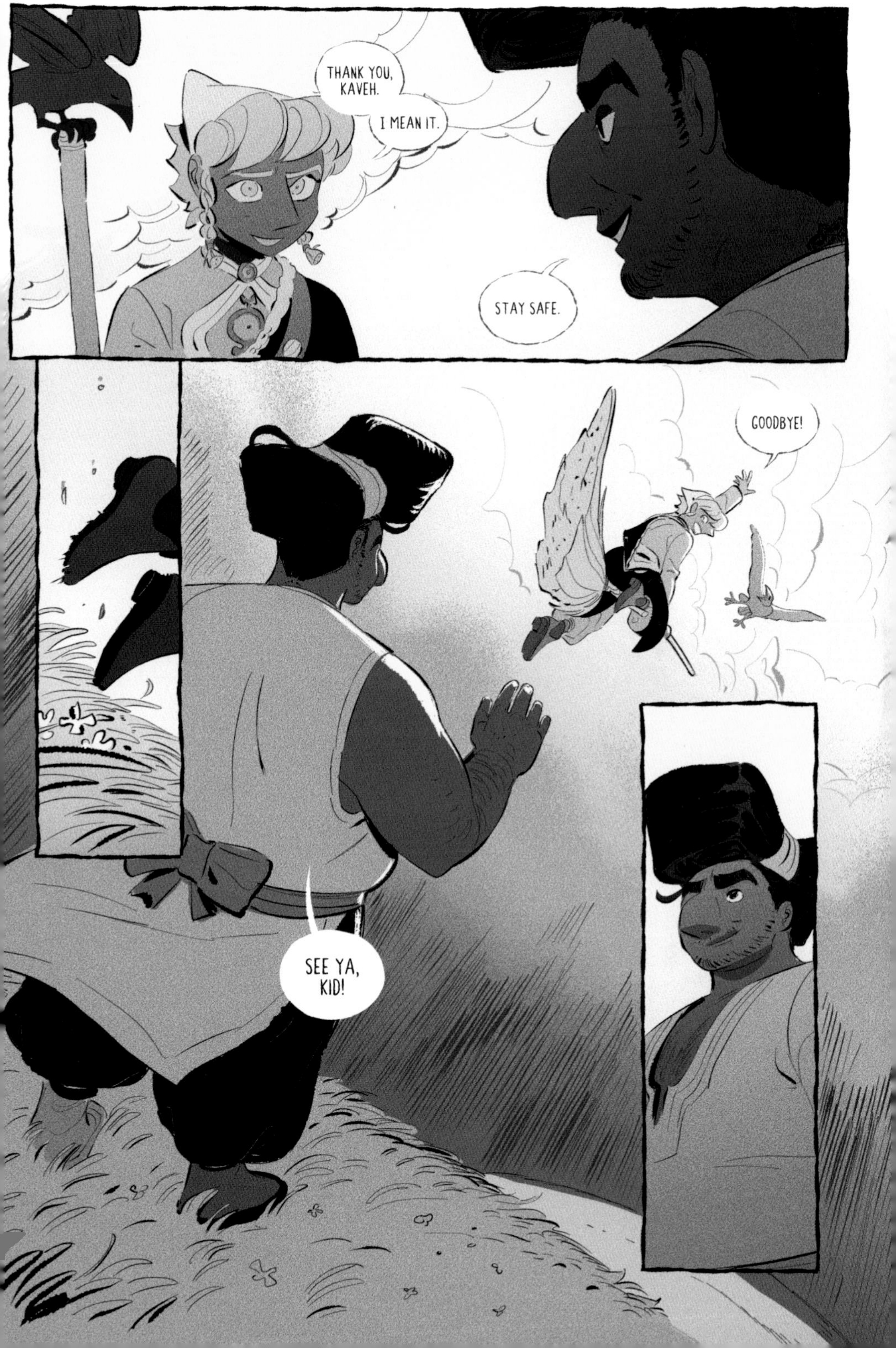
THANK YOU, KAVEH.
I MEAN IT.
STAY SAFE.
GOODBYE!
SEE YA, KID!

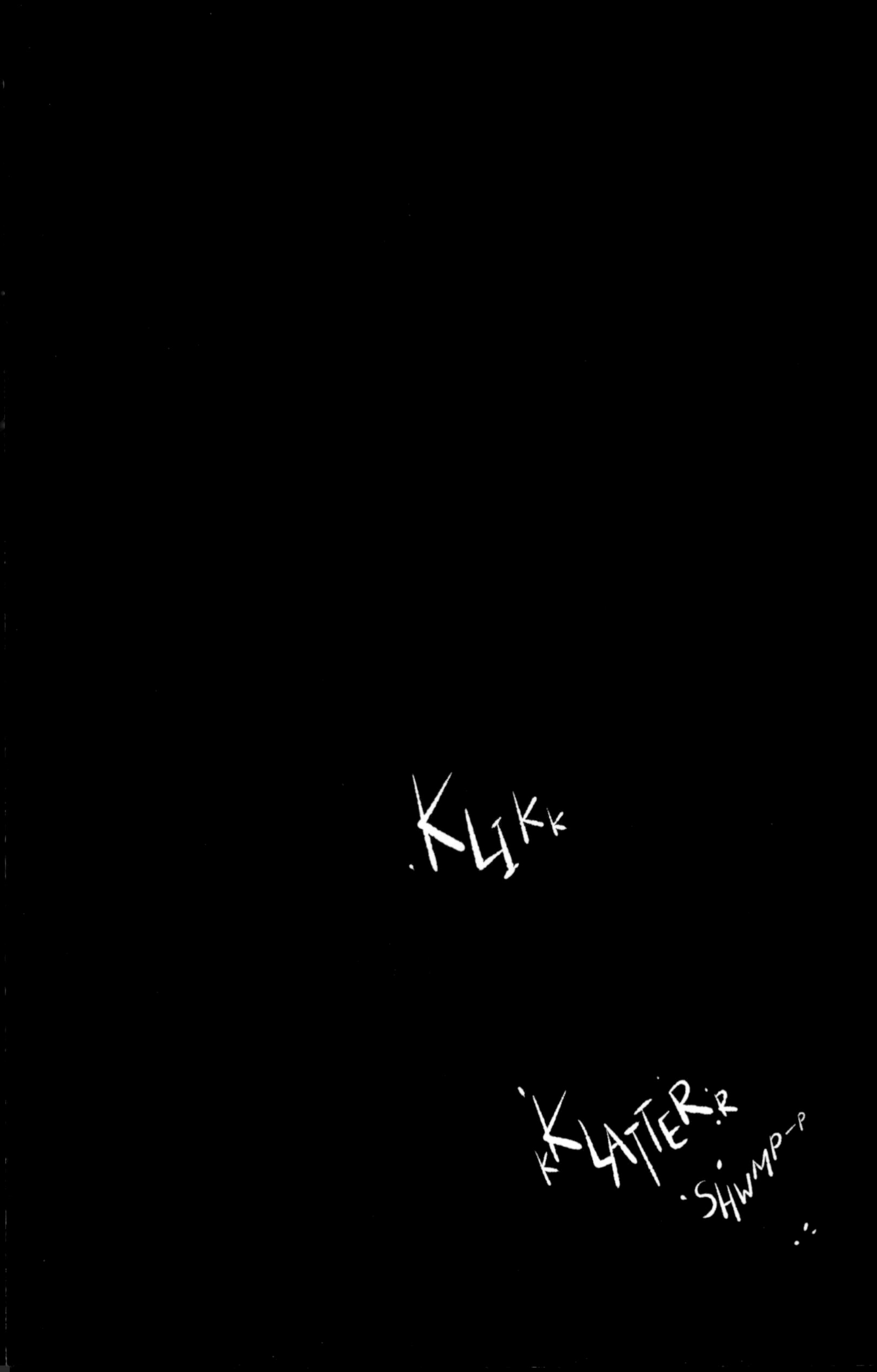
KLIKK
KKLATTERR
SHWMP-P

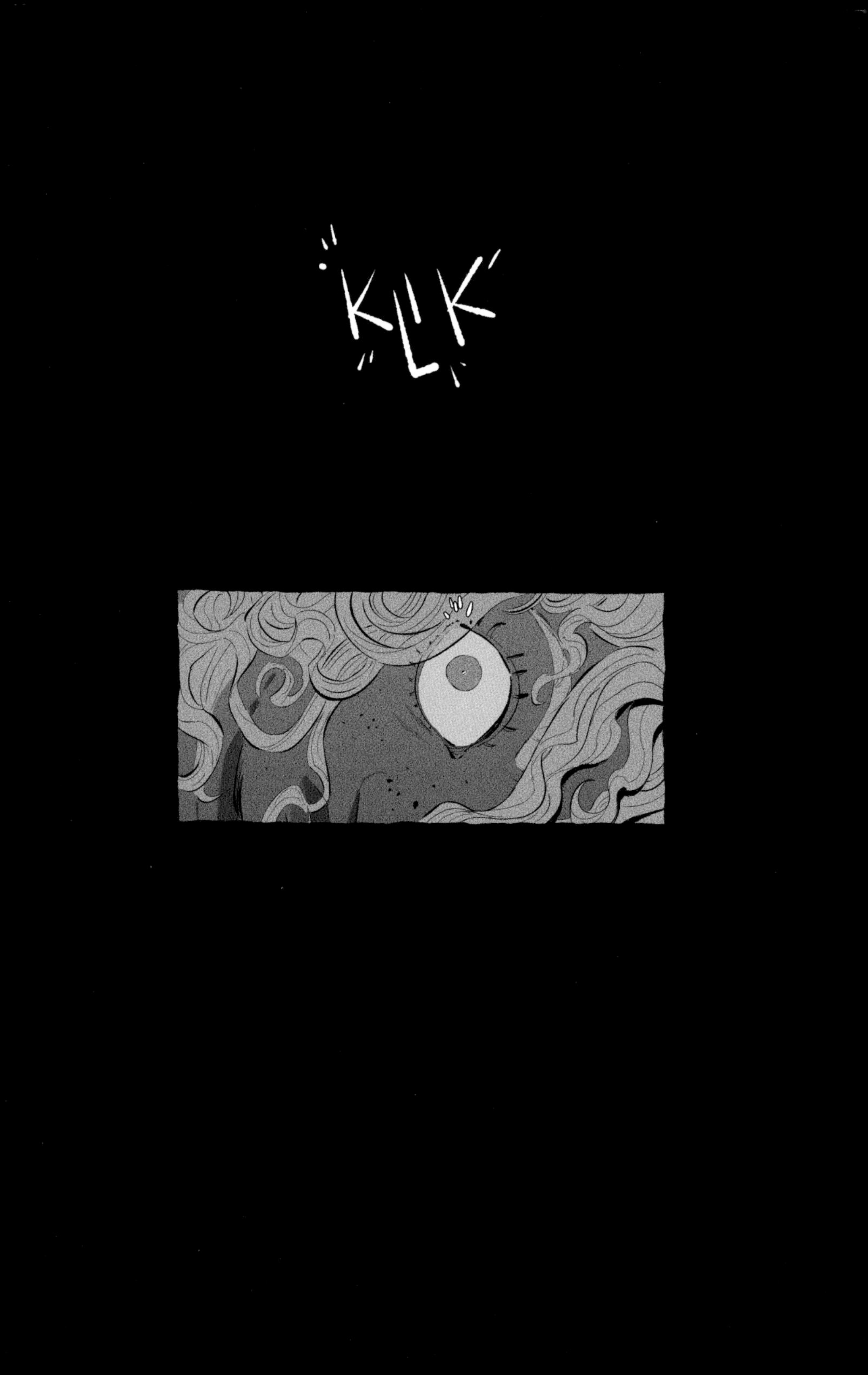
KLIK

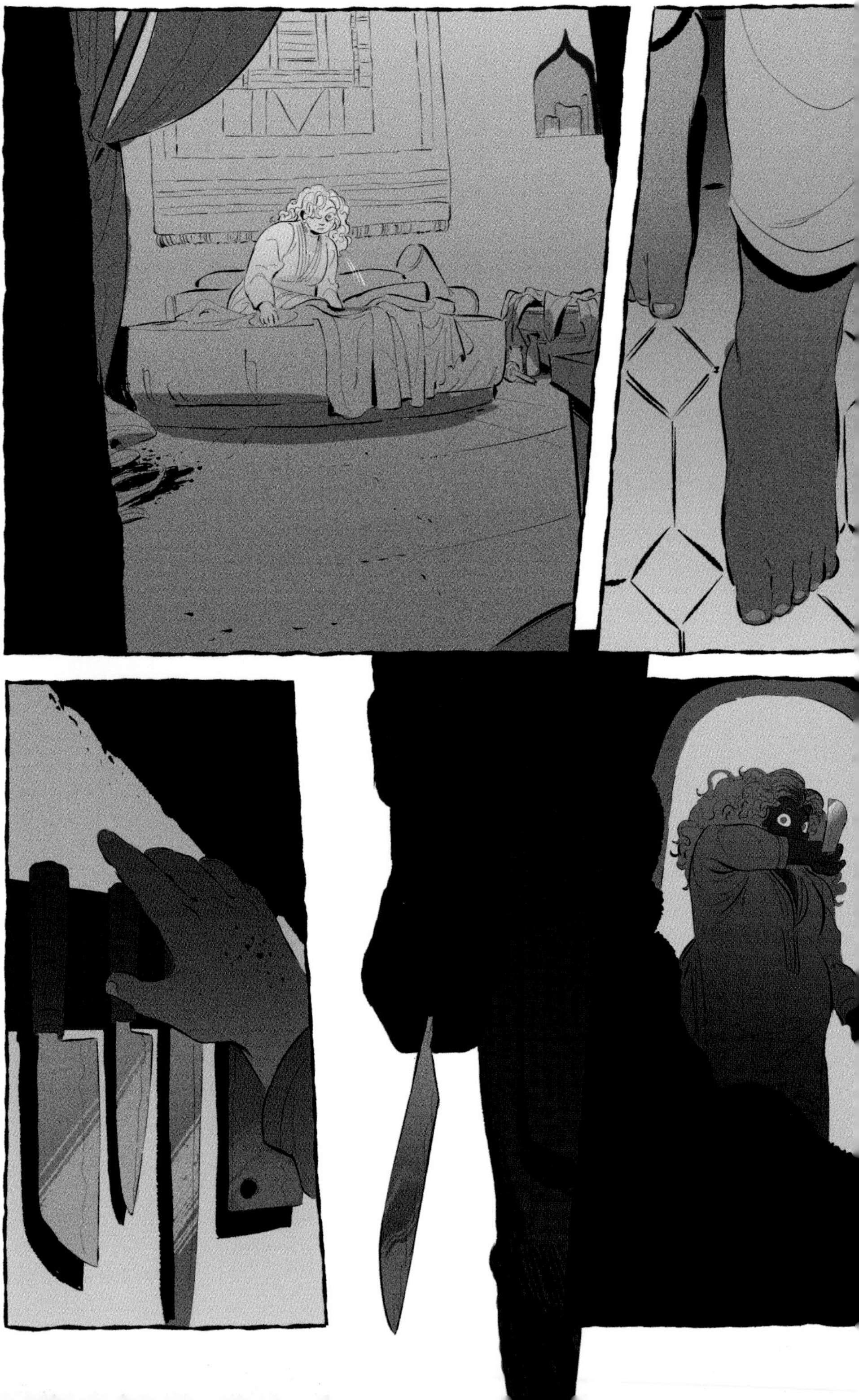

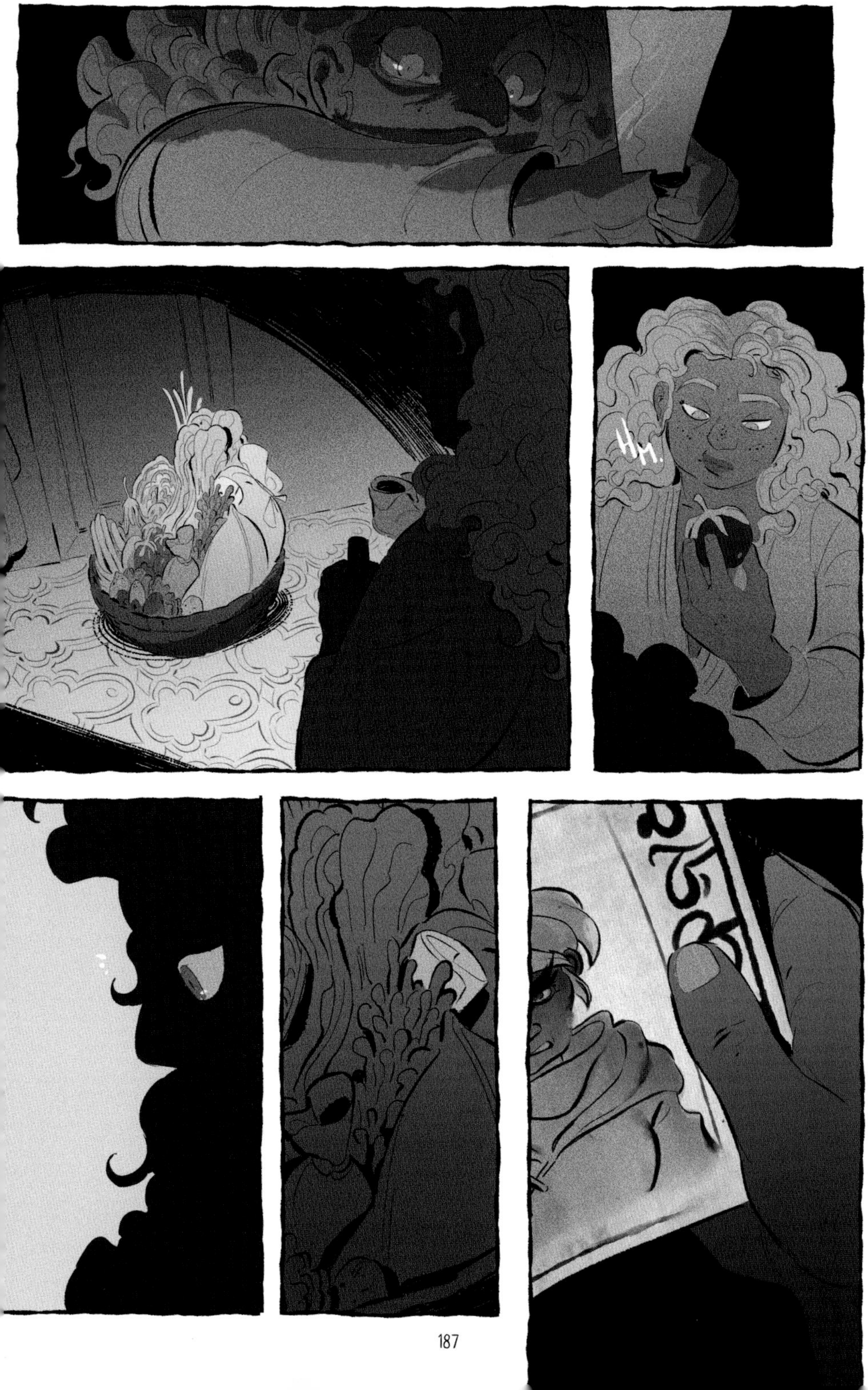
HM.

NEXT TIME...

Nyneve and Banana arrive in Baal only to find
an uneasy air has settled over the once-bustling trade
city. A looming Witch Guard watchtower now occupies
the town center, its knights abusing their power by
extorting the locals wherever they can.

After a disguised Nyneve rescues a young witch from a group
of these impudent knights, she's taken in by their family as
thanks. The family scorns the Guard's influence on Baal, but
when Nyneve's glamour briefly slips in their company,
she finds her plans for settling into a peaceful
new life thrown into turmoil.

Ariel Slamet Ries is an eggplant-human hybrid residing on unceded Boon wurrung and Wurundjeri lands. After studying animation abroad for four years, they lost their degree in the post and unceremoniously bumbled into making comics for a living. Surprisingly, they seem to be making it work.

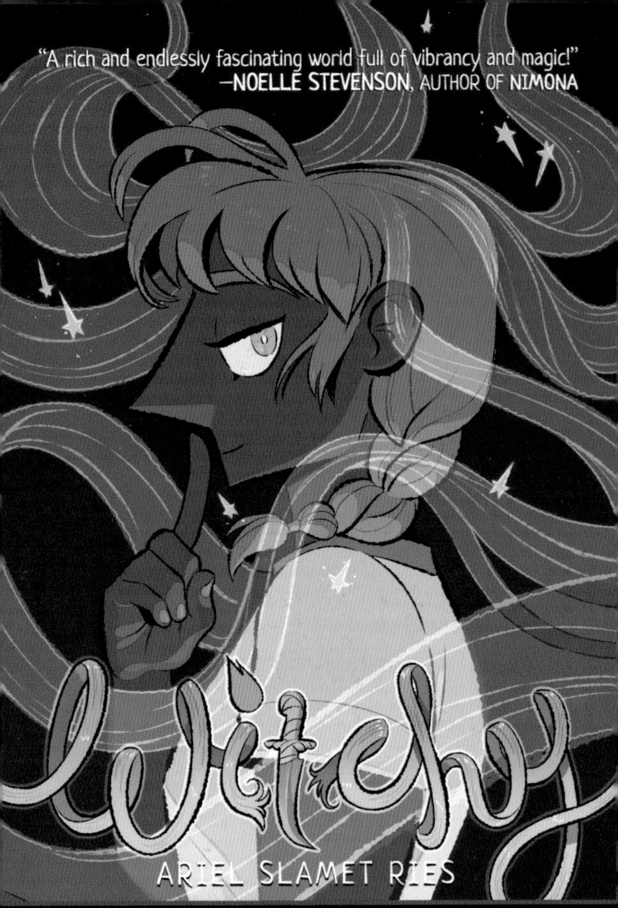
"A rich and endlessly fascinating world full of vibrancy and magic!"
—NOELLE STEVENSON, AUTHOR OF NIMONA
Witchy
ARIEL SLAMET RIES

ıgdom Hyalin, the strength of your magic is determined by the leng
are strong enough are conscripted by the Witch Guard, who enforc
e and protect the land during war. However, those with hair judgec
are pronounced enemies of the kingdom, and annihilated.

This is called a witch burning.

c about the young witch Nyneve, who is haunted by the death of he
Guard poses to her own life. When conscription rolls around, Nyn
oin the institution complicit in her father's death, or stand up for h

ıominated for the 2015 Ignatz for Outstanding Online Comic, the 2C
Web Comic, and the Danish Pingprisen for Best Online Series in 20
Witchy also won the 2020 Ignatz for Outstanding Online Comic.
Witchy will continue in Volume 3!